Surrender to Ecstasy

"If you do not choose to sign the house over to me," Blake said calmly, "I won't throw you in the hold. You will simply stay here, in my cabin — and, I might add, in my bed."

"I don't care about your threats. I am not going to sign that deed!" Lydia cried in defiance.

Apprehensively, she watched him as he walked to the door and rapped softly three times. He looked more like a pirate than ever with that sword in his hand. She bit her lip as she heard a single knock in return, then the sound of boots retreating.

Blake turned back to her. "That was the signal to sail . . . and also, for the guard to leave the doorway. We are locked in together, and I think we'll want no listeners at the door tonight."

For the first time, he smiled at her, a long slow smile that brought a twist of fear and a flicker of heat to her stomach at the same time.

He put down his sword and reached out his hand, taking her chin and gently tilting it upward. "I wonder how many kisses it will take before you are kissing me back?" he murmured.

Lydia gave a startled cry as he caught her in his arms. *How many kisses?* she thought with a kind of wild despair as his mouth came down on hers, *Oh, Blake, just one . . .*

PASSIONATE NIGHTS FROM ZEBRA BOOKS

ANGEL'S CARESS   (2675, $4.50)
by Deanna James

Ellie Crain was a young, inexperienced and beautiful Southern belle. Cash Gillard was the battle-weary Yankee corporal who turned her into a woman filled with hungry passion. He planned to love and leave her; she vowed to keep him forever with her *Angel's Caress*.

COMANCHE BRIDE   (2549, $3.95)
by Emma Merritt

Beautiful Dr. Zoe Randolph headed to Mexico to halt a cholera epidemic. She never dreamed her caravan would be attacked by a band of savages. Later, she refused to believe that she could love and desire her captor, the handsome half-breed Matt Chandler. Captor and slave find unending love and tender passion in the rugged Comanche hills.

CAPTIVE ANGEL   (2524, $4.50)
by Deanna James

When handsome Hunter Gillard left the routine existence of his South Carolina plantation for endless adventures on the high seas, beautiful and indulged Caroline Gillard learned to manage her home and business affairs in her husband's sudden absence. Caroline resolved not to crumble and vowed to make Hunter beg to be taken back. He was determined to make her once again his unquestioning and forgiving wife.

SWEET, WILD LOVE   (2834, $3.95)
by Emma Merritt

Chicago lawyer Eleanor Hunt was determined to earn the respect of the Kansas cowboys who openly leered at her as she was working to try a cattle-rustling case. The worst offender was Bradley Smith—even though he worked for Eleanor's father! She was determined not to mistake passion for love; he was determined to break through her icy exterior and possess the passionate woman who lurked beneath her.

Available wherever paperbacks are sold, or order direct from the Publisher. Send cover price plus 50¢ per copy for mailing and handling to Zebra Books, Dept. 2997, 475 Park Avenue South, New York, N.Y. 10016. Residents of New York, New Jersey and Pennsylvania must include sales tax. DO NOT SEND CASH.

FOREVER PARADISE

MIRANDA NORTH

ZEBRA BOOKS
KENSINGTON PUBLISHING CORP.

ZEBRA BOOKS

are published by

Kensington Publishing Corp.
475 Park Avenue South
New York, NY 10016

First printing: May, 1990

Printed in the United States of America

Chapter One

England, 1685

"By hell, you're the most stubborn woman in England!"

Joshua Lyndham's face was almost purple with fury, as he watched his daughter lift her chin and take his shouted words with a look of insufferable calm. Her cool reply enraged him further.

"Perhaps I am—and a good thing, too. Once I gave in to your wishes meekly enough—and married to please you. This time, perhaps what you call my stubbornness will save me from being sold to the highest bidder twice in a row."

There were startled gasps from all around the room at this unprecedented, unbelievable scene. All the Lyndhams had gathered to lay down the law concerning the important subject of the next marriage for Lydia. They had come expecting to bully, and be meekly answered. They were used to getting their own way, especially Lydia's father, Joshua. No one dared oppose his will—certainly not a mere chit of a girl. And now this! She stood there telling him she had no intention of marrying again!

But Lydia Lyndham Collins was very far from feeling as calm as she looked. She stood in the center of the rococo drawing room of Lyndford Hall, her black widow's weeds a stark contrast to the overelaborate backdrop, gilt furniture, china cupids, and pastoral paintings of fat sheperdesses. With her hands folded in front of her, shoulders back, she presented a picture of unruffled composure.

It was a good thing none of them could see the way that under the gown, she'd slipped off a shoe and was twirling it round and round with one stockinged toe. The old bad habit would be sure to betray her nervousness, she thought.

In a moment, Joshua Lyndham found his voice. "Sold you to the highest bidder?" he roared. "By God—you go too far! *That* is the thanks I get for arranging a most advantageous match for you? With a suitable man any filly'd be glad to have for a husband—" He almost choked on his fury, then started to stand up. "You're not too old for me to take a crop to you, girl, to teach you what your duty is—and the respect you owe your father!"

"I wouldn't fetch your crop, if I were you, Father." Lydia's words were light, but her voice held warning. "May I remind you that as of yesterday, I am of legal age? I am twenty-one. And thanks to my marriage to Baxter, in sole control of what amounts to a fortune. If you lay a hand on me, I promise you all communication between us will cease forthwith."

For a moment, for reassurance, her eyes touched

6

her sister's, wishing she didn't have to witness this. Amy was so sensitive, and Lydia knew how painful a scene like this would be for her.

Lydia hardly glanced at her aunt and her husband, present to lend weight to this family conference. She barely registered their horrified faces, her aunt a voluminous sea of silks and ribbons over an ample frame, her uncle a thinner dark island—but united by their disapproval.

Her eyes came back to her father, and she felt her stomach sink when she saw how red his face was against his crisp silver curls. Joshua Lyndham was a man who didn't inspire fear just in his daughters, but among his tenants, too. With his massive, bullish frame, he strode about his Cotswolds manor lands like a despotic emperor, slapping his crop impatiently against ten inches of shining boot, his pale blue eyes never missing a lazy hand or a haystack carelessly ricked. He'd been content enough to be "just" a country squire—at least, until he'd remarried. Now he was more ambitious, angling for wealth, a baronetcy, a higher social place.

And beside him, her cat green eyes slitted with malice, her sensual red mouth pursed with enjoyment, was the cause of his sudden ambition. His new wife Gwendolyn. All fair curls and awesome bosom in an overfashionable, overtight dress, she obviously expected that at any moment, her husband would crush his daughter's insolent defiance. And from her expression, she was looking forward to it.

Mouth tightening with dislike as she looked at Gwendolyn, Lydia felt some of her courage come back. Well, Gwendolyn was in for a surprise.

"But of course," Lydia continued into the shocked silence, "we need not be so harsh with each other. There is no reason we can't discuss my situation calmly. I think if you'll let me have my say,

7

Father, you will find the plans I have are most reasonable."

Staring as if he could not believe his ears, Joshua Lyndham slowly sank back onto the brocade sofa. He heard the angry indrawn breath from Gwendolyn beside him, and burned at the thought that his expensive, emphatically sensual wife was witnessing this intolerable challenge to his authority from a mere daughter. His eyes narrowed with venom at his daughter. By God, she'd pay for today's work!

But he bit off the roared anger he longed to vent. It was damnably true what the chit said—she was of age, he couldn't force her to do a thing. And that fool of a husband of hers had left his fortune in her control! Her marriage to Baxter Collins had been a triumph. Collins might have been barely gentry, but he'd held an enormous fortune. An estate in Scotland, a townhouse in London, founded on an impressive variety of investments, from shipping to holdings in the colonies.

And after only two months of marriage to Lydia, he'd had the incredibly good sense to die. With her looks and Collins' wealth, Lydia could now easily catch an earl, he considered. With a peer for a son-in-law, with that kind of wealth in his daughter's hands, there was no telling how high the fortunes of the Lyndham family could rise. Yes, Gwendolyn had made him see what an advantage two beautiful daughters could be.

He forced a smile. "Now, now, Lydia—you act as if I were trying to force you into a marriage against your will. I am hardly an ogre. As I recall, no one forced you to marry Baxter Collins. In fact, you acted to me as if you were happy about the match. It now seems that you did not find this marriage much to your liking, but is it fair to blame me? If you'd only spoken of your distaste for Baxter, I'd never have let you marry him."

8

Lydia had to bite back acid words at this speech, delivered in a falsely solicitous, reasonable tone. Forced? It was true she hadn't been tied up and dragged to the altar, but what choice had she had in the matter? Underage, she was her father's chattel to dispose of, and well she knew what happened to those who defied him. He'd chosen Baxter Collins for her and never even asked her opinion. She managed a smile as false as her father's.

"Perhaps that's true, Father. Whatever we both think, my marriage to Baxter Collins is in the past. And before I even think of marrying again, I need some time to collect myself. To decide what I want to do with my life—what place I wish to occupy in the world. To that end, I intend to—"

"What nonsense is this?" exploded her uncle, unable to take another moment. "Damme, Joshua, has the girl gone mad? What does she mean, decide what place she wants to occupy in the world? What other place is there for her, than dutiful wife and daughter? By God, I'll take the crop to her myself, if you don't!"

Lydia turned to see her Uncle Ambrose's thin, owlish face glaring indignantly at her, chins double against his stock. Next to him, her Aunt Phyllida's false front of brown ringlets were bobbing vigorously as she nodded righteous agreement.

"Might I remind you, Lydia," said Phyllida in ringing tones, "of your duty to your family. I can only think that your recent grief has unhinged your senses, to be speaking in such an unfilial manner to your father, and for that I am prepared to forgive your shockingly improper sentiments. As if a girl could be allowed to choose her own husband! What utter nonsense!"

Lydia stopped a grimace just in time. "Her recent grief," indeed! As if Aunt Phyllida had ever been considerate of *that* nonexistent state for even a

9

moment. Too well Lydia remembered that at Baxter's funeral luncheon, her aunt had been the first to approach her and begin harping on her duty to make a second, important marriage. And had even ticked off the merits of some of the attendees as possible eligible husbands, nodding her crepe-trimmed hat at them as they came to pay their respects to the young widow!

But if Aunt Phyllida had been the first, she certainly hadn't been the last. The others had barely let her have a moment's peace since they'd grasped that Baxter really had dropped dead of an apoplexy brought on by too much rich food and drink—and that she was now the mistress of his fortune. It was her duty to marry well, because that would raise *their* social position, too . . . and they didn't intend to let up until she'd done as they wished.

And that's why she'd made up her mind to take the drastic step she intended to take.

She took a deep and steadying breath, but before she could speak, Gwendolyn purred sweetly, "Of course Lydia is quite right, she should have some say in whom her next husband should be." She smiled with false sympathy at Lydia, then turned, and laid an affectionate hand lightly on her husband's coat sleeve, casting him a warm look through half-lowered lashes. "Why, I can hardly speak against marrying for—affection, can I? Though I'm sure Lydia doesn't mean to be quite so indelicate in the way she expresses it, I can sympathize with her feelings—"

Lydia threw Gwendolyn a look of purest dislike. Intolerable to have Gwendolyn pretending to take her side! No more beating around the bush, she thought. *I might as well get it over with.* She took another deep breath, and, acting as if Gwendolyn hadn't spoken, smiled at her aunt.

"Of course, Aunt Phyllida, you are right. I

10

should marry again. But I am quite, quite far from being ready to marry just yet. The trauma of losing my husband so soon after our marriage—" She fetched a sigh. "I feel I must have time to compose myself before I can possibly decide to marry again. That is why I have decided to go and visit my late husband's properties—take a tour of my holdings, so to speak."

Aunt Phyllida blinked, slightly mollified by this plan. "Then you intend to travel to Scotland? Most suitable. And we can open the town house in London while you are gone, and—"

"Not Scotland, no. You misunderstand. I am going to Jamaica."

There was a moment of utter shocked silence, as everyone stared at her anew as if she belonged in Bedlam. Then, they all burst into a storm of exclamations at once.

"You must be mad—"

"Jamaica—it's on the other side of the world—"

"—totally uncivilized, not at all suitable for a woman—"

"—I said I wouldn't beat you, but, by God, this is going too far, and—"

"Haven't I always said that this is what comes of Margaret's soft spoiling of both of them?"

This last was delivered in Gwendolyn's sultry, venomous tones. Lydia, who had stood unmoved, only a slight smile curving her lips, frowned as she caught this last. *Thank God for mother's "soft spoiling!"* she thought. *If it weren't for her, we'd never have known any love!*

As the shouting went on around her, she ignored it to smile at her frightened sister. They both knew all too well that if there was any hope of ever making a better life for Amy, Lydia had to leave. Otherwise she'd never get out from under their rule, and in six months she'd find herself bullied into marriage again. And Amy after her!

That thought bolstered her failing courage, and she turned back to face the battle with renewed energy. It was one she was going to win, if she had to be every bit as stubborn as her silver-haired father, every bit as devious as his mercenary wife. She was going to Jamaica, even if every Lyndham in England tried to stop her.

Chapter Two

"Oh, Liddy, you were wonderful! I can hardly believe the way you faced up to Father—to *all* of them! I should never, never have had the courage to do so myself, not in a thousand years!" Amy stared with awestruck admiration at her older sister as Lydia flopped into a chair with a groan.

Amy was still amazed that her adored older sister had spoken in such a stunningly rebellious way to their father. Neither of them had ever dared to speak up to Father in such a way before, but had lived for years in terror of his autocratic rages, scuttling to stay out of reach of his harsh tongue and heavy hand. But evidently marriage had changed Liddy, even such a short marriage as she'd had. Amy plaited the flowery flounces of her demure muslin dress, convinced now that the mysterious rites that went on between a man and a woman after they'd been joined in marriage must be even more earthshaking than she'd supposed.

She looked through misty eyes at Lydia's rich, dark brown hair, coiled around the crown of her head, the way she held her chin, her squared shoulders. Her black dress and the sun coming in the window gave hints of deep red to her hair, and Amy thought sentimentally that when she'd faced the family, she'd looked as gallant as a queen. Thus might Mary Queen of Scots have faced her executioners, so proudly, with just that tilt to the head. Amy thought the story of reckless Mary most romantic, but as she stared at her sister and compared her to Mary, she didn't pause to think that Mary might have had just such a jaw, delicate but unmistakably square; or such a chin, determined for all its prettiness.

Exhausted, Lydia kicked off her pinching slippers and unbuttoned the top two buttons at her throat. She put a hand to her temples and rubbed them, eyes closed. All the hours of shouting had given her a headache. But it was worth the price of a headache. She'd won.

She managed to smile back at Amy. "I can scarcely believe myself that I did it! When I saw how red Father's face looked—" Both girls looked at each other, then giggled. "Oh dear," Lydia went on, "I thought his heart might just stop then and there when I defied him. Either that, or he would beat me silly while Uncle Ambrose cheered and Aunt Phyllida advised him as to where it would hurt most!"

Amy laughed and threw herself onto the bed in a welter of lace and flounces. "There you go again, Liddy, a story for everything. I wonder how you can laugh when Father really *might* have beaten you

14

silly, or locked you in your room, or—"

But Amy's imagination failed her, and her face sobered suddenly. It was Lydia who had all the imagination. She'd made all the years they'd spent together so fun, and that in the face of the fact that their days were really quite dull. But Lydia always had a story for everything, a trick of exaggerating things so that they were fanciful or funny. But for all Lydia's bravado away from their father, in her heart, Amy had never believed she would really stand up to him, and had certainly not expected that she would actually get her way. It seemed unimaginable. And now . . .

"I know—I know you *must* go, but—oh, Liddy, how will I ever bear it here without you?" she wailed suddenly.

Lydia reached over and took her sister's hand, giving it a reassuring squeeze, trying not to show the worry she felt. Trying to be strong, the way she'd always tried to be strong for Amy. She and her mother had always tried to surround Amy with all the love and gentleness that would make up for her father's coldness and rages. But looking at her sister's innocent, frightened face, she wondered now if maybe they'd sheltered Amy too much.

The sisters had clung together even closer since their mother's death . . . and since Gwendolyn had come to live at Lyndford Hall. She mocked the girls every chance she got, and bullied their father, to their silent amazement. She called lovely old Lyndford "a farm," and railed at the boredom of life in the country.

And sometimes she let her hand linger a trifle too long in the handsome groom's grasp when he helped her mount her mare.

It hadn't been long before Father had packed them all up to London for a taste of the fashionable life. And not much longer after that, Lydia found herself being paid court to by a score of men.

What did it matter if Baxter Collins was stout, with fair thinning hair—and boring? That didn't matter a bit to her father. Baxter was rich.

And somehow, Amy's tears the night before her wedding had kept Lydia from crying her own.

Now, she comforted Amy's tears again. "Amy, darling, I promise you, I won't stay away forever! But you know if I stay here, they'll make life unbearable for me until I marry again. I want to get as far away from them as possible—and Jamaica is all the way across the ocean! Besides, you know Father promised you can come join me on Jamaica the moment I have a suitable house for us to live in. And Baxter left me a house on Jamaica. Why, you may be on the next ship out after mine!"

Amy looked up uncertainly. "But it's a wilderness! There are wild Indians and all kinds of diseases."

"It's not that uncivilized. There are cities there, just like here."

Amy gave a watery giggle, certain Lydia was just spinning yarns again. "Oh, outrageous! You can't tell me that the cities there are anything like London!"

"Well—not London. But as big as any town in this part of England. I'm not used to cities in any case. Yes," said Lydia, warming to her subject, "and I'm sure the house Baxter left me will be a veritable mansion, as fine as any on the Strand. It's called Bellefleur, after all, and that means beautiful

16

flower in French. Oh, I know we'll love it. It will have gilding on the ceilings and statues in the gardens, and we'll have so many flowers in our bedrooms, we'll always smell like roses and we'll never have to buy perfume. Jamaica is supposed to be very beautiful. Seas of flowers, sandy beaches, and ocean all around."

For all her confident description, Lydia really had no clear picture of what any place other than England might be like. She'd grown up in the peaceful green of the English countryside, and even London had been overwhelming to her. But it didn't matter if this place called Jamaica was primitive or paradise. It was on the other side of the world, that was all that mattered.

"But it's hot there! And what about the pirates? They are everywhere! Why, Aunt Phyllida said the last governor of Jamaica, Henry Morgan, was actually a pirate himself!" Amy said, timidly.

"I should rather enjoy meeting a pirate," Lydia said. "Besides, they are called buccaneers, and they fight the Spanish for His Majesty. But the new governor, Thomas Lynch, is most respectable, they say, and I imagine I might even dance with him at a ball at the governor's mansion, some time or another."

But she felt a slight shudder down her spine at the thought of meeting pirates. No one had forgotten the wild rule of the buccaneers less than twenty years before. They'd carved up the islands—English, French and Spanish—in pitched sea battles and bloody deeds. Some of the men who were buccaneers had served England well, even been gentlemen, with a code of conduct. Some had been ruthless murderers, slavers, caring only for money

17

and for rum. Though slightly more civilized governments ruled the islands now, many a pirate ship still plied the waters of the Caribbean.

"Oh! How can you say such things?" cried Amy, with a shudder of her own.

Lydia unpinned the coils on top of her head, and started undoing the braids that fell nearly to her waist. "Maybe it's because life with Baxter was so dull. I'd like to see a little of the world before I marry again — if I marry again. When you're young, you're your father's property. Then when you marry, you become your husband's property. Now I'm finally free — and I'm in no rush to become someone's possession again!"

Amy watched the shadow in her sister's eyes as she spoke, the hectic energy with which she jerked at her hair. "Was marriage to Baxter that bad?" she asked softly.

Startled, Lydia glanced up. She hadn't meant to be so transparent. She'd tried hard to put a good face on her marriage in front of Amy. But, as usual, she hadn't fooled her one bit.

She sat down. "It was awful," she said flatly, glad to be able to unburden herself at last.

Amy blushed. "Was it — the marriage bed that made it so awful?" she ventured, burning to know. She wasn't quite sure exactly what went on in the marriage bed, but knew from her friends' whispers it involved painful indignities and even disrobing.

Lydia hesitated, wondering how frank she should be. She was the only mother Amy had now, and if she didn't talk to her, no one would. Or maybe Gwendolyn might. That thought was awful, and she made up her mind it was up to her to enlighten Amy here and now.

18

Blushing herself, in a few fumbling sentences, she explained to a round-eyed Amy what it was men and women did together that made babies. ". . . And so, he must put himself inside you to make a baby," she finished, her cheeks flaming. "It's most embarrassing, and hurts a bit at first. But fortunately, the whole thing doesn't take very long, and it's done in the dark under the blankets. So you can just close your eyes and think of something else."

"He — he's lying on top of you — *naked?*" squeaked Amy, as if she could not believe such an incredible, undignified thing.

"Well — not *completely* naked. Baxter always left his nightshirt on. But I must warn you, they seem to like to push up your nightclothes and paw about a bit. It's frightfully embarrassing, but it does speed things up. Only a minute or two after that, some panting, and then it's all over. Men seem to enjoy it very much, if Baxter is any clue."

Luckily, Lydia reflected, it hadn't happened more than a few times. Really, there wasn't much to be said for marriage. Baxter had not been much of a conversationalist. He spent his days tending to the fortune he'd made, and never bothered to share the details of his business with his lonely young bride. He'd married her for her beauty, and because she would give him heirs. Not for companionship. When he died, she hadn't shed a tear, but had instead felt the profoundest of reliefs. And though she'd scolded herself that it was sinful to feel so, she couldn't help it.

Now she looked at Amy's bewildered, forlorn expression and felt contrite. Maybe she'd been too blunt, so she searched for a way to soften it. "If you loved your husband—maybe it wouldn't be so bad. After all, I could hardly stand to speak to Baxter, much less have him pawing me. I'm sure the kind of man you'll marry will be sweet and gentle and kind—and ever so handsome. And then maybe it will be different than it was with my husband."

But both girls eyed each other doubtfully.

"Well, if it is necessary for the sake of dear babies—" Amy said after a moment. Then she burst out, "Oh, Liddy, I don't see how you stood being married to that awful man! I just know I would have died, if it had been me!"

"I promise you, if I can help it, I'll see it never does happen to you," Lydia said fiercely. "It's disgraceful, the way they marry girls off to anyone just because they have money or a title. Why, Baxter was *forty!*" Her inflection clearly said that this was an unimaginably elderly age. "I did my duty once for this family—because I didn't know any better—but I tell you, I don't intend to do it again. And I don't intend to let Father marry you off to some old pike-faced lord, either!"

Lydia's eyes glowed with fervor and determination, and she set her chiseled jawline so it was squarer than ever.

"But, Liddy, what about Father? You know he'll make me marry as soon as I'm old enough! He says now that I can come to Jamaica if you find a suitable house for us to live in, but I'm afraid he won't let me leave once you're gone!"

"Won't he?" A cool determined smile curved her lips. "We shall see about that. I beat Father today—and I can beat him again. I learned from that awful marriage to Baxter that you should never let anyone force you into doing something you don't want to

20

do. Father hasn't realized yet just how resolute I can be. One thing that marriage did give me is independence. I'm a rich woman now, aren't I?"

She paused. "And Father wants money for his expensive wife. Very well. I'll give him some of Baxter's property, *if* he'll let you join me. And dangle the prospect of more in front of him every time he tries to thwart me. As long as I'm left with enough for us to live on, what do I care what happens to the rest of it?"

Amy, laughing, threw her arms around her sister's neck. "Oh, Liddy, I should have known you'd never leave me to fend for myself!"

"Never!" vowed Lydia, feeling tears, long held back, prick her eyelids. She held her sister, making a silent promise that somehow, some way, she'd make a new home for both of them in Jamaica.

At the bottom of the great curving staircase of Lyndford Hall, Joshua Lyndham stood, fists on his hips, staring up in rage. So today she'd bested him, a thing he'd allow no horse, hound, or servant to do. Nor wife or child, even though what Gwendolyn did was suspiciously close to twisting him round her finger. At least she paid him in coinage he could understand—in his bed. Whereas this insolent slip of a daughter was worth nothing save how he could barter her in marriage.

He scowled. And no doubt she was upstairs now congratulating herself on how she'd beaten Joshua Lyndham.

Well, she hadn't, by God. She'd learn that lesson well before long. Let her go to Jamaica thinking she'd won! He'd show her soon enough who was

21

master here.

He'd see her married to a lord before he was through with her, or his name wasn't Joshua Lyndham.

He turned and strode out the wide-open front doors of Lyndford Hall, and an unfortunate hound bounded across the graveled drive to meet his master. His boot connected with the hound's ribs and sent him flying across the drive, and for the first time that day, Joshua Lyndham smiled.

Chapter Three

Jamaica.

The sails of the *Sea Lion* were filled with wind above her head, the air full of sounds that had become familiar to Lydia's ears over the last weeks. The deep creaking of rope, the low boom of canvas, the hiss of waves along the hull. She barely felt the rise and fall of the deck beneath her feet anymore; was hardly aware of the constant wind that molded her skirts to her legs and caught at her hair. In the six weeks she'd been aboard, these things, at first strange, had become commonplace to her. Today she was barely aware of the ship as she strained her vision toward the sight on the horizon.

As Lydia stood at the rail, she felt a shiver run through her, half fear, half excitement. There was the island she'd spent so many weeks at sea to reach, leaving England and everything she knew so far behind her.

It was so beautiful, so exotic, and so wild-looking! From the moment the ship had come in sight of the first string of Caribbean islands, she could barely eat or sleep from excitement. How thrilling it had been when they sailed through the Windward Passage, between the islands of the Greater Antilles, Cuba and Dominica! Even the name—Windward Passage—had a romance that spoke to her of Spanish ships and pirate raids. Just like a story! she thought, enthralled.

And now here was Jamaica itself, the eastern point of the island. They had to sail around the tip to reach their destination of Port Royal, on the southeast side of the island. And she'd be on land at last!

Lydia felt the wind tug at the feather in her hat, pull at her full skirts, and knew her hands were gripping the rail tightly in her excitement. The Caribbean sea was like nothing she'd ever imagined, sapphire farther out, clear turquoise closer in. In startling contrast to the blue water, the island was ringed with crescents of white sand beaches sparkling in the sun, backed by lush green foliage, impenetrable and dense.

She saw jungle-covered foothills, green folded ridge after ridge, and behind them soared lofty, cloud-covered mountains. Green in the sun, shadowed purple, and blue. It was the most beautiful place Lydia had ever seen—but she'd felt a shiver all the same. It looked so very wild—so uninhabited! Though she saw the lighter green square of rolling fields, and here and there a glimpse of roof, most of the island looked like untracked jungle.

"Oh, *Madame*—are there no houses in this place? Surely this cannot be Jamaica yet? Is it one of the wild islands no one lives on?"

The voice at her elbow made Lydia turn to find that Brigitte, her maid, had joined her at the rail. Brigitte was French and nineteen, with soft curls and sparkling dark eyes, a pretty, open face, and a bubbly manner that Lydia liked. Lydia adjusted her expression, hoping that none of her dismay showed.

"Oh, no, Brigitte—this is Jamaica. But this must not be a part where many people live. But there are some plantations, I think. See the roofs over there—the cane fields? At least, I *think* it's cane."

"But it is so—so wild, *Madame,*" Brigitte repeated. "Will we be living in such a place, so far away from any towns as that?"

Brigitte was pointing at a distant roof, the peak just showing over surrounding trees. There was a glimpse of a ribbon of road winding along the coast, but otherwise, no sign of civilization.

"No, I'm sure Bellefleur is much closer to town. After all, the warehouses I own are in Port Royal. I'm sure the house is surrounded by lots of other houses," Lydia said brightly, not at all sure.

"I hope so, *Madame,*" said Brigitte, and Lydia heard a quaver of doubt in her voice. *"Mon Dieu! And I thought Lyndford was so buried in the country!"*

None of the servants at Lyndford had been willing to make the journey halfway across the world, and so Aunt Phyllida had produced Brigitte. A housemaid up until now and eagerly anxious to better herself, Brigitte had been willing to go to Jamaica for a chance to be a lady's maid, even willing to sign indenture papers.

But Lydia disliked the idea of indenture—it was all too much like owning another person, she thought. So she'd merely hired the young girl, and was glad she had. Brigitte had an effervescent personality that made her good company on the long,

25

dull voyage, even if she was inexperienced as a lady's maid and rather too free with her tongue.

Now, seeing the expression of horror on Brigitte's face, she wondered if Brigitte would decide to take the next ship back home and leave her here in the islands without a soul she knew.

Lydia laughed. 'Well, I admit this doesn't look much like England. But don't worry—I've heard Port Royal is a sizeable town, and the planters live in mansions, I'm told."

"I'm sure you must be right, *Madame*. After all, what we saw of Port-au-Prince was very formidable, was it not?" Brigitte referred to the city they'd seen on Dominica as they came through the Windward Passage into the Caribbean. It had been reassuringly large.

"I'm sure Port Royal must be every bit as big. And isn't Jamaica lovely, Brigitte?"

For all Lydia's confident words, she felt her own heart sink a little as she surveyed the jungle-clad shores and deserted beaches. How could she bring Amy to a place like this? Take her away from the lovely English countryside, the bustle of London, for a place that looked as if only ten people lived in it?

The voyage had given Lydia six boring weeks in which to do nothing but think—and doubt. She felt very alone without Amy, and even the hours she'd spent talking to Brigitte hadn't helped much. And when she was alone in her cabin or on deck . . . she'd had time to realize how much more Baxter had left her than just a house. There were shipyards and warehouses, coffeehouses. An overseer, servants, hired workers. What would they expect of her when she arrived? She hadn't really paid close attention to the thick reports from Baxter's overseer—but either he or Baxter's local solicitor would be meeting the ship. Would they look to her for direction? Or . . . maybe resent her for coming? Think she was interfering?

How unprepared she really was for managing the fortune Baxter had left her. She'd had lessons from her governesses — but they had spent a lot of time on manners, dancing, sewing, ordering a household. She knew so little of the world, really. She'd spent so much time in the country, where the most exciting part of the day had been taking a long walk to the village to help the vicar arrange the flowers in the church. Fittings for dresses, social calls, painting a watercolor. She knew much more about setting a table for fifty than she did about ships' logs and account books.

In fact, the only thing she really had a talent at was so utterly useless that she felt almost embarassed when she thought of it. Telling stories. Lydia's taste ran to the lurid — stories of ghosts, fairies, murders, pirates, the more adventurous and exciting the better.

How many hours she and Amy had spent, heads bent over stitchery, the gray English rain streaking the windows, while Lydia embroidered shivery tales of haunts or courtly stories of chivalrous love . . .

Suddenly she shook her head, disgusted with herself, with all the fears and doubts she'd been having over the last weeks. After all the tales of adventure she'd regaled Amy with, was she so cowardly she shrank from anything that resembled a real adventure?

Here before her were the fabled islands of the Indies, where maybe there were fountains of youth and undiscovered seams of gold, where pirates roamed and ghost ships plied the waters . . .

"It's going to be wonderful, Brigitte," she said, with a confident ring in her voice. "No matter what

27

happens to us here, we're going to love it. I'm certain of it!"

And at that moment, she did feel sure of it. Even if she hated Jamaica, even if she was miserable here, at least it was an adventure she could tell her children about. She smiled at the thought.

If nothing else — it would make a good story.

Three hours later, a bewildered Lydia stood at last on dry land, Brigitte at her side, surveying a crowd fantastic and varied beyond her wildest dreams. She'd alighted from the ship onto a wharf that was packed with people there to meet the ship.

Port Royal was by no means the small town she'd feared, but a sizeable city with white buildings dazzling in the sun. It looked prosperous and busy, scattered over the high hills around the harbor. There were a number of ships riding at anchor, the waters full of smaller craft. In the narrow streets, foot traffic fought for space with open carriages and wagons. All was noise, confusion, and smells, and a hundred sights strange to Lydia's eyes.

There were men and women in every state of dress and with skin tones ranging from dark to pale. Women in bright cottons with wide baskets and huge loads on their heads, barefoot and graceful in the dust; women in brilliant silks like tropical birds, leaning out of open carriages, shouting and waving to the men. Sailors in ragged trousers, dandies in gorgeous coats, running children, barking dogs. It seemed like she heard ten different tongues on every side, smelled a hundred things. Coffee, flowers, ocean, perfume, sweat, fish all fought in a tide of odors.

All around her, people were greeting those who'd alighted from the ship, shouldering their way with

28

glad cries through the crowds on the wharf.

Lydia looked uneasily at Brigitte, who made a face and shrugged, clutching Lydia's jewel box tightly to her chest. Though they'd been standing on the dock for perhaps a quarter hour, no one had come forward to meet them. Lydia's head was starting to ache from the pandemonium around her.

"It looks as if no one from Bellefleur is here to meet us," Lydia ventured at last. "I cannot understand it. They have known what ship I was arriving on for months."

"Maybe they are at the end of the wharf, *Madame*," Brigitte said hopefully, nodding toward the shore. There a narrow street lined with shops and taverns swept down to the foot of the wharf, and a number of carriages were drawn up along the street. "Perhaps one of those carriages is from the house and they are waiting for us there."

Lydia shaded her eyes, looked down the wharf, not sure whether to wait longer or to stay. But then someone jostled against her, almost throwing her off balance, and she nodded. Anything would be better than standing in this crowd. "Very well— maybe we can hire a carriage down there if no one is here to meet us."

She started off down the wharf, feeling the sun hot on her hat. She could see already that the clothes she was wearing were far too heavy and formal for this climate. She felt hampered by the stiff stays, lace chemise, layers and layers of petticoats, stockings, and high-heeled shoes. Over everything was yards and yards of lavender and yellow brocade, and a yellow felt hat with a rakish sweeping lavender plume. She'd dressed carefully, but as she walked down the pier, she wished she'd worn something lighter.

And maybe something less conspicuous as well.

She felt her cheeks heat up as a group of burly, rough-looking men stopped at the sight of her and stared. One of them whistled, and she caught a glimpse of unshaven cheeks, broken teeth, cutlasses, and pistols at their ragged sides.

Pirates! She felt sure they were pirates. Or at the very least, criminals. As she sidestepped a huge, black-bearded fellow who loitered into her path with an insolent grin, she wished she'd stayed put back at the ship and waited. She glanced back and saw that Brigitte looked decidedly nervous as the men elbowed each other and grinned at her.

"Why, if she ain't the prettiest sight I seen in a long time," Lydia heard one of the men say loudly. She looked down and quickened her pace, pretending not to hear.

"Aye, she's a sight indeed. But don't be in such a hurry! If you're new to Port Royal, little lady, why not see the sights with me?"

One, bolder than the rest, had stepped into her path and was blocking her way. Cheeks crimson, heart beating too fast, Lydia looked up and saw it was the hulking man with the black beard and broken teeth. With a slight gasp, she sidestepped him and started off.

His hand shot out and grabbed her full sleeve. "So the lady's not friendly. I don't like to see a lady who isn't friendly. You're in the islands now, where the sun is hot and so is the blood—and I tell 'ee, you've fired mine!"

Lydia stopped dead and looked around for escape. She swallowed, telling herself there was no reason to be nervous, it was broad daylight, there was a crowd all around her, what could the man do—?

But all the time he was walking toward her.

Panicked, she backed up, forgetting she was on

the very edge of the wharf. And then she felt her heel step on nothing, go down, and catch. For a moment that seemed to last forever, she gasped and pinwheeled her arms for balance, and felt herself going over backward. She had a glimpse of the rowdy men's faces looking startled. She was falling!

She barely had time to feel a tip-to-toe burst of purest panic before she landed with a jolt of sorts, her hat falling over her eyes. The fall was over almost before it had begun, and somehow she'd landed without any pain. Something strong, yet yielding, had broken her fall.

Arms! Someone had caught her and she was being held in someone's arms!

Panicked, she pushed her hat away from her eyes and was transfixed by a pair of the most compelling light gray eyes she'd ever seen. For a moment, she couldn't breathe.

"You—you caught me!" she managed to gasp.

"Indeed. It is my lucky day, it seems," came the gray-eyed stranger's deep-voiced reply.

She stared at him, still bewildered, still breathless. His eyes were amused, and a broad, white smile creased his bronzed face. Windswept black hair curled lightly on his forehead from the humidity and was pulled back and held fast with a black ribbon at the nape of his neck. There were brush-strokes of silver at his temples. And—to Lydia's amazement—there was actually a golden hoop winking wickedly in his earlobe!

Good God—was he a pirate?

All these thoughts went through Lydia's mind in a lightning flash, before she realized that not only was this stranger holding her in his arms—she was being held tightly against his bare chest.

He had no shirt on!

Her face flamed and she stiffened. "Put me

31

down!" she gasped.

The stranger laughed but made no move to let her go, and she heard more laughter—loud laughter from the docks above. Why—all those despicable men were enjoying this spectacle!

He looked up, calling, "Look, Jacques—it's raining women!"

With an indignant little cry, she twisted in his arms to look up at the dock above and saw a crowd of amused faces above them. The one he'd spoken to—Jacques—had a roguishly handsome face, sandy brown hair, and sparkling brown eyes.

"*Oui*, and not just women, but beautiful ones, it seems," came his accented reply from above.

The two men laughed.

Dimly, she felt her hat falling off her head, felt the stranger reach out and make a grab for it with one hand. But she had eyes only for the crowd above and not a thought for her hat. All men, staring down at her.

"Put her down this minute, you beast, and leave her alone!" This came from Brigitte, who now stood beside Jacques on the pier.

"I see she has someone to protect her, no?" Jacques commented, giving Brigitte a focus for her fury.

Brigitte faced off with a laughing Jacques and swung the jewel box at him as her inadequate weapon. "It is not funny, you blackguard," she cried.

Sidestepping the blow just in time, the one called Jacques called over his shoulder, "You'd better do as she says, or she will kill me with her carrying case!"

Lydia turned back to her captor, struggling, but the arms holding her didn't give at all. "I told you to put me down at once!" she demanded.

"Such ingratitude for the man who saved you from a nasty fall," was the cool and infuriating reply.

"I thank you for that, sir—but I do not thank you for making a public spectacle of me!"

"And I saved your hat, too," he said, clearly laughing at her, and making her suddenly aware of his hand at her waist holding her hat against her. "You are sorely in need of rescuing." He glanced down. "Perhaps you will be more grateful to me if I save your shoe as well?" he suggested smoothly.

Her shoe was loose and dangling on the end of one toe, and she made a grab for it, but then had to grasp the stranger around the neck instead to keep from falling as he moved his arm. His free hand was sliding down her leg!

And then he cupped her shoe to the heel of her foot and slid his arm up under her knees again, stopping her from falling—but also taking her skirts up to her knee! "How can I believe you want me to put you down when you hold onto me so tightly?" She narrowed her eyes at him, giving him the most venomous look she could manage. "I'm sure you think this is very amusing, but this is *most* improper! I demand that you put me down this instant!"

"Right here?" he asked, and the laugh in his eyes made her lose her temper. "And this instant?"

"Of course, right here and at once, you simpleton!"

An eyebrow lifted at the term *simpleton*.

"Very well—if you insist," he said regretfully, and with a flourish he set her down.

In a foot of water.

Until that moment she hadn't realized they weren't on the shore, but that man who'd caught her had been standing in the water, loading crates

33

into a waiting boat. She felt her heavy skirts soak with seawater almost to the knees, shoes sinking into the sand, and gasping, clutched the stranger's arms to keep her balance.

"Oh — you — you *blackguard!*" she cried, righting herself and staring at him in utter disbelief. "You put me down in the water!"

"But you insisted," he said, and held out her hat. She snatched it, and then heard the guffaws and calls from those watching on the docks above.

For the first time she noticed that not only was he bare to the waist, but his rather ragged white trousers were rolled up over his knees. Strong, muscled thighs supported the rest of his hard-lined frame. The water lapped at his calves, which were as well-formed as the rest of him. Then her inappropriate and brazen appraisal of his physique made her shake with fury. Why was she standing here gaping at him? Practically taking inventory?

Her cheeks flamed, and, pulling at her skirts, she started to wade through the water to the shore.

And then her anger got the best of her. How dare this man made a laughingstock of her in front of this crowd of brigands? She waded back, weighted down by her skirts, and slapped him across the cheek. Then she turned, and trying her best to stalk away through the water with dignity, realized she'd need both hands to hold up her heavy skirts. She put her hat back on her head and felt the wet clinging of the plume stick to her cheek, felt a trickle of water run down her neck. Good God! She'd been dragging the hat in the water without noticing! From the cheers of those on the dock, she knew her slap followed by donning the wet hat was the final comic touch the whole humiliating scene needed.

There was a splashing at her side, and the man

she'd slapped ran up to her. She'd hardly begun to turn her head to glare at him when she felt herself being swept up once again into his strong arms. She cried out and struggled, but he had her, dripping skirts and all, and was striding through the breaking waves to the shore.

"Oh! You—" she cried, fighting him.

"It is no use to struggle, you'll find," he said, in a voice that brooked no argument. "It was shameful of me to put you down in the water, and the least I can do is set you safely on shore. You're being met?"

"I am going to hire a carriage. You may put me down when we reach shore and leave me alone!"

"But the least I can do is find one for you. You are in no condition to walk anywhere alone. Your clothes are soaking wet."

"For which I have you to thank!"

"And besides, as you may have noticed, the crowd on the docks is rather rough. No place for a lady like yourself."

"As I can see! Aren't we at shore yet? I must admit this is the first time I've ever been manhandled by a pirate!" She spoke with all the scorn she could manage, but was greeted by a laugh.

"Pirate? So you know what a man does for a living by simply looking at him?"

He waved an arm at a passing carriage—and if Lydia had not grasped him tightly around the neck, she would have fallen.

As the open carriage rolled up, he grinned down at her, making no move to replace his supporting arm.

"I can see you are feeling more friendly to me by the way you are clinging to my neck," he remarked.

"Oh! If you would have the decency not to let go—"

"So, it's being clasped in my arms you are yearning for . . ."

But she had no time for a stinging reply to his sally. He was opening the coach door and swinging her inside. He settled her on the seat and leaned in, looking down at her for a moment.

"And now, shall I claim my reward for finding you a carriage?"

Before she realized what was happening, he'd bent his head and warm lips brushed hers for an instant.

"Mon Dieu! What has happened to you?" came Brigitte's voice.

Jerking away from him, Lydia caught the rakish grin on the lips that had just dared to kiss her own. Her cheeks were flaming as he stepped away to make room for Brigitte to scramble into the carriage. Still chuckling, he turned and walked to a respectful distance where his friend Jacques was waiting for him, grinning.

"Brigitte! Tell the driver to leave at once!" Lydia gasped, averting her eyes from the pair of them.

Brigitte leaned out and spoke to the driver. "The Grand Inn, driver!" The carriage started with a jerk, and Lydia, looking away, did not see the flirtatious smile and wave Brigitte bestowed on the two watching men.

Lydia looked at Brigitte as the girl settled across from her, not looking the least upset. In fact, she looked as if she were trying to put on a properly solemn face over great excitement. "The Grand Inn? How did you know a name to tell the driver? Do you think it will be respectable enough to stay in for one night, until we can arrange to go out to the house?"

"It's the best inn on the island, *Madame,*" Brigitte informed her. "That man—the friend of the man who caught you—told me so."

"You *spoke* to him?"

Brigitte shrugged her shoulders. "I could not save you from the other, so . . ." She sat forward, and her eyes sparkled. "He was truly most civil. He told me he is Jacques Noir, a French privateer. I heard of him on the voyage here. He is said to have plundered every ship and every female in the Caribbean. I believe it. He is handsome, is he not?"

"Brigitte!" Lydia was shocked. But then her curiosity got the better of her. The carriage was moving slowly in the traffic, and she twisted in her seat to look back. The pair of them were still standing there, and though what Brigitte had said was true—they were both very attractive men—she had eyes only for one of them.

She had a last glimpse of him standing in the street, smiling after her, handsome and wild as the devil himself.

My God. She hadn't been in Jamaica but minutes—and she'd already met a pirate!

Chapter Four

The next morning, Lydia stood on the steps of the Grand Inn, reading once again the note that had arrived yesterday evening. The boy who'd brought it panted that he'd scoured all the inns until he'd found her. It was from Blake Spencer, her late husband's overseer, and it apologized for not being able to meet her ship or come to the hotel. The unexpected arrival of an important shipment had detained him.

The note finished by suggesting that she come out to the house Bellefleur, where he would join her as soon as possible, so they could discuss her affairs. She would see something of the island on the way, and the servants would make her comfortable.

Now she was awaiting the arrival of a hired carriage. Spencer. The name rang a bell from the interminable papers she'd had to go over when

Baxter died. She frowned, thinking that it was a singularly cavalier way to treat your new employer.

Well, she'd see soon enough, she thought, as the carriage arrived. She felt good this morning and was looking forward to an outing and to seeing something of the island.

She settled back into the cushions of the open carriage. She'd left Brigitte at the inn to await their trunks, and the driver would return later to fetch her to Bellefleur.

"How long will it take to drive to Bellefleur?" she called to the driver, and he turned and gave her a grin as white and friendly as the clouds sailing overhead.

"Not long, Mistress, these horses they fast, the roads they smooth. Maybe an hour, we have you there." With a flourish of his whip, the driver cracked it over the horses' heads and they broke into a trot. In a few moments they were rolling along a shade-dappled coast road, and for the first time, Lydia got a good look at Jamaica.

It was beautiful.

Everywhere, amid the rich green tropical plants, trees, and vines, were flowers. Orchids, hibiscus, bougainvillea, azaleas. Brilliant birds, as strange to her as the plants, flashed in and out of the sunlight and shadows. She'd never imagined a place could be so lovely — it was like paradise!

Sometimes she caught glimpses of great white houses high among the green. They were enormous and graceful, and she wondered if Bellefleur would be as grand. She knew that many of the owners had come here in irons — wrongdoers indentured for some crime. And imagine, pirates as respectable citizens! The thought of all those criminals, now part of society, was slightly unsettling.

Perhaps under the floral-splashed beauty, behind

the white walls, there was ugliness. It would take a strong person to survive in this new, raw land. Here one might be exposed to harsh realities that were hidden in the more civilized land of England.

Am I strong enough? she wondered.

The memory of sun-bronzed arms with iron muscles and a pair of light gray eyes flashed into her mind. Impatiently, she tried to put the thought of the pirate away, but instead found herself remembering him in all-too-vivid detail. That hard, hawk's face with the arrogant curved nose, the slash of dark brows, the wide firm mouth. The fascinating tautness of his chest muscles, slick with sweat. She remembered the way his tied-back black hair had fallen against the muscles of his neck. No doubt, that man was strong enough for a world like this.

And being in his arms had made her feel so very weak, helpless.

Not able to stop herself, feeling a guilty pleasure, she let herself wonder what would it have been like if he had kissed her more thoroughly than just the slight brush of his lips on hers. If she'd let her head drop back slightly while being held against his chest like that, if she'd lifted her arms and twined them around his neck, felt his shoulder muscles under her fingertips? Maybe brushed her hands along the silver wings at his temples?

With a start, Lydia recovered herself and felt her cheeks flame. What was she doing, having fantasies about a common criminal? It was mad.

She lifted her eyes to the horizon, where great white masses of thunderheads drifted, tinged with purple and gray beneath, the blue of the sky startling between them. The warm, humid wind slid over her skin, the sun danced on the clear, clear water, and all around the deserted shores, the beaches were dazzling. Instead of being hot like

40

she'd feared, the air was heavenly, with a freshness that spoke of flowers and the sea, with a warmth that was delightfully cooled just the right amount by the puffs of breeze.

It must be the tropics, she thought, *affecting me already!*

She smiled, amused. Why not admit it? That pirate had done more to her senses with his arms around her, his killing smile, his light kiss, than any man ever had in the past. All of Baxter's touches had made her want to turn her head away.

It was a good thing she wasn't likely to see him again.

"Mistress, you look now. We coming to where your house is built. This part of the road not far from where you live, so you look that way and then you see the house." The driver's words brought Lydia out of a daydream that was in danger of becoming too pleasant, and a little startled, she looked up. With his whip, he was pointing out toward the sea, but all Lydia could see was dense foliage and waving palms.

But she could see ahead where the road curved, and beyond it would be Bellefleur.

She leaned forward eagerly, anxious to see what the land around her new home was like. As they came around the bend in the road, she saw a jutting peninsula thrusting out into the sea. Where it joined the mainland, purple blue, smoky mountains rose, their feet in steaming jungle. The peninsula itself soared steeply out of the sea in green slopes on all sides, some of them forested and some cleared fields and lawns. At their feet, the green cliffs were girdled with white sand beaches that surrounded tiny turquoise inlets that cut into the peninsula. It had an air of utter peace and privacy, a tiny kingdom, a small paradise. She caught the silver thread of a waterfall falling through a jungled cliff to the beach below.

On the top of the peninsula stood a white house.

It was long and low, the front pillared and surrounded by a verandah, many windows open to the sea. Its stucco was brilliant white against the smooth emerald lawns that sloped in front of it, against the tall darker trees that were set against it at back. Even in the sudden far-off view she had of it from the coast road, she could see from the splashes of color that the gardens surrounding the house were masses of flowers. Graceful of line, Bellefleur was well named, the loveliest house she had ever seen.

"Oh," she breathed, overwhelmed. "Is that really it?" She could send for Amy right away, she thought excitedly. How Amy would love this gorgeous, gorgeous house!

"That's it, Mistress," the driver said. "Not so big as some, but very pretty she be."

Pretty! thought Lydia, staring entranced. An understatement if she'd ever heard one. "Oh! You must be able to see the sea from every room!"

"See it—and hear it, Mistress. House that was there before, she blowed down in a hurricane!" He threw her a sly grin. "But don't be scared, Mistress, they build this new house strong."

If the driver was hoping she'd be unnerved by his disclosure, he must have been disappointed, because an enthralled Lydia, eyes sparkling, was leaning all the way out the carriage, craning her neck for a last glimpse of the house before the trees and the curve of the road cut off her view.

The doors of Bellefleur swung wide, and a middle-aged man with a sunbrowned face that was creased in lines of cheerfulness came down the steps, bowed legs pumping briskly.

He reached her side as she alighted, in time to extend a guiding hand to her elbow and to smile up at her. "Mistress Collins? Am I correct? Daniel O'Hare at your service, most pleased to welcome you to Bellefleur!"

He bowed low and Lydia smiled down at him, warmed by his friendliness and evident pleasure in greeting her. She'd been nervous as they'd turned up the steep, shaded drive, but now that nervousness disappeared. Dan O'Hare was sturdily built but short, dressed in neat black trousers and waistcoat, and a wide-sleeved white shirt. Though the top of his head was bald, the fringe of silver hair around his ears was unashamedly pulled back into a clubbed ponytail. His voice held a sunny Irish lilt that Lydia warmed to at once.

"Thank you, Mr. O'Hare. I am pleased to make your acquaintance. I take it you received my letter? I don't believe in unexpected visits."

"Indeed we did, Mistress, and might I say we're all most pleased to welcome you to Jamaica. It's a rare privilege to welcome anyone from home—especially, if I might be so bold, such a lovely visitor as yourself. It's grace the island, you will!"

He beamed at her, then suddenly clapped a hand to his head. "I was forgettin' myself!" he exclaimed with a stricken look. "May I offer you my sympathies on losin' your fine husband, Mistress Collins? Such a shame—a rare tragedy—so soon after the two of you were joined in holy wedded bliss and all!"

Lydia barely hid a smile at O'Hare's exaggerated dolor. He was a comic little man—and one who evidently didn't stop for breath much. But it wouldn't do to smile when offered condolences. It was already scandalous enough, no doubt, that she'd left off wearing mourning.

"Thank you, Mr. O'Hare," she said gravely. "It was, indeed, a sad loss." She paused, wondering if O'Hare's intelligent-looking eyes missed the fact that she was hardly a grief-stricken widow. "So, Mr. O'Hare, you are the overseer?"

"No, not the overseer!" O'Hare smiled again, his earlier mournful expression evaporating as quickly as mist in the sun. "Saints preserve me, but that's one job too tough for the likes of me! No, I'm more of a butler, and me dear wife Moira's the housekeeper. Indentured I am, a seven-year indenture, of which I've served four," he said proudly.

Lydia wasn't sure how to respond to this. Should she ask him how he came to be indentured? Willingly? Or had he been kidnapped and pressed into signing the papers? Or—she threw him an uncertain glance between her lashes—was he a criminal? Impossible to imagine that his open, almost childlike face hid a criminal past!

But O'Hare spared her the need to reply. Again, he clapped his hand to his head in what seemed to be his stock gesture of self-reproach. "But Mistress Collins! Forgive me! What am I thinking of, keeping you standing out here in the hot sun? My wife Moira'd have me head off at the shoulders if she knew! She's been in a bother all week, getting ready for your visit, and she'd say I don't have the manners of a pig, and right she'd be at that! Come in, come inside!"

With a half-turn, Lydia smiled at the coachman, who tipped his hat to her and gave her a wide grin, and allowed herself to be led by the still-talking O'Hare across the wide sweep of gravel drive up to the front steps.

But she wasn't hearing a word the voluble O'Hare

was saying . . . instead, she was looking at the house. It dazzled the eyes, so white its walls were in the sun. A wide collonaded verandah ran the length of the house front and was shaded by blooming vines that screened out the tropical sun. There were chairs and tables on the verandah, many doors and windows. It was all open and airy, and on this side, overlooked a spectacular view of climbing mountain slopes and spreading gardens filled with flowers. The other side of the house would look to the sea.

They climbed the wide steps to the verandah, and with another bow, O'Hare ushered her inside the house.

". . . and 'tis heartbroken she'll be that she wasn't here to greet you, but we had no way of knowin' which day your ship would come in, of course, and expected a message when you got here. But today's Moira's day to market, and so it's off she is to town. Doesn't trust the other servants to bargain for the best, but then, she's a Scotswoman, she is . . ."

Lydia turned all the way around, scanning the wide reception rooms O'Hare had led her to. Ahead of her, a double row of French doors opened onto a balcony, and the view was of ocean everywhere she looked.

"It's beautiful," she breathed. "The house is so much more than Baxter—" She blushed. "I mean, the late Mr. Collins—ever told me. You must forgive my unexpected arrival. It's just that I was so anxious to see what the house was like, and whether I'd like it enough to stay or not."

"Stay?" She turned to find Dan O'Hare goggling at her. But he recovered himself quickly. "Please, Mistress Collins, you must be fatigued with the drive. Excuse me for a moment, I'll go and give orders for tea to be brought, and send word to Mr.

45

Spencer that you're here. He was most specific—
wanted to greet you himself, he did. Welcome you,
like. Excuse me."

And with a third bow in as many minutes, Dan
O'Hare was gone before she could ask him any
questions.

She looked after him, feeling slightly out of
breath, then decided she liked Dan O'Hare very
much. He might be too free with his tongue by
English standards, but obviously things were more
relaxed in the islands—and she liked not having to
be on her dignity all the time.

Besides, she was sure she could find out a lot
about Bellefleur and the people who lived there
from such a dedicated talker.

In a few moments he was back, along with a
servant who set out tea. He sat across from her and
beamed at her. "So—how long have you been here?
Have you seen your holdings yet? What did you
think of the warehouses?" he asked.

"I came here first. I was most anxious to see the
house. I'm afraid I haven't seen anything else yet,
for I just arrived yesterday. In fact, I'm eager to be
shown over the house. It looks to be a most adequate size."

For a moment, Dan O'Hare wrinkled his brow.
Did he look puzzled? But the expression was gone
as quickly as it had seemed to appear.

"But I'm afraid Mr. Spencer wishes to show you
the house himself. We've sent word to him, and he
should be here soon enough."

"What kind of man is Mr. Spencer?"

Again O'Hare's face registered surprise. "You've
not read his reports to your husband? A fine man,
he is. Not polished, perhaps, but there's no one like
him when it comes to managing a business. Why,
it's he who turned your late husband's holdings

46

from just a single ship into the richest exporting business in the islands. It's because of Mr. Spencer your late husband rarely had to make trips here to see to things himself. A luxury not many absentee owners have."

"It sounds like we're lucky indeed to have such a man. How long has he worked for—us?" Lydia wished she'd paid more attention when going over all the endless papers and bills of lading. But it had all been so incomprehensible . . . and boring.

"Well, he's been in the islands nearly ten years, I think. He'd be about thirty-five now, I'd guess. The first five years here he spent as an indenture. Your late husband bought his papers from a cane-cutting crew, I gather. Looking for muscle and sinew to work on the docks and warehouses, Mr. Baxter was. Well, it wasn't long before Spencer was running things and making Mr. Baxter more of a profit than ever before. Your late husband made him the overseer. And when his indenture was up, he agreed to stay for a stake of his own. He's worth it, I think you'll find, Madam. Men of his abilities are hard to find."

Lydia was taken aback. "Cane-cutting crews? Isn't that where they send—"

"Convicts? Aye. But don't let it worry you, Mistress Collins. There's many who came to the islands in that way, but for some trifling offense. The laws in England are harsh for offenses like debt."

"Oh—debt. Was that it?"

Lydia's relief must have shown in her face, for O'Hare hesitated before he answered reluctantly. "Well, I don't rightly know. I never dared ask him. But Spencer is an honest man, I can vouch for it. A mite rough-hewn, perhaps, for a lady of your background. Arrogant as Lucifer and sometimes hard, but then, he has to be to thrive here. But a fair man, one I'm proud to call my friend. Why, 'tis he who insisted there be no slaves or forced indentures working for your late husband's holdings—only free indentures like myself and my wife Moira. We came here to find work. Beats starvin' in Ireland. Here, we eat well every day and when we're through, we'll have enough saved to buy us more acres than a squireen would have back in Ireland!"

Lydia was relieved that O'Hare and his wife were willing indentures, but unnerved that her overseer might be a criminal. He didn't sound like a man she was going to enjoy dealing with. But she reminded herself that she had to learn to be firm, if she really meant to stay here and oversee all these businesses.

"I'm glad to hear there are no unwilling servants here, Mr. O'Hare," she managed.

His look approved her. "If I might be so bold, Mistress Collins, I'd say that's why the businesses have done so well. Spencer has a generous system of bonuses set up, and I believe folk work harder when they have a hand in things."

"It . . . it sounds like a lot to learn," Lydia said uncertainly.

"I'll wager you'll do fine with Mr. Spencer's guidance."

Lydia returned O'Hare's warm smile, all at once feeling welcome and at home. She wondered what his wife was like. If all the people she had to deal with were as friendly and likeable as O'Hare, she'd be at home here in no time. Emboldened by O'Hare's warmth, she decided to venture a question that might make her sound foolish, but one she'd been dying to ask.

"Mr. O'Hare—after my husband died—well, all the lawyers and their papers were so confusing, and of course, I wasn't really at my best—"

"Naturally not," he put in sympathetically.

"I'm afraid I'm confused. Exactly what do I own in the way of things like ships and warehouses?"

He laughed. "I know just what you mean! I've no head for lawyer's jawings, either, they'd try the patience of a saint! Well, for starters, here on Jamaica you own four warehouses and all the land they sit on, two here in Port Royal and two across the island. We ship to the colonies up North as well as to Europe, and import goods scarce here in the islands, like good building wood, pitch, and tar. And, of course, you own several coastal schooners, and four oceangoing ships. Makes trade monstrously profitable, owning your own ships."

Feeling slightly overwhelmed, Lydia ventured, "That's all?"

He laughed again. "Isn't that enough? Of course, there's more. Your late husband had his finger in plenty of profitable things. There's a coffeehouse he owns a portion of, and a couple of taverns he has an interest in — all most sound investments."

It sounded like so much! Lydia set down her cup of tea and stood, smoothing her dark green moire silk skirt. She looked down at it ruefully. Yards and yards of bustled silk were rustlingly draped over many stiff petticoats. With stockings and shoes, and lace jabot at her throat, she was stifling and feeling too warm. She walked to the window. "Quite a view — and a breeze. I can see I am going to have to learn to dress differently for this climate," she said.

"Aye, it takes a bit of adjustin' to, after the cool climate that England enjoys. Well, Mistress Collins, I'm afraid I must leave you for a bit. I've me duties to see to, and with Moira gone — but Mr. Spencer should be here soon, and feel free to explore the rooms down here if you like. If there's anything I can get to make you comfortable, you have only to ring. And might I say again, welcome to Jamaica!"

Lydia watched him go, a warm smile on her face. It seemed she'd found a peaceful haven at last.

The sun was dipping toward the horizon, and still the overseer had not arrived. Lydia had explored the house, then been served luncheon by Dan O'Hare. But she was too happy to be annoyed; she had started mentally composing a letter to Amy, telling her all about the house.

Great, gold-tinged clouds hung above the calm sea, and the breeze came over the waves and lifted Lydia's hair. She stood on the seaward side of the house, in the door to a verandah that was built on high wooden stilts above a green slope that fell to the sea, so that she seemed to be standing on air above the sea itself. Behind her was an echoing ballroom. Its French doors stood open and gauze curtains blew in the wind. Almost half the house on this side was taken up with this ballroom, with its polished wooden floors under crystal chandeliers.

Simple but lovely, she thought. That's what all of Bellefleur was like. The rooms were open and airy, with a feeling of casualness that suited this relaxed island paradise so well. At every hand were windows and doors, open to the ocean, to the breeze, framing scenes of flowers and palm trees and blue sea. The verandahs that ran around the house seemed as much part of it as the rooms inside.

What sparse furniture there was showed a taste that surprised her. White walls, beautiful colors, everything so lovely for all it was spare. Crystal bowls overflowing with flowers. Mahogany polished until it was like mirrors. As she'd been shown through its rooms, she'd wondered again and again at the contrast to Baxter's other houses. The house in London was crammed with the overly ornate, French furniture, stiffly formal. The estate in Scotland was stuffed with heavy furniture, gloomy with ancient paintings of hunting scenes and red velvet draperies. But Bellefleur was a house to be lived in, not looked at.

She loved it.

Impulsively, she stretched her arms up toward the serene sunset, feeling absurdly glad to be here, glad to have had almost a half hour alone to look at the rooms. It had been the right decision to come to Jamaica!

Amy would love it here. They could make a new life together, far from their father's tyranny. Here they would find happiness and a new freedom neither had even imagined before.

Suddenly she was so happy she had to speak aloud.

"I'm so glad to be here — a home of my own — at last!" she laughed, stretching her arms up over her head and feeling the breeze mold her dress against her and play in her hair. "Baxter, I never knew you had such taste, but thank you at least for Bellefleur!"

"He didn't, Madam."

The deep voice coming unexpectedly from behind her startled her horribly, and with a gasp, she jumped, then whirled around.

What she saw startled her even more, so that she gave a small scream, her hand going to her throat, eyes flying wide.

Across the ballroom stood the pirate from the docks.

He was dressed this time in black knee breeches that clung to his muscled thighs, spotless white stockings. A loose white shirt with full sleeves open at the throat to show a bit of his bronze chest, a

51

hint of lace at the wrists. Slung around his lean hips was a leather sword belt, and a long, service-able-looking sword hung at his thigh. His hair was pulled neatly back and tied with a black ribbon. He looked like a gentleman, nothing like the half-naked savage who'd caught her in his arms.

But there were the same silver touches at his temples, and those were the same light eyes, so startling in his bronzed hawk's face. There was no doubt about it—it was him.

"What are you doing here?" she gasped, her heart beating far too hard in her throat as her eyes met his and held. "You—I don't know what you want, but I warn you, the house is full of servants! I have only to scream, and—"

A black brow quirked upward, and his dark face seemed amused. He took a few sauntering, lazy steps toward her, then stopped, one fist resting on his hip above his sword. She realized he moved silently, like a cat. No wonder she hadn't heard him approach. What on earth was he doing here? She couldn't seem to think at all when his eyes were on hers.

"Why would you do that, Madam? Was our brief meeting so distasteful to you? It didn't seem you disliked it at the time." His words were a drawl with an edge to them she didn't like. He was mocking her fright.

She drew herself up, regaining her calm from being startled. "I know that you are a pirate, sir, and you have no business here at Bellefleur. I—"

Once more he startled her. He threw back his dark head and laughed. She watched him, backing up a slight step, comforted by the fact that the open French doors were behind her.

Those disconcerting eyes came to rest on her once more, lit with amusement.

"I am no pirate—though some might say it. I am your overseer."

There was a pause as she stared at him. Her overseer! She felt dizzy all at once, as if she might faint.

He bowed slightly. "Blake Spencer, at your service. And indeed, Madam, I have every business here at Bellefleur. I own it."

Chapter Five

Lydia stared at this apparition in front of her, trying to make sense of what he'd just said. He stood with folded arms, regarding her impassively, waiting for her to speak, but she thought she saw a gleam of amusement in his eyes.

"Now wait. *You* are Mr. Blake Spencer, the overseer?" she said, her gaze fastening on his gold earring.

"That is correct." He gave the slightest — and most mocking — of bows.

"And am I to further understand," Lydia asked frostily, "that you claim to *own* this house?"

A grin was her answer, a flash of white teeth against his brown skin. "That, also, is correct, Madam. And may I add, I regret I was not here to welcome you to Bellefleur in person? Business detained me. But I am happy to have you here as a visitor. Especially," he added, and she saw the glint in his eyes, "since we don't often have such—lovely—visitors." His gaze went over her, taking in her silk dress and every curve beneath it.

Not to be intimidated, Lydia smiled back at him, her best duchess-to-stableboy smile. She lifted an arm and waved toward some chairs, giving him her gracious permission to sit in *her* house. "I believe you are operating under a misapprehension, Mr. Spencer. Perhaps you would care to sit and discuss it?"

One black brow was lifted cynically at her. It seemed her grande dame performance would be wasted on him, for he stood his ground, purposely ignoring her invitation to be seated. "A misapprehension, Mistress Collins?"

"A terrible misapprehension, I'm afraid. I am the owner of this house. My late husband left it to me. The solicitors in London were quite clear on that point, and I have seen the deed."

"I see." He raised a negligent arm gracefully toward the chairs that stood in an embrasure near the windows, politely granting *her* permission to have a seat in *his* house. "Then perhaps we *should* sit and discuss this comfortably?" With the ironic air of a gentleman, he walked to a chair and waited for her to join him.

Lydia clenched her fists against her anger of his blatant parody of her. He didn't seem a bit shaken by her declaration of ownership. He was as cool and unruffled as any pirate about to scuttle a ship.

She walked rigidly to the chair. He waited for her to sit before taking his place opposite hers. "Comfortable?" he asked.

She took a moment to compose herself and the folds of her gown before meeting his eyes with deadly calm. "Quite."

55

He leaned back in his chair. "You mentioned a deed. Do you have it?"

Lydia thought frantically. There had been so many papers! Uncertainly, she shook her head. "No, I believe the deed was left in London — Whitehall — and it was definitely in my name. But, Mr. Spencer, certainly you don't think I would travel halfway around the world if I believed I had nowhere to live when I arrived?"

This time she could clearly see twin sparks of amusement dancing in his eyes. "Not knowing you well, Mistress Collins, I cannot say what you might or might not do. But I would hazard from our earlier meeting that your temperament is quite impulsive indeed." Ruefully, he rubbed his cheek, as if remembering the stinging slap she had planted there.

Lydia felt her cheeks heat up. The rogue! How dare he refer to the fiasco of their last meeting! No gentleman would dare to allude to what had happened between them — but then, it was clear Mr. Blake Spencer was no gentleman. A criminal and a pirate. And now, simply because she was what he thought of as a helpless widow, no doubt he believed she would be easy prey. She opened her mouth to tell him just how mistaken he was, but he went on smoothly, clearly enjoying her discomfiture.

"As to why you came to Jamaica, your properties here *are* quite extensive. However, this house does not number among them. I don't know if you are aware that I was indentured for seven years in your late husband's service?"

Lydia again felt a rush of discomfort — almost embarrassment. He was so composed about it, speaking almost as if he were *proud* of the fact he'd been indentured for some crime! She wondered exactly what hideous deed had earned him the heavy sentence of seven years' indenture, and decided he looked capable of anything. "I am aware of it," she said coldly.

He flashed a grin at her, seeming to read her thoughts, and to be entertained by them. "Yes. Well, at the end of my indenture—nearly two years ago—your late husband was most anxious to retain my services. It saved him from having to take up residence here on Jamaica, and there were other advantages."

Well, at least the rogue wasn't going to brag about those "other advantages," Lydia thought. Now that she'd seen him, she had no doubt he'd been well paid for these services. And his next words confirmed it:

"In any case, your late husband and I came to an arrangement. I had no real use for money. I am desirous of establishing my own fortune here, and to that end, property and goods serve me better than money. In addition to my salary, every six months Collins deeded me a piece of property, a coastal schooner, a piece of waterfront footage, and this house."

"I am sorry, Mr. Spencer, but I hold the deed to this house. My solicitors—"

He held up a hand to silence her. "Naturally, I don't expect you to take my word without proof." He walked out of the room and came back in a few moments with a folded piece of paper.

She took it, heart sinking.

Could it be a more recent deed to Bellefleur than the one the solicitors had shown her? Without a place to live, her father wouldn't let Amy join her. And housing on the islands was scarce because of the great expense of shipping lumber and building materials from North America. It might take months for her to find a new place to live, or have a house built. Trying to contain the sinking feeling, she unfolded the document and began to read.

It was a letter from Baxter to Spencer, dated March 1682. She recognized Baxter's hand at once, and knew it was no forgery. She scanned the perorations about their business, and at last found the key paragraph.

"As we agreed, at the close of this period, I shall file the deed to the house called Bellefleur, on the island of Jamaica, in Whitehall, in your name, as recompense for your services. Yr. grateful servant, Baxter Collins."

She looked up. "And when was this agreed-on period to be up, Mr. Spencer? The letter does not say."

"It was last April, Madam."

"But, Mr. Spencer, I have only your word that the agreed-on period actually elapsed. And secondly, whatever you *claim* my late husband's intentions were, the fact remains that he did *not* file the deed, which is still in my name."

"Perhaps, Madam, that is true, since I believe the time period we are speaking of was around your wedding?" She nodded. "Then I can understand how a man with a new bride as lovely as yourself might well forget all about business matters for a time. And he died soon after the wedding?"

"Two months," Lydia said shortly.

His eyes went slowly over her green dress, and the corners of his mouth lifted mockingly. "My condolences on your sad loss, Mistress Collins. I am sure you feel it deeply."

"Mr. Spencer, I fail to see—"

"In any case, this letter proves your late husband had a business agreement with me and intended to file the deed to the house in my name. He perhaps put it off due to the wedding, and he could not have expected to die so soon. As you are already aware, all property transactions for the Crown Colonies are filed in Whitehall in London, and they often take a number of months to complete. Doubtless your late husband filed the deed in my name and word of it has not yet reached your solicitors. Mister Collins was never behindhand where business was concerned. And even if he did not—"

It was Lydia's turn to hold up an imperious hand for silence. Rising, she said, "Further discussion on this point seems fruitless, Mr. Spencer. We cannot solve it by arguing between ourselves. It seems we need a legal opinion."

He rose, too, and stood for a moment looking down at her. "I would agree. As you have just arrived, I do not imagine you've yet met Andrew Ames, your late husband's solicitor here and man of business?"

She shook her head. "I have heard of him, and intended to call on him when I got settled."

"Then I suggest we send someone to fetch him now. He'll have finished dining, and his land adjoins Bellefleur—he is, in fact, our nearest neighbor. I think we'd both feel better, if this matter was settled as speedily as possible, don't you agree?"

He continued to stare down at her, and she was all at once aware of him again as a man, remembering what it had felt like to be clasped in his arms against his bared chest.

"I think that would be best," she said, drawing in her breath and seating herself again.

Feeling slightly dizzy, she watched him as he crossed the room to ring for a servant. He walked with the grace of a panther, and her eyes traveled over the width of his shoulders, the narrowness of his hips, his long legs. He looked, she thought, provocatively uncivilized. With that black hair caught back on his neck, the small gold hoop gleaming against his tanned skin, and those light gray eyes under straight dark brows, he was nothing like any of the men she'd met in polite London society. Uneasily, she wondered if she was going to like it here on Jamaica.

And more to the point, how much of her opinion of the island would depend on the trouble this man would cause her.

He crossed the room and sat opposite her again. As if he could read her mind merely by reading her expression, he said, "I must admit I'm thoroughly puzzled. What brings a delicately bred London lady to the wilds of Jamaica?"

Lydia stared at him. *"If* it is any of your business, Mr. Spencer, I am sure you are aware that properties require efficient management to continue to be successful. I came here to look them over."

He sat back, and she could almost feel the intensity of his eyes on her. But his face remained bland. "Aware? None more so, Mistress Collins, seeing that it was I who bought most of those properties for your late husband, and have been running them very efficiently without your help for several years."

"I am completely aware of your management abilities, Mr. Spencer. But I was very active in my late husband's affairs, and I intend to remain so," she storied, not wanting him to know the real reason for her need to settle in Jamaica. It was none of his affair, and furthermore, he was being unbearably confident. She wasn't going to give him any room to consider her a meddlesome incompetent, as his comment implied.

"But it still seems strange to me that a lady like yourself would travel so far to dirty her hands with trade, particularly in this part of the world. I'd

60

think the healthy balance sheets you receive each quarter would be more than enough to keep you safe in London, buying gowns and jewels."

Lydia gave him a frigidly scathing look. "Some women, Mr. Spencer, have more on their minds than simply gowns and jewels. Why do you find it so strange that a woman would have an interest in what belongs to her?"

But it seemed she would have to wait for her answer. At that moment a servant walked in, and they both looked up, distracted.

It was Dan O'Hare. "Evenin', Mistress Collins." He beamed at Lydia, giving her a broad wink, then turned to Spencer. "And what would you be needin' this fine evenin', sir?"

"Mistress Collins and I have a matter to discuss with Mr. Ames. Would you kindly send a servant to fetch him for us?"

"With pleasure, sir. Might I bring some refreshments for yourself and the lady?"

Spencer nodded. Dan O'Hare bowed to them both, and with a final twinkle for Lydia, left. She turned back to Spencer who was standing near the terrace doors now, his back to her, looking out into the night.

"You haven't answered me, Mr. Spencer. Why do you find my idea of living on Jamaica so laughable?"

He pushed open the terrace door and said, "Come here. I want to show you something."

Reluctantly, Lydia rose and preceded him out onto the balcony.

The sky had turned to delicate shades of apricot and robin's egg green, the clouds salmon pink to mauve. A great white star bloomed in the deepening night sky to the east. She could hear the thunder of the surf below and see the beach gleaming pale as a bone in the moonlight. The jungle trees and palms along the shore were full of mysterious murmurings, leaves moving in the night breeze, and she heard the strange cries of nightbirds. Far out to sea, a ship's riding lights twinkled. The breeze filled her nose with the heady scent of a thousand flowers and the tang of salt water. Except for the ship's lights, she could see no other signs of civilization.

Spencer's voice came from behind her. "It's a wild land you see before you—raw and as yet untamed. It's no place for a fine London lady whose white hands have never known the feel of labor, whose sensibilities are easily offended."

Lydia turned, indignant. "And how would you know what I am accustomed to, Mr. Spencer? We have barely met, and you know nothing at all about me. It is the height of—"

"Ah, but you keep forgetting. This is not our first meeting." His voice came out of the scented dusk, low, and she saw the flash of his teeth and the gleam of his eyes in the moonlight. He was grinning, the devil!

"Oh! you are indeed a reprobate to bring that— that *incident* up, but still, you learned no more of me in that meeting than this one, for I have told you little about myself, and—"

Warm hands clasped hers, then moved to her wrists. She tried to pull her hands away, but he was too strong for her to resist.

He turned her palms upward. "I don't need to be told to know things about you. These are the hands of a London lady." He laughed softly, as she tried to jerk out of his grasp, and then ran his thumbs over her upturned palms. "Skin as soft and white as a camelia. And I learned something else about you in that first meeting that you didn't tell me."

Lydia stopped struggling, realizing it was undignified and useless. Maybe once he made his point he'd let her go—and the sooner she let him, the sooner she could get away. His caressing thumbs were causing strange sensations to shiver all the way up her bare arms, raising gooseflesh.

"What was that?" she asked coolly, when he didn't go on.

For an answer, he raised her hands and bent his head to meet them. She felt a shock as his warm lips met her palm, then slowly traveled over her skin to her wrist. She gasped as his mouth brushed the skin on the inside of her wrist, slowly and burningly. She tried again to jerk her hands out of his grasp, and he raised his head. He was laughing softly.

"I learned you need kissing," he said.

At last he let her free, and her temper got the best of her.

"And just what makes you think I need kissing?" she cried.

"Your pulse is racing. And this morning when I held you so closely in my arms, I could feel you trembling—with excitement."

"How dare you, Mr. Spencer!? I was trembling with fear, not excitement! And if my pulse is racing now, it's because I'm so furious, not because—"

"You want to kiss me as much as I want to kiss you?"

"Oh!" Anything she said, he turned it around. She brushed past him, and heard him say with a laugh in his voice, "You need kissing—and I promise I'll see you get it, if you stay. There are wolves on Jamaica who will eat you up, lovely Lydia, and I intend to be the first to do so. We need not be rivals, my love. I would prefer quite another relationship with you than the one we have now. One much warmer."

She broke away from him and rushed to the wide-open balcony doors, only to be brought up short.

A tall, brown-haired man stood staring at her, startled as she was — an obvious witness to the whole humiliating scene.

From behind her, Blake Spencer's hateful voice drawled, "Ah, I believe you have not yet met our solicitor, Andrew Ames. Mr. Ames, may I present Mistress Lydia Collins?"

Cheeks afire, Lydia whirled to glare at him, lounging in the doorway, arms crossed, one shoulder against the frame, cool and insufferable as the devil himself.

Chapter Six

Lydia gave Blake Spencer the most scathing look she could muster before turning to Andrew Ames, a gracious smile on her face. She extended her hand to him, and, as if the previous incident had never occurred, said sweetly, "Mr. Ames, it is a pleasure to make your acquaintance." She heard Spencer's low chuckle behind her and willed herself to ignore it.

Ames politely took her hand and kissed it, bowing slightly at the waist, "The pleasure is mine, Mistress Collins."

She was about to offer him a seat, when she noticed Dan O'Hare standing in the doorway, gaping at the three of them, a pewter serving tray in his hands. No doubt he too had heard and seen everything, she thought, and felt nettled all over again at Spencer for embarrassing her in front of Ames *and* the servant.

She addressed the Irishman. "Thank you, Mr. O'Hare. Mr. Ames has only just arrived. You may serve us now."

O'Hare snapped to attention and placed the tray on a low table in front of a dark green velvet settee in the middle of the room. While he poured the wine into pewter goblets, Lydia took the opportunity to consider Andrew Ames, checking off his qualities as a possible ally.

First off, his kiss of her hand had been appropriately genteel, and she felt a rush of relief to know that other men on the island were not all as forward as Blake Spencer. Apparently, fine etiquette had not been completely abandoned here.

Ames was as tall as Spencer, but of slighter build, with long brown hair tied at the nape of his neck. Without seeming too obvious, she leaned slightly to one side to check his ear and was relieved to find no earring there—he was no pirate, thank heavens! He appeared to be a few years younger than Spencer and nearly as handsome, but less dangerous-looking. Ah! That was the difference. Ames' green eyes and even features gave him the face of a man she felt she could trust. She doubted if he would ever think to kiss a lady's wrist. He seemed a perfect gentleman—the complete opposite of Spencer—and one who would not allow that pirate to take advantage of her. She came to the conclusion that Andrew Ames and Blake Spencer had nothing more in common than their residency on Jamaica.

Lydia gestured to the settee as O'Hare excused himself. "Mr. Ames, won't you please take a seat?"

Ames looked from her to where Blake was still standing in the doorway, and smiled broadly. "I will in a moment, Mistress Collins, but first I'd give a hearty welcome to my good friend, Spence, here."

To Lydia's consternation, Ames crossed the room and took Spencer's hand, shaking it fiercely, and slapping him on the back—like a long-lost relative.

"Spence, old boy, but it is good to have you back from Barbados! I see you've found all the furnishings you wanted for the house, but tell me, what of the copper bathing tub? Were there any in Bridgetown to be had?" Here he turned to a shocked Lydia. "He's been looking for one for months—says the springs are too cold for bathing."

Spencer laughed. "I found one, Ames. A big, oval copper tub on feet, with a plug in the bottom for draining. And I'd say it's large enough for the three of us!"

Lydia blushed and sank to the settee. She could barely believe her ears. All this talk of private grooming, and in front of a woman! Nor had she missed the mischievous quirk Spencer's mouth gave when he bragged about the tub's size—as if she'd ever climb into a tub with him! This wasn't turning out as she planned at all. The two of them seemed as thick as thieves.

Spencer was going on. "It was the sole possession of a Frenchman I met in Bridgetown, and he wouldn't part with it. Seems he slept under it when it rained. When he heard my offer, though, he gladly handed it over. It cost me dearly, I admit, but it will be such a pleasure to have a hot bath after a day's work."

"I'd have to look at it, if you don't mind. I fancy one myself," Ames said.

"Not at all. It's out back in the kitchen. Moira has been scrubbing it—"

67

"Pardon me for interrupting, Mister Spencer." Lydia could no longer hold her tongue. "We do have a matter to discuss with Mr. Ames, or had you forgotten?"

"I nearly had," he replied innocently enough, but the impish sparkle in his eyes told her he was enjoying making her wait. "It will keep until we've seen the tub. Andrew and I haven't seen each other for some time, and I wouldn't want to burden him with business first thing. It will take only a moment, and you can join us if you like."

Before she could reply, Spencer had grabbed two goblets of wine and directed Andrew Ames through the door toward the kitchen. Lydia sat there shocked, kicking herself mentally for thinking Ames would have taken her side. Why wouldn't the two of them be friends? They were neighbors. And, she'd wager, Ames was Spencer's solicitor, too.

"Mistress Collins?" she heard the scoundrel call after her from the kitchen. "Are you coming? It is a handsome tub."

She bridled at the mocking tone in his voice. "In a moment," she called as sweetly as she could and rose from the settee. He wouldn't make a fool of her in front of Andrew Ames, she vowed, and stormed after them, determined to take care of the business of Bellefleur, and *immediately*.

Once in the kitchen, though, she stopped dead in her tracks, unable to comprehend what she saw. Not only was Ames friends with Spencer, but he was completely addlebrained, too!

He and Spencer both sat in the huge copper tub, facing each other, drinking the wine and talking about crops of all things! So much for her opinion of her solicitor's maturity.

Ames was speaking. "I took your advice about planting the cane in the east field and the indigo in the west. Both crops are doing splendidly. You'll make a plantation owner out of me yet, Spence."

"It's the least I can do for the counsel you give me," he replied, giving Lydia a smug look over his shoulder. It was obvious he thought he had Ames squarely on his side. He nudged Ames with his foot. "What do you think? Is it big enough for Mistress Collins, too?"

Ames looked at Lydia, and the smile faded from his lips. He stood up and stepped outside the tub, looking very embarrassed. "Perhaps, but from her expression, I'd say we'd have a difficult time getting her in here. Mistress Collins, I beg your pardon. We have been acting like utter fools and ignoring you. And I've been terribly remiss in not having offered my condolences straight off on the passing of your husband. A fine man he was. Mr. Collins and I worked closely when he visited Jamaica, and I was very sorry to hear of his passing."

"Thank you, Mr. Ames," Lydia said, grateful for a chance to speak with him at last. "Your condolences are—"

"Mr. Spencer!" A woman with flame-colored hair and a face full of freckles swept into the room, her face puckered with indignation. This must be Moira O'Hare. Lydia sighed in exasperation. Would there be no end to these constant interruptions?

Moira held a wooden bucket of clean water in one hand and a scrub brush in the other. She signaled to the kitchen door with the brush and addressed Blake who still sat in the tub. "Remove yourself from that tub, mon, and this very moment if you want to take another breath. I havna had a

69

chance to properly scroob it, and I don't take kindly to launderin' your breeches because you've a mind to sit in the filthy thing."

Blake scrambled out. "Come now, Moira, you know you enjoy 'scroobing' my shirts and trousers," he teased, then flinched when she threatened to throw the scrub brush at him.

"You're enough to provoke the Devil," Moira muttered, and Lydia had to agree. She almost wished Moira had thrown the brush at him. A nice lump on the head would serve him right for making her wait so long to talk to Ames.

"Now, out of here," Moira commanded, setting down the bucket. "The kitchen's no place to entertain guests. Where have your manners gone, mon? This is what comes of not having a woman around to see things done proper."

He took Moira's hand and spun her around. "I would marry you, sweet Moira, but you're already taken."

Lydia thought the Scotswoman would commit murder. Moira brought her arm back ready to fling the scrub brush at him, but before she could let it fly, he had ducked out of the room, laughing.

Ames nodded in the direction he had gone. "He is a lively one."

"He's demon-possessed, that one is," Moira muttered and knelt to dip the brush in the bucket to finish cleaning the tub.

Lydia spotted her chance to address the solicitor without interruption. "Mr. Ames, would you care to accompany me into the drawing room? There is a matter between Mr. Spencer and myself that distresses me terribly, and I would be very grateful for your expert opinion. I'm afraid it can't wait any longer."

Ames turned and started to say something, then stopped and merely stared at her face for a moment. Then his gaze dropped appreciatively to view the rest of her. From the way his mouth nearly dropped open, Lydia knew she now had his complete attention. And, she thought, she would use it to her best advantage as Spencer had used his friendship with Ames.

"It w-would be my utmost pleasure t-to assist you, Mistress Collins," Ames stammered in reply. "If there's *any* advice I can offer you, I'd give it gladly. Again, I must apologize for my rude behavior. I'd blame it on Blake—he has such an infectious nature, you know—but it'd be a poor excuse for having abused such a gracious and lovely lady as yourself."

"Your apologies are unnecessary, Mr. Ames. No one understands better than I the excitement of seeing an old friend after a long absence." She slipped her hand through his arm and eyed him coyly through her lashes, giving him a smile she didn't feel. She hated playing games like this, and knew she would regret this flirtation later. Oh, hang Blake Spencer for making her do this! But one way or another, she'd tip the scales back in her favor, and show that arrogant vagabond that Lydia Lyndham Collins was not to be trifled with.

The ticking of the white and gold porcelain clock on the mantelpiece almost drove Lydia mad. She glanced at it for what seemed the hundredth time that evening. Nearly a quarter of an hour had passed and still Ames hadn't spoken. Nervously, she

71

twirled her shoe around and around with her big toe beneath her skirts, then looked to where Blake, arms crossed over his chest, sat watching Ames with an intensity that could have burned holes into the poor solicitor's head. Ames had patiently listened to both sides of the story with little comment, and now stood pacing the room, rubbing his jaw and shaking his head.

"Well?" boomed Blake, obviously past all patience.

Ames shrugged. "I'm not sure."

"Not sure? I've shown you the letter. It makes it perfectly clear who owns this house."

"There are other things to consider, Spence." Ames turned to Lydia. "Men like your late husband are notorious for employing several solicitors to handle their business matters. It's a means of keeping the full extent of their properties and holdings in confidence. I know for a fact that there were certain matters Mr. Collins entrusted to me, and others to Mr. Brunbury, Jamaica's other solicitor. It's possible he handled his affairs in London in the same way."

Lydia felt sick to her stomach. It was more than possible—it was a certainty. How well she remembered the endless parade of solicitors with their clerks, secretaries, and recorders calling on her after her husband's death, each to discuss some new piece of business.

She looked at Blake, who had risen and was now standing behind his chair. With each new possibility Ames had named, he'd nodded his head, his smile growing wider, as if Ames had confirmed his right to the house. How dare he be so confident!

"But all this is merely conjecture," Lydia stated

72

flatly. "We can speculate until the end of time, but the face remains that no other deed has surfaced as of yet, and until such time, the house is mine."

Ames looked doubtful. "In essence, yes—"

"You've heard it from his own mouth, Mr. Spencer. The house is mine until a more recent deed comes to light." It was Lydia's chance to be the confident one, and she enjoyed the look of horror on Blake's face.

Ames raised his voice. "Mistress Collins, you didn't allow me to finish. Yes, in essence, the house is yours, until another deed is brought forth, but we cannot ignore Mr. Collins's letter to Mr. Spencer, stating his intentions. In some cases, a letter of intent is as valid as any other document."

"Then the house is mine," Blake stated firmly.

Ames was apparently at his wits' end. He took a handkerchief from his pocket and wiped his forehead. "That's not what I meant at all."

Blake exploded. "Then say what you mean, damn it! All this verbal seesawing is making me dizzy. *Who owns this house?*"

The solicitor sighed heavily, his shoulders slumping forward. This evening had been extremely difficult. Never before had he dealt with two such mule-headed people in all his life! Each one was determined to claim ownership of this house and claim it *tonight*. And what he had to tell them next would make neither of them happy.

Ames took a deep breath before plunging into his final assessment of the situation. "At the present time, neither of you have proved ownership beyond a doubt. Nevertheless, you both have an equal claim to Bellefleur. Until I'm able to write to Whitehall and present your case there . . . investigate the possibility of the existence of another deed . . . obtain a ruling on the letter of intent as a binding document or not, your *claims* to this house are on equal grounds. However, I cannot determine ownership tonight from the evidence at hand."

When Ames finished, he sat on the settee, wiped his forehead again with his handkerchief, and wondered when the shouting would start again.

But both Lydia and Blake were silent.

Finally, Lydia rose from her chair and addressed the solicitor. "Mr. Ames, it was very kind of you to come here and apprise us of the situation. I am most grateful to you for your opinion, and I'm sure Mr. Spencer is, too."

A doubtful grunt came from Blake.

Lydia ignored him and continued. "When could Mr. Spencer and I expect to hear the final outcome of your investigations?"

"Since you both seem rather anxious to have this matter settled, I'll send a letter by ship no later than the end of this week. I'd say it would be no longer than two or three months before we'd receive an answer."

"Two or three months!" Blake burst out.

Ames appealed to his friend, "It's the best I can do, Blake."

"And that's all we can ask," Lydia proffered, rising. "I think we've taken up enough of your time, Mr. Ames. Again, I thank you for speaking with us. And now, may I show you to the door?"

Ames bowed. "It would be a pleasure." He turned to Blake, offering his hand. "Good evening, Spence. As always, it's been interesting."

Blake crossed to Ames and shook his head. "Yes, it has, Andrew. I would like to offer my thanks, too, and an apology for being so hot-tempered."

"No apology necessary. I know what Bellefleur means to you." He gave Blake a knowing smile, and Lydia felt a pang of guilt. She hated causing all this trouble, but Bellefleur meant a good deal to her, too—everything depended on it. And if it turned out that the house was hers, she would fully reimburse Spencer for any of his expenses, perhaps deed him some other tract of land that he could build on. It was the least she could do. This satisfied her for the moment, and she turned her attention to Andrew Ames. "Follow me, Mr. Ames."

She led the way out into the hallway and toward the front entrance. At the door, she stopped and faced him. Lydia offered her hand to him, saying, "It's been a pleasure meeting you. I'm only sorry it couldn't have been under more agreeable circumstances."

Ames kissed her hand again. "Perhaps—no, never mind. It's not important."

"What is it, Mr. Ames?" she asked, smiling sweetly. He was going to ask if he could see her again. She could see it in his eyes. Heaven forgive her for encouraging him, but if it meant gaining his confidence . . .

"Well, it's only—I was thinking—I could show you the island sometime, Mistress Collins. It's a wild place, but very beautiful. I'd show you some of the more interesting sites Jamaica has to offer. And it would give me great pleasure to have your company on such an excursion."

She laughed and touched his arm. "You flatter me, Mr. Ames. It's very kind of you to ask. Perhaps when I'm settled." She opened the door for him.

"I'll call on you at a later time?" he asked.

"I anticipate your call."

"Good evening, Mistress Collins."

"Good evening, Mr. Ames."

Lydia closed the door behind Ames and let out an exhausted sigh. Yes, she was definitely going to regret this flirtation.

Blake's voice brought her up short.

"And where do you think you're going?"

"If it is any of your business, I thought I would retire for the evening. It's been a rather grueling night." She began to mount the stairs. Really, the man was impossible!

"Not in this house," he stated firmly.

Slowly, she turned to face him. "And why not?"

"Because *I* intend to stay here." He smiled at her from the bottom of the staircase.

"Well, we *both* can't stay here."

"Exactly my point, Mistress Collins. I'll send O'Hare around with the coach. He can drive you into Port Royal, back to the Grand Inn." He left her standing on the stairs and made his way to the kitchen.

Lydia stood stunned for a moment, before heading after him. She caught up with him in the kitchen, where he was talking to O'Hare. Moira was still kneeling beside the tub, but had stopped scrubbing.

"Have the stableboy prepare the coach to take Mistress Collins into town. She'll be staying there for the night," ordered Blake.

O'Hare nodded and started to leave.

"Don't you move a step, O'Hare." This came from Moira, who struggled to her feet to face Blake. "What's the meaning of this, sending a fine

76

lass as Mistress Collins to stay in Port Royal? Tisn't enough room for her here? You've been as testy as a boar pig this evenin', Mr. Spencer, with manners to match. And if I wasn't but a wooman, I'd—"

"Thank you, Mrs. O'Hare, but I'll handle this myself," Lydia interrupted. "Would you and your husband be so kind as to leave us alone?"

When the servants had gone, Lydia rounded on Blake. "My things will remain here, as will I, until the matter of who owns this house is settled, Mr. Spencer. I think, however, for propriety's sake, if anyone should stay elsewhere, it is you."

"I have an equal claim to this house, Madam. You heard Andy—"

"Oh, it's *Andy* now, is it? Do you think you can use your friendship with *Andy* to claim Bellefleur?" she burst in, and when he looked shocked at her accusation, she continued, "Don't think I didn't notice the way you pandered to Mr. Ames when he first arrived—the two of you sitting in that tub, chattering away like a pair of magpies, laughing it up, making me wait all the while. It was a blatant attempt to sway Mr. Ames in your cause, and I dare you to deny it."

"And I suppose I should have accepted an invitation for a tour of the island instead. Perhaps that would have served me better!"

Lydia's mouth popped open. "How dare you eavesdrop on my private conversations! And for your edification, I accepted Mr. Ames invitation out of . . . politeness—not, as you may have erroneosuly surmised, in the spirit of advancing my claim."

"Hah!" he scoffed.

"Think whatever you like, Mr. Spencer. It matters

not to me." She crossed her arms and lifted her chin primly. "As for the matter of who stays and who goes, I think it best you leave tonight."

His dark brows settled over implacable eyes. "I am not leaving tonight, or any other night. This is my home, and I will not be chased out of it by a woman. Since you are a newly arrived visitor and have not had a chance to settle in, it only makes sense that *you* should be the one to stay in Port Royal."

Lydia felt panic rising from the pit of her stomach at the mention of Port Royal. She would have gladly backed down, if she could find lodgings anywhere but there. The port was rife with all sorts of thieves and cutthroats. Why, she'd be frightened half out of her wits to stay there for two or three months! She'd be lucky to walk away with her life, not to mention her virtue. No, she would rather take her chances with Blake Spencer. "You're being completely unreasonable, although from my experience with you, I don't find that surprising in the least. I am not staying in Port Royal. I am staying right here. Do you understand?"

He clenched his fists in anger and looked as if he wanted to strangle her. For a moment Lydia thought she'd gone too far. But then the tension left his body, as a smile spread across his lips, and that already familiar devilish spark replaced the anger in his eyes. He took a step toward her, and she felt her knees go weak, her stomach start to flutter.

"Stay if you like—as long as you like—but stay at your own risk, lovely Lydia."

"Stop where you are. Take another step and I'll call the servants," she warned, remembering their earlier encounter. But he continued to move toward her. She sidestepped him quickly, then stood with her back to the wall nearest the door to the hallway, ready to dash through it if he came any closer. "Do you think you're so clever that I haven't figured out your game, Mr. Spencer?"

"And what game is that?" he purred.

She pointed a steady finger at him, but beneath her dress, her shoe had slipped from her foot and was twirling around in mad circles on the end of her toe. "You think these—these advances of yours will frighten me into leaving Jamaica and Bellefleur behind, but I'm not foolish enough to leave, Mr. Spencer."

"Your leaving is the furthest thing from my mind right now, my love. Stay."

"And do you always change your mind so quickly?"

"I've merely remembered the advantages of having you stay."

Lydia's cheeks flamed at his insinuation. "How indecent of you to say such a thing! I really wonder how far you would carry this ridiculous charade, if I called your bluff."

"Call my bluff and find out."

"I'm not afraid of you—not in the least." Although she sounded confident, she was sure the noise of her shoe scuffing the floor as it went round and round betrayed her real state. It was almost deafening to her, but Blake seemed not to notice.

He was only a few inches away from her now, and although he hadn't laid a finger on her, the power in his presence had her nearly pinned to the wall.

"You're trembling again," his voice was soft and

caressing, and a shiver ran through her, almost as if he'd touched her.

"I'm not afraid of you," she repeated.

He towered over her, bracing himself against the wall with one arm, blocking her escape. With his other hand, he reached up and brushed a strand of hair from her cheek.

At his touch, she felt herself melting. Her shoe came free from her toe and skidded out from beneath her skirts, scudding across the kitchen floor.

Blake's eyes followed its progress, then peered inquiringly into hers. "If it isn't fear that makes you tremble, my sweet Lydia, then what do you suppose it is?"

She swallowed hard. This had gone far enough. If she didn't stop him now, heaven only knew where this would end. And the way she felt now, she doubted she'd have the presence of mind to stop him.

She gathered her wits and smiled sweetly. Then laid a hand gently on his shoulder. "Do you really want to know why I'm trembling, Mr. Spencer?"

She'd caught him off guard, for he backed away from the wall, looking suspiciously at her hand that was now pressed against his chest.

Lydia looked him squarely in the eye, and raising her foot, she brought her bare heel down as hard as she could on his toes. "It's anger, Mr. Spencer. Pure and unbridled anger! Nothing more."

He leaped back and let out a howl.

Lydia quickly bolted through the door, nearly colliding with Moira and leaving her one shoe behind. She brushed past the housekeeper and headed for the stairs, calling out, "I'm staying, Mr. Spencer, and there's nothing you can do to stop me."

"Then stay if you like, but I'm *not* moving out!" he shouted after her.

"That's fine with me, Mr. Spencer," she shouted back, and he heard her bounding up the stairs.

"Damn woman," he muttered to himself.

Moira came through the kitchen door to find Blake, leaning against the table, one shoe and stocking off, rubbing his toes with his hands, a nasty scowl on his face.

Moira put her fists on her hips. "Och! I heard every disgustin' word of it."

Blake groaned. The last thing he wanted right now was a reprimand from his housekeeper. "Moira, not now," he pleaded.

"You ought to be ashamed of yourself for abusin' a fine lass like that when there's plenty of room for her here. It's your stubbornness and pride that makes a brute of you." She grabbed his foot roughly. "Let's take a look at the damage. Hmmm. You're lucky you got off with just a few bruised toes. If it'd been me, you'd be lookin' out the backside of your head." And with that, she smacked his foot solidly with her hand.

Blake howled again. "Confound it, woman. Leave me alone."

Moira crossed to Lydia's shoe and picked it up. "I think I'll take myself upstairs to see after *our guest*."

"Fine. And put *our guest* in the Rose Room where the guests belong," he grumbled and turned his attention back to his foot.

As soon as Moira left, Dan O'Hare stuck his head through the kitchen door. "Mr. Spencer?"

"What is it, O'Hare?" He winced as he tested his smarting foot. Damn the woman! She'd made a cripple of him. Who would have thought such a dainty foot could cause so much pain?

O'Hare stepped sheepishly into the room. "It's about the women, sir."

Blake sighed. "What about the women?"

"They're gettin' mighty uppity, sir. Mistress Collins ordered me to find her things and bring them upstairs. And Moira slapped me just now in the hallway for no apparent reason." He rubbed the offended cheek with his hand, and then regarded Blake with a look of pretended confusion. "I was wonderin', Mr. Spencer, who's the master of this house now? You or Mistress Collins?"

O'Hare's goading was enough to renew Blake's anger. He'd been upset from the first that she was coming out to meddle in the businesses—and now this! His plan to intimidate her yesterday and today had failed. But damned if he'd give up!

"As long as I remain here, I am master of this house. Mistress Collins is a guest and nothing more!" This last he shouted at the ceiling, hoping she would hear him. He collected his dignity and turned to O'Hare. "I'm going into town—on business."

"And will you be back this evening, sir?"

"You can count on it, O'Hare." Blake grabbed his sword that hung from a hook by the back door, and without even buckling it on, he swung out the door, leaving a satisfied O'Hare behind. The heavy wooden door slammed shut with a bang that rattled the windows.

Upstairs, Lydia heard the door slam shut and congratulated herself for having got rid of him for

82

the moment. She leaned against the wall at the top of the stairs to catch her breath. She was still trembling from being so near him, and her heart was positively racing. When she'd told him it wasn't fear that made her tremble, she wasn't lying, but it certainly wasn't anger either. It was something entirely different. How could he make her so furious one minute, then have her heart tripping so fast the next that she was dizzy? It was the way he looked at her, not unlike the stares Baxter'd given her.

But Baxter's leers had repulsed her. Not this man's. His left her absolutely breathless.

"What are you doin' standin' up here all by yourself in the dark?"

Lydia jumped at the sound of Moira's voice. The housekeeper struck a match and lit a lamp that sat on a small table in the hallway, throwing a bright light on the walls.

Lydia laughed. "Oh, Moira. I was so angry with Mr. Spencer, I just ran up the stairs without a thought as to where I was going. I don't even know which room will be mine."

Moira handed Lydia her shoe. "Doncha give another thought to Mr. Spencer. He's a decent enough mon — aye stubborn, but decent. If you do like I do, and just give it back to him, he'll learn to respect you. You'll see."

"I hope you're right," Lydia said doubtfully, taking the shoe from Moira.

"Of course, I'm right. Now where's your baggage?"

In all the confusion with Blake, she'd completely forgotten about Brigitte! "My maid stayed in Port Royal to arrange to have my bags brought here, but that was this morning. You don't think anything's

83

happened to her?"

Moira rolled her eyes at the ceiling. "And you've lost your maid, too? Ye wee poor lamb! We'll send into town to inquire after her. You'll be stayin' down the hall here."

Moira took the lamp from the table and led the way. They passed an open door, and Moira continued on. But Lydia stopped to look in, curious to see more of Bellefleur.

The room was well lit by a lamp on a nightstand next to the huge canopied bed. The bed was hung with a sheer pale blue curtain that fluttered from the breeze that blew through an open window. A velvet throw of a deeper shade of blue covered the bed, and at least a dozen velvet pillows in reds and golds were propped against the mahogany headboard. She liked what she saw and stepped into the room to get a better look.

Near a mahogany overmantel on the opposite wall, two high-backed patterned chairs faced the hearth. A Persian rug of royal blue, burnished gold and deep red, picked up the same hues in the chairs and almost covered the entire floor. And the windows! Four in all, they nearly reached from floor to ceiling, and were topped off in gracefully decorated arches. A long writing table of polished mahogany gleamed in the lamplight from in front of the open window. The high ceilings and white walls gave the room a spacious and airy quality that she couldn't resist. It was obviously the master bedroom.

And she fell in love with it immediately.

She called after Moira. "Is this room empty?"

"Aye, for now. But Mr. Spencer was goin' to move in once the curtains were hung."

The housekeeper appeared in the doorway, and

after she saw the impish smile on Lydia's face, a look of horror spread across her own. "No, Mistress, you can't be thinkin' what you're thinkin.'"

"But I am, Moira."

"Mr. Spencer will have—"

"I don't give a farthing for Mr. Spencer. I intend to make this room my own. When Brigitte arrives, instruct her to have my belongings brought here." She surveyed the room again. "Yes, this will do nicely."

She turned to find Moira shaking her head. "You've got the nerve of a lion, Mistress, to be going up against Mr. Spencer this way."

Lydia winked at the housekeeper. "Just 'givin' it back to him', like you said, Moira."

Chapter Seven

That same evening in Port Royal, a couple stopped beneath the sign of the Coq D'Or.

"And so, you will step inside my lodgings and allow me to give you a glass of wine?" Jacques Noir smiled down at the woman on his arm—his most persuasive smile.

"Mais non! And what kind of woman do you think I am, sir, that I would enter a gentleman's room in an Inn on such very short acquaintance?" Brigitte said indignantly, stopping in the street and removing her arm from his grasp.

But a most beautiful one, *cheri,* that is the kind of woman I think you are! he thought, looking down at her and noting with approval that though her red lips were set in a quite delicious pout, the sparkle in her blue eyes hinted that she was flattered, not insulted, by his suggestion. For at least the hundredth time that day, his eyes caressingly swept her tumble of shining raven curls, her petite, full figure, and the tip-tilted nose that leant mischief to her pert, heart-shaped face. *Oh, indeed, a beauty,* he thought, *And if you think I would insult you by giving up so easily—!*

He put his hand on his heart in mock affront, and raising his eyebrows, protested convincingly, "But, *cheri,* how you insult me! I swear I would never dream of taking advantage of a lady such as yourself! I only wanted to offer you some refreshment after these dusty, hot hours we have spent seeing the markets. How ravished I am that you consented to allow me to show you around your new city, and never would I dream of spoiling it by crude behavior. You are new on Jamaica to be sure, or you would have heard by now that Jacques Noir is a perfect gentleman where ladies are concerned! Why, I would run any man through who even dared to offer you the slightest insult!" His hand went to the sword at his hip in a dramatic demonstration of his willingness to spit any rogue who looked at her sideways.

Brigitte dimpled, tilting her head back so she could meet his eyes. He was so very tall—and strong—and handsome! With his sandy blond hair tied back, his dark brown eyes, and his sparkling white smile, he was quite irresistible, she reflected. Still, it would never do for him to believe she was *too* easily persuaded. She knew the rules of the game better than most, and played them with superb skill.

"I *am* dreadfully thirsty," she conceded prettily. "Perhaps we could step into the common room together. That would be acceptable, for it is public."

Jacques made a horrified face and raised his

eyebrows. He was as adept at this game as she was. "But *cheri!* The common room! Perhaps in England or France, a lady might enter an inn's common room, but in Port Royal! No, here the worst kind of rogues, drunkards, and pirates swill rum all day! No respectable lady would dream of entering an inn's common room and exposing herself to the trash who frequent such places!"

"Pirates?" she said softly, with a flirtatious and knowing smile. "But *monsieur,* in that case I believe I am in most desperate danger at this very moment."

He smiled back, his dark eyes dancing. "Ah, but I am no common pirate, *Mademoiselle.* I am a buccaneer, and there is a world of difference. I merely plague the Spanish for the sake of my country—with their approval. So you see, you are in no danger at all. In fact, you are safer with me than you would be with the governor himself."

"Oh, I doubt it," she laughed softly. "I understand the last governor, Henri Morgan, was a pirate too—or buccaneer, if you shall have it so! But I see that here on Jamaica, I must perhaps learn new ways. I shall go up to your room for a short time and refresh myself—if I have your solemn word that all I will get is a glass of wine."

"You have my word that you shall get only what you desire," he said gravely, offering his arm.

As she took it, she reflected, *Ah, I shall have to watch my step with this one!*

And as they entered the inn, she stole a glance at him under her lashes and added to herself, *Especially because he's so handsome. I believe he could talk an angel into temptation!* She sighed. Sometimes, temptation was so much fun.

* * *

Blake Spencer strode angrily through the crowded streets of the waterfront, brushing past burly seamen without seeing the occasional insulted looks he engendered, the hands automatically reaching for knives hanging at belts. Fights were all too easy to start in Port Royal. But a look at his grim, set face, and something made those same hands relax and drop from the knives. At no time did Blake Spencer look like a man most men wanted to tangle with — and just now, he looked dauntingly formidable.

At the sign of the Coq D'Or, he turned into the doorway and strode through the common room to the stairs, then took them two at a time. Without bothering to knock, he flung open a door.

"Oh!" With a startled squeal, the black-haired girl in Jacques's arms jumped backward. It was the girl who'd defended Lydia Collins at the dock, and then shared her carriage to the Grand Inn. They must have been shipboard acquaintances, he surmised.

Jacques looked up, bemused, and when he saw who it was, gave a rueful grin. Blake noted the wine bottle on the table, the two empty glasses. Doing his best to conceal a grin of his own, he bowed and started to back out. "My apologies, Mistress, Jacques. I see I have come at an inconvenient time — "

Sniffing (but not blushing, Blake noticed), the girl patted her curls straight and said coolly, "But do not leave on *my* account, *Monsieur — whoever-you-are*. I was just leaving myself. The hour is late and I have overstayed here as it is."

This last was said with a rather simmering glance at Jacques, and again Blake had to suppress a smile. Well, whoever she was, she was a decidedly pretty baggage, and French to boot. Jacques would no doubt have his head for interrupting his tryst, but Blake had been so angry when he'd climbed the stairs, he hadn't even thought to knock. And now, from the look in the girl's eyes, it seemed both of them were to be beset by woman troubles this day.

Jacques had opened his mouth to speak, but before he could, Blake put in smoothly, "Then allow me to give you back the privacy I have so rudely interrupted to make your farewells. Again, *Mademoiselle,* my apologies." And he was backing out, pulling the door shut as he went.

But she was quick, this girl. Across the room in a flash, she had the door yanked wide and her hat on her head in a moment. *"Monsieur,* I have no need of privacy to say my *adieux,"* she said tartly, giving him a rather murderous look. She turned. "Goodbye, *Monsieur* Noir," she said stiffly. "I thank you for showing me the sights this afternoon."

Jacques was quickly at her side, taking her hand to kiss it. "But you must allow me to accompany you home! It is unthinkable you would go unescorted in these streets!"

"I think not. But—you may escort me to my carriage, and see me into it." Blake was relieved to see she softened her words with the glimmer of a smile. *"Au revoir, Monsieur whoever-you-are."* And she sailed from the room, a rather sheepish Jacques following behind her.

Blake now allowed himself a grin, momentarily diverted from his troubles by the ones he had just caused Jacques. He strolled to the table near the window and poured himself a glass of wine. If he knew Jacques, it would be some time before he bid his farewells to the pretty wench. Jacques would be doing his best to smooth her ruffled feathers and

90

set up another meeting with her. And in Blake's estimation, the girl would take some time to smooth.

But Jacques was back before he'd finished half his glass of wine. Blake looked up as Jacques walked in and leaned in the doorway. "So what was it, *mon ami,* that could not wait, so that you must come tearing down my door without even a knock?"

"For that offense, you have my permission to call me out. For I admit it was unpardonable," Blake said ruefully.

"Call you out? I think not. The last time I did that, our duel landed us both in trouble that we still are in to this day." Laughing, Jacques walked to the table and sat down, lifting his boots to the tabletop where they were displayed to best advantage. He poured himself a glass, then tilted his chair back, and regarded Blake through narrowed eyes. "I tell you truly you could not have burst in at a more inopportune moment. She was just beginning to soften, after a most delicate campaign that took most of the afternoon!"

"That long?" Blake raised his eyebrows in mock disbelief. "Then she must be as enchanting as she is pretty, for that is an unbelievably long attention span for you." At Jacques's snort, he grinned. "But at least ease my conscience. Did she relent?"

It was Jacques's turn to look disbelieving. "But of course, *mon ami.* What woman can resist me? We meet tomorrow afternoon—so I can show her my ship. Dead boring, *naturellement,* but this one is worth a bit of trouble. But come. Enough of my *affaires.* What made you burst in here as black as a storm cloud?"

Blake shrugged, and his mouth tightened. "That

woman. What else could make one so angry?"

"So. She made you angry? But this is most strange. It is true that women have a way of making the best men furious, but *you?* I would not have put money on *that* bet. It has been many years, *mon ami,* since you gave a woman more than a passing thought. Myself, I believe that is why they pursue you so relentlessly, for a more surly, less charming man with women I never did see. Still, they always want what they cannot have, and it is obvious to all they cannot have your heart. So my little diversion at the dock failed to make her meek as a mouse? Never tell me she could be this paragon of a *wife* you claim to be searching for?" This last sentence was delivered with the heaviest of sarcasm.

Blake scowled. "No, damn it, it's no love affair. And she's certainly not a woman I would consider for a wife. She's the most damnably stubborn wench I've ever laid eyes on, and even though she looks like the most luscious of wantons, she's as prim as a reverend's wife!"

Jacques made a lascivious face and rolled his eyes. "If I had not already been distracted by my sweet dark-haired one, I would have made every effort to snatch that one out of your arms! She was gorgeous!"

"Gorgeous, yes, but she's got the temperament of a mule, I tell you!"

Both men stared at each other across the table for a few moments, and then Jacques began to laugh softly.

"What's so funny?" Blake growled.

"Ah, but this is too priceless! The first woman I have seen you take an interest in in years, and she turns out to be the one you have been cursing about all these months, sure she was coming to stick her nose in your affairs, and try to take things over, and run everything while knowing nothing—"

"Which is exactly what she is doing!" Blake exploded.

"But then why are you so angry, when this is no more than you expected? At least her beauty should make the situation *piquant,* no?"

"If that was *all* she was doing, maybe. But listen to this, Jacques! The vixen showed up claiming that *she* is the one who owns Bellefleur!"

Jacques gave a low whistle, and listened while Blake explained the imbroglio over the deed.

"And the worst of it is," Blake finished, "I'm afraid she may be right. Baxter, damn his eyes, may have *forgotten* to file the deed, and then died, hang him! After all, he'd just married her, and—"

"And she is enough to make any man forget business for awhile," Jacques finished for him.

"Exactly!"

Both men sat thinking, Blake scowling into his glass, Jacques with a knit brow. Then Jacques's expression cleared. "But can you not simply *buy* the house from her, if the decision goes against you?"

"I'll try." The words held grim promise. "But I have a feeling she is not the type to care that I spent a year of my life slaving for that house. She's just the type of stubborn woman who cares for nothing but what she's wearing, and doesn't understand business."

"You say *she* is the stubborn one, but I say that there is no one more stubborn than you. Is that not what brought us to Jamaica in the first place—your cursed stubbornness? That you would accuse *me,* Jacques Noir, of cheating at cards—and then refuse to take those words back! It was your very stubbornness that forced that damned duel between us in the first place!"

Blake quirked a brow cynically. "In the first place, you know damned well that you *were* cheating at cards with me. After all, that's how you were earning your living at the time, as I recall. And in the second place, your name wasn't Jacques Noir then—but Phillipe DuNoir Charles St. Jacques, and you were making a living by dishonest gambling simply because your family had disinherited you!"

"And were you any better? I seem to recall you were in exactly the same boat, black sheep of your family, and you, too, were making your living at the tables!"

"Ah, but I did not have to cheat to—"

Jacques lifted a hand. "Let us stop this ridiculous argument before it lands us in another duel! As I was saying, you are every bit as stubborn as that woman. Let me illustrate my point. When we were caught dueling and thrown in prison to be sentenced, you were too stubborn to let the Paris magistrate know who you were, or to contact your family. If only you had, you would never have been sentenced to indenture at all."

"Go begging to my family after they'd thrown me out? You still don't know me, if you think that I would have gone to them. And besides, I didn't see you writing any letters to your father the *Comte.*"

"Oh, I know you well enough, and that is just what I have been saying. Besides, what good would it have done me to write to old Henri? As you know, I was born on the wrong side of the blanket, and even if I was at one time his favorite son, I'd not seen him in four years. He would rather die than be dishonored, and I don't think he would have looked kindly on my gambling and dueling."

"Let's get back to the point, Jacques. What the hell am I going to do about that damned woman? I haven't told you the worst of it yet! She's going to live in the house until word comes from London—and that could be months!"

"So? I myself would not think it a hardship, but instead an opportunity, to live alone in a house with a so-beautiful woman. I think I would find ways to influence her." Jacques grinned modestly. "Why not marry her? She's rich and beautiful, and then you would surely own the house without bothering with lawyers and deeds."

Blake ran his hands through his hair, letting it fall into disarray. "Haven't you been listening to me? I tell you, I wouldn't marry that frigid, stubborn shrew if she were the last woman on earth! I'd die of frostbite on our wedding night!" But even as he spoke, Blake had a momentary vision of holding her in his arms at the dock—and how warm she'd been for a few moments. That desire that had leaped between them for a moment had been startling.

"So she is not of a sensuous nature?" Jacques's question broke into his thoughts. "Strange. I would have been willing to bet a bag of doubloons that she was. Women with those wide, full mouths and lids that look half-closed by the weight of their eyelashes, usually are the most passionate."

"No, she's certainly not passionate. In fact, when I tried what you suggested, she went as stiff as a board. Her lips were as cold as ice. I have the idea she fears men."

"Then it *is* your answer! Chase her around like a satyr, and never give her a moment's peace! I wager she'll go running back to England on the next ship—if she's really as cold as you say."

"I am afraid it won't work. She has enough spunk to fight back, and a temper to match the red lights in her hair. I think it will take more than a few stolen kisses to dislodge her."

"Then why bother with all that?" Jacques laughed. "Why not just take your pistol, point it at her, and *force* her to sign over that deed to you? If you are afraid of the law, I am sure you can scare her into keeping her mouth shut."

Blake smiled. Jacques was always full of such rash plans. "I will wait until we receive word from Whitehall before I do anything. It's likely Baxter Collins filed the deed in my name as he promised to, and all this will be settled in my favor."

"Then why, *mon ami,*" Jacques asked patiently, "did you have to burst down my door and ruin a whole afternoon's work for me? I know, I know — do not answer. It is because this woman made you so angry, and you could not see straight. What was her first name again?"

"Lydia." The name came out sounding like a curse.

"Hmmm. Well, if you want my opinion, chilly or not, you are more than interested in the beautiful Lydia. Otherwise she would not make you so angry. So relax and enjoy living in the same house with her, and go ahead with your plan to make Jamaica too hot a place to handle by chasing her all over the house. But I suppose you are determined to do it the lawful way, and there is no use my trying to talk you into something more interesting?" Jacques added wistfully.

Blake shook his head, and Jacques sighed. "Too well I know your penchant for doing things the lawful way, Blake. After we were both clapped in irons and indentured, it was your good fortune to become my friend on the voyage, while we both lay chained in that stinking hold. But then, when we arrive on Jamaica and I offer you a chance to escape with me and become a pirate, what do you say? No!" Jacques sounded as if he could still hardly believe it.

"But you know that if I'd escaped with you, I'd still have to live as you do, a buccaneer—"

Jacques laughed derisively. "And what would be so different? At least you'd have money, and not have had to slave for this Collins pig for seven years, and—"

"I'm making money. I'll be one of the richest men on Jamaica before long, and free to enjoy it."

"I still cannot believe you chose seven years of indentured service instead of escape, just to preserve your good name, when look how cavalierly you treat that very name now!"

Both men laughed.

Jacques swung his boots down from the table and landed his feet on the floor with a thunk. He leaned forward, eyes glinting with deviltry. "But I think I can help you in your problem with the beautiful widow."

"You can? I'm not sure if I want any more of your help," Blake said suspiciously.

"The black-haired beauty you drove out of my arms just now?"

"Yes . . . what about her?"

Jacques' eyes gleamed with triumph. "She works for Lydia Collins. That was her maid, Brigitte. So you see, *mon ami,* maybe I can be of help after all with your problem."

Chapter Eight

The next night, only a few lights showed in the windows as Blake climbed the front steps of Bellefleur.

He'd spent the night at the Coq D'or, and today business had kept him in town. And then it hadn't seemed worthwhile to him to rush home—not with that woman waiting for him. Maybe, he'd reasoned as he'd gone back to the inn to dine with Jacques again, she decide to pack up and leave, and when he got home she'd be gone.

It was late, but his steps didn't betray the amount of drinking he'd done with Jacques. A close look would have shown his shirt unbuttoned, cravat in his pocket, jacket slightly rumpled. And his eyes held a determined glint.

Damn that woman! he was thinking, as he fumbled with the latch. *Why did she have to decide to come halfway around the world just to make my life miserable? Why didn't she stay in London where she belongs?*

The door swung wide, and he looked up to see the anxious face of Dan O'Hare peering at him over a brace of candles.

"Ah, there y'are, sir! By the saints, 'tis about time you got here. I've been lookin' for you all day, and waitin' up for you t'get home."

"You have? And why is that? You haven't suddenly taken a notion to act as my valet, have you, just because we have a *lady* in the house?" Blake said sarcastically, as he stepped into the foyer.

"No, sir, saints forbid it!" answered O'Hare fervently, as he locked the door and followed Blake down the corridor to the library door. "That's just the trouble I was meanin' to broach with you, sir. This business of having Mistress Collins and all her quality ways in the house as it were. Everything's at sixes and sevens."

Blake threw himself down in a leather wing chair and looked up at O'Hare bleakly. O'Hare's red, guileless face carried a look of anxiety—even trepidation. "Like that, is it? I thought so. She's a meddlesome jade if I ever saw one. Well, out with it, man. What's she done that's so terrible?"

"It's like this, sir. Bless your heart, we've never had a mistress in this house, and we've all got comfortable with your ways. Know what you like, and what you don't. There's nothing like a mistress for turning a house upside down, I always say, and many's the time I've praised the saints that you're a confirmed bachelor. Moira's too many for me sometimes with her passion for giving orders and suchlike, dear as she is to me, but she isn't the lady of the house and there's much to be said for that when you and I want to get around her orders."

Blake suppressed a smile, but pretended impatience. He was used to O'Hare's rambling way of getting to a point. "Come on, Dan, tell me what she's done without all the preamble. And I can't say I agree with you about a mistress. A lady of the house is exactly what Bellefleur needs—the *right* lady, that is. And I intend to marry in the near future, as you well know. But when I marry, she'll have a sweet temperament, and she'll know who the master is here. So you don't need to fear things will change too much. Except that, of course, she'll keep you in line, which you're sorely in need of."

O'Hare raised his eyebrows skeptically, but Blake couldn't guess whether he doubted that a "sweet" mistress wouldn't turn everything upside down anyway, or that Blake would ever marry.

For too many years now, O'Hare had watched young ladies set their caps at Blake with no results. And many of them had been as sweet-spoken as angels, O'Hare reflected. Somehow, he had his doubts that the master *really* wanted to get married at all, at least not to an angel. And weren't things comfortable just as they were, with no mistress for Bellefleur? Why ruin a good thing? He heaved a sigh and went on.

"Well, Mistress Collins has already got m'wife Moira, bless her, twisted round her finger like a piece of string. They're thick as thieves, those two, and you never saw such cooing and billing and polite words as they have for each other, I swear. What I want to know, sir, is whose orders are we to follow, yours or hers? It fair puzzled my head this afternoon, I can tell you."

"My orders, of course, O'Hare. I'm the master here, and it's still my house until proven otherwise."

"But, sir, she says it's her house until proven otherwise, and there lies the rub." He looked apprehensive again, then blurted out in a rush, afraid of the famous Spencer temper, "It's that she's had all her things moved into the master bedroom, sir."

He was not disappointed in the reaction. "What!" Blake sat up, brows drawn together, hands gripping the arms of the chair. "Did you say she's moved into the master bedroom?"

"I did say that, sir."

"But damn it, it's just been finished! I was going to move in there myself as soon as they hung the damn curtains!"

"Just what I told her myself, sir! And the curtains were hung today. Seems my wife Moira could get those lazy workmen moving so everything would be perfect for *her*, and so she bullied them into getting the drapes up."

O'Hare added this final twist of the knife triumphantly, knowing Blake had been waiting almost two weeks for the workmen to hang the curtains. " 'Tis wonderful what a woman can do when she sets her mind to it," he added piously.

"Moira had the drapes hung — for *her?*" Blake's words were spaced slowly and evenly, and O'Hare was glad to note the glint in his eye.

"That she did."

"And what did Mistress Collins say when you told her it was my room she was moving into?"

Ah, yes, there was a dangerous tone to the master's voice now, and that was all to the good, because the sooner that widow learned who wore the breeches in this house, the better for all concerned, O'Hare thought.

"She told me that it was the master suite, and since she was the owner of the house, she was entitled to it. Oh, and I believe she added that since you've been sleeping over the stables all these months, obviously the odor of animals suited you, and she was sure

101

you'd be much happier in the surroundings you were used to than in the house," he embroidered with an innocent air.

This was too much for Blake. He stood up, and there was a murderous gleam in his eyes. "It seems," he said deliberately, "that Mistress Collins and I have much to discuss."

As Dan O'Hare watched him stride out of the library, a satisfied smile creased his face at the sight of his master's rigid shoulders.

Now things would be set to rights, for he'd never known anyone to get the better of Blake Spencer when he wanted his way, and he wasn't going to lay any money on a mere woman doing what strong men had failed to do. Yes, tomorrow everything would be back to normal, thank the Lord.

Lydia sat in the center of the great four-poster bed, brushing her hair. She was tired. All in all, it had been an exhausting day, meeting all the servants, dealing with Moira, and getting everything moved into her bedroom. Thank God that at least Moira O'Hare was understanding. She seemed the only civilized human being in this house.

She was relieved that Blake had chosen to absent himself, for she knew he'd never have taken her move into the master bedroom meekly. But now that she'd done it—she smiled. Well, now it was too late. There would be nothing he could do other than make a few predictably vulgar remarks.

Blake Spencer. As they had many times that evening, her thoughts turned to her adversary. The man was disgusting! Obviously without moral scruples of any kind. And the most arrogant man she'd ever met. He acted as if nothing mattered to him— and that included manners. But then, what could she

102

expect of a man who numbered pirates among his friends, and might even be a pirate himself?

It was easy to picture him on the deck of a burning ship, bloody sword in hand, that long black hair tinged with silver loose to his shoulders, earring gleaming as he robbed innocent passengers. For a moment, her old story-telling habit came back, and she saw herself on that tilted deck, facing him bravely.

"Sir, you are a coward!" she told him in ringing tones, lifting her chin high. "To rob women and children. Are you afraid of men?"

In the daydream, she could see him quite clearly as he walked forward, those light gray eyes cold as steel, his sword pointed straight at her heart. In the daydream, she faced him boldly, a true heroine, as his eyes raked her from head to foot. She wasn't afraid, not even when he lifted a lock of her hair from her shoulder with the point of his sword.

"Ah, but Madam," the dream-Blake said softly, "Robbing you was not what I had in mind."

Lydia sat up straight in bed, her eyes flying open. She felt a rush of embarrassment at the sudden direction the daydream had taken, and more so at the thrill that had run through her at the way the dream-Blake was looking at her when he said those words.

What's wrong with me! she thought angrily. *He's a boor, and I hate him, and he's horribly arrogant!*

But he's so handsome, a little voice in her mind answered before she could stop it.

Because Lydia was honest with herself, she realized that she had developed a dangerous attraction for Blake Spencer. It wasn't just his looks, spectacular as those were. No, it was the way he made her feel alive. It was the challenge of besting him, she realized.

She had enjoyed battling with him yesterday, if the truth be told. Oh, this standing up to people was becoming a habit! First her father, and now Blake

Spencer. She smiled as she thought of how mousy she had once been, and how now she was learning she could get her way, if she only fought for her rights.

And she would enjoy showing Blake Spencer just how hard she could fight. Until they heard from the solicitors—in her favor, she was certain—this house was hers. Not his. Yes, she would simply have to make that clear from the beginning, and she was glad all over again that she'd moved into this room right away. It would show him and all the servants, that she intended to be treated as the mistress of the house.

Yes, it was rather fun to stand up to Blake Spencer. What he didn't realize was that she'd faced down her father. And after Joshua Lyndham, Blake Spencer looked tame.

Smiling again, she resumed brushing her hair, looking around the room in satisfaction. At last her gaze fell on the curtains, and her smile widened to one of triumph.

Her hand froze in mid-stroke at a sound.

Eyes widening with horror, she watched as the door was flung open, so violently it crashed against the wall.

Blake stood in the doorway.

"Oh!" she cried. "What are you doing here?" *Why hadn't she had the sense to latch it!*

He walked into the room as if he owned it, to the side of her bed, and stood towering over her. Hastily, she snatched the covers to her chin, covering up her white lace nightdress.

"I might ask you the same question," he said evenly. He looked positively frightening, with his dark brows drawn down over his eyes, his square jaw set. With a little jolt, she saw that his shirt was open at the throat, coat rumpled. He'd been drinking!

"Get *out* of my bedroom!" But instead of sounding like the brave heroine on the deck, her voice came out

104

sounding frightened.

"It is you who are in my bedroom, Madam. And since I find you in my bed wearing such a delectable nightdress, I can only presume this is your way of telling me you wish to spend the night making love to me. What else can a man think when a lady crawls into his bed and waits for him? So I'll be glad to oblige you. I've always heard widows were—"

As he spoke, he shrugged off his jacket and began unbuttoning his shirt. Lydia gasped at his words and his actions, but finally found her voice.

"Don't move! How dare you! If you do anything more, I shall scream!"

"Of that, I have no doubt, my dear Lydia. Women tell me that I'm most accomplished at making love, and often they cannot hold back their screams in the moment of passion," he said outrageously, opening his shirt all the way. Swift as a panther, he lifted the covers and started to climb into the bed.

"Ohhh!" she shrieked, moving over to the very edge of the bed and dragging the bedspread with her. "Get out of my bed this minute!"

He was grinning at her, the devil, as she stretched himself prone on his side of the bed. She had a disconcerting glimpse of bronzed, muscled chest before she hastily averted her eyes and stared straight ahead. "If you don't remove yourself from my bed this moment, I swear I shall scream for the servants!" she repeated.

"And as I have mentioned, the fact that you are in *my* bed might make them a trifle unsympathetic. They would think what I think, that you are here because you needed consoling in your widowhood. Except, perhaps, Moira—and I must warn you, she sleeps like the dead. Do you *really* want to summon all the male servants on the place and find out whose side they'd take?"

Her fear was being replaced by a blazing anger. *How dare he!* And yet, there might be some truth to what he said. How did she know whose side the servants would take? It was only her second day here. No, this one she'd have to handle herself, if she expected to be able to hold her head up tomorrow morning. And damn him for knowing that!

She turned to face him, giving him her coldest look. "Mr. Spencer, I deplore the undignified manner you have chosen to try to demonstrate to me that you believe this room to be yours. You must be drunk. Sir, you were not living in this room — it was vacant. And it is the master suite. Since I am the rightful owner of this house, I moved in here — as is my right! If you wish to discuss this matter further, you may talk to me in the morning about it."

There! That should fix him!

"A capital suggestion," he grinned. "I agree that we should waste no further time talking tonight. I am sure that after a night spent loving each other intimately, you will be of a sweeter temperament in the morning, in any case. Of course, you are welcome to move into this room for your stay here — *I* should have no objections — but do you really think it would do your reputation any good? Or doesn't that matter to you, perhaps?"

His hand reached out and caught a corner of the bedspread. With a yank, he pulled it out of her hands and down across her lap.

"Oh!" she gasped again, snatching at the bedspread. But he was laughing, and clearly enjoying the tussle. And she couldn't wrest it out of his hands. Good God, this was so undignified! Giving up, Lydia scrambled out of the bed. She wouldn't stay in that bed with him one more minute and listen to that kind of talk! She stood, shaking all over, glaring down at him.

106

"You—*bastard!*" she burst out. "Get the hell out of this room this minute—or I will shoot you!"

He lounged back on the bed, at ease, his eyes gleaming up at her. "With what? You don't seem to have a gun," he remarked, and let his eyes travel slowly over her. "At least, none that I can see, and with you standing in front of that lamp, I can see most everything. Very nice. Curves in all the right— and most tempting—places. Do come back to bed and stop tantalizing me by showing them to me so clearly."

Hastily, Lydia stepped away from the lamp behind her. "Mr. Spencer," she ground out between clenched teeth, "I am *not* going to bed with you. Not now, not ever. So get out of my room."

He sat up, pretending surprise. "You are not? But what else was I to think when I found you in my bed? Ah, well, it seems there has been a misunderstanding, then. Perhaps someone showed you to the wrong room. Your bedroom is the rose one down the hall. And let me get one thing straight with you."

Suddenly he was menacing. She thought she'd never seen a more determined face. "This is *my* room, and if you stay here, you're going to be up all night making love to me. If you really don't want to be my mistress, as you claim, then I suggest you go along to your own room before my control runs thin. For you are very tempting indeed, my Lydia."

"Of course I won't sleep here with you! How dare you suggest such a thing!" she shouted.

"Then I suggest you get your pretty little bottom to your own room, Mistress Collins, before I truly test your resolve!"

"I'm not leaving—*you* are!"

He was on his feet in one fluid motion, striding to her side. She turned to run, dodging his grasp, but iron arms came around her waist and her knees and she was scooped up off her feet into his arms.

She kicked wildly. "Put me down!"

But his arms were hurting her, stilling her struggles. He was too strong for her, and his face was too close to hers. "Where? In my bed—or in yours?" he grated.

This was too much. She felt heat course all through her, fury, embarrassment—and something else. A feeling that was the most dangerous of all the strong emotions running through her. She was too aware of the feel of his bare chest against her, the way his muscles rippled, his scent filling her nostrils. Oh God, this had to end *now,* she thought desperately.

She stopped struggling, and lifted her head to stare defiantly into his eyes. She might have to let him have his way, but she'd never let him think he'd really won.

"In my bed," she said angrily.

"Very well," he breathed.

But he didn't move. Their eyes locked. For a moment, neither could look away. Something leapt between them, a strong and hot current, and Lydia felt her lips open as her breath caught. His chest was rising and falling as he held her tightly, and it was as if every curve of hers was melded by heat to every hard plane of his chest. She saw his silvery eyes take on a passionate darkness, saw his lips part as slowly, so slowly, their mouths were drawn closer as if by irresistible magnetism.

And then she realized what was happening. She was about to let this despicable man kiss her! She stiffened and jerked her head back, letting her hands come up against his chest to push him away, hard. Caught off balance, he almost stumbled, and when he regained his footing, his eyes blazed down at her with a mixture of fury and what might have been frustrated desire.

"Very well then, Mistress, your room it is," he snarled, and whirling, strode from the room carrying her.

Thank God none of the servants were in the hall, drawn by their shouting! Her cheeks were blazing, her heart was beating too fast, and she felt that at any moment she was going to faint, as he carried her down the hall. He reached a door three doors down from his and didn't even break his stride as he kicked it open.

The room was dark, the light from the moon coming in the windows. All Lydia could see was that it was large, and she could make out the silhouette of a great bed near the windows. He was across to it in a few steps, where he stopped.

And unceremoniously tossed her down into the middle of the bed.

He stood over her, panting, his fists on his hips, and then, without a word, turned on his heel and stalked out of the room.

The door slammed.

Lydia pressed her fists to her burning cheeks and felt her chest hitch in a dry sob that was half a hysterical laugh.

And she'd thought Blake Spencer would be easier to tangle with than her father! Well, thank heavens he'd gone and left her alone! One more moment locked in his arms and—

And what?

She shook her head wildly, a curtain of hair falling around her face. It was a question she couldn't answer, didn't *want* to answer. All that mattered was that he was gone.

But he wasn't. The door was flung open again, and her head flew up. To her astonishment, she watched as he walked into the dim room, carrying some sort of a large, irregularly shaped bundle. And then she saw what it was. The bedspread from his bed, filled with—

"Your things, Madam. From the dressers. I'll have your clothes moved in the morning," he said, and with no further ado, shook out the bedspread onto the floor. She heard the clink and rattle of glass and silver as her hairbrushes, cosmetics, and jewelry boxes fell in a tumble. There was a brittle sound of shattering glass and a sudden overpowering wave of perfume filled the room.

"Ah. I see I owe you a bottle of perfume," he said blandly. Then, slinging the bedspread over his shoulder, he walked to the door. There he paused and turned, a black outline. "Sweet dreams, dear Lydia. And if you change your mind about sharing my bed, you know where my room is."

With that, the door shut behind him, leaving an outraged and open-mouthed Lydia on the bed. But as she sat there in the dark trying to tell herself what a bastard he was, all she could think of was the way the bare, warm skin on his chest had felt when she'd tried to push him away with her hands.

Chapter Nine

Lydia woke to the sounds of someone moving around in her room, and opened her eyes with a start. She sat up, her gaze falling on Brigitte, who was going about the business of hanging clothes in the wardrobe.

Brigitte turned with a smile. "Oh, good morning, *Madame*. I thought nothing would wake you this morning. You must have been very tired."

"Brigitte! Where did you get my clothes?" Lydia demanded, her memory of the past night coming back all too clearly.

Brigitte's smile turned into a positive smirk. "Oh, but, *Madame,* it was most amusing! You see, I thought you were in the master bedroom, so I go in to open the new drapes and bring your tea, and instead I find the *master* is in the master bedroom!" She giggled, vastly diverted, and Lydia could have hit her.

111

"Such a surprise it was!" Brigitte went on, and now there was a sly twinkle in her eyes. "For him, too, I may add. *Dieu! That* one is a man! He sat up in bed without his shirt on, and I must say I was not sorry to see such a sight!" She rolled her eyes appreciatively. "But, *Madame,* may I be permitted to ask *when* you changed rooms? For I myself helped you to bed last night," she added with an appearance of innocence.

Drat the girl, Lydia fumed, embarrassed once again. It seemed everything Blake Spencer did landed her in some sort of humiliating situation! "There was a misunderstanding," Lydia said coldly, lifting her chin. "Those rooms belong to Mr. Spencer—at least until my claim to the house is verified. Which it will be."

"Then . . . he must have come to your door last night?" Brigitte asked, eyes twinkling.

"No! He—" Lydia cast around frantically. Heavens! She just wasn't awake enough yet to deal with this, that was the problem! But she wouldn't have the whole household talking about her, and if she had to lie, so be it. "He sent Mrs. O'Hare to tell me." There! She'd have a word with Moira later about it.

Brigitte's eyebrows quirked. "Ah? That is a shame. Myself, I would have preferred that such a handsome man come himself to my room in the night, no? And so you just moved in here, *Madame,* yourself? I would have thought you would have argued about it—or at least insisted on moving today instead of in the middle of the night. But, oh, I see. You must have been half-asleep." And her eyes went pointedly to the mess in the middle of the floor where Blake had dumped her things last night.

Damn it! Obviously she didn't believe Lydia's story—but Lydia had a feeling that elaborating on it would only make things worse. "Brigitte, you still haven't answered my question. Where did you get my clothes?" she said sharply.

Brigitte tossed her head. "But did I not tell you, *Madame,* that I went into the master's room this morning? He woke up, and was most ravishing about it, I must say."

Probably kissed her, Lydia thought acidly, *By the way she's preening!*

"And he told me you'd moved, and to which room. So he got out of bed and helped me put your clothes into a trunk, and carried it down the hall for me. It's right outside your door, and I've been bringing your dresses inside in armloads and hanging them up so they don't wrinkle." This last was said virtuously, as if Lydia should be impressed with Brigitte's devotion to her wardrobe. But all Lydia was thinking of at that moment was an all-too-clear picture of Blake getting out of bed with no shirt on (and what did he have on on the bottom? she thought before she could stop herself) and assisting a giggling Brigitte to pack her clothes. Indeed, how many kisses had the rogue stolen from her maid? And the damnable thing was, Brigitte was glowing from her encounter with him!

"I see. Well, please fetch my tea before you finish hanging the rest of the clothes, and then you may assist me to dress."

"Yes, *Madame.* But, *Madame,* may I ask you one more thing?"

"Yes?" Lydia said curtly.

"The master—he is the same man who caught you when you fell off the dock! The one I saw you kissing?"

Lydia sighed. She liked Brigitte, but the girl was so very pert. Sometimes it was a trial, having a maid who spoke her mind so baldly. "Yes, he was the same man. But *he* kissed me. I did *not* kiss him. He is an unbelievable brute with absolutely no manners. But maybe that's the way all the men are on Jamaica."

"Oh, no, not all the men!" Brigitte said eagerly. "But that is what I am telling you. You see, *Madame,*

113

things are different here on the islands. People are freer. Why, they do things that would shock us at home, but here they are quite acceptable! I think you should revise your opinion of Mr. Blake Spencer, *Madame*. A man like that doesn't fall into one's lap every day of the week!"

"No, thank God! But how do you know so much about the men of Jamaica already? And by the way, where did you disappear to all day?" It was nice, Lydia reflected, to see Brigitte squirming for a change.

"Oh, but it took ever so long to arrange to have your trunks fetched from the docks!" Brigitte said hastily. "Now I must bring you your tea, *Madame,* for I am sure you are dying for it!" And with that, she hurried from the room.

Lydia smiled after her, feeling that perhaps now this business of how and when she moved into her new room would be dropped.

As Lydia let Brigitte lace her into her stays after she'd gulped her tea, she thought about her coming collision with Blake Spencer. For collision it would be. After that outrageous scene last night, she was more determined than ever to lay down the law. When she found that her thoughts had a tendency to turn toward certain moments of their encounter last night, she turned them firmly toward just what words she would use to let him know how things would be from henceforth.

"Madame?" Brigitte's voice broke into her thoughts.

"I have asked you twice, *Madame,* if you will wear the gray faille or the bronze?"

Shaking her head, Lydia turned her attention to the two morning dresses Brigitte held out. The gray faille was the more dignified, to be sure, and she would need all her dignity this morning. But—

"The bronze," she said. It was the more flattering.

Brigitte slid the layers of silk over her head and stood behind her looping each tiny hook up the back. The dress was a dark bronze silk with a slightly scooped neckline that just skimmed her collarbones. A filmy mock collar of cream-colored lace was settled around her shoulders and across the tops of her breasts, veiling them discreetly. The full skirts were caught up to reveal a dark green petticoat, and the tight sleeves ended at the elbow in a burst of cream lace. Brigitte wove a dark green velvet ribbon in and out of her curls, tying them back so they fell in a cascade behind her shoulders. Checking the mirror, Lydia was pleased with her reflection. She looked prosperous, dignified — and ready to do battle.

When she reached the door of the breakfast room, she paused, then heard a low rumble of male voices. So he was in there! Good! She'd hoped to catch him before he left on the day's business, so she could tell him a thing or two. She put her hand firmly on the latch, squared her shoulders, and marched through the door.

He was sitting at the long mahogany table, obviously finished with his breakfast by the litter in front of him. A steaming cup of coffee sat before him, and its delicious aroma filled the room. Dan O'Hare stood at the sideboard, arms crossed over his chest, probably receiving the day's orders, she surmised.

Blake looked up. "Ah. Good morning, Mistress Collins. I was beginning to despair of you. I trust you had a restful night? Was the bed to your liking?"

She nodded to Dan O'Hare as she crossed the room, and imagined he was trying to hide a grin. Had Blake just been regaling him with their adventures last evening? Already she was having to fight to keep her composure, but she vowed to herself that nothing he'd say would make her lose it.

"Good morning, Mr. Spencer. Mr. O'Hare. Since you asked, the room was adequate. Though not the

115

room I intend to occupy when it is finally proven that this house belongs to me."

She sat down with a rustle and looked up at Dan O'Hare. "Perhaps you'd be so kind as to fetch me a pot of tea from the kitchens, Mr. O'Hare. I do not drink coffee — and I require a moment alone with Mr. Spencer to discuss some business. Pray do not hurry over your errand," she added smoothly, as O'Hare shot a startled look at Blake, then ducked his head and started out of the room.

She turned to find Blake regarding her with an amused expression.

"I suggest you develop a taste for coffee if you plan to stay on the islands. Not many here drink tea, you'll find," he commented.

"I think I have made myself clear on the fact that I do intend to stay in the islands. But I will come straight to the point. I found your behavior of last evening intolerable, Mr. Spencer. I will not tolerate anything of the kind again. If you ever enter my room without permission or lay a hand on me, I shall have you clapped in irons. In fact, I will see you hang and smile at your hanging. Do I make myself quite clear?"

"You do. But since you're new to Jamaica, I feel it's my bounden duty to point out to you that Governor Lynch is a good friend of mine. I doubt he'd hang me for pursuing a beautiful woman, even if the pursuit was a trifle ardent." He grinned at her, and she steamed, reflecting that he probably told no more than the truth!

"If the law will not hang you, I promise I shall shoot you myself," she promised coolly.

"Then I suggest you buy a pistol and start practicing, my darling Lydia, for I have decided I find you too enticing to resist. I add the warning that as long as you live under my roof, I intend to continue my pursuit of you. The idea of you sharing my bed — which, by the way, *you* put into my head last night — is

116

one I cannot seem to forget. I suggest that if you have objections, you might find a stay in one of Port Royal's inns more comfortable, until this little matter between us is settled."

"If you are determined to pursue me, I promise you, you shall be disappointed. There is absolutely no likelihood I will ever regard you as anything but a despicable, arrogant brute. And of course I shall not be removing to any inn. This is my house, and here I will stay until you are forced to leave."

It would be too galling to back down in the face of his efforts to intimidate her—which was obviously what he was trying to do. She didn't allow her mind to touch on the fact that she'd admitted to herself just last night that she found these clashes of wills stimulating.

"But I am willing to forget last night's fiasco," she went on, "in light of the fact that we must live here together for some time. There is no use quarreling like children. I am sure that if we lay down a few ground rules, we will have no more such clashes. In fact, I promise I will see as little of you as is possible."

He grinned. "If you are willing to forget last night, I am not. Yet I will concede that what you say has merit, if you really mean to stay here. Very well then. Here are my rules. Stay out of my way as much as possible, unless you are interested in ending up in my arms. Don't give any orders to the servants—except the most minor ones—without checking with me first. And don't interfere in the way I run the business."

Lydia's lips tightened. "I see you have a sense of humor, Mr. Spencer—something I had not previously suspected. Your first request will be easy enough to accede to, since I would rather spend time in the company of a viper than with you. Your second I will adhere to only to the extent of making decisions or alterations that might affect the house. Which I will also expect you to adhere to. Nothing about it should be altered until the affair is decided. I am sure Mr. Ames will agree."

She allowed herself a tiny inner smile as he glowered. Good! She'd scored at least one point off of him. "As for your third request, I do not plan to interfere in *your* businesses. However, you run a great many of *my* businesses at the moment, and I will spend the coming weeks becoming fully acquainted with them."

"Damn it! I won't have you sticking your nose in, changing things you know nothing about! If that's the way it's going to be, Mistress Collins, I shall resign as your overseer!"

This gave Lydia pause, for it was indeed a meaningful threat. She knew nothing about her holdings, and right now, she needed him to run them for her. Later, she could find a trustworthy—and polite!—replacement, or perhaps she'd even be able to run them herself. But if he resigned today, she would be in a mess. The galling thing was that he obviously knew it.

"My, how easily your feathers are ruffled, Mr. Spencer," she said in a light tone designed to irk him. "I merely said that I intend to *learn* about the businesses, not to interfere. At least not at this time. As an owner, that is reasonably within my rights. You needn't storm at me like a child having a temper tantrum. And I would remind you that I prefer not to hear oaths at breakfast. May I make a suggestion? You remain as my overseer until this matter of the house is settled. I imagine we may come to a parting of ways then in any case."

Blake glared at her across the table. Hell take it! This wasn't going at all the way he'd planned. His attempts to drive her away by being as crude to her as possible were only making her all the more determined to stay, that was obvious. And it was equally obvious he'd handled this woman all wrong from the

118

beginning. He'd underestimated just how stubborn she was—and how very willing to stand up to him. But then, he'd never before met a woman who had the spine to listen to the kind of rudeness he'd been dishing out and give it right back.

And there was the problem. He ought to have charmed her right from the start, he realized now. A little soft flattery, a kiss of the hand, and she would have probably been clinging to him and pretending to be unable to make a decision. Deferring to him, the way women usually did. Blake had no illusions about his own power to charm women, and in fact felt rather cynical about it all. He despised the way some women would act all syrupy and sweet and helpless just to gain his attention. For a moment, the paradoxical thought that a sweet, helpless woman was the type he was looking for to marry crossed his mind—but then he dismissed it impatiently. The woman he would marry would be different, after all. Sweet, yes, but it would be an unaffected sweetness, not that false dependent act that turned his stomach.

It's been far too long since I've had a woman, that's the problem, he thought, staring at Lydia, remembering the way he'd been unable to get to sleep for hours last night. He'd sat up, thinking of the way she'd felt in his arms, all those soft, lace-covered curves pressed against him. Or the moment when he'd come so close to kissing her. Just for that moment, he thought he'd seen a heat in her eyes that matched the heat he was feeling through his whole body. But he must have been crazy—imagined it, he thought, looking at her across the table. She was as cool and composed as an iceberg. Speaking to him like a nurse would to a wayward child.

But cool or not, she was beautiful. No, she was gorgeous. That, combined with the fact he'd been so long without a woman was enough to explain his sudden, almost uncontrollable flare of passion last

119

night.

Feeling a discomforting renewal of last night's lust tugging at him now, he shifted in his chair and said, "Very well, then. I agree to stay on as your overseer until Bellefleur's ownership is settled. And to show you what you need to know of the business. But if we're going to avoid each other, what shall we do about rooms such as this one or the dining room? We shall inevitably meet there."

The door opened, and Dan O'Hare cautiously popped his head in, then, when Lydia nodded, came in carrying the teapot. He was followed closely by his wife Moira.

"Your tea, Mistress Collins," said O'Hare, setting the pot before her. "And is there anything else you'll be requirin'?"

"Just what I was comin' in to ask myself," said Moira, before Lydia could answer. "I am sure you'll be wanting to go over all your orders for the running of the household. And high time it is too that a woman took a hand in running this place, Mr. Spencer. There's a great deal I must ask you about menus and linens, if you have time after you've breakfasted."

Lydia smiled as Blake's eyebrows shot up at this obvious defection of his housekeeper to Lydia's side. "Thank you, Mrs. O'Hare. Of course I shall have time after breakfast to discuss household matters. I am certain you and I will find much that needs changing. In fact, Mr. Spencer and I were just discussing the matter of how the house will be run until the ownership is settled."

"Now just a moment! I thought you and I just agreed that nothing would change!" Blake said in a warning tone.

"We merely agreed that major changes to the house would not be made, and I hardly think that linens and menus qualify."

"That's right, Mr. Spencer. I've been after you and

120

after you to pay more attention to household matters, but with you so busy in the business, you never had time. It's thankful I am that Mistress Collins is here to attend to such things, for I assure you this house is in dire need of attention!" Moira put in forcefully.

"Wife, it's forgettin' your place you are, speakin' to the master in such a way!" cried Dan O'Hare, leaping in on Blake's side.

For a moment, all four were glaring at each other. Then Blake spoke up in a measuredly dangerous tone.

"If we are not to have war in this house, then now is the time to finish the ground rules you and I were speaking of. Go ahead and tinker with the menus and the linens, if that will amuse you. That domain will belong to you and Moira. Dan and I will have charge of the grounds, stables, and outbuildings. Now, as for the rooms we must share, such as the breakfast room and the dining room—"

Here Blake got up and stalked to the middle of the room, pacing a line horizontally along it as he spoke. "They will be divided evenly in half. You may have the south halves, while I will take the north. *That* is your half of the table. If the rooms face another direction, you'll take east while I take west. And in *my* halves of the rooms, Mrs. O'Hare," he stated, whirling to face her, "things will be conducted as they always have been. Meals will be the same and so will everything else. What goes on in Mistress Collins's half I care not. Do I make myself clear?"

Lydia gaped at him open-mouthed, and then, suddenly, had to stifle the urge to laugh. It was so ridiculous that it made a kind of asinine sense!

"You do, Mr. Spencer," she said. "Very well then, we will divide the commonly used rooms in half. Do you suggest painting a line down the middle so no mistakes are made? And by the way, what is the penalty for stepping over the line?"

Cool and determined gray eyes met hers. "I think I

will be able to devise one you will not like," he said, then let his eyes drop meaningly to her lips.

Lydia colored, half angry and half affronted. But she was not so easily cowed. "And which rooms exactly are only your territory, which mine?"

"I only claim exclusive use of my bedroom and my study. You may have your bedroom, sitting room, and the morning room. Satisfactory?"

"Satisfactory," Lydia agreed, still trying to stifle her amusement. Dan O'Hare was simply gaping like a beached fish, while Moira was glowering at Blake. "But also rather ridiculous, Mr. Spencer. But if it takes such drastic measures to have peace in this household, so be it."

Blake stared at her, feeling a frustrated sense of having just lost a skirmish. How he'd lost he couldn't put his finger on, but he had the uncomfortable sense she was the victor this time.

And it was a good thing they'd decided to divide up the house, he thought, as he continued to stare at her. It was becoming all too clear that not only couldn't he remain in the same room with her long without losing his temper, but worse, losing the battle against the attraction he felt for her.

There were things about her he found it almost impossible to ignore. Her coloring, for one. She had a warm, inviting look with that bronze touch to her dark hair, those huge, slanting greenish eyes under dark brows. Her skin was as warm as a sun-ripened apricot, Blake thought. He kept wondering how she'd look in the firelight with all that rich, shining hair loose over her shoulders.

If that wasn't bad enough, he found it hard to concentrate on what she was saying when she talked. Her mouth was full and wide enough to give her chiseled features a sensual touch, a mouth that promised passion in a cool English face.

But most distracting of all was her figure. Though

122

overall she was slender, with one of the narrowest waists Blake could ever remember seeing, she had full breasts generous enough to make a man forget everything else when she was wearing a low-cut dress. Including the business his mind should be on.

Now he scowled as he stood up, cursing her for having such a damnably spectacular figure, and cursing himself for not being able to forget that fact for even a moment. It gave her an advantage.

As she nodded regally to him and swept out of the room, followed by Moira, he wasn't aware that the advantage wasn't all on her side. Because as Lydia settled down to the business of counting linens, discussing menus, and meeting the maids, her mind wasn't really on such subjects.

Instead, she was trying not to think about how unbelievably handsome Blake Spencer had looked as he strode around the room, dividing it up. His long, long legs, his wide shoulders. It was hard not to think about how wonderful the silver wings made his long, tied-back black hair look. Or how arrestingly light his eyes were in contrast to his dark brows and long lashes. Or how very good tanned skin looked on a man, not like the pale faces she was used to in England.

She was even beginning to like his earring.

Yes, Blake would have smiled in triumph had he known how matched this aspect of the battle between them was.

Chapter Ten

Lydia sat alone in the breakfast room, looking out into the gardens, emerald green and bordered by masses of flowers, the sky a faultless blue overhead with only a few giant white clouds massed on the horizon. Beyond, the sea sparkled.

The weather on Jamaica hadn't ceased to amaze her. Though it was hot, there was always a breeze from the ocean that made the air comfortable. Rains came with a tropical violence and suddenness, but often in a few hours they passed and the sun shone again. It truly was like paradise here.

Two months had passed since her arrival on Jamaica, and each day had been utterly fraught with activity. Somehow, Brigitte had managed to find a competent dressmaker in Port Royal — she had the most mysterious connections already! — and Lydia was being fitted for a cooler wardrobe.

Then there were her long, daily letters to Amy, reassuring her that in only a few months, she could set sail for Jamaica herself, describing what little Lydia had seen of life here; and her consultations with Moira on household matters. And, of course, the ever-maddening Blake Spencer to contend with, day in and day out.

She'd had barely a moment to herself. But this morning, for a change, she was utterly free.

Moira was busy supervising the hot and messy business of making soap. Brigitte was in town picking up the dress stuffs they'd ordered, and if Lydia knew anything about it, she'd be gone most of the day. What the girl got up to—! Lydia was certain Brigitte had found some swain in town. And Blake was nowhere to be found, along with Dan O'Hare. Doubtless they were overseeing the unloading of some smuggled shipment from a pirate ship, Lydia thought with a frown. She'd come to suspect that Blake's supposed genius at trade matters was a polite way of saying he dealt with pirates . . . if he were not actually in league with them.

Then she shrugged her shoulders. What did she care where they were? For once, she had a whole day to do as she liked and not be bothered with any of them. And she hadn't had any time to explore the peninsula Bellefleur was built on. The miles of beaches white in the sun were beckoning her.

In a few moments, she was up in her room, deciding what would be best to wear. She didn't want the tropical sun to burn her, but if she was going to do much climbing and walking, she wanted to be cool. Finally she settled on a thin, white muslin dress that was one of the new ones she'd had made up. It had long sleeves that would protect her

125

from the sun. She quickly tied her hair into a knot and put a wide, shady straw hat on her head. She pulled on her sturdiest pair of walking shoes. They were of pale brown kid and looked odd with the dress, but what did it matter? No one would see her.

Soon she was out in the gardens, heading for the gap in the wall that she knew led to the beach path. Bellefleur was almost a fortress, the way it was surrounded by steep, jungle-covered cliffs, but in one place an easy path down to the beach had been built in the cliff where its slope was gentler. She found as she started down it that steps had been cut in the steeper spots, so it was quite an easy climb down to the beach.

She reached the bottom and took a few steps out before stopping to marvel at the sight before her.

She might have been alone in the world. An unmarked beach of glinting white sand stretched to the margin of the ocean. Turquoise waves clear as crystal broke into foam one after the other. Farther out, the sea was dark as sapphires all the way to the place where the dazzling blue sky met the ocean.

The beach was thickly fringed with overhanging palms and riots of flowers in bloom. A small silver waterfall cascaded down black sheer rock not far from where she stood, spilling over the beach in a small river that ran to the sea. Delighted, she walked down to the waterfall, entranced by its beauty. It fell sparkling into a small pool that gathered at the rock's foot, and all around the pool and climbing the rocks, a profusion of flowers grew. Hibiscus, fuchsia, and many she didn't recognize. It was a fairy grotto.

Lydia stopped and cupped her hands in the clear

126

water of the pool, seeing a shadowy reflection of her wide hat. Smiling, she turned back to the beach, wanting to see what further beauties lay in store.

As she meandered down the beach, she began to feel hot. The sand was so smooth under her feet that she decided she could dispense with shoes and stockings. But when she had them off and was carrying them, the sand was scorching. So she ran, laughing, to the water's edge and walked along the cooler wet sand where the waves teased her ankles.

Her skirts were getting soaked around the hem, and for some reason, this delighted her. She felt so free, the worries of the past weeks vanishing. The worries of her life vanishing, too, she realized with a start. Why, all her life she'd been at the beck and call of other's whims! Obedient, sticking to the conventions because people like her father and Aunt Phyllida said she must. How shocked they would be to see her at this minute, her feet bare and her skirts wet, and how scandalized to know she was enjoying it!

Why, now that she thought of it, she'd never really known a moment's freedom until now. If it hadn't been her aunt or her father, it had been Baxter telling her what to do. And now Blake Spencer trying to dictate to her. Well, she wouldn't have it, that was all. She was a grown woman now!

From now on, Lydia told herself firmly, *I shall do as I please, and if it doesn't fit the conventions, too bad! I don't care if everyone is shocked or not!*

Feeling happily rebellious at these daring resolutions, she stopped to stare at the sea. She'd walked perhaps a mile in the hot sun, and had come upon a sheltered cove. It was small and surrounded on two sides by rocks, on the side she stood on by smooth white sand. Barely a ripple marred its aquamarine surface, and she could see through the clear water that the bottom here was clean sand unbroken by seaweed or rocks. It was the most inviting sight she'd ever seen, and she was hot.

With a glance all around her, she made sure she was alone and out of sight from anyone. To her satisfaction, she couldn't see the house, and the cliffs above were a deserted expanse of thick jungle. The palms screened her from view on either side, and there wasn't a single footprint in the sand. This was her place, alone!

She would go swimming.

Smiling, she untied her shady hat and set it on top of her shoes and stockings. Then, with another glance around, she quickly shed the white dress. Underneath, she wore only a thin petticoat and a chemise with lace straps. These days, she only wore stays and the full complement of petticoats and garters when she had to, such as when dressing for dinner. The rest of the time, she'd taken to the island custom of wearing as little as possible in order to stay cool. Though at first it had seemed vaguely indecent, Lydia had been surprised how rapidly she'd grown used to putting comfort over propriety.

And wouldn't Aunt Phyllida faint if she could see me right now! she thought with a grin.

Standing, she flung her arms wide to delight in the breeze that flowed over her bare skin and through her thin garments. Oh, this was heaven! And she was still so hot. Wouldn't the water feel wonderful?

She waded into the azure cove, slowly at first as

the warm ocean rose to her knees. Then she laughed and uncoiled her hair from its knot, and dove under the water like a mermaid, to emerge wet, gasping and laughing. Yes, this *was* heaven on earth!

From the shade of a palm tree, Blake Spencer stood, hand on the trunk, watching Lydia. He grinned as she looked all around, obviously trying to see if she was indeed alone. This was getting interesting. And his grin widened when she started unhooking her dress. So she was going to go swimming.

He'd followed her down to the beach when he saw her start down the cliff path, annoyed that she would think of going down there alone. There were places where the rocks were treacherous to the unwary, and he'd meant to warn her what spots she should keep away from, if she wanted to explore the beaches. When he'd reached the beach, her footprints clearly told him which way she'd gone, and he'd breathed a sigh of relief. Luckily, the way she'd chosen was away from the more dangerous rocks. But still, he'd have to follow her to warn her not to go the other way when she came back.

And now, he thought, he was glad he'd come. His annoyance with her foolishness at going down to the beach alone had vanished the moment she'd started removing her dress.

He drew in an involuntary breath. She stood, clad only in a slip and chemise, and spread her arms wide. It was a sight he knew he wouldn't soon forget. She was beautiful enough in her clothes, but out of them—! Blake swore softly under his breath as she waded out into the water, then laughed when she let her hair fall down her back and dove under.

This was a side of Lydia he'd not seen before. In the house, she was as stiff as a starched collar, all prickly, tight-lipped dignity. He hadn't suspected that she had the ability to let that dignity go and play like an uninhibited child.

Which was what she was doing now. He smiled as he watched her splashing in the water, ducking herself and coming up again, for all the world like a five-year-old child. He reflected that it was a good thing she was playing where she could stand in the water, because it was obvious she knew nothing about swimming.

And with that thought, he had an idea. It was true his crude treatment of her wasn't working. Maybe, he thought, lips curving in a small smile, it was time to try a different tack. Time to see what effect his charm could have on her.

But a thoughtful frown creased his brow. The trouble was, how to approach her while she was swimming, without scaring her half to death so that she screamed and ran?

He had an idea. *It just might work,* he thought, taking a path through the trees that would keep him out of her sight until he reached the beach. And as he went, he was busy slipping his shirt over his head.

Lydia floated on her back, eyes half-closed against the sun above. She knew she shouldn't stay in the water much longer, if she didn't want to get burned, but it was too marvelous to leave just yet. She was just turning over to find her footing when

130

she heard a tiny splash and felt the water move against her in a wave. Eyes flying open, she gave a small scream as something brushed smoothly against her legs under the water and she struggled to find her footing on the bottom.

With a laugh, shaking his wet hair out of his eyes, Blake Spencer came up from under the water right at her side!

"Oh my God!" she gasped, standing, shock almost making her fall again. What a trick to play on her!

"I didn't mean to startle you. I promise you no harm. I was simply worried about you, that's all." He lifted both hands wide to show his harmless intent, and Lydia's own eyes widened as she suddenly grasped the fact that he was wearing no shirt whatsoever!

"You! Oh! How dare you sneak up on me, and—dressed like that! I—" she spluttered.

"I repeat, I am sorry I startled you. But I didn't know another way to approach you without risking harm to you. I was afraid that if I stood on the beach and hailed you, you might swim out farther." He flashed her a grin that acknowledged the fact that she had every reason to swim away from him.

"You see, these coves look very peaceful, but they can be dangerous to those who don't know them. Just a little further out is a current that's very strong. It could have swept you away, if you'd gone much farther. I promise you, I was only concerned for your safety. I have no dishonorable intent."

Lydia stared at him, narrowing her eyes. He sounded so reasonable—so polite! What did he want? Before she could think of anything to say, he went on.

"And as for my—ahem—attire, I don't generally swim in my clothes. I did leave my breeches on in deference to your sensibilities," he informed her.

His words made her suddenly realize that she was standing, facing him in water that came only to her waist, and not only was her hair streaming down her back to her waist, but her white chemise was clinging to her like a transparent second skin. With another gasp, she sank down into the water up to her neck, realizing as she did so that, unbelievably, he'd kept his eyes on her face and not indulged in any of the suggestive leers he was usually so fond of.

"I demand you go away and leave me this minute!" she cried.

"If you wish. But truthfully, Lydia, I meant you no harm. I followed you to warn you not to walk the other way along the beach. There are dangerous rocks that way. And if you wish to go swimming, it is safe as long as you know which places to swim in. For example, this cove is fine as long as you stay close to shore, but as I told you, farther out there are currents. They aren't bad, if you know how to swim, but I believe you do not?"

"How would I know how to swim when I'm from England?" she said testily.

He smiled. "I thought not. If you'd like, I can teach you how. It's not very difficult, really, and then you can come and swim in this cove without worrying me half to death. I promise to be the perfect gentleman while teaching you. In fact, I'm glad I had this chance to see you alone. I'm tired of fighting you. I'd like to apologize for the damnable way I've been behaving to you, and to suggest a truce."

Lydia gazed at him, astonished. Could this really be Blake Spencer speaking? Then she frowned with suspicion. "And why should you want a truce? What is it you're hoping to get from me now?"

He grinned down at her, and she felt her heart give a little jerk. Lord, he looked like a Greek god standing there in the sunlight, the water gleaming on his brown arms, the skin over his muscles smooth as bronze silk!

"I am not trying to get anything from you. I don't blame you for not trusting me. I see I shall be forced into honesty. When you first came, I was angry—both at the thought that a woman would want to meddle with the business, and then more so at the fact that you claimed to own the house. And I admit that I decided that if I made your stay at Bellefleur as unpleasant as possible, maybe you'd just pick up and go back to England, deciding Jamaica wasn't for you. So I—"

He suddenly looked half-ashamed, Lydia noticed with astonishment. He went on. "I must admit I tried pestering you with my attentions. I thought that might make you hate it here, if you believed me and other men on Jamaica to be vulgar ruffians. But you have too much backbone to be driven away by my futile attempts at rudeness. I have been a boor. And if you wish me to leave now, I shall. But if I can make it up to you by teaching you to swim, you have only to say the word."

Lydia stared at him, weighing his incredible words. Did he mean it? Or was he just trying a new way to get around her?

And then she decided it really didn't matter what was motivating him. In the end, the house would belong to her, and in the meantime, it would be

133

much more pleasant to live with a polite Blake Spencer than with the suggestive, seductive blackguard she'd had to put up with.

She smiled up at him. "Very well, Mr. Spencer. As unbelievable as your confession is, it is a welcome sound to my ears. I had grown very tired of your unwanted attentions and insinuations. Whatever your motive is now, I shall be more comfortable living with a gentleman than with a knave."

He smiled back at her, his eyes dancing. "And will you allow me to teach you to swim?"

She considered. She really did want to learn. But it seemed more than a bit scandalous to be in the water with him, and both of them practically unclothed. The image of Aunt Phyllida's face rose before her and decided her. After all, hadn't she just vowed to do what she pleased and be damned with propriety? Besides, no one would know of this except the two of them, for there wasn't a soul in sight, thank God!

"You may . . . that is, if I can remain underwater. And if you can remain the gentleman you claim to be now. You may tell me what to do."

A deep dimple appeared in one cheek. "I shall be the soul of propriety, Mistress Collins. Very well then, the first thing you must do is learn to float on your back."

"I can do that already."

"Show me."

She eyed him uncertainly, then turned over and stretched out on her back in the water, letting her feet float upward, her arms out.

Blake looked down at her, glad she couldn't see herself through his eyes, or she'd be putting an end to this lesson so fast his head would spin. The

134

water did little to cover her—and neither did her soaked undergarments. Steeling himself against the sight presented to him, he had a moment of deeply regretting he'd promised to play the gentleman now and wasn't still doing his best to seduce her. But then, he'd never have been treated to this sight if he was still acting the Knave of Hearts. Truly, politeness had some advantages.

"Very good." Managing to sound unmoved, he walked through the water until he was at her side. She jerked her head up and started to put her feet hastily down on the bottom. "No, don't stop floating. The next step is to teach you how to swim on your stomach. The strokes you must use. For that you must turn over, and if you don't let me hold you up at first, you'll sink. I'm still being the gentleman, remember?"

Lydia hesitated, then turned over in the water. How else could she learn to swim? She must trust his promise, and if he broke it, he'd soon feel the sting of her fingers on his cheek!

She started to sink right away as she turned over, but strong hands came up under her and lifted her to the surface, holding her up. One hand was just over her rib cage above her waist, the other on the bottom of her stomach. Her face flamed at being held in such a way, and she was about to protest when he commanded, "Now stretch out your arms in front of you—that's right—and let your legs float behind you." His voice was brisk and businesslike, and she relaxed a bit. "Now, the first thing to learn is how to kick. Kick your feet up and down, just a little. That is what will propel you through the water. Try it."

Lydia kicked, setting up a spray of splash, and

135

Blake laughed and shook the water out of his eyes.

"Do you have to drown me? No, smaller kicks. Back and forth. Can you feel the way your feet are pushing the water? That's right. Excellent!"

Lydia smiled up at him, forgetting for the moment anything but the fact that she was mastering swimming. He grinned back at her, one lock of raven hair dripping water down his forehead, and then went on with his instruction.

"Now your arms. Wait. I am going to put you down for a moment, so I can show you what you should do. It's easier than telling you." He set her on her feet and she stood, watching him as he dove gracefully under and came up swimming.

His arms cleaved the water in powerful curves, one at a time, coming over his head. She could see how he was pulling himself along in the water. Now and again he turned his face up to breathe. And his feet barely broke the surface at all with their powerful kicks. So that was how you swam!

He stood and strode toward her. "Now you try it."

Eagerly, she laid down in the water again, not even embarrassed when his hands came up to support her. First, he showed her how to hold her breath under water, and breathe only when she turned her face to the side, then made her practice the arm motion. Finally, he had her do all three things at the same time, and Lydia struggled with trying to coordinate the motions until it was coming easily. All her self-consciousness was, for the moment, forgotten.

But it was a good thing she couldn't see Blake's face. He was trying his hardest not to look down too often at the sight he held in his arms, but he

136

was losing the battle. The lines of her back and the curve of her buttocks were all too clear under the wet white material. And her legs were stunningly outlined. But that wasn't the only problem. He was far too aware of the feel of her in his hands, the stretch of her rib cage, the curve of her stomach, and the way her breasts just brushed his hand as she swam. It was maddening. And if he were holding her any lower against him, she'd not be long in knowing just how strongly she was affecting him.

"Here. Try it on your own now," he said harshly, and let her go.

She turned in the water, finding her footing and being careful to leave the water up to her neck, surprised at the brusque tone of his voice, but he was only smiling down at her in that kind way that put her suspicions to rest.

"You think I am ready?"

"I think so."

He stood and watched her as she struck out on her own, then followed after her, critiquing and correcting her technique. But Lydia barely heard him. She was swimming! Knifing through the water under her own power, why, it was wonderful! She was as unfettered as a seal or a mermaid. She would do this every day!

At last she came to a stop, feeling the ache in her arms. "That was wonderful, Mr. Spencer! Thank you so much for teaching me! It is so easy!"

"Well, you will need to practice, but I think you have the idea. And since we are friends now, why not call me Blake? I've never been comfortable with 'Mr. Spencer,' " he said, watching her. Her smile was radiant, her hair a dark waterfall. It was all he could do to keep himself from pulling her out of

137

the water and into his arms.

"Then, Blake," she murmured, with a shyness he found delightful, "I should get out of the water so I don't turn into a fish," she finished gaily. Lord! She was so attractive when she didn't have her mouth pursed up like a prune! "So would you be so kind as to go up on the beach and turn your back, until I finish dressing? Now that you are a gentleman?"

"I won't turn around until you call me." He walked out of the water and up the beach to where his own clothes were folded. He didn't put his shirt on yet—the sun would dry him off in a few moments—and he listened to her as she splashed out of the water. The temptation to turn around was great, but he knew she was probably watching him. *Besides, you've had enough of that for one day, my lad,* he told himself. If he didn't find some female companionship soon, he was in for another string of restless nights thanks to this little interlude.

"I'm dressed!" she called, and, carrying his shirt and shoes, he walked down the beach to join her.

"I am afraid I am still wet," she said ruefully, holding out the folds of her skirt where the water was soaking through from her wet undergarments beneath. "And my hair!"

She'd put on her wide hat, but her hair hung in wet ropes down her back, wetting her dress further.

"I suggest we both sit down for a little while and dry off," Blake said, collapsing on the sand. "I don't want to put on my shirt until I've dried, and my pants are still soaking. It won't take long in the sun. Then we can be presentable when we go back to the house."

She sat down next to him on the beach, and clasped her arms around her knees, staring out at

138

the sea. He saw she still hadn't put on her shoes and stockings, and she was burrowing her bare toes into the warm sand.

"It's so beautiful here," she said after a few moments.

"That it is. I wasn't happy when I was first forced to come here, but now I wouldn't live anywhere else."

Lydia turned to study him curiously. His profile was to her, and gave no hint of what he felt. "You mean—when you were indentured?" she asked, voicing something she'd long been curious about. "How—how did it happen?"

He looked at her, a rueful set to his lips. "It was a duel. In Paris. I was caught and had to pay the penalty, along with my friend Jacques. I was given a choice—prison or indenture. Indenture seemed the lesser of two evils."

"You mean—you were dueling with Jacques Noir?"

He laughed, a trifle grimly. "Yes. In those days we were not friends. We learned to like each other when we were chained in the hold of the ship that brought us to Jamaica."

She shivered a little at the image. "But what on earth did you two duel about?"

"He was cheating at cards," Blake said with a shrug, as if there was nothing unusual about facing a man with a sword over such an incident.

She was chilled, though the warm sun was on her arms. It had been so easy to forget for a few moments how ruthless this man was. Imagine, to want to kill a man over a card game! Why, in the water, he'd seemed gallant, lighthearted. And—attractive. She blushed as she thought of the way it

139

had felt to be held against his strong body, his wet skin against her. Quickly, she said, "So you think nothing of killing a man over a card game?"

He lounged back on the sand, turning to face her and propping himself on one elbow. Golden grains of sand clung to his back, dusted his forearm, glinting a little in the sun. She caught herself staring and directed her eyes to a safer vista—the sea—as he answered her.

"It seems you know little of dueling. It's true some duels are fought to the death, but those are usually over dire insults, such as stealing a man's wife. Most are merely matters of honor, such as the one Jacques and I fought. The first to draw blood is the victor. I'd just nicked Jacques's arm when we were arrested. He's never forgiven me for that to this day. But the authorities don't make distinctions over the intent of the duel. It's still unlawful. I suspect you think me the worst of savages, but I assure you I have never killed a man."

Lydia felt warmer at his words, but aloud she said, "I still think it's barbaric!"

"That I have never killed anyone?" he teased.

"No, dueling. And your friend Jacques is a pirate. If he was indentured with you, how did that come about?"

"Because he escaped soon after we got here. He wanted me to come with him, but I refused. I preferred to serve out my indenture rather than live as a fugitive with a price on my head. And I'm glad I did. Now I'm a free man, free to build my own business empire here in the islands, marry, and start a family."

Lydia was surprised at this revelation. Why, he almost sounded respectable! It would be so easy to forget that he was probably building this business of his on dealings with smugglers and pirates, which made him no better than they were, after all. And he wanted to marry! That was another surprise. Somehow, she couldn't reconcile the Blake she knew with the image of a family man, children on his knee.

"Now I have told you how I came to the islands. It is your turn. I admit to a great deal of curiosity about why you really came here. It seems strange to me that you wanted to give up your London life for this primitive place."

Lydia hugged her knees and stared at the glittering sea. He'd been honest with her. Why not be honest with him?

"I came here because my family is determined that I marry again," she said.

"And what is so bad about that? I would think you would wish to be married again."

"I do *not* wish to be married again. At least, not unless it is of my own choosing!" she said fiercely. "I was forced into my first marriage, for I was underage. My father gave me no say in the matter. And Baxter was—" She turned and looked at him. "Well, you knew him."

"Yes. I would imagine that he was not a young girl's dream of a husband," he remarked, thinking, *So that's why she's so afraid of men! Why didn't I see it before! I never gave a thought one way or another what it must have been like for a young girl to be married to a fat oaf like Baxter!* But he kept these thoughts to himself, for she was talking again, looking out to sea, her eyes clouded.

"My father has always dictated everything to me. And when Baxter died, the whole family was behind him. They were at me morning, noon, and night to make a second marriage. They want me to marry a peer in the most desperate way. That would increase their social standing, you see. So my father wanted to take me to London where I might catch the eye of some earl or duke or lord, and then he could marry me off a second time." Blake saw how a determined set came to her jaw. "But I was of age by then, and Baxter had left me everything. So I beat them at their game by coming here. Here, they can't hound me and make my life miserable until I marry again—and I won't let them dictate to me ever again. Nor, to my sister," she finished, sounding most resolute.

"Your sister?" he prompted, not wanting her to stop.

"Yes, Amy. She is only fifteen, but soon she will be old enough to marry. I won't have her forced into a horrid marriage either!"

"But how can you stop your father?"

"She will come here and live with me on Jamaica. My father wants money, and I will give him the money he wants, only if he lets me have charge of Amy's life. That is why this house matters so much to me."

Blake didn't answer, but thought, *And you have money enough to build yourself a palace, my girl, while I spent a year of my life slaving for this place. If you think your story about your sister will move me, you are much mistaken.*

Aloud, he merely said sympathetically, "It seems you have had a trying time with your family."

Lydia shook herself mentally. "Yes, and what interest can my troubles hold for you, Mr. Spencer? I am sorry for bending your ear so shamefully."

"Ah, but you do interest me, Lydia. And I thought you promised to call me Blake."

The soft tones of his words made her look at him, startled, and when she met his eyes, she couldn't look away. They seemed to burn her, they were so ardent.

"I—I think we are dry enough to go back now," she said nervously, looking away from him and getting up.

He stood quickly, close to her, and still she looked down, not daring to raise her eyes and meet that scorching gaze again. A gentle finger came under her chin and lifted her face.

"Call me Blake," he murmured.

Frozen, she stared up at him, transfixed by the tenderness she saw in his expression. It was as if she was captive to his will, and her lips parted on his name.

"Blake . . ." she whispered, to find him lowering his head to softly capture her lips with his own.

A shock coursed through her at this unexpected kiss. The warm touch of his lips over hers was blissful, as his lips pressed against hers with utmost tenderness. This was nothing like the kiss he'd taken at the dock! Lydia was dizzy with the sweetness of it, and felt a warmth start deep inside her, a feeling of a strange pleasure that made her limbs feel heavy.

His strong hands were pulling her closer, moving up over her arms and around her back to tangle in her damp hair. Before she knew what was happening, he'd pressed the length of his hard body so tightly against her that she could feel the muscles of his thighs through her thin wet dress, of every inch of him molded against her. And as he drew her against him, she could feel the intake of his breath as his kiss became less gentle and more demanding.

Her head spun as his mouth opened hers further beneath his, his tongue creating little trails of fire where it touched her lips and penetrated her mouth. She felt the warmth blaze into a flame of intense longing and hot desire, feelings so new to her that she could barely grasp that they were happening to her. For the moment, her mind was lost under the touch of his mouth and body on hers, and she was all sensation.

She realized that somehow, her own arms had lifted to twine around his neck, and he was kissing her with a passionate intensity now that had nothing to do with gentleness, but everything to do with raging desire!

She gasped under his mouth and straightened, pulling her hands down from his neck to push against his chest. At once, he released her, standing away from her. But his hands were still on her shoulders, and she was shattered by the expression she saw in his eyes. There was a light in them that took her breath away.

"Oh! I should have known that your gentlemanly behavior was all an act!" she cried, fury at her own behavior and his rushing through her where passion had sizzled just a moment before. She reached up and slapped him ringingly, then turned and ran, stumbling, down the beach.

"Lydia!" She heard his footsteps behind her, and then felt him seize her arms and stay her wild run. She stopped, chest heaving, unable to meet his eyes.

She couldn't look at him, aware that her face must be crimson.

And she couldn't speak.

He said nothing for a moment, and then: "You have left your shoes and your hat behind. Let me go get them for you. You can't turn up at the house barefoot and hatless."

She nodded, and his hands fell from her arms. She heard him walking away down the sand, and by the time he rejoined her, she had some of her composure back. But she was still too embarrassed to meet his eyes. She took her offered hat and put it on, then collected her shoes and stockings. She couldn't put them on in front of him, so she just carried them as she started walking.

She felt him at her side.

"I can see you are angry. I—"

"Please, Mr. Spencer, let's just forget it happened. I'd prefer not to discuss it. I will pretend it never happened, I promise."

He didn't say anything then, just walked in silence at her side. Lydia was in an agony of mixed emotions, embarrassment and anger at herself uppermost. Why, she'd let him kiss her as if she were no better than a lightskirt! She cringed as she remembered the wanton way her arms had wrapped around his neck, the way she'd opened her mouth under his and returned his kiss eagerly! Oh, right now all she wanted was to be alone! She'd never wanted anything so desperately. Maybe then she could sort out the confusing feelings that were raging inside her.

At last they reached the cliff path and started up it. She stopped after a moment and asked him evenly to turn her back so she could sit down and put on her shoes and stockings. She needed them now that they were off the beach, and besides, she couldn't go into the house barefoot!

145

She struggled with them, thinking that she looked a sight, and praying they would slip in unobserved. Her dress was still wet, her hair a tangled mess down her back. And he looked as bad as she did, with his wet breeches and hair. God knew what the servants would think if they saw them come in together in this state! At least, she amended, she knew what Brigitte would think, and she'd be too close to the truth!

Blake waited patiently for her to finish, back turned, and still he said nothing, for which she was grateful. They started up the steps again without a word, and at the top, she took a quick glance around to assure herself the gardens were empty. They were. Maybe they would be lucky. They could go in the verandah doors that led into the library, she decided with relief.

They crossed the lawn together and reached the house without incident. Blake stopped at the library doors and opened one of them. At last she briefly met his eyes, and he gave her a rueful smile.

"After you, Lydia," he said.

She stepped inside quickly, squinting against the dimness. And felt a jolt of horror as she realized someone was in the room!

Andrew Ames stepped forward, startled as she was, just as Blake came in through the doors. His eyes went over the both of them, shocked, and Lydia thought despairingly, *Oh God! Not again! Why does he always have to catch us in embarrassing situations?*, as he said, "Miss—Mistress Collins! Uh, Spence! I—forgive me, I see this is an awkward time. Had you forgotten, Mistress Collins? I've—uh—come to take you for our carriage ride!"

Lydia winced. "Mr. Ames! I—I am afraid I had

146

an accident down in the cove, and Mr. Spencer—"

She looked at Blake, and saw that he was standing with his arms folded over his chest, one dark brow raised, waiting for her to go on.

And the look in his eyes!

There was no way he'd back up whatever story she'd been about to tell, so why try? Despairingly, she said quickly, "Excuse me, Mr. Ames. If you'll wait down here, I shall go change. And then we can go on our carriage ride."

As she fled the room, she didn't know which of three evils was worse. The way Andrew Ames looked at her, completely shocked? The way he and Blake had stared at each other across her in enmity—like a pair of bristling dogs?

Or the utter cold fury she'd seen in Blake's eyes, for a fleeting moment, before she'd fled the room?

As she ran up the stairs, she had the feeling that she had just seen the curtain ring down on the brief appearance of Blake Spencer in the role of gentleman.

Chapter Eleven

It had been months since her ill-fated carriage ride with Andrew Ames, and Blake was avoiding her.

Lydia sat at the dressing table in her room, brushing her hair, making ready for the busy day ahead of her. As she pulled the brush through her hair, she sighed at her reflection in the mirror.

She missed the oddly comfortable routine the two of them had fallen into. A routine that had consisted of alternately avoiding each other, and then clashing occasionally so neither would forget the other was there. Strange as it was, she enjoyed their confrontations and looked forward to locking horns with him on any occasion she could manage. She had to admit it was amusing to catch him crossing the imaginary line that divided the house, and see the look of anger on his face when she pointed it out. And when he caught her trespassing, it was a triumph to apologize profusely, retreat to her territory, and then watch his expression change from a gloating one to a brooding one when he saw how little she was bothered by it.

But the game seemed to be ended on his part. He'd been cold, formal, and brief when he'd seen her, leaving the room almost at once.

He was taking her on a tour of one of the warehouses on the wharf this afternoon—an excursion she'd gladly have forgone, having only a minor interest in the trading business. But she was determined once and for all to learn how Blake conducted his business. Maybe such knowledge would help her lay to rest these troubling feelings she had for him.

Then after the warehouse, she had to hurry back and dress for the dinner party she'd planned for that evening. There wouldn't be much time, but she'd have to make do, she thought, as she laid her brush aside.

Brigitte came bouncing through the door, humming a tune. She stopped humming long enough to say, "Good morning, *Madame,*" then proceeded to Lydia's wardrobe and flung open the doors.

"Good morning, Brigitte," Lydia returned, trying to arrange her hair on top of her head, and frowning at the results.

Brigitte pulled two gowns from the wardrobe and turned to her, displaying them for her approval. "The rose satinet or the blue ducape for *Madame's* trip into Port Royal?"

"The satinet will do fine, Brigitte," Lydia answered. She stood, wearing a pale blue and rose floral petticoat which ended in a hem flounce of the same lace that edged the ivory-colored chemise she wore. Brigitte slipped the gown over her head and

149

arranged the skirt, which was open in front to show the petticoat underneath. Where the dress was pulled back, large ivory ribbon bows held it in place at her hips.

Brigitte tugged at the bows. "Will *Madame* need me tonight for the soiree?" She gave Lydia a furtive glance, then began lacing up the brocade stomacher.

Lydia studied Brigitte. No doubt, the girl had a tryst planned with some scoundrel in Port Royal tonight, and wanted the evening free to meet him. Brigitte was never around when she was needed, and was always making excuses to run into town. But Lydia really had no use for her tonight, and heaven knew the girl would find some way or another to keep her rendezvous.

"I suppose not," she said, sighing. "Moira and the others will be serving dinner. There won't be much need for you until I'm ready to retire. But, Brigitte, do you think it possible to make it home from Port Royal in time to undress me?"

Brigitte blushed and stammered. "*Madame,* I—I will be in my room all night . . . embroidering!" She'd finished the lacing and looked up wide-eyed and innocent, then quickly turned away and began straightening the room. She continued, "I—I will remain in my room all night long. When you are ready to undress, you need only call for me, and I will lay aside my needle and thread and come running."

Lydia suppressed a smile at this obvious lie and sat at the dressing table to arrange her hair. She watched Brigitte from the corner of her eye, as the girl carelessly tossed the blue ducape gown into the wardrobe and shut the doors on the hem of the dress. Domesticity was not one of Brigitte's strong points, and the thought of her engaged in embroidery was laughable. Lydia strongly doubted the girl could thread a needle, let alone manage a stitch.

She cleared her throat. "I see. Embroidery . . . a far more preferable occupation to frequenting the streets of Port Royal, I should hazard?"

"Oui, Madame," Brigitte answered, trying to look professional, as she tugged at the coverlet on the bed and fluffed the pillows. "That is no place for a decent young girl such as myself."

For all intents and purposes, Lydia supposed the girl was trying to make the bed, but the mangled pillows were tossed back into odd positions with about as much concern as had been given the coverlet which hung unevenly from the foot of the bed.

Lydia managed to keep from laughing and pointed to the bed. "Brigitte, could you please straighten the coverlet? And you've shut the wardrobe on my gown."

Brigitte looked genuinely contrite. "But how careless of me." And she set to the task of straightening the cover and putting the gown to rights.

"Your mind is on other things, no doubt?" Lydia offered.

"Oui, Madame."

Her lover, she would bet. Lydia shook her head. She should have given more consideration to her choice of a maid. Brigitte was completely inept at housekeeping. Anyone in their right mind would have let her go long before now. But lately Lydia was finding she had all too much sympathy for Brigitte's preoccupation with her lover!

How could Brigitte lead a double life—one that led her into the streets of Port Royal at night and back to Bellefleur to play the not-so-perfect lady's maid? But she had to admit she was also fascinated by it, often imagining herself in Brigitte's place, roaming the dark and wicked places of the harbor town. She would have loved to hear the stories

Brigitte could tell of her late-night carousing with her lover, but at the same time, she was sure she would faint from hearing them.

She looked in the mirror and frowned. "Brigitte, come here and help me with this mess," she exclaimed, referring to hair. It had fallen to one side of her head in a huge mass of mahogany curls.

"Ooooh. That will never do, *Madame*." Brigitte removed the pins that had been haphazardly placed in Lydia's hair and began brushing out the tangles. "Is *Madame* so nervous about her dinner party tonight that she cannot arrange her own hair?"

"You know full well you do a much better job of it than I. And no. I'm not nervous at all. I am looking forward to playing hostess for the first time on Jamaica . . . but I do wonder if I should have invited the Reverend Galdy."

With deft fingers Brigitte twisted a portion of Lydia's long hair into a loose knot that she pinned just below the crown of her head. "The Reverend Galdy? But he is so very sour, *Madame*."

Lydia sighed. "Yes, and prone to sermonizing I'm afraid, but he was so nice to have invited me to tea my first week here that I didn't have the heart to exclude him. But at services he at least introduced me to the Van de Meents. I invited them right off."

Brigitte clapped her hands. "Such a robust and lively pair, *Madame!* What fun they will be tonight. Very amusing."

"And *very* honest. Do you know, they gave me a full account of the previous year's business of their dry goods store and the groghouse they run in Port Royal? And right there on the front steps of the church, directly after services. I'd only just met them!"

"But, *Madame,* they didn't!" Brigitte rolled her eyes and shook her head. "And what do the owners of a groghouse think of the people of Port Royal? A different opinion than the Reverend, eh?"

"Indeed. They think Port Royal's residents 'charming and colorful' to put it in their words. And with good reason. The groghouse's profits for which those charming and colorful people were responsible exceeded those of the dry goods store by threefold!" She looked at Brigitte in the mirror. "Can you imagine?"

"Oui, Madame, I can. I have seen such drink —" she stopped in the middle of her sentence. "I have *heard* of such drinking and carousing in Port Royal," she corrected herself, and tended with complete concentration to the business of looping a ribbon into her mistress's hair.

Lydia bit her lip to keep from laughing, and not to embarrass Brigitte further, who was turning redder by the minute, she went on, "Sir Thomas Lynch is by far the most interesting guest for tonight's party."

"The governor will be here tonight? But, *Madame,* what an honor."

"The Van de Meents introduced me to him in their shop. Sir Thomas didn't have much time to talk, but he thinks his post here tiresome and dull. From what little he told me, it seemed anything but that. I'm anxious to ask him more about his duties here. And, of course, there's Mr. Ames."

Brigitte caught her mistress's eye in the mirror. *"Monsieur* Ames has developed a *tendre* for *Madame,* no? I have seen the looks he gives her, and did he not invite her for a carriage ride in the country?"

Lydia frowned at the mention of the carriage ride. What a nightmare it had been — though, not entirely Andrew Ames's fault. The roads they'd taken had been dry and dusty, and the wheels of the carriage had thrown the dust back in their faces. Conversation had consisted of intermittent coughing and sneezing fits, watering of eyes and waving of hands to ward off the clouds of dirt. They'd gone a good distance from Bellefleur in this manner, when it had started to rain. In a mad rush they'd raced back for the house, but not before getting soaked to the skin. When at last the rain stopped, the dust had settled, but the insects came out in full force to plague them. At this point, conversation had been reduced to more waving of hands, swatting of mosquitoes, and scratching of bites.

Ames had apologized over and over again at his utter failure to treat her to a pleasant ride. He was genteel enough, but he'd not given her one breathless moment, nor had he sent her heart racing at being near him—not at all like another who could make her knees knock at the sound of his voice in the next room. But wobbly knees and loss of breath were no indication of a man's suitability. A woman would be mad not to acknowledge Ames's attributes as a suitor—and the other's obvious lack thereof. She should give Ames another chance, she decided.

She frowned, not wholly convinced.

Brigitte's voice interrupted her thoughts. "But *Madame* does not have a *tendre* for *Monsieur* Ames. That is obvious. Perhaps there is another who makes her heart beat faster, one who takes her breath away? One much closer, more passionate."

Lydia looked up to see her maid smiling at her in a very vexing manner. It was apparent who she was referring to. Why was it the two least trusted people in her life—Brigitte and Blake Spencer—had a penchant for reading her thoughts?

Nettled, she brushed Brigitte's hands away from her hair, and began rummaging through her jewelry

154

box. "Don't be absurd, Brigitte. I have no feelings for Mr. Ames one way or the other, and if you're referring to Mr. Spencer, I would think our animosity for each other would speak for itself."

"*Oui, Madame,* and in the most interesting language, I have noticed." Before Lydia could reply to this, Brigitte continued. "You and *Monsieur* Spencer have put aside your animosity for the soiree tonight? He is attending, no?"

"No. I assume he's made alternate plans for this evening."

"That is strange."

Lydia turned to face a puzzled Brigitte. "How do you mean?"

"Only that *Monsieur's* best justacorps and breeches are being brushed and pressed. And he has ordered O'Hare to make his special rum punch. I heard him say he wanted only the finest for dinner."

"Rum punch? Are you certain?"

Brigitte nodded. *"Oui, Madame."*

Baffled, Lydia turned back to the jewelry chest and pulled several pieces from it. "Oh. I only assumed he had no intention of attending. When I told him of my plans, he seemed not to care a whit . . . told me I could do as I pleased. I admit, I expected one of his tirades, but he was *completely* indifferent. I never even imagined he would want to join us, and I feel terrible not extending a formal invitation to him."

Brigitte's voice held a note of warning. "I would not feel so terrible, *Madame.*"

But Lydia seemed not to hear. She was stunned to consider Blake Spencer would actually *want* to be at dinner this evening. Could this mean his cool treatment of her was coming to an end? She found herself hoping so. If she wasn't convinced, she'd be an utter fool to imagine it. It had almost seemed to her as if he'd been *jealous* of Andrew Ames. But that was a ridiculous fancy on her part, she knew. Well, whatever the reason, she would welcome the thaw between them. Could it be that he wanted to make amends for all their previous battles?

"How thoughtful of him to think of punch," she said out loud. "Well, it is a bit sudden, but I suppose it makes no difference, one more or one less. Be sure to tell Moira to set the table accordingly."

"And how would that be, *Madame?*" Brigitte asked hesitantly.

"For nine. It will make an uneven number at the table, but we shall have to make do."

"How for nine?" persisted Brigitte.

Lydia heaved an exasperated sigh. "How else does one set the table for nine—with nine place settings."

"Anywhere else, this would be a silly question, *Madame,* but at Bellefleur . . . where rooms are divided . . ."

Lydia glanced in the mirror at Brigitte who shrugged her shoulders.

A thought crossed Lydia's mind, but she immediately dismissed it, saying, "No. Don't be ridiculous, Brigitte. Mr. Spencer would not be so rude as to allow the divided house rule to reign tonight with guests at Bellefleur. He's attending dinner after all—and he's ordered up the punch! It would be absurd and completely unreasonable of him, and I give him a little more credit than that." She turned back to the jewelry chest, and drew out a brooch of pearls and aquamarine.

But the nagging doubt was still there.

"What do I know? I am sure you are right," Brigitte said. "But he does so enjoy angering *Madame,* and he has been most strange to her all week long."

Yes, Lydia thought, staring at Brigitte. Why hadn't he mentioned his intentions to be present at dinner tonight?

It was preposterous! Did he expect her to crowd her guests into one half of the dining room, and one half of the drawing room? Were they supposed to come in one half of the door and keep to one side of the hallway, too? He could play this game with *her,* but he wouldn't dare expect it of her guests.

Or would he?

She gasped out loud, as it all became very clear. Make amends?! Blake Spencer, the most infuriating, stubborn mule of a man she'd ever met? Not in a million years! These last months of peace were a fraud. Of course he planned to be at dinner—and of course he planned to enforce the rule! Nothing would give him more pleasure than to make her look like a fool! And, she would wager, the detestable jackanapes was sitting downstairs this minute having a good laugh at how he planned to dupe her.

She slammed the jewelry chest lid down hard, setting her perfume bottles and jars to rattling. She spun around on her chair. "Brigitte! Will you kindly ask Mr. Spencer if he does indeed intend to be at dinner tonight."

With a curtsy, Brigitte ran from the room. Lydia drummed her fingers on the table. *That insidious snake! That conniving slyboots!*

She heard Brigitte racing down the stairs to find Blake, and shortly afterward, her noisy return. Brigitte stood panting in the doorway " 'Of course,' he says, *Madame.* He is looking forward to the soiree."

No doubt, he is—and looking forward to making an idiot of me. "Will you ask him if he intends to dispense with the rules for our guests?"

"Oui, Madame." Brigitte was gone again. Lydia

157

waited patiently, her eyes narrowed and hard on the doorway. *Scoundrel. Beast.*

Brigitte appeared, fanning herself with her hands. She blew a stray strand of hair from her face. *"Monsieur* Spencer says no."

"Is that all? Just no without an explanation?"

"Just no, *Madame.* I asked him if he intended to dispense with the rules as you asked." She stopped to take a breath. "And he said no."

Lydia rose from the dressing table. "Will you kindly inform Mr. Spencer that I *request* we disregard the rules tonight out of deference to our guests?"

Brigitte sighed and curtsied again, then turned and sped down the stairs, though not as fast this time.

Lydia began to pace. *Blackguard. Monster. Lucifer!*

Before long Brigitte was back, completely out of breath. "No he says again, *Madame."*

This was no surprise to Lydia. "And no reason for his denial?" She was amazed at how calm she sounded.

"Monsieur Spencer says, 'Rules are rules.' " Brigitte leaned against the doorway. "Is that all, *Madame?"*

Lydia willed herself to remain steady. It was far too late to call off the dinner party. Moira had been cooking since early this morning, and her guests would be offended if she canceled on such late notice. Besides, she wasn't going to give Blake Spencer the satisfaction of knowing he'd gotten the best of her. It was exactly what he wanted. Instead, she decided, she would observe the silly rule, act as if nothing were wrong. She would be the most gracious hostess Jamaica had ever seen. And if all went well, it would be Blake who would come off looking like the buffoon.

Resolved, she addressed Brigitte coolly. "Please inform Mr. Spencer that I am ready when he is to leave for Port Royal."

Brigitte curtsied a final time and left.

Lydia arranged the folds of the rose satinet gown, tugged at the spill of lace at her elbows, and with one last glance in the mirror, prepared herself mentally for her afternoon with Blake Spencer.

Chapter Twelve

Port Royal was always hot, but it was hotter today than any other day Lydia could remember. As the carriage made its way along Wharfside Street toward the warehouses on the harbor, it seemed to her as if they'd driven directly into an oven. The red-tiled roofs of the many brick houses and shops that haphazardly crowded the street shimmered in the noonday heat, and testily she wondered at the residents's good sense to build here where the island was most stifling. There was no sea breeze to speak of to stir the stagnant air that hung about the harbor, and the stench of refuse, livestock, and rotting fish was nearly overwhelming.

And so was her anger.

Blake Spencer sat at her side in the carriage, leaning out to now and again direct Dan O'Hare, who guided the coach through the crowded streets. During the ride to Port Royal, Blake had made no mention to her of the dinner party, and his very nonchalance grated on her. How could he appear to be so cool when she was so damnably hot?

"This is it," he said and jumped from the carriage before it had even stopped.

O'Hare had halted in front of a warehouse, a large wooden structure, drab and weather-beaten. Not much to look at, she thought. And it was set so close to the water, it seemed to rise directly out of the harbor. She saw a ship docked nearby rocking gently on the rolling waves, and the goods that would be unloaded and stored in the warehouse. Great piles of carpets, furniture, barrels, and crates were all heaped on the quay, and men moved about bringing even more from below.

Ignoring her, as he had throughout the ride, Blake addressed Dan O'Hare. "Show Mistress Collins the office inside. And give her the ledgers. I am certain she will want to see that all is in order. Perhaps she can help us later logging in the new inventory. I'll return later to give her a tour of the warehouse." He grinned roguishly at Dan, then turned, and walked off toward the quay.

O'Hare got down from his perch. He handed Lydia down. "Follow me, Mistress Collins. It's through this door."

He tugged at a wooden door and opened it. A blast of heat more suffocating than that of the harbor hit her, and she hesitated before following the Irishman into the dark office. The door banged shut behind them, plunging them into total darkness.

"Curse that door," she heard O'Hare mutter as he moved around the office.

"Mr. O'Hare, where are you?" she asked timidly,

taking a careful step into the room. Something brushed her face, and she froze in her tracks, pulling the cobweb from her cheek.

"Just openin' some windows, Mistress Collins. Stay where you are. Jesus, Mary, and Joseph, it's hot in here." She heard him moving about, and then sunlight filled the office as he lifted a huge wooden panel on hinges out of the window space and propped it open with a stick. The window overlooked the harbor and through it she could see Blake on the deck of the ship, supervising the unloading.

From near the door, she gazed around the office. It was small and very cramped with a desk and chair sitting below the window and a cabinet on the opposite wall. Everything was covered in dust. O'Hare moved to the cabinet and opened it, rifling through its contents and stirring up the filth with his movements.

She sneezed.

A moan came from somewhere in the office.

"What was that?" she asked in an alarmed whisper.

"It's only Cappy."

"Cappy?" she managed to squeak out.

O'Hare glanced at her, then motioned to the far corner. There on the floor on the other side of the desk was an old man, curled up, half-naked, and hugging an onion bottle. He moaned again and turned toward the wall. Liquid spilled from the bottle and the recognizable reek of cheap rum filled the room.

Her eyes widened in disbelief. "My God! What's he doing here?"

O'Hare pulled a large leather-bound book from the cabinet and turned to her. "Sleepin' it off, I would guess. Here's the ledger. You can make

162

yourself comfortable and have a look at it. As for myself, Mr. Spencer will be needin' my help." He handed her the ledger, bowed his head, and crossed to the door.

"You're not going to leave me here with him?" she pointed in horror at the sleeping figure.

"With Cappy? Nothin' to fear from him. He's gentle as a lamb, Mistress. He wouldn't hurt you."

O'Hare was gone.

If Lydia was angry before, she was absolutely livid now. Blake and O'Hare had known how stifling the office would be, and they definitely knew this character would be inside. The two of them were probably sniggering amongst themselves this very minute, patting themselves on the back for subjecting her to yet another torment.

Determined not to let it bother her, she took out her handkerchief and dusted the seat of the chair off, then the top of the desk. Ignoring the sleeping figure in the corner, she sat, and with as much concentration as she could muster, she opened the ledger and began poring over its contents.

She started with the inventories. One neat row of figures followed another, with notations in the margin, small initials that meant nothing to her. She made a note to ask Blake what they stood for and continued her review of the records of the year's business. Everything had been logged, down to the last item, in a very comprehensible and orderly way, she noticed. Blake Spencer may have been the most infuriating man she knew, but he was also a very good businessman. She could find no fault with the way he'd managed Baxter's records, and she wondered where an indentured servant had learned so much about the keeping of ledgers and the management of a warehouse. Had he been schooled, or had Baxter taught him the business?

163

With a new sense of curiosity about him, she compared the expenses with the income which were logged in another section of the ledger and drew in her breath slowly. She checked the figures again to make sure she hadn't been mistaken.

She closed the ledger and looked thoughtfully out the window.

No wonder her solicitors in London had spoken of him with awe, and no wonder Baxter had sought to keep him at on at any expense. She saw him in a different light now, a self-made man, ambitious, and shrewd in his dealings. And though she hated to admit it, she felt a sense of admiration for him for overcoming his poor beginnings to establish such a business in this place.

She fanned herself with a piece of paper, thinking about him from a new perspective. Her anger at him over the dinner party seemed small and foolish to her. Her plans for the evening meant nothing to him really. It was all part of the game he was playing in the battle for Bellefleur. And if she had any inkling of his personality, she'd guess he was enjoying this. He was a man who liked challenges. Merely possessing the house wasn't his goal; he wanted to win this game.

Maybe he'd told her the truth after all. Maybe he wasn't the criminal she'd thought him, doing his best to connive against a woman. Maybe Baxter *had* owed him the house. Uncomfortable at the thought, she shifted her shoulders.

That would mean she was wrong, and he was right.

It would mean that soon, she'd have no house to live in . . . and nowhere for Amy to come.

It was something she was going to have to think about.

But then, a small, persistent voice said, *you*

*know so little about him — and all you do know
points to the fact that he's a ruthless man, more
than capable of taking you in!*

Had her head been turned by the attraction she
felt for him? she asked herself guardedly.

Her eyes focused on the scene on the docks and
Blake's figure coming down the gangplank of the
ship, carrying a carpet over his shoulder. If his
mental capacities had impressed her, his physical
ones unnerved her entirely.

He'd stripped off his shirt and boots, and was
barefoot with his breeches rolled up over his knees.
His bare chest gleamed tanned and powerful in the
afternoon sunlight, and sweat rolled down the sides
of his face. He shifted the weight of the carpet and
the muscles in his shoulders and arms flexed with
the motion. Her breath caught in her throat and
the familiar flutterings began in her stomach as she
remembered her first encounter with him not far
from here. Even then she'd felt how powerful he
was, and this display of him at work was making
her positively dizzy.

In long loose strides he was down the plank and
moving toward the warehouse.

She couldn't help herself. She rose, looking out
the window, and followed his progress. He disappeared to her left inside the building. Through the
wall she heard him moving things around in the
warehouse and stared at the wall, listening.

Then silence.

A long snore from Cappy startled her. And as he
appeared to be rousing, she quickly stood, having
no wish to confront a drunken old man. Gathering
the ledger to her chest, she walked to the door and
stepped out into the sunlight.

Blake emerged from the warehouse and saw her.
He threw her a devilish smile as he walked up to

165

her. "I take it all is in order with the ledgers?"

He stopped directly in front of her, and the impact of all that bare flesh nearly knocked her off her feet. She swallowed hard, her throat incredibly dry. "The ledgers? Yes." She looked down, aware that she'd been staring. Opening the pages of the book, she thumbed through them. "Everything seems to be satisfactory here. You've managed the business well, Mr. Spencer. I can understand Baxter's reluctance to let you go."

She stopped and looked up at him, trying unsuccessfully not to gape at him. He was saying something, but it was impossible for her to concentrate on his words. His lips were moving, but she could only watch them. Full lips that had touched hers more than once.

She blinked, breaking the spell. "Pardon me?"

"I asked if you had any trouble in deciphering my system of accounting. Do you have any questions?"

"I'm sorry. It was so stifling hot in there, I've seemed to have lost my train of thought."

He laughed. "I should have warned you." He paused and appeared to be waiting for an answer to his previous question.

She racked her brain for what she had wanted to ask him. And then she remembered. She opened the book to the lists of inventories. "I do have a question, Mr. Spencer, about this." She pointed to the initials that had puzzled her earlier.

Blake moved beside her and peered over her shoulder. He was so close, she could feel his bare chest brushing against her arm, and the sweet scent of his perspiration filled her nostrils. She took a deep shaking breath. "These markings here. What exactly do they denote?"

"They are the initials of the ship from which the

166

cargo was taken. See here." He pointed at one of them. "That stands for the *Silent Lioness*."

He pulled away and Lydia breathed a sigh of relief. "An English merchant ship. I see."

He raked his fingers through his hair and gave her a wicked smile. "I've heard them called many things, but not merchant ships. The *Silent Lioness* is a privateering vessel, Mistress Collins."

"A privateering vessel?" The shock in her voice was clear.

"Yes, and if I remember correctly, she was packed to the gills with Spanish booty. And these notations to the right," again he pointed to the book, "refer to where the cargo was shipped to and sold. As you can see some was shipped to London, some to the Americas, and the rest to Hispaniola. Sold back to those it was taken from, you could say."

"*Stolen* from!" she corrected with indignation. He seemed completely unembarrassed about these shady dealings with pirates, as if it were the most natural thing to do—steal from the Spanish and then sell them back their own goods. And to think, only moments ago she'd admired him for his business sense. What a lot of rot that was! Her opinions of him seemed to change with the wind, but from now on, she vowed, she'd be more careful about what she allowed herself to believe of him.

And she'd let the solicitors—not her treacherous body—decide who had the right to the house!

She snapped the book shut and whirled on him. "And I suppose this is the way you've been conducting *business* for my late husband all these years. Stealing from the Spanish."

It seemed his mouth tightened at her sarcasm. "Mr. Collins was completely aware of how trade is conducted here on the islands. I merely handled

167

the details for him."

She sniffed. "And you expect me to believe Baxter knowingly dealt with pirates? You may have been able to keep him in ignorance as he was far away in London—but I am here, and will not condone such criminal dealings!"

"It was not my place to offer moral judgment on the matter of how *your* late husband wanted his business conducted." The words were a whiplash. "I was an indentured servant, Madam, and bound to serve your husband. I continued to run the business as he wanted it to be run." A devious glint came into his eyes. "But I thought you were aware of all this. You did tell me you had been actively involved in your late husband's affairs."

She cringed at the mention of the story she'd told him the night she'd first arrived, but she quickly recovered. "I am aware of his dealings in England, *not here*. That's why I *came* here. And now that I *am* here, I am thoroughly appalled!"

She turned from him and approached the ship. "You there," she called to one of the workers. "Put that back. We're taking none of it."

The worker stopped what he was doing and looked to Blake for an explanation.

Blake chuckled softly behind Lydia and shouted up at the worker. "Do as the lady says. The rest of you, remove the things that are already in the warehouse."

The workers stared at him in disbelief.

"Don't stand there like a bunch of louts. Move, I tell you," he commanded them, and they jumped to work.

She heard Blake's voice from behind her. "You've lost a pretty fortune today, Mistress Collins. I can't expect to demand the return of payment for that shipment."

Slowly she turned to face him, determination in her eyes. "It matters not to me, Mr. Spencer, but that my business be run honestly, and my wealth gained honorably. I wish to leave now. I have a dinner party to prepare for."

She brushed past him for the coach.

The open carriage sped precariously fast along the unpaved roads that led to Bellefleur. Lydia gripped one side of the carriage with both hands so tightly that her knuckles turned white. The vehicle struck yet another pothole, and she held on for dear life as she was nearly bounced out of the carriage. If she didn't know better, she'd guess that O'Hare was seeking out every possible bump and hole in the road and steering for it, with the express purpose of irritating her.

The events of the afternoon had proved too much for her, and then there was the evening ahead. She wanted nothing more than to be back home where she could compose her frayed nerves and try to salvage as much of the already doomed dinner party as she could. She craned her neck over the side of the carriage to see if Bellefleur was any closer. She groaned. They were passing through a grove of trees, and the house was still nowhere in sight.

"Mr. O'Hare," she yelled above the clattering of the horses' hooves and the creaking of the carriage. "Mr. O'Hare, do you think it possible to slow down?"

From the driver's perch, Dan O'Hare glanced back at Lydia over his shoulder. "I'm afraid not, Mistress Collins. Wouldn't want to be late for the party tonight, now would we, Mr. Spencer?"

"Not on your life, Mr. O'Hare," Blake shouted.

Then with a wink at Blake, O'Hare cracked the whip above the horses' ears, urging the animals on to greater speeds.

Lydia cursed the two of them under her breath and clutched at the side of the carriage again to keep herself from being jolted into Blake's lap. *Hang Spencer and O'Hare from the highest tree for this hellish ride!*

With pursed lips, she turned to find Blake smiling at her. Despite the jarring and jostling of the vehicle, he seemed completely relaxed and annoyingly content. With one booted foot propped on the seat opposite him, his hands resting lightly on his thighs, he was the perfect picture of calm. She, on the other hand, was nearly crammed into the corner of the carriage, trying her hardest to have as little bodily contact with him as possible, and still fuming about what she'd learned at the warehouse.

The carriage hit a large bump in the road and tilted to one side, throwing Blake up against her shoulder for nearly the hundredth time since they'd left Port Royal. She heard him laugh softly, as he took his time in regaining his seat. *Hang him from the nearest belltower!* She gave a disgusted sign and slid even closer to her side of the carriage.

"Are you comfortable, Mistress Collins?" Blake inquired with apparent feigned concern.

"I'm fine, Mr. Spencer."

"You're not still angry about the warehouses, are you?"

She glared at him. "Of course, I am. I want all the warehouses cleared of those ill-gotten goods."

He put a finger to his lips. "And what business would you suggest we replace it with?"

"I don't know, nor do I care, as long as it's honest," she answered tersely.

170

"Consider it done. Sugar and rum."

"Pardon me?"

"The sugar mill and distillery you own are near completion, and you'll need a place to store the goods they produce. The warehouses can be converted easily. A wise choice, Mistress Collins, this change." He leaned back, thinking out loud. "Of course, it will take time and money to make the switch, but in a couple of years, you won't even miss the ship trade business. And as I see things, the sugar and rum trade is where the real fortune is. This situation with the Spanish can't last forever, but sugar cane . . . it takes root here and grows like weeds."

His eyes seemed to light up at the prospect of another challenge, and she remembered her earlier assessment of him—and the warning she'd given herself to be wary of him. Slightly mollified by his proposal to ship rum and sugar, some of her earlier wrath dissipated.

She nodded her head. "Sugar and rum it is, Mr. Spencer."

"Very good, Mistress Collins." He winked at her.

The carriage rocked again and she gritted her teeth.

"Are you sure you're comfortable? You look rather . . . cramped in that corner you've taken a liking to."

"I'm very comfortable, and I can't remember ever enjoying a ride as much as this one," she said, sending him a look that would wither a stone.

"I've always found that if you relax and take the bumps as they come, the ride can be very enjoyable." And to prove his point, he stretched out his long legs and laced his fingers behind his head.

The carriage lurched again, throwing him up against her. He looked her straight in the eye and

171

repeated, "Very enjoyable."

This time he made no attempt to right himself, but remained pressed close against her. She could feel his shoulder against her arm, one of his thighs alongside hers. His face was only inches from her own, his lips drawn into a rakish smile. And those eyes—light gray but growing dark with meaning. He lowered his arm to rest it on the back of the seat behind her, and her heart skipped a beat at the feel of his arm on her neck.

Quickly, she slid away from him, managing somehow to rise and flop onto the cushioned seat opposite him.

She fixed a cold glare on him. "Since we've decided to divide the house, I suggest we do the same with the carriage." She described a line across the middle of the vehicle with her finger. "This side is mine, and that is yours."

"Are there penalties for trespassing?" he inquired, flashing her a broad grin.

"Try it, Mr. Spencer, and that smile of yours will be missing a few teeth."

He threw back his head and laughed heartily. "I do imagine you could give me a sound thrashing, Mistress Collins, if your punch is half of what your temper is. But if you were to cross my line, I promise no penalties that you wouldn't enjoy."

"You're impossible!" she spat at him and looked away.

"Not impossible. Quite willing, in fact."

"Detestable!"

"I think you'd change your mind, if you gave me a try."

"Conceited!"

"And with good cause to be so. Let me show you."

Lydia clamped her mouth shut. She wouldn't say

another word. Anything she said, he'd just twist into some knew suggestive insinuation. She wouldn't even look at him. She knew he'd be grinning at her, confident and cocksure, and it made her blood boil to think she'd allowed him to provoke her.

She was grateful for the silence that ensued, and she hoped it would last until they reached Bellefleur, but before long she heard Blake's voice. "Hmmm. But the view has improved immensely with the dividing of the carriage."

She looked at him and nearly regretted having moved opposite him. It gave him a full view of her, and he appeared to be taking liberal advantage of it. Starting with her feet, his gaze traveled to her waist where it stopped. He lifted both eyebrows and waggled them up and down, then continued until his eyes settled on her shoulders. There he sucked in his breath slowly between his teeth, and let out a low whistle. At her lips he moistened his own, and at her eyes, he tilted his head to one side and heaved an exaggerated sigh, rolling his eyes to the sky. He let his head fall back to rest on the seat behind him, then clasped his hands to his heart, and brought his head back up. "Oh, Lydia. What you do to me."

There had been nothing lascivious in his perusal of her. In fact, it had been quite comical—and an attempt to goad her into another argument. But instead of calling him names, she merely stuck her tongue out at him and looked away. And then she couldn't help smiling, and soon she was laughing. It was all part of the game. How ridiculous the two of them must have seemed, bouncing along, tussling, and bickering in the carriage, like a pair of ill-behaved children. And in his own way, he was letting her know just how ludicrous they appeared.

Blake leaned forward. "Are you laughing, Mistress Collins? Don't tell me I've actually made you laugh? I do believe you're laughing, Mistress Collins, and I think I'm responsible."

She kicked his leg playfully with her foot. "Don't flatter yourself." She shook her head, still smiling. What a rogue! Infuriating her one minute, making advances on her the next, and then making her laugh about it. Tonight would be more interesting than she first thought. Who could possibly guess what he had in store for her. If she was any judge of him by now, this pleasant interlude would have little bearing on the evening to come.

Regarding him from the corner of her eye, she said coolly, "Don't think that because I laughed just now, that I've forgotten about this afternoon or forgiving you for not bending the rules for tonight. The rules are still the rules. Correct, Mr. Spencer?"

He leaned back in the seat. "Positively, Mistress Collins. And don't think that because I've made you laugh that I won't be as trying as ever tonight."

"I wouldn't have expected anything less of you, Mr. Spencer."

Chapter Thirteen

"Mr. Spencer, I have heard all the island gossip about your feud with Mistress Collins over Belle-fleur, but don't you think this is carrying it a bit too far?" drawled Lady Grandmire dryly.

It was an hour before dinner was to be served, and Lydia smiled in satisfaction, looking across the drawing room where Blake sat all alone. Lord and Lady Grandmire, Governor Thomas Lynch, Peter and Anna Van de Meent, and Lydia all sat at *her* end of the room, closely packed but comfortable. The Reverend Galdy had not arrived yet, and neither had Andrew Ames, though Ames had sent a message indicating he would come later.

Blake shrugged his shoulders in response to Lady Grandmire's question. "Both Mistress Collins and I agreed that the house should be divided. We've even divided the carriage."

175

"Really?" Lady Grandmire raised her eyebrows and looked to Lydia for some response.

Lydia nodded her head in agreement. "It's quite true. Until Mr. Ames hears from Whitehall, one half of the house and coach are mine, the other half belong to Mr. Spencer."

She tried to read Blake's expression to see if he was the least bit uncomfortable under Lady Grandmire's questioning, but he was as relaxed as always.

He had made no excuses when the guests had arrived, merely instructed them all as to where they could and could not go. And he'd had the nerve to greet them in the same shirt and breeches he'd worn that afternoon at the warehouse. His shirt was sweat-stained and wrinkled, and he was in desperate need of a shave. It was a blessing to have him on the other side of the room, she thought, for no doubt, he stank as well. And from the smug expression on his face, she could tell he was perfectly aware of how much his appearance embarrassed her in front of her guests. But she decided she owed her guests no explanation for his poor manners. It was far better to let him answer for his own actions.

Lady Grandmire, an imposing but handsome older woman, continued, "Have you also divided the servants? Which half of Mr. O'Hare is yours?"

Blake chuckled. "All of Mr. O'Hare is mine. Mistress Collins has laid claim to Mrs. O'Hare."

"I see." Lady Grandmire was not without a sense of humor and smiled at this. "It must make their marriage very difficult."

176

"I believe their marriage has always been difficult," Blake quipped in return.

"Perhaps Mr. Spencer and I have improved the
situation by separating them," Lydia added.

There was general laughter from the other
guests.

Blake lifted his cup in mock salute to Lydia's
quick wit. She returned the salute with one of her
own and smiled to herself. Her guests were the
least of her problems tonight, and it came as no
surprise that they were all familiar with Blake and
his stubborn ways. They seemed to be taking the
divided house in stride. Instead of being shocked
by a man and woman sharing a home, they'd
been very interested in the arrangement and thoroughly amused by it. But there was still Blake to
contend with, and she knew he would have a few
tricks waiting for her before the night was
through.

She didn't have long to wait. She noticed the
governor's punch cup was empty. Without thinking, she rose and began to cross the room into
Blake's territory, where the punch bowl sat on a
small table next to his chair. Before she'd gotten
halfway, Blake's voice brought her up short.

"You've crossed the line, Mistress Collins."

She stopped and looked down at her feet, then
stepped back across the imaginary boundary, her
cheeks burning in embarrassment at the amusement of her guests.

She held her head up and looked Blake directly
in the eye. "Sir Thomas's cup is empty, Mr. Spencer, and since the punch is on your side of the
room, would you kindly pass it to me, so that I

177

might refresh his drink."

Blake didn't move. "Since the bowl is on my side, then the bowl belongs to me." He looked at the others. "What do you think?"

There was agreement from the other men in the room. Anna Van de Meent and Lady Grandmire jokingly protested in Lydia's favor. Still Blake made no move to pass the punch bowl to Lydia. He only watched her.

But Lydia was prepared. She turned and walked to a window in the corner of the room. From behind the draperies, she retrieved a long pole with a crook at one end. She'd counted on this kind of behavior from Blake and had brought the tool in from the stables where it was used to break up hay bales. Her guests cheered as she maneuvered the crook around the leg of the table from her side of the room, and pulled it across the dividing line. She grasped the big crystal bowl, holding it aloft in victory. There were cheers, and from across the room, the sound of Blake's applause.

Blake was glad of the chance to laugh out loud—his plan of serving O'Hare's incredibly strong concoction was going better than he'd anticipated.

Lydia bowed to her guests and finally to Blake. "The punch appears to be on my side now, therefore, it must be mine."

She poured for the governor and sat back down, pleased to have gained a small triumph in the game against Blake Spencer. She settled back to enjoy the conversation.

Before long, she spotted Lady Grandmire eyeing

178

Blake's mussed hair and clothing and wondered what the older woman would have to say about it. Lydia knew she would say something and impishly hoped it would be as embarrassing to Blake as his disheveled appearance was to her.

Lady Grandmire didn't disappoint her. "I'm flattered, Mr. Spencer, that you and Mistress Collins invited us for dinner, but really you shouldn't have dressed just for us."

"Winnifred, dear, let up on the man, for heaven's sake," Lord Grandmire cried. "No doubt, he's been working all day. I must say, your comments are embarrassing Mr. Spencer. You've been at him since we arrived this evening."

"It's quite all right, Albert," Blake said. "Lady Grandmire and I have been going at each other since you first came to Jamaica over a year ago."

"And we do so enjoy it, don't we, Mr. Spencer?"

"I know of no better verbal sparring partner than you, Lady Grandmire . . . with the possible exception of Mistress Collins."

All eyes turned to Lydia. Lady Grandmire eyed her from head to toe.

"Has this young lady boxed your ears soundly with a word or two?" Lady Grandmire inquired of no one in particular. "Yes, I imagine she's quite capable of it." She turned back to Blake, and look of mock hurt on her face. "I'm jealous, Spencer. How am I to compete with such a lovely young woman?"

"There's no competition, Lady Grandmire. You may have the dubious title of Blake Spencer's verbal sparring partner. I find it far too exhausting," Lydia sighed.

"But he is challenging?"

Lydia looked at Blake. "Oh, yes, very challenging. But then so is an angry bear. And, frankly, I do not know which is worse. An angry bear or an angry Mr. Spencer."

"An angry Mr. Spencer," the governor chimed in. "I've seen him in Assembly and he can be a very formidable opponent. To be sure. I think I'd rather go up against an angry bear any day."

Their laughter was interrupted by the entrance of Dan O'Hare. O'Hare signaled to Blake who rose.

"It seems my bath is finally ready. If you will excuse me, I will take my leave and prepare myself for dinner. I do apologize for greeting you in these clothes, but the tub I purchased in Barbados takes a good deal of water, and it requires some time to haul it up to the house and heat it."

What a perfectly reasonable and charming liar he could be, Lydia thought. He'd had all afternoon to fill the tub and take his bath. He could fool their guests, but he didn't fool her.

"Why ruin your barbarian theme for the evening by taking a bath and changing clothes?" she called. "We were all so looking forward to you eating with your fingers and swilling wine straight from the bottle."

Lady Grandmire clapped her hands amidst the laughter of the other guests. Even Blake smiled and chuckled, but Lydia didn't miss the *I'll-get-even-with-you-later* gleam in his eyes.

"Very good, my dear." Lady Grandmire perused

the two of them carefully. " 'Tis a shame the two of you are on opposite sides of the fence. What an interesting coalition you would make. Your conversations would never be dull, that is for certain."

"No thank you, Lady Grandmire," Blake raised a hand. "I think an angry bear would inflict far less serious wounds than Mistress Collins. I prefer a more peaceful coalition."

"Of *course* you do," said Lady Grandmire, but her tone indicated she didn't believe a word of it.

Lydia watched Blake leave, almost sorry he would be gone, even if it was for just a little while. Lady Grandmire was right. Conversation was never dull with Blake around.

Lydia turned to Sir Thomas. "Please do tell us about being governor here. I imagine all sorts of interesting problems come your way in a day's passing."

The governor sighed. He was a melancholy sort of man, she thought, thin and drawn-looking. "It's not interesting in the least I fear, Mistress Collins, all rather boring and trying at the same time. Lord Grandmire can attest to that. We get no support from the Crown, and nothing but complaints from the local Assembly, no offense intended, Mr. Van de Meent. Mr. Van de Meent is a member of the Assembly, Mistress Collins. Though I understand the problems of the local merchants, I'm always caught in the middle between them and the Crown. It seems I can please no one. And then there are the continual attacks on our ships by the Spanish, and the retaliatory sacking of Spanish ships by the French and by

181

our own countrymen."

Lydia's interest was piqued by the governor's last statement, as she recalled Blake's association with the French pirate, Jacques Noir. "But I thought the treaty with Spain would have put an end to pirating?"

"To be sure, it hasn't."

"It is a matter of—" Peter Van de Meent stopped mid-sentence, searching for the right word. "A matter of ec-o-nom-ics, Mistress Collins. Vithout the pirates, Anna and me, ve have no business. Ve go back to Amsterdam."

Sir Thomas nodded his head in agreement. "The buccaneers are keeping this island alive. They sack the Spanish and spend their pieces of eight in the local groghouses and brothels. The merchants are happy, the doxies are happy, and to be sure, the pirates are happy. But Whitehall can't let this go on forever. The Spaniards will inevitably declare war again over the attacks on their galleons. Trying to develop agriculture on the island is near to impossible. The King won't support us, and the young men who come here to plant are soon lured away to the pirate ships by tales of Spanish gold."

Lydia opened her mouth to comment, when a horrible sound came from elsewhere in the house. All conversation stopped, and her guests turned around in their seats as the sound continued.

It was Blake, singing at the top of his lungs from the kitchen.

"Good heavens! Is Mr. Spencer singing?" Lord Grandmire exclaimed. "No wonder we never see the man at Sunday services, Winnifred. He'd

182

frighten the other worshipers off with that awful racket."

A nervous titter escaped from the other guests. Blake's singing was so loud, it was impossible to continue any further conversation.

Peter Van de Meent smiled as he listened. "That is no hymn he's singing."

Lydia blushed when she was finally able to make out the words to the song. It was a bawdy tune about a sailor and a young woman who sells fruits. The double entendres in the song were shocking, and when Blake had come to the part where references were made to the young lady's melons, Lydia rose in indignation, ready to storm into the kitchen and give Blake a piece of her mind. She'd expected him to be trying, but not crude!

She started for the door.

"Where are you going, my dear?" Lady Grandmire asked.

Lydia stopped, remembering her guests. She turned back to them, not knowing what to say.

Lady Grandmire laughed out loud. "There's no need to be embarrassed, dear Lydia. The song does not offend me in the least, and knowing Mr. Spencer as I do, his singing it for his guests does not shock me as I think you imagine. We're all very aware of the game you and Mr. Spencer are playing here. But I'd say he's winning at the present moment."

Lydia bristled, not because Lady Grandmire had drawn attention to her embarrassment, but because the older woman was right. Blake Spencer was winning. Then an idea struck her—doubt-

183

less, induced by the punch.

She fixed a very gracious smile on her face. "I only thought you might enjoy seeing the tub that Mr. Spencer brought back with him from Barbados. It is a very fine tub, made of copper, and as Mr. Spencer boasts, large enough for three."

Lady Grandmire jumped to her feet. "Well done, my dear!"

Moments later, the group of giggling guests had gathered outside the kitchen door. Blake's off-tune singing came in sporadic bursts from the other side, mixed with sounds of splashing water.

Lydia pressed a finger to her lips for the others to be quiet, then put her hand on the latch, lifting it slowly. It clicked, and Blake's singing stopped. She waited for what seemed years, and then he began a new off-key chorus, even louder than before.

Lydia swung open the door and swept into the kitchen with her guests following quickly behind her. The look of surprise on Blake's face as he first registered their sudden appearance, and then his own nakedness, was an expression Lydia wanted to remember always.

Lydia boldly crossed to the tub, and Blake slid up to his neck in the soapy water. He sputtered. "What the hell are you doing in here?"

"I'm showing our guests the new tub you purchased." She rapped its side with a knuckle, saying to the others. "It's as I said . . . made of copper."

The others were roaring with laughter, but Lydia kept a straight face as she pointed out the tub's many features. She pointed to a pipe that ran from the tub's drain into the floor of the kitchen. "This was my idea," she said, pushing one sleeve of her dress above her elbow, then bending and reaching into the water at Blake's feet. She made a tugging motion and pulled up the cork that kept the water from draining into the pipe. She held it up out of Blake's reach for the others to see.

Lydia stood with her back to Blake, but she could hear him struggling to stuff a cake of soap into the drain. And fortunately, he was laughing, too, as the soap kept slipping from his hands.

"You see, dumping the water was a problem," she began. "You can imagine how heavy the tub was to move with water in it. Since it already had a hole in the bottom for draining, I suggested that a pipe be run below the house and out onto the grounds."

"How clever of you," commented Lord Grandmire between chuckles.

"Thank you, but Mr. Spencer engineered the entire thing. We're planning to install its own water pump, but we haven't quite figured out how to heat the water. Mr. O'Hare suggested we build a fire underneath the tub, but the idea of keeping the fire going while Mr. Spencer was in the tub was too tempting."

The men launched into another fit of laughter at this, and were nearly hanging onto each other to keep from falling over. Mrs. Van de Meent's bubbling giggles escaped from behind the fan she held in front of her face, and Lady Grandmire crowed, "That's showing him!"

"Please, Mistress Collins," Blake said from be-

185

hind her. "Now that we've all had a good laugh at my expense, do you think you could continue your lecture in the drawing room? The water is getting immodestly low. Unless you care to stay and see something more."

"No thank you, Mr. Spencer, we only came to see the tub." Without turning around, Lydia dropped the cork into the water and led the way out of the kitchen. Her legs were shaking at her brazen display, and though she'd tried not to look directly at Blake sitting in the tub, it had been impossible not to catch a glimpse of his bare chest, gleaming above the water. And how it had set her heart to hammering! She only hoped no one had noticed the effect the sight had on her.

On their way back to the drawing room, Lady Grandmire moved to her side and whispered in her ear, "My word, what a chest that man has. I should have liked to have stayed and seen more, wouldn't you?"

A shocked gasp was all Lydia could manage for a reply. By the time Blake had dressed and rejoined them in the drawing room, the Reverend Galdy had arrived and was boring everyone to tears with his incessant grumblings on his favorite subject—the moral licentiousness of the island's harbor folk.

Lydia looked gratefully at Blake when he walked into the room. Perhaps now they could have dinner. The change in scenery would hopefully result in a change of conversation.

Lydia crossed her fingers and led everyone into the dining room.

Eight chairs were crammed to one side of the

table, and a single chair sat at the head of the other end. Moira O'Hare stood nervously to one side, fidgeting with her apron. Lydia's eyes met hers, and the frazzled housekeeper shrugged as if to say, "I've done my best!"

Lydia signaled to her to begin serving dinner. Moira disappeared through the door into the kitchen.

The others seated themselves, but the poor Reverend looked confused. He watched Blake cross to the single chair and sit down, then looked back at the other six guests and Lydia.

"Please, won't you have a seat." Lydia indicated a chair on her right. The Reverend sat down, all the while glancing suspiciously around the table.

Lydia suppressed a smile. None of the others had commented on the unusual seating arrangement, because they understood the rule. But the Reverend had no idea what was going on and was too polite to mention it. Perhaps it was best to keep him in the dark, she thought. At least he'd stopped preaching to them.

With knitted brow, the parson watched in silence the strange ritual of serving dinner. First Moira served Lydia and her guests, then set the steaming dishes in the center of the table. Here, Dan O'Hare, who had entered the room with Moira, would take over and serve Blake. As each course was dished out, the parson would look at the others, searching for some kind of confirmation from them that he was seeing what he thought he was seeing, but no one let on that anything was out of place. It seemed everyone was grateful for his silence.

The Reverend's confusion was increased when Vande Meent spoke up. "Spencer, vould you mind passing the gravy this vay."

Blake grinned and stroked his chin. "The gravy is on my side of the table, therefore—"

"It belongs to him!" the Grandmires and Sir Thomas finished.

Lydia heard Moira muttering under her breath from her corner of the room. Quickly, before Moira could charge Blake, Lydia got up and walked to the middle of the table, then bent over and reached for the gravy boat. Her fingers had just grasped it when Blake pulled it backwards out of her reach with a grin.

"This manner of table service has its rewards," he commented, his eyes going to Lydia's bodice.

She straightened up at once when she realized that her breasts had been in peril of spilling out of her bodice.

"I see there is a method to your madness, Spencer," Lord Grandmire said approvingly.

Blake looked at Lydia mockingly, enjoying her discomfiture. She reached for the gravy again, her napkin held protectively over her cleavage. His hand came down over hers.

"Not so fast, Mistress Collins, you've already stolen a bottle of wine from me. I won't have you stealing my gravy, too."

The Reverend's eyes widened in disbelief. "Thievery!" he exclaimed suddenly. "Port Royal abounds with thievery of the worst kind!"

Nearly everyone had to stifle a laugh. Lydia covered hers with a cough and sat down, grateful for once for his diversion. The poor man was so terribly puzzled by the evening's events, that in his attempt to make some sense of the bizarre occurrences, he'd grasped onto the only subject he knew well. And, obviously, he'd been sampling the punch too freely.

Lydia gritted her teeth.

"Port Royal is the dunghill of the universe, a receptacle of vagabonds!" The parson's face was red with passion as he continued, and Lydia thought he'd surely burst a vein. "Such a godless, heathen pack of wolves never to be found anywhere else on the face of the earth. Port Royal will surely be punished for its sins."

A silence so thick ensued it could have been served for dinner, she thought. Lydia's guests shifted uneasily in their chairs. Lord Grandmire cleared his throat, Anna Van de Meent's fan began waving vigorously back and forth in front of her face, and Blake—she was sure he'd be no help in this situation, especially after the tub incident.

Lydia steeled herself for another attempt to steer the conversation away from the Reverend's favorite subject. "I find Port Royal fascinating, though a trifle hot. I've never known such a climate in all my life. So different from London—the sun always shining, clouds that threaten then disappear to let loose on some other part of the island, yet it's always cool and breezy in the evenings. The sunsets are quite stunning."

The tension eased and the other guests nodded their agreement. Lady Grandmire quickly added, "Lord Grandmire and myself never miss a single one. The day's heat is easily forgotten in the splendor of the sun's setting."

"Ven Peter and I move to Jamaica, ve glad to leave behind cold vinters in Amsterdam. No skating here, but ve take up new pastime—svimming!" Anna Van de Meent made paddling movements with her hands and laughed. She beamed at her husband who bobbed his head up and down and said, "Like fish, me and Anna."

Blake's eyes locked with Lydia's across the wide expanse of the table as the rest of the guests laughed.

"But wherever did you learn to swim?" Blake asked them, without taking his eyes off hers. The rogue! She felt a flush start at his mocking question, meant for her, and she deliberately turned her attention to Anna, praying the conversation would lead somewhere else!

Anna's eyes grew large and round. "I have best teacher in all Jamaica."

"Who?" Lady Grandmire piped up. "Peter?"

"No. Peter say to me, 'Anna, I teach you to svim.' But Peter no teach me to svim. He take me to beach. Ve go into vater. I see big fish mit big fin svimming to me. Shark. I learn to svim very fast. Shark teach me."

A new round of laughter circled the room.

Lydia looked at Blake. "I *have* heard," she stated, "that there are sharks in these waters."

"And I have heard," he replied, "that there are mermaids."

"A sailor's tale, Spencer!" put in Peter merrily. "The only mermaid, I ever see is my Anna!"

"Mit my figure some mermaid I make!" She

190

indicated her ample curves, and shot her husband a fond look. "Ven it get too hot, Peter and I close the shop and go svimming. No one shop ven it get hot anyvay."

The Reverend grunted in disgust. "But you never miss an evening at the groghouse—serving rum to the reprobates who frequent your establishment, do you, Mrs. Van de Meent?"

No one said a word. Lydia wished she could ask the parson to leave, but a voice from across the room came to her rescue.

It was Blake. "It's not hot enough to swim in the evening. Besides, after a warm day even reprobates get thirsty, Reverend."

Again the others chuckled. But the parson persisted. "I see nothing humorous in promoting the lack of morality on this island through the sale of rum, and turning a profit on it at the same time."

Blake countered. "But, and correct me if I'm wrong, Mr. and Mrs. Van de Meent, it was those profits that helped pay for the building of Reverend Galdy's church."

Mrs. Van de Meent nodded, her curls bouncing. "Ya. Ve give very generously to the Church."

"And I know the Van de Meents are not the only merchants in Port Royal who have donated funds." Blake went on, "I suppose one could say your church, Reverend Galdy, belongs to those vagabonds and reprobates. They are the ones who paid for it."

His comment was met with a hearty burst of laughter from all sides. To her surprise, Lydia was truly glad Blake was there. He was making

191

the difficult parson's presence easier for everyone to bear.

The Reverend opened his mouth to argue in his defense, but Blake cut him off again. "Enough about that. Mistress Collins, won't you please tell us all one of your delightful stories?"

Lydia looked up at him across the table in shock. "I don't know what you're talking about, Mr. Spencer. I don't tell stories, delightful or otherwise."

"Don't be modest. I hear you telling them to Moira all the time."

"And I never thought you were listening, hiding behind your books. Shame on you, Mr. Spencer, for eavesdropping," she chided him.

"Well, your stories were a sight more interesting than some of the books I've read lately. Go on, tell us a story. Don't make me beg you."

Blake's request had come as a pleasant turn of events. Was he only trying to keep the Reverend from monopolizing the conversation, or did he truly want to hear a story?

It didn't matter. Everyone was waiting on her. She thought for a moment, then remembered a story about a ghost ship her dressmaker had told her one day when she was in Port Royal. Soon she'd forgotten everything as she became involved with the tale.

Blake leaned back into his chair, comfortably listening to Lydia's voice. When it wasn't loaded with verbal darts, he found it could be very soothing. As the story unfolded, he thought it

There was an interested murmur around the table.

Lydia found her fingers were clutching her napkin.

"In any case, Spence, I should know one way or another by the morning. If you and Mistress Collins will call on me then, perhaps we can get this matter settled at last."

Lydia's eyes flew to Blake's across the table. And she saw that all the warmth was gone from them—and all the cold challenge was back.

Later that evening, Blake stood on the veranda off the drawing room, leaning against the door to the balcony. Their guests had left, and he was watching Lydia as she bent over the oil lamp in the drawing room to turn the flame off.

She pivoted and saw him standing there. "Shall I leave the light on?"

"No," he answered. "I can find my way in the dark."

She straightened up, looking across the room at him. "So tomorrow, we will have our decision," she said softly. "No more divided house."

"Yes—tomorrow we will know, one way or the other."

Was that regret she heard in his voice? Or was it anger? She felt strangely awkward, almost ill at ease with him, now that there was no longer any reason to treat him as a rival to be outwitted at all costs.

She almost felt sad. "Well," she said with a small laugh, "I suppose tonight's dinner party was

194

sounded like a melody, rising and fallin
gentle rhythm, growing soft, then racing e
ahead, tinkling like bits of broken glass. I
he'd only wanted to keep the Reverend at b
deep in his heart he knew he'd wanted her
a story, just so he could listen to her vo

The candlelight flickered, throwing a
glow around her face and shoulders and g
in her hair. Her eyes grew big and round,
the suspense of the story. This was the p
liked best. First she would smile, then gas
finally give a wave of the hand, as she dr
listeners to the tale.

She had no conception of how lovely sh
All the beauty and innocence of a new ro
thought. He smiled to himself and finish
analogy.

Complete with thorns.

But Lydia was not destined to finish he

"Mistress Collins! My apologies for bei
late!"

Blake scowled as everyone looked up, s
for it was Andrew Ames who'd just burst
room.

And was kissing Lydia's hand. Blake
deepened at the way his friend was starir

"Forgive me for missing your dinner,
Collins, but perhaps you will underst
you hear what's kept me," Ames said,
ing. Then he turned and looked at Bla
received word that a ship from L
sighted this evening—and aboard, I
be a letter from Whitehall. I hope it
a decision as to the ownership of

193

a fittingly ridiculous end for the fued we've conducted."

She saw him smile ruefully. "It *was* ridiculous, was it not? I fear I've blackened your name in Port Royal for good, though here that will probably only add to your popularity."

She smiled back at him. "You were a good sport about the tub and very charming all evening—with a momentary lapse now and then. Wherever did you learn that horrible song?"

He couldn't help but laugh. "A friend taught it to me."

"Never introduce me to that friend. I might be forced to give him a piece of my mind. In any case, I was glad you were here. I enjoyed myself."

"Does that come as a surprise?"

"Not entirely," she admitted. "But tell me, when the Reverend started in, why didn't you just let him ruin my party? It was what I was expecting," she asked him.

He thought for a moment. "We did put our rivalry aside and join forces toward the end of the evening, didn't we?"

In the lamplight, he saw her brow furrow slightly, as she considered this. "Yes, we did." Then she turned the lamp out and the room slowly grew dark as the flame sputtered and died.

He could see her shadow moving through the doorway where she stopped. She didn't turn around, but said softly over her shoulder, "Good night, Blake."

"Good night, Lydia."

And then she was gone.

He jammed his hands in his pockets and turned

to stare out at the night, and a fierce love for the beauty of his house filled him. The house he'd built as a labor of love.

He hardened his heart against all soft feelings, against the coming day. No matter how much he was finding he liked Lydia Collins, no matter how her beauty was entrancing him, it didn't change the fact that she was doing her best to take the thing he loved most in the world away from him. Bellefleur.

He'd not forget it again.

Chapter Fourteen

"I am ready to make a plan."

The words were bitten out one by one, and Jacques looked up from the charts he was studying, slightly startled, at his open cabin door, aboard the *Tiger Lily*.

It took only a glance at Blake Spencer's face to make Jacques think that he knew that look all too well. He'd seen those same steel gray eyes across a card table once, and soon after, above a sword.

He smiled and leaned back in his chair, pushing aside the charts with a negligent hand. "Ah. So she has the house? I can think of no other reason for you to storm aboard the *Tiger Lily* like I would a Spanish galleon—that is, unless you intend to scuttle me. No?" He smiled. "Then you had best shut the door and sit down."

He watched without speaking as Blake closed the door and took a chair across from him. This was a very different Blake Spencer than the one who'd months ago burst into the Coq D'Or with that woman under his skin. Blake angry was one thing . . . but when he was cold as ice, *Dieu!* He almost felt sorry for the woman, she did not have the advantage of knowing Blake as he did . . . of knowing that *this* Blake Spencer always got his way. Such knowledge could save a person a lot of unnecessary trouble.

"It's lawfully hers. Baxter never filed the papers. Before you ask me, I offered her an outrageous price for it—though why I should have to do that when I already worked a year to own it—Enough." Blake cut off his sentence with an impatient gesture. "She would not sell me the house. She wanted to offer me another tract of land and some money, as if she doesn't know it's Bellefleur that matters to me! I have one week to move everything out. She even owns the O'Hares indenture papers now . . . and refuses to sell me Dan's for Moira's sake. Or let me buy him his freedom. There was a rare scene, my old friend, with Moira and Dan shouting, and Moira going to *her* and sobbing on her shoulder—" A momentary shudder ran through Blake, Jacques saw, at the memory.

Blake shook his head as if to clear it and the cold glint came back. "Dan swears he's running away to become a pirate . . . but I told him to do nothing until I had a chance to think."

Jacques gave a low whistle, putting on a mock

sympathetic face that hid the fact that he wanted to laugh. Just at the moment, he knew, laughing would not be a wise thing to do.

"I can see why you came here. Tell me, Blake — are you still opposed to the obvious solution? Why not marry her?"

"I will if that is the only way I can get my house back," came the even reply. "But if you think I'd let myself be forced into marriage without a fight — that is a last resort. I think I will see what persuasion can do first." Blake smiled, and it was a smile Jacques knew also of old. "I will make her see reason."

Jacques brought his fist down with a thump. "At last! It is what I told you from the first. If you just hold a gun to her, scare her, force her to sign the deed over — "

"Oh no. You mistake me, my friend. She will sign it of her own free will. I have not sunk so low that I would resort to terrorizing women. No harm of any kind will come to her. I must make that clear from the start, Jacques."

Blake's voice held a warning note, and Jacques nodded, albeit a trifle reluctantly.

"I have your word?" Blake pressed.

"You have it."

The two men clasped hands over the table, and Blake seemed to relax. He, too, sat back in his chair, and lifted a boot to the table.

"Good. Then this is what I mean to do. I think I can persuade her to sign the deed if I use a certain . . . leverage . . . I have in mind."

"Blackmail?" said Jacques, interested.

Blake grinned. "No, nothing so drastic. Just

the threat of something that I think would make her see she can buy *another* house with the money I give her."

"But I thought you just said you were not going to use threats!"

"I don't plan to frighten her . . . at least, not more than I have to. What I plan to do is bluff her. She does not have to know that she is in absolutely no danger. She only has to believe that I will carry out what I say I am going to do, if she does not allow me to purchase the house."

"That sounds very much like terrorizing women to me, *mon ami*," Jacques pointed out.

"Ah, but I do not intend to offer her any violence, or even real threats. Just choices she is free to make."

"It is not very fair," Jacques laughed. "And if I may say, most strange of you. I always thought you put your honor and your sense of fair play above everything else, such as going to prison, for example, or serving an indenture. But, *alors*, people change." His eyes twinkled at his friend.

Blake stood up, and the cold look was back. "But you forget, Jacques, that she has treated *me* unfairly and dishonorably. I worked for one year of my life for that house . . . for her as well as for her husband. I slaved to keep her in the dresses she looks so damned fetching in. She saw the letter of intent Baxter wrote. None of this mattered to her, and she stole that house from me as surely as if she were the one with the pistol and I at the other end. I overlooked all that and still offered her a fair price for the

200

house, and for Dan, too. So do not talk to me of fairness! I have come to realize she is my adversary, and the fact that she is a woman has ceased to matter to me. Her sex may keep me from calling her out, but it won't keep me from getting back what's rightfully mine. I shall just have to use different methods than those I'd use with a man, that's all."

Blake stopped his striding up and down and looked at Jacques. "So, are you still willing to help me?"

"I am."

Blake gestured to the charts. "Looking for a rich prize in the next weeks?"

"The Spanish will always be there." They could wait, Jacques thought happily. Planning ways to plague Spanish ships was amusing . . . but this promised to be much more so.

"Then how would you like to spend some time with Brigitte aboard my schooner—without a crew around to bother you?"

Jacques gave a wolfish grin. "My old friend, I knew helping you with your little problem would be diverting, but not *this* diverting!"

Blake raised an eyebrow. "She is that—?"

"That delightful. I too am learning new things every day about women that I never suspected before. I shall have to watch myself with this one, or I shall find myself at the altar."

"You?" They both laughed. "But it is up to you to get her to agree to our little plan. That is the first thing I will need from you."

"I believe this thing is within my power," Jacques said with mock modesty. "And the second?"

Blake smiled, and his arm came up to sweep the cabin. "This. I should like to borrow the *Tiger Lily* while you and Brigitte are gone."

Four days later, Lydia sat at the desk in the study, trying to concentrate on the letter she was writing to Amy. She read the first few sentences with a small frown.

"My dearest Amy, at long last I am able to send good news. The matter of the house has been settled in my favor. Bellefleur is now *ours,* and so you can book passage on the next ship to Jamaica! I have just finished my letter to Father, and I am sure he won't object. But of course, if he does, you must write me immediately and I will come back to England myself to straighten it all out . . ."

For the fourth time, she disgustedly set aside what she had written and pulled out a new sheet of writing paper. She just couldn't seem to strike the right tone. She wanted to sound joyful that she had won the battle over the house, that Amy could come to Jamaica now, and to convey her confidence that there would be no problems with their father she couldn't handle . . .

She put the quill back in the inkstand and looked around the room. That was the trouble. It was hard to write with a confident air when she didn't *feel* confident.

"And just exactly what is your problem, Lydia?" she asked herself irritably. "You have won what you fought for. Amy can join you here.

You should be overjoyed."

The masculine interior of the study seemed like an unspoken reproach. The late afternoon sun was muted by the gauzy drapes and lit the leather chairs and dark wood, as if to emphasize the comfortable feel here she had always liked. The faint aroma of one of Blake's cigars hung in the air.

She got up and walked restlessly over to the windows, filled with a tumult of conflicting emotions. She'd won, hadn't she?

Then why did the house seem to belong to Blake more than it ever had before?

If only he'd accepted her offer, she wouldn't have to feel guilty.

She turned her back on the view of ocean and green cliffs to shut her uneasiness out. But the thoughts kept coming. She should be triumphant right now . . . but the house felt so empty. It had been four days since Blake stormed out, and she'd not seen him since. Only a formal note to let her know he'd arranged to have his belongings moved at the end of the week. It wasn't that she *missed* him — but it was so quiet! Moira and Dan were barely speaking to each other, and Brigitte was suddenly unbearably polite, keeping her eyes cast down and her comments confined to *"Oui, Madame,"* and *"No, Madame."*

Again Lydia frowned. Well, she really didn't care what they all thought, did she? The best thing would be to release Dan and Moira from their indentures right away, and let them decide what they wanted to do between themselves, without her interference. It was just that everything had happened so fast, she hadn't had time to think of what was right or wrong. She resolved to call them in directly after dinner tonight and tell them the news. That would at least get her out of the middle of a domestic problem she had no right to be involved in.

And Brigitte? Lydia felt a slight twinge of regret, but tried to shrug it off. True, she liked Brigitte, but if the girl was not happy in her service, she would help her find a post elsewhere, if that was what she wanted.

Why, she wondered with a touch of despair, did she seem to have more problems now than the ones she'd struggled with back in England? And why didn't making decisions to solve them make her feel any better?

There was a tap on the door, and with a sigh, she called, "Come in."

Brigitte opened the door and regarded Lydia with that new expressionless face of the last four days. "Will *Madame* be needing me before she goes on her evening walk?"

Lydia stifled her irritation, thinking that there could be no complaint in the fact that Brigitte had made it a point to study her habits. "No thank you, Brigitte. I am finishing a letter to my sister, and I may not go on my walk if I do not complete it first," she said pointedly, expecting Brigitte to merely nod her head and close the door.

But instead, Brigitte took two steps into the room. *What now?* Lydia thought wearily. She steeled herself to be gracious. "Yes, Brigitte?"

"So *Madame* is writing to her sister? She will

be coming here to Jamaica now?"

"I hope so. That is, she will," Lydia amended.

"And Mr. Spencer—he will be moving his things soon?" This was said with a chilly air.

"You know perfectly well that he will. I can see you think that—" With an effort, Lydia controlled herself, and stopped.

"I only ask, *Madame,* because I imagine you will be doing a great deal of redecorating."

It seemed now was the time to sound out Brigitte's feelings, after all. As kindly as she could, Lydia said, "Brigitte, if you are not happy here, we can come to another arrangement."

Brigitte's eyebrows rose in a look of affronted surprise. "Perhaps *you* are not happy with me, *Madame?*"

"It just seems clear to me that you have been very quiet—not yourself—since Mr. Spencer left, and I thought perhaps you no longer wanted to remain in my service."

"Pardon me, *Madame,*" Brigitte said stiffly, "but I have been quiet because I did not think you wanted to hear what I had to say. It is not the servant's place to give opinions to her mistress if they are not asked for, no?"

Oh, this was too much, Lydia thought, exasperated. As if Brigitte had ever been shy about offering unsolicited opinions in the past! "And what is it that you wished to say to me? I am ready to hear it."

Brigitte gave her a quick unreadable glance through her lashes, then, with the air of one burning her bridges, remarked, "It is just that I

205

think *Madame* has been very unhappy since *Monsieur* Spencer left the house. I think *Madame* is not aware she has developed tenderer feelings for him. Perhaps fallen in love with him."

"Brigitte, that is outrageous! I should dismiss you for such insolence! And it is quite, quite untrue. He is—"

"Oh, I know you think he is a bad man," Brigitte cut in. "But permit me to say I have experience in such matters. I mean no insolence. It is simply that a woman's heart does not always listen to reason, and it is possible to be in love with a man, even if you don't approve of him. And also, there are many kinds of being in love, not just the true love we all look for." Brigitte gave Lydia what looked to her like a slightly pitying smile. "Sometimes a woman's body may say things to her she does not want to hear. Her heart may race faster at the sight of a man when he is a man as beautiful as *Monsieur* Blake Spencer. And I think you may hate him, but you are still upset that he is gone . . . and now, *Madame,* if you like, I will leave your service."

Lydia struggled for a moment with the hot words that were springing to her lips, but Brigitte's last words made her feel slightly ashamed. After all, hadn't she just been wishing Brigitte would talk to her again in her old way?

"I—I don't wish you to leave my service, Brigitte—unless you are not happy with me. I . . . maybe you are right, and in a way I do miss Mr. Spencer. I don't really wish to discuss it right now, for I don't know what I really feel about anything . . . but I am not angry with you for speaking honestly to me."

"Then—perhaps *Madame* will still be going for her walk? It is a good way to think." Brigitte smiled at her for the first time in four days with what looked like warmth, and Lydia was relieved that at least *one* problem seemed solved. She rose, glancing out the window. The earliest blue dusk was falling, looking impossibly inviting.

"Yes—you're right. I do need some air, and some time to clear my head. The letter can wait. Thank you, Brigitte," she finished, striving to sound much more decisive than she felt, and then, giving Brigitte what she hoped was a friendly nod, she walked toward the study door.

As she went out into the hall, she heard Brigitte say softly behind her, "Have a good walk, *Madame*," but Lydia didn't turn to answer. She simply had to be alone to think. She couldn't cope with another crisis today.

Brigitte smiled as she watched Lydia walk out of the study, quite a different smile than the sympathetic one of a few moments earlier. She waited a few moments, listening to the retreating footsteps in the hall, then casually strolled over to the desk where the unfinished letters lay. Picking the latest version up and reading it, she gave a small shrug, and put it in her pocket.

Then, briskly, she left the study and went in search of Moira.

"She's not *gone?*" Moira's tones were of the

most outraged affront. "After everything that's happened?"

"Just for a day or two—perhaps a week, I do not know. My mistress simply told me to tell you that she felt the need of a few days away after all the trouble there has been, to rest. She requires me to pack a bag for her for a few days' stay at a friend's, and has instructed me to join her there."

"A friend's? What friend? Surely not Mr. Ames? But no—he'd never lose his sense of propriety so, and I willna believe it of her, either!" Moira said warmly.

"Do not distress yourself so, Mrs. O'Hare." Brigitte raised her eyebrows to show that she thought of this incredible assumption on the part of the housekeeper. "I do not know where they met, perhaps in town when she was on business, but she has been invited by the *Comtesse* Deveaux to spend a few days with her on Barbados. Her ship sails in an hour, and if I am not there—*Dieu!* Why am I wasting the time I need to pack talking to you? If you do not believe me, here is a note she wrote to you." Brigitte proffered a piece of paper covered with Lydia's flowing handwriting.

Moira waved it away, agitated. "There, girl, you know I canna read! I never thought the mistress'ed be so flighty as to just up and leave me with everythin' at sixes and sevens, but there, the poor wee lamb has had a hard time what with Mr. Spencer and all, and—the *Comtesse* Deveaux you say? It's just the sort of acquaintance she *should* be making here. I don't

208

wonder she accepted it—"

As she spoke, Moira reached a decision and suddenly shooed Brigitte with both hands. "Well, what are you standin' here for, girl? Go and pack your mistress's things and I'll order the carriage to take you to the docks."

Brigitte was already running lightly up the stairs, but she turned to give Moira a brilliant smile. "The carriage is already waiting for me, Mrs. O'Hare, I have ordered it."

Moira stared at her for a moment, dithering, then started up the stairs after Brigitte with a look of decision. "Then hurry, me lass. You can read me her note while you pack for her. I hope she's left me instructions. Is she staying until after Mr. Spencer's belongings are moved out?"

Moira wrung her hands as she hurried rather breathlessly up the stairs, then broke into a smile. "The *Comtesse* Deveaux! Och! Just imagine!"

The sun was ablaze behind a bank of red and golden clouds when Lydia reached the beach. She stopped for a few moments to watch the spectacle, but then reminded herself she wasn't here for sunsets, no matter how beautiful, but to think. Darkness fell very quickly here, she knew, once the sun sank below the palms, and she didn't want to make the climb back up to the house in the dark.

So Brigitte thought she was in love with Blake Spencer.

Was she?

As Lydia walked slowly toward the ocean's edge, no longer seeing the sunset or hearing the rustle of the palms, she realized that Brigitte had been speaking the truth.

She was in love with Blake Spencer . . . Lord help her.

Knees weak, Lydia sat down all at once on the sand and tried to think clearly. What did that mean? Was she *really* in love with him? Or was she just feeling those . . . *physical* feelings Brigitte had referred to?

The waves rolled endlessly and the sky deepened to crimson, but Lydia lost track of time, trying to sort out the unsettling discovery she'd just made . . . and in trying to think what to do about it.

Nearly half an hour passed before she glanced around and saw that dusk was stealing beneath the palms behind her, though the ocean was still dazzlingly light. Slowly she rose and started back to the house, still thinking about Blake.

I miss him, she thought, *and my heart races every time he walks in the room. I want him to kiss me! But what difference does any of that make? He's dishonest, and I may never even see him again—*

Never see him again! Lydia stopped, her heart sinking. For a long time she stood, staring up at Bellefleur's roof, outlined against a copper sky.

At last she started walking again, a decision made. It didn't matter whether what she felt toward Blake Spencer was love, desire, or hatred, at least not right now. And she didn't know. What mattered to her was letting Blake buy the house back.

It was the only right thing to do.

Because even if she was a fool, her *heart* had come to believe in Blake, to believe he loved this house as much as she did, and—

One more time, very near the trees now, Lydia stopped. A lump formed in her throat. How much she had come to love Bellefleur. The thought of giving it up was an unbearable ache in her throat. But if she felt that way, how must *Blake* feel? She could build a place as beautiful . . .

There is no other place as beautiful as Bellefleur, a small forlorn voice said inside her.

But she shook it off and stifled the tears. What mattered was that she be able to live with herself, and not feel as if she'd taken advantage of Blake. Amy could still come. She'd make the sale contingent on their not having to move until her new house was finished, even if it took a year. Blake could go stay at the Coq D'Or, and probably happily enough, if he knew he'd get the house at last.

And as for this matter of whether or not she was in love with Blake Spencer, time would tell her that. It was a feeling that would probably be best to stifle. After all, Blake Spencer was not exactly her idea of an eligible husband!

Feeling much relieved, Lydia reached the bottom of the stairs and started to climb up. By now it was dark and there were mysterious rustlings and noises in the jungle on either side of the stairway, but she steeled herself. A few mysterious noises were nothing compared to what

211

she'd just been through!

But suddenly, the rustling behind her was much louder, almost like a large animal. Lydia whirled around with a small shriek of fright, just in time to see the dark shape of a man looming out of the bushes, before the sack came down over her head and cut off her screams.

Chapter Fifteen

Lydia stopped struggling. She'd been picked up and thrown over the man's shoulder, bundled in the sack, and her screams and kicking were having no effect on him at all. The breath was being jolted out of her lungs with his every step, and the rough sacking was covering her mouth. Her heart pounded with terror, but panic wasn't helping her. She had to try to be alert, so she would have a chance to get away from him.

She felt him stop, and she struggled again as his rough hands lifted her off his shoulders. The breath came out of her in a gasp, as she was swooped through the air and landed with a thump on some kind of seat.

Without ceremony, the sack was dragged off her head, and coughing and ready to fight, she tensed.

213

A man she had never seen before sat calmly across from her in the bow of a longboat, holding a pistol pointed at her heart. Her eyes widened, then she twisted to look at the other man, the one who had carried her, who was calmly stowing the sack in the stern of the beached longboat. He grabbed the gunwales and shoved off, leaping easily inside the boat. As he sat and took the oars, the longboat rocked so that Lydia clutched at the gunwales with a small cry, almost overbalancing off her seat.

When she had herself righted, she sat up as straight as possible to face the man seated across from her in the bow. He was only a dark shadow against a thousand stars, but though she couldn't see his face, she could still see well enough the glint of the gun barrel.

She willed her words to come out as calmly as possible. "What are you going to do to me?"

The voice that answered her out of the blackness was accented in French. "Do not be afraid. No harm will come to you, if you do not do anything foolish. We are not going to do anything to you. We are just sailors, under orders to take you to our *Capitaine*."

She saw his arm describe an arc against the stars, and for the first time she noticed the twinkle of the riding lights of a ship at the head of the cove. The point had hidden the ship from her as she walked on the beach, but now the longboat had rounded the headland.

"Your captain! You mean—you are *pirates!*" Lydia felt a welcome surge of fury replace her terror.

"Do not distress yourself, *Mademoiselle*. I must

214

tell you, I can answer none of your questions. You will wait to speak to the *capitaine*."

"Perhaps you will at least tell me the name of the ship to which I am being taken?" she said scathingly.

But the man merely sat across from her impassively.

"You hope to get a ransom?"

Silence again was her answer. There was only the steady swish of the longboat's oars, the riding lights of the ship at anchor drawing closer and closer.

Lydia twisted again in the seat to look back at the shore. High on the hill she could see the lights of Bellefleur. But there was no stir of activity. Obviously, no one had seen them take her . . . and as obviously, this had been well planned. They must have watched her for a time, known of her habit of taking evening walks on the beach.

And known she was rich.

She willed herself to concentrate. When she didn't come back—a surge of relief swept through her. Moira and Brigitte were expecting her back at any moment. They would raise an outcry, start a search.

"You cannot hope to get away with this. My servants expect me back at any moment, and—"

At last he broke his silence. There was a trace of patient amusement in his voice. "And by then we will be long gone. I think they will not search for you on ships. I tell you, *Mademoiselle,* wait to speak to the *capitaine*. He has promised you no harm, and he is an honorable man."

"Honorable!" Lydia spat, but then gave up.

They were nearing the shadow of the ship now. It rode easily at anchor, masts tall against the night sky. The detestable pirate was right. The last place anyone would search for her was aboard a ship, and by the time they thought of it, she could have been sailed to any of a hundred islands. And where would they even get help in searching for her? Port Royal was regrettably lawless, and even the governor might not be able to do anything—

The longboat scraped against the side of the ship, and she could see men on deck, letting down a rope ladder. Her hands went to her hair, down around her shoulders, then gave up, realizing it was a wild tangle from her ride in the sack. One of her captors steadied the boat, while the man with the pistol rose as if to help her onto the ladder.

"I can climb it myself."

She stood, realizing she only had one shoe on; the other must have been lost in her struggles on the beach. With as much dignity as she could muster, she gathered up her voluminous skirts in one hand, climbed onto the ladder, let her skirts drop, and started up.

It was a terrifying thing to do, and that, coupled with the thought that the pirates below were probably looking up her skirts, kept her panic at bay. She tried not to look down, just up, and found it was actually an easier climb than she'd anticipated.

And quickly over. She reached the top, and a man was waiting there to grasp her hands and haul her over the top onto the deck.

"Take your hands off of me, you filthy brute!"

The moment she had her footing, Lydia angrily wrested her hands away from the man's grasp and looked him over scornfully. He was a bear of a man, and the flickering, chancy light of the ship's lanterns did nothing to conceal the fact that he was unshaven and had very few teeth left in his mouth. If that weren't bad enough, her nose told her he hadn't washed in a long time, and that he reeked of rum. A flicker of fear went through her lightning-fast at the thought of this man — or any other of these brigands — touching her.

But he merely dropped her hands at once and stood back a few steps. If it wasn't impossible, he looked nearly as frightened as she was. He ducked his head in a clumsy mixture of a bow and a nod, and said, "Zis way, please, *Mademoiselle*. I show you to *le capitaine*."

The words came out in a French accent so heavy she could hardly understand them, and well slurred with rum. "Captain? I refuse to go to him!"

The man, clearly ill-at-ease, stared at her, obviously at a loss as to what do to about her refusal. So they were afraid of her! Lydia felt a small dart of triumph that was short-lived as guffaws and appreciative whistles broke out around her.

She whirled indignantly to find that the men from the longboat had climbed onto the deck and had joined a group of others that were standing around, watching the fun. They were a motley bunch of all ages, shapes, and sizes, united only by their exceptional filthiness and general state of drunkenness. She heard a number of rapid, low-voiced French and English comments and saw

217

grins, quickly hidden, as her eyes swept them. It was all too apparent that though they were being rather polite and respectful, and keeping their distance, they thought this spectacle was vastly amusing.

The only one who wasn't laughing at her was a slip of a boy who couldn't have been more than twelve — and he was scowling.

She turned frigidly back to the man who had spoken to her, and saw that his cheeks were as red as hers, but whether from the rum or the comments she didn't wish to hazard. "Very well. Take me to your captain," she capitulated.

At once, he smiled at her as if relieved by her sensible decision, and turned, walking quickly. She followed — anything to be away from the men on deck! — and her jailer stopped at a door to a cabin, opened it, and motioned her inside.

So this was the captain's cabin! It was hardly the luxurious den of a pirate she had pictured, but rather small and cramped. The overhead lantern illuminated no golden spoils of the Spanish Main, but rather a bare scrubbed plank floor, some sea chests, and a built-in bed that was the only thing not austere about the cabin. On it were tossed a rich jumble of bedthrows and pillows, in dark red damask shot through with gold threads.

There was a table littered with maps and charts, some rolled neatly and tied with a length of rawhide, some open, their curled edges weighted with instruments such as sextants and a spyglass.

Hoping to find some clue about the pirate who held her captive, she crossed quickly to the desk

218

and scanned the papers hurriedly, rooting through them without a care for how she was disturbing them. She knew she might have only moments before the pirate captain joined her, and she was determined to make use of them.

But to her disappointment, all the writing was in French, even on the maps and charts. She could recognize charts of the Spanish Main, of New Spain, the Virginias, and of the coasts all the way up to the New England colonies.

"Curse it, why did I never learn to read or speak French?" she murmured aloud, as she scanned the maps. Obviously this one had tired of preying on Spanish treasure galleons and turned to what might be a richer prize . . . ransom . . . and ransom of the Caribbean's wealthiest widow.

She gasped at a thought. "What if he wants to force me to *marry* him?" she whispered aloud.

She turned, frantic to ransack the cabin and find some clue about its owner. But the sea chest at the foot of the bunk was banded with brass, studded, and locked. As were all the drawers in the desk built into the wall across from the bed. She had just turned to try the drawers under the bunk when another unwelcome thought struck her and made her stand stock still. A suspicion so ridiculous that she couldn't credit it, but—

What if Blake Spencer had something to do with this?

Lydia's knees went suddenly weak, and she was forced to sit down on the bed. Not Blake, she told herself. Not when the moment she'd been kidnapped, she'd just realized she was in love with the rogue, and—

219

Listen to me! I am calling him a rogue in my mind already, when—

When that is exactly what he is, another part of her mind answered firmly. It just seemed so right—so much what Blake *would* do. And so wrong—not what the Blake Spencer she was falling in love with would do.

But the anger refused to be stifled, as much as she tried, and the furious voice in her mind shouted, *Well, damn him, if he had anything to do with this, he'll never lay a hand on Bellefleur! I'll keep it and with good conscience!*

A key turned in the lock and Lydia's head flew up as the door opened.

"I am glad to find you in my bed, because that is where I intend that you stay tonight."

Blake stood in the doorway, plain white shirt, black breeches, jackboots, hair tied back carelessly. The earring winked in the lantern light. And resting easily balanced in one strong hand was a drawn rapier, pointed at her as surely as the pirate's pistol had been.

"And I am not in the mood for fighting," he said coolly, shutting the door behind him.

Chapter Sixteen

"I *knew* you were a pirate!" Lydia leaped to her feet, her dumbstruck amazement that it really *was* Blake after all dissolving in a blaze of anger.

His face didn't change at her shouted words. His eyes were as silver as the blade he held, and every bit as implacable. For a long moment he looked at her, then he turned his back on her and walked to the chart table, still holding the sword on guard. She saw he held something in his left hand; she'd only had eyes for the rapier and his face until he turned.

A leather sack hit the charts with a heavy clinking sound, along with a scroll of parchment. "Think what you want about me," he said indifferently, turning back to face her again. "But if you are wondering why you are here, the answer is simple. I mean to have the house, and there on

221

the table is more gold than I offered you before. And a deed of sale. I believe you'll find a quill beneath the mess you seem to have made. All you need to do is sign."

He uttered these outrageous threats in a cool and reasonable tone. As if he actually expected her to walk over to the table and sign the deed as calmly as he was speaking!

"Sign—and what?" Lydia burst out. "And you will let me go? This is robbery, pure and simple! So you cannot bear the fact that the house was found to be lawfully mine, and have decided to resort to force! Abduction. And from my very own beach! If you think for even one moment that force will make me sign over the house to you—!"

Lydia turned her back on him and paced up and down in front of the bed, so furious that she had completely forgotten to think about how she looked, an unusual state of affairs when she was dealing with Blake. She whirled back to face him, eyes snapping sparks, and went on, "No wonder your despicable henchmen would not even tell me whose ship they were taking me to, or even the name of it! So *this* is what you are doing with the ships Baxter was foolish enough to deed over to you! 'Making a fortune' for yourself, you told me—and now I know how! As a pirate! Preying on innocent sailors and ship's passengers—and now, on me!"

As she stood glaring at him, she was glad to see the slightest tightening of one jaw muscle, as otherwise his face still remained completely unreadable. But if she had indeed struck a nerve, he didn't join in the argument, the way he usually

222

did.

"The name of this ship is the *Tiger Lily*," he answered. "And now do you want to hear why you are here? It is not—precisely—abduction."

"I don't care what word you use to ease your conscience. I tell you, you will never force me to sign over Bellefleur to you. You can hold me here as long as you like! Go ahead, throw me in the hold! If you think Moira won't be raising an outcry soon—"

The rapier caught the lantern light in a dazzle as Blake braced his boots wide apart and lifted it lazily until it was at the level of her throat. He stood a good six paces away from her, and even though Lydia wasn't in the least afraid that he would hurt her, the gesture was sufficiently unnerving in the small, locked cabin to make her close her mouth abruptly.

"I am not going to force you to sign that deed," he said, quietly enough, but there was something new in his eyes that made Lydia hold her breath. She was beginning to get the feeling that Blake meant every word he said—that this was no game. "It is your own choice. You may choose to sign it, and sell me the house for an outrageous profit. If you do, we shall toast the transaction with a glass of wine and you'll be rowed instantly back to Bellefleur—where you can pack your things."

"My *choice?*" She laughed scornfully. Then she added through clenched teeth, "And if I don't?"

"If you don't . . ." Without taking his eyes from hers or lowering the sword, he sat down in a chair and negligently lifted his boots to the table. Leaning back, he let his eyes slowly rove over her hair, her shoulders, and down the length of her body.

She stiffened under his perusal, for even though she had endured this from Blake before, this time it was somehow different. She was all at once aware of the disgraceful state of her hair, and had to will herself not to raise her hands to straighten it and twist it back into a knot as she suddenly longed to do.

". . . If you do not choose to sign the deed," he was going on, "I won't throw you in the hold. You will simply stay here, in my cabin—and I might add, in my bed."

"Oh!" Lydia was so outraged that for a moment she couldn't speak. "Stay here . . . and in your bed? Are you threatening to take me against my will, Blake Spencer? What makes you think I would share your bed—*or* give up my house?"

He shrugged. "I would recommend you think it over well, Madam. In case you have not noticed it, we are getting underway now. The crew is under orders to sail to a certain island with an extremely hidden cove . . . where I have some business to conduct. You and I can go on a pleasant voyage together. That would suit me, for I think I have made it clear to you how very desirable I find you . . . and I have need of a mistress at the moment."

Lydia stifled an outcry as she clearly heard the rattle of the anchor chains, and felt the ship suddenly shift. She swayed, momentarily unbalanced, and she angrily wondered if that was why Blake had had the foresight to sit a moment ago.

He was going on, not giving her a chance to speak.

"I advise you to think well about your choice. Don't count on help from Moira. You see, your

224

servants have all been informed that you have gone on a visit to the *Comtesse* Deveaux, who lives on Barbados, and they are not expecting you back for some time. If you arrive home in the morning, your respectability will remain unscathed."

"And they believed this lie?!"

"They believed me." There was the smallest of pauses. "And so will all of Jamaica—and the Caribbean."

The words sank in. All of the Caribbean didn't know Blake for the rogue he was, as she did; even the governor thought him an honest businessman and actually respected him to the point of admiration.

She saw a glint in his eyes that told her he hadn't missed the effect of his words on her, and cursed herself for giving him even this slight advantage. She forced herself to make her face as bland as his was, as he went on, "Besides, the *Comtesse* is a friend of mine. An *old* friend. She has agreed to say you were indeed at her house for one night . . . or four nights . . . or however long it takes you to make up your mind to sign the deed. Of course, if you never sign it, eventually I will take you back to Bellefleur, and you can explain your absence however you like." Again, he paused. "But I do not think the wolves on Jamaica whom you fear so greatly, lovely Lydia, will ever treat you again as the *respectable* widow you so enjoy . . . portraying."

His last sentence was heavy with mockery, and there was a sudden challenge in his eyes as he spoke it. She knew he was deliberately reminding her of the willing kisses she had given him. She saw a sudden and humiliating picture of herself, standing up in the ocean, her chemise and petticoats clinging to her.

But fiercely, she thrust away the humiliation. Now she knew what he was threatening her with, and she focused on that. He was using her fear of losing her reputation against her! She had to admit she'd held propriety over his head more than once. Well, what Blake Spencer didn't know was that she'd decided not to care about convention anymore . . . or that she'd made that decision the morning he'd surprised her swimming on the beach . . . and later, kissed her. To think she'd been fool enough to believe there was tenderness in that kiss!

With narrowed eyes, she considered her adversary. Who could blame the *Comtesse?* He was handsome enough that probably half the women on the islands wanted to share a bed with him, shameless as they seemed to be. Oh yes, that part of his story rang all too true!

And the rest of the servants? Would they really believe him if he showed up with some plausible story? She had to admit that they would, except possibly Moira, who might be suspicious . . . but who would do nothing, Lydia surmised, simply to protect the very reputation Blake was threatening to destroy.

Nevertheless, for a few moments of silent struggle, she quailed at the thought of being the talk of the Caribbean.

I doubt the Comtesse *cares about her reputation much,* she thought and then was surprised to recognize jealousy in the thought.

She came to a sudden decision.

"I don't give a damn about my reputation. I am not going to sign that deed."

She had hoped to startle him, but he answered only, "Very well. As I have said, I have long wanted you as my mistress." He swung his boots down and stood, letting his sword drop to his side.

Apprehensively, she watched him as he walked to the door and rapped softly three times, thinking he looked more of a pirate than ever with a sword in his hand. Now—what would he do? She bit her lip as she heard a single knock in return, then the sound of boots retreating along the deck.

He turned back. "That was the signal to sail . . . and also, for the guard to leave the doorway. We are locked in together, and I think we'll want no listeners at the door tonight."

For the first time, he smiled at her, a long slow smile that brought a twist of apprehension and a flicker of heat to her stomach at the same time.

The sword came up again, in a motion as unhurried as his smile. "Take off your dress." The smile deepened. "I fear I am impatient to see what I have so often imagined—and even dreamed of."

Lydia raised her head defiantly. "I will not."

"Then," he said with deliberation, "I shall have the pleasure of taking it off."

He took a few paces toward her, then stopped. "I assure you this is no game, Madam. It would be far easier for you to take that dress off, then to make me cut it off you. And more pleasurable for both of us, as well. I think you will find you will enjoy this more if you will just relax—for I know I am not mistaken in the fact that you have enjoyed my touch and my kisses in the past."

His words were producing a heat Lydia did not

227

want to feel, and she fought it with anger. "Then cut it off if you must—but I shall not help you take it off me," she dared him, standing with her fists clenched and shoulders thrown back, unable to believe Blake would do a thing like this—unable to believe he really meant to take her in the face of her refusal. Even in all his outrageousness, he had never forced his attentions on her once she had told him to stop. At least—not *physical* attentions, she reassured herself.

The sword flicked lightly upward and then down, and there was the sound of tearing cloth. It was over so quickly that Lydia had time to do no more than gasp.

She looked down to see the amber silk of her dress gaping open from bodice to hem, revealing her chemise and petticoats beneath.

She grabbed the edges together ineffectually at her breast, but was aware that the silk and lace of her underclothing was showing above and below her hands. The dress was cut so cleanly that she knew his blade was honed razor-sharp—not dulled as she had guessed. She whipped her head up to stare at him. "You mean it!" she cried.

"I mean everything I say, Lydia, and the sooner you learn that, the sooner you and I shall be making love . . . or completing a business transaction." She watched him with astonished wariness as he added in a huskier tone, "Now . . . are you going to finish taking off that dress? Or must I finish cutting it off you?"

She took a step backward and felt the backs of her knees hit the bed. She looked around for something to throw at him. But there was nothing in sight, her hands were busy holding the dress together, and besides, he stood not five feet away with that cursed sword.

"Shy? Perhaps I shouldn't hover over you. I don't think we need this anymore, do we?" She looked up to find him grinning smugly at her, and then he strolled to the chair, as if this type of incident were the most everyday occurrence in the world to him. There he sat down again, stretching his long legs out in front of him and carelessly tossing the sword onto the table.

He looked at her.

"And besides, from here I shall be able to enjoy the view."

She squared her shoulders and faced him, giving him the proudest and most disdainful look she could muster. It seemed there was no way out of this situation . . . she was locked in here with this madman. She could fight, but she knew he was more than capable of fighting back. Once again, she had underestimated the lengths to which he would go.

But he had underestimated her, too.

She could really only see one way to find out whether or not he meant to go through with this. He had to be bluffing! Her heart could not believe Blake would really harm her, much as her mind was screaming at her to be cautious.

She let her hands fall and felt the dress gape open.

It was the hardest thing she'd ever done in her life, to keep her eyes on his face, but she managed it. His gaze slowly traveled down the length of her body and back up to her face.

"A lovely sight," he said softly. "The dress?"

She took a deep breath to compose herself. Her

nerves were singing, her hands trembling, but she didn't want him to see that.

Lifting her hands to the rent sides of the dress, she shrugged it off like it was a greatcoat, and tossed it carelessly on the floor. She saw that slow hot smile of appreciation start, and his gaze on her exposed shoulders and arms were counteracting any chill she might have felt without the dress. It was as though the thin lace straps of her chemise had vanished; she felt as if she were standing in front of him completely unclothed.

He shifted in his chair, and she saw his lips part on an intake of breath. "Beautiful," he murmured. "You are indeed made to trouble a man's dreams."

His eyes met hers again with a heated shock she felt all the way through her body. "Untie your ribbons," he said.

She raised her shaking fingers to the ribbons that tied her chemise at the bodice, and slowly pulled the long ends downward. She didn't want to look away from him — that would be to let him win — but looking at him was making her feel so warm. It was suddenly hot in the cabin, and she was having trouble drawing her breath. She could feel her breath coming more rapidly, her heart pounding in her throat, as the ribbons slipped through the knots and the bows fell loose.

She let her hands drop. She couldn't stand here in front of him loosening the crisscross lacing of the ribbons down the front of her chemise — doing so while he watched was making her feel too strange. She knew she should be keeping her gaze coldly and challenging on his eyes, but her eyes seemed to have a will of their own, distracted by details about him; to be seeing the firm cut of his

230

mouth, the way his black brows contrasted with his tanned skin, the faintest shadow of beard on his clean-shaven jaw. It was as if his male presence was something she could feel tangibly, something that was robbing her of her ability to stay angry.

Some sound she could not identify brought her back to her senses, and she suddenly realized the only sound in the tiny cabin was her shoe on the wooden floor. Mortified, she abruptly stopped the twirling of the lone shoe she still wore, and angrily kicked it away, as she'd slipped it off her foot in any case.

"Now that you've dispensed with your shoes, perhaps your stockings will follow?" came the insinuating suggestion.

Relieved to have something to distract herself with from these unsettling feelings, she bent, letting her hair fall in a curtain that hid her face and fell almost to her knees, as she lifted the skirt of her petticoat above her knee. There! she thought smugly. *That* should block his view!

But as she was unfastening her garter, she heard a low appreciative laugh that caused her to whip her head up, only to find his eyes devouring her.

"You are a most seductive sight."

She followed his gaze and saw to her dismay that her untied chemise had gaped open at the top, and from where he sat, her hair had done nothing to hide it. In fact, she was inadvertently giving him a view that must look deliberately enticing!

She whipped up, and this time, she couldn't keep a cool face anymore. She glared at him.

"If you want me to disrobe any further, it will be you who will have to do the rest. I don't

231

believe you will go through with this . . . this misguided attempt at extortion, but if you mean to take me against my will, it still won't get you the house."

His hand made a polite gesture, and one brow rose as he indicated the deed on the table. "I must confess, Lydia, at this point, I am hoping you will not decide to sell me the house until at least tomorrow morning."

It was time to call his bluff.

"Very well, then, let it be on your conscience," she said with her best air of defiant abandon. "Do your worst!"

And she stood there, heated and trembling inside, waiting to see if he would call hers.

Chapter Seventeen

"Do your worst!" Blake sat for a long moment unmoving, hearing the unbelievable words

Now what was he going to do?

Inwardly, he cursed—first Lydia, and then himself, and both for treachery. This was much harder than he'd thought, and in more ways than one. He'd thought he had her, when he'd heard her shoe going in circles on the floor . . . a habit of hers when she was nervous, though he had been careful never to show her he'd noticed it. Yes, and she'd been trembling, just the way she always had when he took her in his arms. So afraid of a man's touch, of her feelings, that he'd been certain that any moment, she'd give up and sign that deed.

And then he'd pushed her just a bit too far, fool that he was, and she'd gotten her anger back. To his dismay, he realized that now he had a damnable choice: to give up and admit defeat . . . or to go on with it . . . and make her believe that he meant to go through with it.

But already too much time was passing in silence. If he wasn't careful, she would know in a moment that he had no intention of forcing her into his bed. To buy time to think, he made himself smile at her, as if he was delighted with this sudden turn of events, and heard himself say, "A wonderful suggestion. This—ah—performance has been most delicious, but it has made me on fire to touch you . . . and to have you touch me."

The problem was, those words were only too true. Watching her tonight in the small confines of the cabin had stirred a desire in him stronger than any he'd ever felt for her before, and that from the very first moment he'd walked in and seen her facing him, her hair an unbelievably rich river of mahogany falling around her shoulders, down her back, and to her waist, her eyes wild and sparkling with anger.

He'd barely been able to keep his reactions to her off his face, and he'd felt his breath tighten in his chest at the sight of her, fury narrowing the long lashes around her eyes—they were as amber as her dress, he saw—and her gorgeous breasts looking like they'd spill out of her low-cut bodice every time she shouted at him or took an angry breath.

And that had merely been the beginning of his torture.

When he'd cut her dress open, it had been a matter of will not to fling the sword aside and crush her to him in a kiss. To have to let his eyes roam over her body and to try not to see the curves was torment indeed.

But when she'd straightened her shoulders and clenched her fists to face him, looking at him so proudly and flinging her dress aside with the air of a queen going to the stake . . . that was when he'd almost really done it . . . taken her in his arms and

234

the consequences be damned! A wave of admiration so strongly mingled with desire had come over him that he suddenly realized he had never wanted *any* woman as much as he wanted her.

And when she began slowly pulling those ribbons, when her chemise had opened so that he could see how soft her skin looked, how white and glowing, when she bent over to unclasp her garter, that was when he'd known if this little charade didn't end in the next moments, it might not end at all, because right then he wanted her more than he wanted the house.

And now—God help him—he had to go on with it!

He stood up. "Shall I take off my shirt . . . or do you want to do it for me?"

"*I* won't do it!" She moved as if to run away, then stilled herself.

So he *was* getting to her. He opened his shirt as he walked toward her.

Since he'd begun this, he'd had to sit down more than once, or he knew she'd have seen the effect she was having on him all too clearly. Now as he saw her eyes measure him, shoulders, waist, hips, and when they widened and flew to his face, startled, he knew he'd kept that secret from her no longer.

Good, he thought, setting his jaw against the anger he felt at himself for frightening her. Now maybe she would sign the damned deed and be done with it.

His shirt was open to where it was tucked into his trousers. He stopped in front of her and reached out a hand, taking her chin and gently tilting it upward. He saw her mouth part, heard the inrush of breath . . . and smelled her perfume.

"I wonder how many kisses it will take me, before you are kissing me back?" he murmured, and saw her lips tighten as if she were determined to resist his kiss.

Angry or laughing, she had the most beautiful mouth in creation, and he found that he couldn't take

235

his eyes off it. And, hell take it, he knew well enough he was no longer concealing the way he felt from her. He knew the desire he felt was showing in his eyes, and he cursed himself for being unable to stop it, unable to take a breath as he watched her.

He had to kiss her . . . he wanted to kiss her. He steeled himself to kiss her. Just a few more moments, and it would be over, he promised himself. He could hold on that long.

He let his arms go around her and swept her into his embrace.

Lydia gave a startled little cry as Blake caught her in his arms, pulling her against him so abruptly she was not prepared, well though she knew he meant to kiss her. When he'd stood above her, staring down at her with his beautiful light gray eyes, she had felt all her resistance to him melting away, had been able to think of nothing but the fact that she wanted to feel his mouth on hers, wanted his arms around her, wanted to run her fingers through his black hair and touch the strands of silver at his temples.

How many kisses? she thought with a kind of wild despair as his mouth came down on hers. *Oh, Blake, just one—*

And she was kissing him back as fervently as he was kissing her.

So this was what desire was like, she had time to think as his hands plunged into her hair, as his kiss deepened, spinning her mind away as sweetness flooded her body. His arms were crushing her close against him, she could feel the bare skin of his chest against hers, and she wanted to lift her own arms and wrap them around his neck—

But that was madness. It was mad enough she was letting him kiss her, reveling in his kiss!

And then he broke the kiss with a ragged intake of

breath, and she saw that he was staring down at her almost angrily. She could feel his heart hammering against her, and then he smiled and bent his head again, his lips brushing her hair.

"I knew," he breathed, "you would make the most desirable of mistresses."

Lydia stiffened, recalled to herself, but his arms tightened around her like iron. He gave her no time to protest as his lips found her neck. A thousand thrills shot through her as he kissed her neck, trailed his lips over her collarbones, and then found the hollow of her throat.

Mistress, he'd said, she thought, frantically fighting the incredible sensations he was producing in her. *I can't—he won't—*

But his mouth, hard and demanding, was on hers again, his hands were moving up her rib cage, loosening the ribbons of her chemise, making her breath come faster and faster, and she thought, *But I want to—whether this is love or merely desire, I have never felt anything like this before—*

She relaxed in his arms, in his kiss, and realized her arms, with a will of their own, had come up around his neck and were drawing him closer. As desire dizzied her, she had a last fleeting thought for propriety and found it just didn't matter, not when Blake was kissing her until she couldn't think, not when his hands were opening her chemise and she felt the searing heat of his skin against her bare skin . . . *Besides, who would ever know?* she thought. She heard Blake make a rough noise that sounded like a groan, and sent shivers all through her.

His hands moved from her breasts to her shoulders, and she felt his fingers tighten there in a convulsive grip. Then he broke their kiss again. Shaken, she stared up at him, wondering what would happen next, wondering why his mouth was set in such a grim line, wondering if now he would carry her to the bed and . . .

Blake stared down at Lydia, utterly shaken by her response to his kisses. She had been stiff in his arms at first, and that had been bad enough. To feel his hands in her hair, the silkiness of her shoulders, to taste the skin of her neck, to kiss her . . . He was lost. When she'd started to kiss him back, he knew it was time to end this, and *now,* or he'd have picked her up and carried her to his bed, and he'd never forced any woman in his life!

And wasn't going to start now. But damn it, why did she have to kiss him back? Didn't she know that he was about to take her? Pulse pounding in his throat, he stared down at her and realized he had to end the game now. Leave the cabin, get some fresh air, get his control back.

"Lydia," he said hoarsely, wishing she would take her arms from around his neck, wishing she weren't so close, "I must—"

To his shock, her fingers came up, touching his lips softly, stilling his words. "I know," she whispered. "I—I'm not afraid."

And to his utter disbelief, her hands went to his chest, running shyly across it and under the shirt, as she pulled it free from his trousers. Her eyes dropped in a charming expression of timid shyness that clutched at his heart, and she glanced tentatively up at him, saying, "I thought you wished me to take off your shirt."

This time, Blake's groan was one of utter defeat as he merely pulled her tightly against him, arms around her, and stood holding her head against his shoulder, unable to let her go.

Chapter Eighteen

Her cheek against his shoulder, Lydia gave herself up to the wonderful feeling of being held so possessively by a man — that man, Blake Spencer.

Being held by Baxter had never been like this. It was only Blake who seemed to be able to stir these irresistible and delightful feelings in her, who could make her forget everything except the need to be touched by him, held by him, kissed by him.

But still, in the midst of the passion he was awakening in her, she knew a twinge of shyness. What would come next? Would everything be over quickly?

And what . . . what was she expected to do?

She had a wild moment of regretting her inexperience, and then being glad for it, glad that Blake would be the man to show her what love between a man and a woman could be.

She wanted him to kiss her again.

A little shyly, she turned her head and brushed her lips along his neck, as he had done to her.

She had not known what to expect, but his reaction to her simple action startled her. He pulled back from her as though her lips had burned him, and almost roughly took her face in his hands. She had never seen eyes so intense, a mouth drawn in such a stern line.

"What's wrong?" she whispered, sure she'd done something terribly wrong by being so forward.

"Wrong? God!" He laughed, a grim laugh, and she stared up at him, wondering if he were angry at her. "Nothing except that I have never . . . ever . . . wanted a woman as much as I want you . . . desire you . . . at this moment."

His words were evenly spaced, and Lydia thought she would faint at the expression she saw in his eyes, faint if he didn't kiss her soon. She looked away in confusion, lowering her lashes against the heat in his eyes, feeling a blush start as she murmured, "I . . . I think you have made me feel the same way."

He kissed her then.

And he was kissing her senses away as, somehow, they were falling to the bed together. She had a fleeting moment of disappointment, wondering if now it would be all over in moments. But she soon learned that Blake was in no hurry; he was taking his time.

His kisses now were as tender as moments before they had been hard and demanding; and the slow, soft way he was kissing her was exquisitely sensual, melting her fears. She became hazily aware that as he was kissing her, his hands were slowly opening her chemise, moving down to her waist to unfasten her petticoats, up her legs to untie her garters until

240

she was lying in a welter of half-open lace and silk.

He broke the kiss. "Let me look at you," he said softly.

She reached her hand up and ran her fingers through his hair, where one long dark strand had loosened. "If I can look at you, too," she whispered.

He gave her a slanting smile. "I promise you, you will . . . but first, let me look at you, I beg you . . . for I didn't lie to you when I told you I have been dreaming of this."

He ran a leisurely finger down her neck and over one half-exposed breast, then caught the silk of her chemise. It whispered aside, and then he did the same to the other side, baring her breasts to his gaze. She saw his breath catch, his eyes darken as he looked at her, and now he was drawing down her silk stockings as he molded the curves of her legs lovingly, pulling her petticoat off so that she hardly felt it go, only feeling his warm hands caressing her skin, every inch, as he stripped her last garments from her.

"You are more beautiful even than I imagined," he said, his voice hardly a breath, and she wanted to blush, he was looking at her so shamelessly—but he wasn't giving her time to feel ashamed. His hands were running along the line of her hip, up her rib cage, over her breasts, and she gave a startled gasp as his fingers brushed her nipples and she felt them tighten.

Emboldened, Lydia reached up and ran her hands over his chest to the sides of his shirt, pushing it off his shoulders until it too had vanished as mysteriously as her clothes; their bare skin seemed to be exchanging a silken heat as he held her close and stroked her back and her tumbling hair.

241

She was dimly aware that his pants and boots seemed to be in the way, and he must have felt it at the same moment, for he gently caught her hands and brought them from around his neck to his mouth, where he kissed them as his eyes locked with hers.

He smiled at her, a smile that made her heart turn over, and then he stood next to the bed. For a moment, he just looked down at her, but this time she felt no embarrassment as he let his gaze travel over her; she was too busy looking at him to care.

Had there even been such a man? she thought. The width of his shoulders, narrowing in a sharp line to his waist, took her breath. He was perfectly made, his tanned skin taut over his muscles, and in the dim lamplight, the faint sheen of sweat on his chest turned to bronze.

She watched as he bent to pull off his boots, then he straightened and his hands went to his belt. Lydia bit her lip, feeling a mingled fear and thrill at the knowledge that he was going to stand there and take off his pants in front of her—not under the covers as she had imagined it would happen.

She realized she was glad, though her cheeks were heating as she watched him.

He was magnificent. His legs long, as muscled as the rest of him, his hips slim. Fascinated, as he straightened to face her for a moment, she let her eyes boldly sweep all of him, as his had swept her, and had to look away at the sight of his eager manhood, as breathtaking as the rest of him.

He was beautiful . . . and he was frightening. He climbed into the bed, and she shivered with pleasure at the feel of his long, lean body against her softer one, as he gathered her into his embrace again. "Don't be frightened, Lydia darling," he said tenderly, as if he had read her mind. "I promise I shall make it as sweet for you as it is for me. . . "

Their lips met in a searing kiss that seemed to stretch to eternity. Time lost all meaning. All that existed for Lydia was Blake, and what they were sharing together, something so new and so untamed that she felt her blood sing in her veins and her heart expanding with some emotion that was as wild as it was loving.

And she knew the desire she had felt before was only a shadow to what he was making her feel now. Dear God, she had never imagined she could feel like this! His mouth was doing incredible things to her breasts, to her neck, and his hands were roving over her hips, her legs, all silken sensation and impatient passion.

She yielded to him completely, letting her hands rove over him, delighting in the shape of his back, his legs, and even in the way his breathing was becoming harsher, more ragged sounding, as she touched him. So she could do the same to him that he was doing to her! It was a wonderful discovery, but one he didn't give her long to savor.

She felt his hands gently move her legs apart, felt his touch between her legs shooting a sharp thrill all the way up her nerves. For a moment, she stiffened, embarrassed by this intimacy, but the persistent movement of his fingers soon melted her resistance, until she arched against him with a cry. What was this he was doing to her?

She hugged him closer, twisting in his embrace, but he was merciless, not letting her hide her face against his shoulder, finding her lips for another kiss. The sensations he was creating were building up to an unbearable pitch; she longed for some release that she knew nothing of, and she gasped under his lips, and heard him answer with a low sound. Just as she knew she could bear no more, she felt him move above her, his maleness hard against her, and then he slid deep inside her.

A shock of pleasure jolted every nerve she possessed.

He seemed to fill her whole soul, and she cried out as she tightened her arms around his neck. He was murmuring something in her ear, kissing her eyes and her face, moving in a slow rhythm that was sending waves of pleasure through her body beyond anything she had ever imagined.

A tide of feeling bound her to him as he moved inside her, faster and harder, and she could hear his breathing speed to match the rhythm of their motion. Then she heard something else that for a moment she could not identify. As the world exploded into joy, she realized it was her own voice calling out . . . she was saying his name over and over again, just as he was saying hers.

Chapter Nineteen

It was one of the loveliest nights the Caribbean could offer, with a slim crescent moon almost dimmed by the dazzle of stars in the cloudless black sky. But the couple on deck of the small schooner anchored just off the point at Bellefleur were not watching the sky, glorious though it was. They had eyes only for the distant riding lights of the *Tiger Lily*, anchored at the head of the nearby cove . . . and for each other.

Jacques laughed and slipped an arm around Brigitte's waist. She turned to look up at him, and he enjoyed the sight of the balmy breeze lifting her black hair, the way her eyes sparkled mischievously at him. "I grow impatient, *cherie,* to learn whether or not we will be sailing together tonight . . . or whether I shall have to return you to that house at once. What can be taking them so long?"

"But I have told you! In fact, you will recall that we have even bet a gold piece on the outcome. My mistress is the most stubborn of women. She will not return to Bellefleur tonight."

"The gold piece matters nothing to me . . . in comparison to the thought of not spending some time alone with you. I hope it takes her days to make up her mind to sell the house to him! However, I am betting on Blake to win this one, for I have never yet seen him lose."

"I did not say she would *not* end by selling him the house, Jacques darling. I *said* she would not return home tonight. So never fear, we shall have at least one night aboard your ship, and I can see these lovely deserted beaches you have told me so much about. I am so glad to be at sea, and seeing something of the islands at last!"

She laughed, feeling happy and free . . . and utterly in love with Jacques. For a moment, she wished she could tell him how much she loved him, but she knew that if she did, he would sail over the horizon and out of her life so quickly, it would be as if she'd never met him. Brigitte had set her sights on marriage, nothing less, but she knew Jacques would take some convincing before he could be brought to realize he loved her as much as she loved him.

She sighed, then looked up at him and saw that he had raised one quizzical brow at her statement.

"Yes . . . you will love this place we are going to, but, *cherie,* why do you say she will not return home tonight? Just because she is stubborn? For I tell you, *he* is stubborn, too."

She gave him a playful tap on the arm. "Men! You have no intuition! I doubt she will sell, no matter what he threatens her with . . . but I only agreed to do this for one reason. She is in love with him. And I think he is falling in love with her, too. I thought some time alone together might show them that there is no reason to fight over this silly house, and show her that she need not fight her feelings for a man. After all, she is a

246

widow! Free and rich! Why should she not do as she pleases? These English!" Brigitte shook her head in amazement at the strange behavior of her mistress.

"In love?" He laughed. "Perhaps on her side, but Blake? I think he cares for nothing except winning the battle with this woman. I have never seen him care about anything so much before. So I suppose you could say he has a passion for her . . . but I do not know if I would call it love."

Brigitte flashed him an irritated look. *Why is it so hard for them to admit that they feel anything with their hearts, and not just with their bodies!* she thought.

"But she is not the only stubborn one," he went on in an insinuating tone, pressing a kiss near her ear. "Why must you go back into her service at all? You and I could sail to Barbados together, right now . . . I know some beautiful places I would like to show you, *cherie.*"

Brigitte laughed lightly, and sent him a slanting look. "And what future would there be for me, as a mistress to a pirate?" she said virtuously. "You forget I am a respectable woman. *L'amour,* that is one thing . . . but to depend on your faithfulness! Where would I be, stranded in Jamaica, my reputation ruined, when you tired of me?"

"But I begin to suspect I shall never tire of you . . . not when you are so charmingly practical and so desirably elusive. Though I still cannot understand why a woman of your beauty and talents should be wasting her time as a lady's maid—"

Jacques felt a twist of something new for him—jealousy—at her answer, still lightly spoken: "Ah, but I do not imagine I shall be a lady's maid forever, my darling Jacques. And my mistress has done very much for me. Here on Jamaica, I am meeting so many more people than I would as a maid in France, where things are so much more strict. Who knows what may come of it?"

247

Jacques tightened his hold around her waist, for he knew well enough what might come of it! Marriage. Jamaica was short of respectable women — marriagable women — and it was as she said, social standards were much more relaxed here. A woman as beautiful, as intelligent, and above all, as charming as Brigitte might hope to marry far above her station, perhaps to a planter or a politician, or to a younger man well on the way to establishing a fortune . . .

The rattle of an anchor chain came clearly over the water.

"They are sailing!" he cried, momentarily distracted from his jealousy, and relieved. Now he would have Brigitte alone, and perhaps he would drive all thoughts of those planters out of her head, or even succeed in convincing her to leave that woman's service and explore the islands with him.

"What did I tell you?" she laughed, staring out across the water as the sails of the *Tiger Lily* caught the wind. "I did not think she would go home!"

Jacques turned and swept her into his arms. "And you and I shall follow in time, *cherie,* but first —"

He bent his head to kiss her.

For a long time, they stood locked together at the rail, each overjoyed that their trip would not be postponed. And then suddenly, Jacques picked her up as she shrieked and laughed and demanded to be put down.

His eyes were dancing, and she knew he was the handsomest man she had ever seen. "But we are in no hurry, are we, my darling?" he said, before kissing her again. "We have all night."

It was, indeed, much too beautiful a night to be wasted, and Brigitte threw a last glance of gratitude at the departing sails of the *Tiger Lily* as Jacques carried her down the deck to his cabin.

Chapter Twenty

What a wonderful dream this is, Lydia thought. She dreamt that she and Blake had made love and were now lying in each other's arms in a bed that seemed to float on air. She nuzzled her cheek against the dream-Blake's chest and thrilled at how real the sensation was, and when she inhaled she thought she could even smell his scent.

She wondered if she concentrated hard enough if she could will the dream-Blake to put his arms around her, and no sooner had she thought of it, then indeed in her dream, she felt the pressure of his arms as they slid around her back, pulling her to him.

"That was nice," she murmured. "Do it again." When she felt herself held tighter to him, she was amazed at the sensual reality of the dream. She could actually feel the hairs of his legs tickling her own legs, and his lips kissing her forehead.

Perhaps she could even will the dream-Blake to make love to her again, and the thought made her giggle in her sleep.

"Lydia," she heard him call softly, but his voice seemed to come from somewhere beyond the dream. "Lydia," he called a little louder.

She opened her eyes, and from beneath her heavy lids, she thought she saw Blake's face. She couldn't really bring it into focus, because it was so close to her own. All she could do was watch the lips move as they spoke to her.

"Lydia, it's getting late. We really must get up."

She furrowed her brow and closed her eyes again. "Oh, do be quiet. I'm having the most delicious dream about you," she mumbled, trying to recapture the warm feeling once more.

But Blake's voice came to her again in a singsong warning. "Lydia, if you don't wake up by yourself, I'll be forced to do it for you."

She groaned. "Be quiet."

"I'm warning you," he sang.

She ignored the voice this time, and wished the dream-Blake into blazing a trail of kisses that ran from her neck to her—

There was a sudden shove and soon after the sensation of falling.

She hit the floor with an unladylike thud, her eyes popping open and blinking in confusion at her surroundings. When she finally came fully awake, she found herself sitting naked in a puddle of sheets and pillows on the floor of the ship's cabin. Blake lay on his side in the bed above her, as naked as she was.

It hadn't been a dream at all! she thought, as the events of the previous night came flooding back— all the warm passion that had flowed between them, the deep kisses, and tingling friction of their bodies tightly pressed together had been real, and she'd actually experienced it all, every wonderful, splendorous moment of it. She wanted to leap up from the floor and fling herself back into bed with him to experience it all over again, but she noticed he was grinning at her, then remembered he'd just tossed her out of bed.

She wasn't angry with him for doing it, but he really did deserve a lesson for being such a brute.

She smiled back at him, then shyly brought the sheet on the floor up around her to cover herself. Grasping the pillows in her hands, she knelt beside the bed, bringing her face within inches of his. She kissed him softly, lingeringly on the lips, murmuring, "That was for last night. And this—" She brought her arm up with the pillow in her hand and landed a good solid smack with it on his head "—was for pushing me out of bed at such an ungodly hour!" Whumph. "Late indeed! The sun's barely up." Whumph. "This one is for kidnapping me!" Whumph. "And these are for the months of absolute torment you've put me through." Whumph. Whumph.

A laughing Blake brought his hands up to shield himself from her blows, and finally succeeded in snatching one of the pillows from her. Then rising, he started after her.

"I'll get you for that!"

Lydia's eyes grew round when she saw that he meant to fight back. She tried to scramble away, clutching for the other pillows that had spilled onto the floor, but not before Blake's foot came down on one edge of the sheet that covered her. The cloth slid away as she rose and ran naked to the other side of the room.

With as much dignity as four pillows would allow, Lydia covered herself as best she could, by hugging them to her, and then faced off against him.

He lunged for her, and she flung one of the pillows, then quickly another at him. Dodging the first, Blake reached for his sword—the nearest thing he could find to ward off the flying missiles. The second pillow hit him in the chest when he brought the sword up. He laughed and taunted, "Fire away, m'lady! I gladly face this battle for the pleasure of disarming—and disrobing you—completely!"

"Just try it," she giggled and threw another pillow at him.

He sliced it clean through. A shower of goose down burst from it and fluttered in a frenzy around his head.

Lydia had one pillow left, and it was the only thing she had between her modesty and Blake's attack. When Blake, arms waving to clear a path through the snowfall of feathers, made another lunge for her, his sword carefully held out to the side, it was obvious her defense was far more important than her modesty.

She threw the last pillow with all her might, aiming for his head.

Blake saw it coming and raised his sword, spearing the pillow dead center. It slid with a loud rip along the blade and came to a halt, limp and lifeless, at the hilt.

He feigned a solemn look as he held it up for her to see. "Another pillow sacrificed in the battle against m'lady." Then he looked at her. "But I see I have achieved a victory!"

Lydia felt the blood rising to her cheeks. She was completely disrobed and felt vulnerable under his gaze. Quickly, to divert his attentions, she grabbed one corner of the speared pillow and pulled it off the sword, ripping the casing and sending a new storm of down swirling around his head.

He sneezed, and Lydia took the opportunity to smack his bare bottom with the new empty casing, as she darted past him. He howled and spun around, tossing the sword aside.

As she ran, Lydia grabbed the sheet that had fallen on the floor and held it up to her chest with one hand. With her other hand she snapped the pillow casing at him each time he took a step near her. Every time the casing cracked within inches of him, he quickly jumped back and waited for another opportunity to advance. Feathers were swirling in the air from their movements, and both were sneezing and coughing and laughing at the same time.

He advanced once more, and when she whipped the casing at him, she realized she hadn't been quick enough. He caught it in his hand.

"Now I have you," he said in a husky tone. "And I mean to have you entirely."

She found herself slowly being reeled toward him, as he pulled at the casing hand over hand. She resisted now and then, just enough to tease him, keeping her gaze on his and sending him messages of the same passion she saw in his eyes—a passion that made her stomach flutter, her skin tingle in anticipation of his touch.

Finally, his free arm slipped around her waist and drew her to him. The pillow casing slid from her hand to the floor. He smiled down at her, his lips parting slightly, and pulled the sheet from between them. Gently brushing an errant feather from her cheek, he drew his hand around her neck and into her hair.

"This was not my plan for this morning," he said and smiled again.

"But it was mine," she murmured.

He bent and pressed his lips against hers, brushing them lightly, running his tongue along them, as if he were savoring the taste of her. She tried the same, and thought he tasted delicious. Imitating his movements, the way his hand slipped down her back to her waist, and pressed her hips to his, she found that touching him was as exciting as being touched by him. The smooth feel of his muscles beneath his skin, the softness of his lips under her tongue sent thrills coursing through her.

His kiss deepened, and soon he was devouring her, his breath catching in ragged gasps that matched her own. And then he was lifting her onto him as he was standing. She wrapped her legs around his waist, longing to feel him inside her. With a searing thrust, he filled her, and she heard herself cry out in ecstasy. She rocked against him as he buried his head in her breasts, sucking one nipple and then the other. Hugging him to her, she felt her nipples rising in rigid peaks filling her with singing vibrations of intense pleasure. He thrust against her and the tension she'd fought to liberate the night before began again, tugging at her center, pulling her toward its release. Her rhythm increased in energy, the tension building with each of his thrusts until like a wave rolling toward the shore, she was carried up and delivered in a gasping moan. He echoed that moan with a shudder, and she felt the throbbing of him inside her as he spilled his seed.

Weak and trembling, she loosened her legs from his waist and slid her feet to the floor. He held her up, clinging to her, showering her face with kisses. "Lydia," he whispered into her hair. "My Lydia."

He pulled her away from him and looked into her eyes, questioningly. "What a mystery you are to me."

She brushed back the silver hair at his temples, and smiled. "I would think all the mystery was gone after last night."

"I feel I could search for years and never uncover it all." He pressed his lips to her forehead and held them there for a moment.

She inhaled his scent and let out a sigh. What a mystery *he* was to *her*. They'd just made love like — a pair of animals! How could he arouse her so quickly, and make her forget everything but the satisfaction of their desire?

She looked into his eyes and saw them twinkling devilishly. "I have an idea," he said. "I know of a place, a private place. I want to take you there."

"What about your plan for this morning?"

"To hell with my plan! I've got a better one. Get dressed. We're going ashore."

Lydia looked over his shoulder to where her dress lay, nearly in tatters from the night before. "You seem to have forgotten that you used my dress for fencing lessons last night."

With a slight frown, he let go of her and crossed to a trunk at the foot of his bed. He lifted the lid and threw it back. Pulling a few articles of clothing from it, he eyed her for a fit, then tossed the clothes at her. "Those should do."

She looked at the breeches and shirt he'd given her. "But these are men's clothing. I can't be seen in these."

"No one's going to see you where we're going . . . and who knows, you may not have them on for very long." He laughed and began dressing himself.

She huffed in mock indignation. "We'll see about that," she said and turned to begin dressing.

An hour later, Lydia looked at the sight before her and uttered a sigh.

"Blake, it's beautiful."

They'd taken a smaller craft ashore and had landed on a deserted beach, fringed by huge palm trees, twisted overgrowth, and a riot of flowers. Blake had grasped her hand and headed across the sandy beach for the bushes.

"Where are you taking me?" she'd screamed. "There's no path."

"Stop your caterwauling and follow me."

She had. Blake had pulled her along behind him as he'd picked his way through a tangle of jungle, pulling aside vines and branches, trekking across thick mosses, and climbing over boulders, until they reached the large clearing where she now stood.

It was a paradise. A deep pool of water spread out at her feet. The sound of rushing water tempted her ears, and she looked up. At one end of the pool, a solid face of rock rose in monstrous sloping steps to a height far above them. Jets of water careened down the slope and fell in a hundred little waterfalls into the pool. The foliage surrounding this paradise was lush and green, dotted with palm trees and hibiscus that filled the air with their perfume. The morning sunlight danced on the greens of the undergrowth and sparkled in the blues of the pool, giving the site a dreamlike quality.

"How did you ever find this place?" she gasped.

"By accident. I was lost once and trying to find my way back . . . to my ship, when I found it."

She eyed him suspiciously. The way he'd paused before saying ship gave her reason to believe he wasn't being completely honest with her. "Where is this place?" she asked. "Jamaica?"

"No. On one of the other islands."

"Near Jamaica?"

He smiled at her. "Why do you ask? Are you planning an escape?"

She smiled back. "Not yet."

He furrowed his brow, looked out over the pool, and changed the subject. "I wasn't sure if I could find this place again. You've a very trusting nature."

"I was thinking the same thing as you dragged me through the jungle."

"Was it worth the journey?"

"Yes. Entirely."

"What do you say to a swim now that you know how?"

She glanced down at her clothes. "But I have nothing to swim in. My . . . undergarments are on the ship."

"Undergarments? Who needs undergarments! If you're worried about being discovered, there's no one around for miles and miles! You weren't shy with me last night or this morning. I want to see you now. All of you. Why are you so afraid?"

Lydia didn't know how to answer him. How could she put into words how awkward and unsure she sometimes felt about her own body? How unprotected she felt beneath the full force of his gaze? In the dim light of the ship's cabin, under the spell of passion, it had somehow been different. But here in broad daylight, swimming nude—would he see her flaws and turn away?

She shrugged, averting her eyes. "Why do you need to see me? I'm too tall, much taller than most women. My hair, uncooperative. Look at how it sticks out." She pulled at some stray strands at her temple and searched his eyes, dreading to see confirmation there.

He gathered her into his arms, reaching around to pull the pins from her tresses, then running his

257

fingers through the loosened curls. "Your hair is like this waterfall. The feel of it against my skin, mussed or combed, is like cool, clear water. And if you were any shorter, I wouldn't be able to gaze into your eyes like this. But it's not your hair or your height that you're afraid to let me see."

She sighed and offered lamely. "But I'm bruised from being carried like a sack of potatoes."

"Where are you bruised?"

She pointed to her shoulder, and he peeled back the shirt to see. He kissed the spot she had indicated. "I love this bruise," he said and kissed it again. "It is the most tempting shade of purple and becomes you immensely. What else are you afraid of?"

She frowned. "My skin's so pale, like . . . paste."

He unbuttoned her shirt and pulled the cloth off her shoulders, sliding it down her arms, until it fell to the ground. Then he pressed a line of kisses from her collarbone to between her breasts. "No, Lydia. Your skin is like cream, rich and silky, sweet to taste." His tongue played at her nipples, urging them into peaks. She gasped, then giggled when she heard him say, "Mmmm. Strawberries!"

He pulled her to the ground. "Strawberries and cream you are, Lydia." He gazed into her eyes and kissed her, as he undid her breeches, sliding them along her hips and thighs. She kicked off her boots in a mad rush, while pulling at his shirt, undoing the buckle of his belt, sliding his breeches free, until she and he were both lying naked. She looked up at him, eager to make love with him again. She waited impatiently, but he made no move.

An impish smile parted his lips. "Don't be so quick to finish what we've started. I want to know what else you are afraid for me to see."

She gave a slight frustrated laugh and said, "My

258

hips. You don't think them too wide?"

Pressing himself against her, a look of mock consideration on his face. He shook his head once, and smiled down into her face, his eyes burning with passion. "Like a cradle. Your hips are perfection, beautiful. But your true beauty comes from here." He laid a finger against her temple. "When you know and understand that, then you will no longer be embarrassed to let me see who you are."

He kissed her lightly on the forehead and stood up. Despite his reassuring words, she felt shy again with him standing over her, looking down at her. She started to cross her arms over her breasts, but he held out his hand for her. She took it. Then he pulled her to her feet and held her against him. And she felt safe once more.

"No sense rushing things. We have all day in this place," he said.

She groaned. She'd wanted nothing more than to make love with him again, and now he was going to make her wait. She reached up to kiss him, hoping to entice him back into their previous mood.

But he raised his hand and pressed his fingers to her lips. "Save it for later. Trust me. You'll find more pleasure in the wait."

Whatever did he mean by that? she thought, but before she could consider it further, she found herself being swept off her feet and up into his strong arms. He held her there. "This is our place, Lydia. Yours and mine. We can be anyone and do anything we want here. And right now, you are a water nymph, and I am Neptune!"

With a whoop, he ran to the edge of the pool and jumped in, taking her with him. The cold water hit her with such an impact that it took her breath away. She came up sputtering, crying out in protest. "You brute!" She splashed water at him furiously.

He dove beneath the surface of the water, and soon she felt his hands around her ankles. She took a hurried breath of air and submerged as he dragged her under. Then, just as suddenly, his arms came around her waist, and he pulled her to the surface again. He was laughing, water trickling down his face, his eyes wide in imitation of the expression on her face. "I had to cool you down. You were getting so hot, I could see steam rising out of your ears."

"If there was steam coming out my ears, you should have seen the billows of smoke coming out of yours."

"There was not," he protested, spinning her around once in the water.

"Yes, there was. And little flames coming out of your nose."

He laughed. "Your very flesh was so hot, it seared my arms. I bet I have scars."

"How you exaggerate! Throwing me in was completely unfair. You gave me no warning," she pouted, bringing her arms to rest around his neck.

"I don't have to give you any warning. It's one of the rules here."

"Not another one of your silly rules?" she said, then slyly brought her hands up to the top of his head and pushed him under the water in a quick dunk. She swam away from him as fast as she could toward the falls, but he caught up with her quickly and swam beside her. She stopped and tread water, watching him as he swam past her. Then he climbed up onto the rock beneath the falls.

He turned and faced her brazenly. His proud lion's body glistened as the water crashed against his shoulders and rushed the length of him. How uninhibited he was, standing there, no shyness whatsoever, no attempt to cover himself. He held his body erect, his arms outstretched to catch the water in his palms, powerful and struggling against the force of the water. Seeing him this way made her shiver with excitement. She wished she could stand next to him, hold his hand, and feel as strong and sure of herself.

Blake smiled at her, as if reading her thoughts. "It's wonderful! You should try it."

Embarrassed at having been caught looking at him, she shook her head. "No. I'd rather swim."

"It's your loss," he called to her and dove back into the pool. As he swam past, he taunted, "Did you enjoy the view?"

Her cheeks flamed, and she splashed water in his face with both hands. "No. There was this naked man, blocking my view of the waterfall!"

He splashed back at her and kept it up. "But what did you think of the naked man?"

She laughed, defending herself by setting up an equal spray in his direction. "I don't know, I was trying to see the waterfall."

"Was he the most handsome naked man you've ever seen?"

"As handsome as naked men go."

He leaped up out of the water and dunked her head under.

When she came up he was swimming away. "Where are you going?"

He called over his shoulder, "Since I'm not appreciated, I think I'll go sun myself." He climbed out of the pool and stood at its edge, stretching, tauntingly displaying himself for her. "Peacock!" she yelled and dove under the water.

When Blake opened his eyes, he leaned up on one elbow, looking around. He'd been sunning himself

261

for a quarter of an hour, drowsing from time to time. He scanned the pool for Lydia, and found her just where he thought he would. He knew, given enough time and enough privacy, she would find her way to the waterfall.

Lydia was draped across a rock, eyes closed, her face uplifted into the falling water, obviously enjoying the feel of it as it tumbled down around her. The water sparkled in the sunlight like diamonds against her pale skin. Her long hair hung in dark wet ribbons across her breasts and shoulders. Her peaks rose in pink rosebuds between her hair, and he warmed at the sight of her. She turned her head into the water slowly and let it fall onto her face with its full force, where it ran in rivulets between her breasts, pooling between her thighs. Like a cat she stretched her legs out and lifted her hands into the jetting water, showering herself anew. Then her hands went to her hair and smoothed it along her head and shoulders, and he imagined the soft, cool feel of it in his hands. Her languid movements, her long lithe body, and his memory of their lovemaking made him feel as if he could stay here and watch her forever.

She was the most breathtaking woman he'd ever encountered.

And she had no idea that he was watching her. Not wanting to spoil her enjoyment of the waterfall, he lay back down. He turned his head to keep an eye on her, and hoped she wouldn't notice. When she finally looked up and saw him, he was immediately sorry, for she sat up with a start and moved away from the falling water, her arms crossing over her chest to cover herself.

He leaned up on one elbow and called, "No. No. Don't stop. You were enjoying yourself. Don't even think about me."

262

"How can I not think about you, when you're there gaping at me?"

"I was not gaping. I was enjoying the sight of a beautiful woman, who felt beautiful and was delighting in it." He stood up and entered the pool, gliding toward her. He came to the edge of the waterfall where she sat above him, her eyes downcast.

"You make me sound so vain," she said, her hands clutching her shoulders tightly.

"If I thought what I saw was vanity, I wouldn't have been so pleased by the sight of it. What an odd opinion you have of yourself. It's as if you think of your body as another person."

"Sometimes it feels that way," her voice was barely above a whisper. "And I'm not sure I want you to see that other person."

"What person is that? The Lydia who is warm and alive, strong and vibrant. The Lydia who has the power to make me feel weak as a lamb."

She said nothing, and he rose up out of the water and bent down on one knee in front of her. He reached for her hands and took then in his and began pulling them away from her shoulders. She resisted. "Trust me," he said and brought her hands to his lips. "I want you to know that other person as I know her."

Guiding her hands to her cheeks, he pressed her palms against her own skin, moving them gently along her jawline and slowly back up, pressing her fingers lightly when he reached her cheekbones.

Lydia closed her eyes, savoring the warm feeling of his hands on hers, as they moved upward to her temples and across her forehead in one satiny stroke. Her fingers tingled and grew warm under the feel of her own skin. Was this what he felt when he touched her?

"Do you feel how soft your skin is?" she heard

263

him ask. She nodded, then felt him take the index finger of one of her hands, and together they traced the outline of her lips. She found that her mouth was moist and yielding beneath her touch, and smiled at the thought of the pleasure they brought to him when pressed to his. She opened her eyes and saw that he was smiling back at her, his gentle dove gray eyes encouraging her to explore further.

He brought her hands down along her neck to her shoulders and back up into her hair, which was smooth and cool against her fingers. Together, their hands crossed at her shoulders, then whispered along her upper arms, grasping once in a small hug. The first stirring of passion tugged at her center to find that she was desirable to him. She wanted to experience more.

Her lids fluttered shut and she leaned back against the rock she was sitting on. In one slow silken movement, he placed her hands on her thighs and guided them back and forth along the surface and up to her hips. She gasped and felt him quickly bring her hands along the ridges of her pelvis to her taut belly where he let them rest a moment. He murmured words of encouragement, soft and low, hypnotizing.

The heat from her hands radiated through her, as they were pulled to her rib cage with a fluid sweep, her skin whispering beneath her palms. She wanted to feel her breasts as Blake felt them, wanted to know the sensations he experienced when he touched her there. And as if he'd guessed her thoughts, together, they cupped her breasts. He ran her hands over the firm mounds, applying pressure to grasp them softly, and she heard his breath catch, confirming his delight of them. Her nipples grew firm and grazed her palms as their hands passed over them together. The sensations of feeling and being felt coursed through her blood and brought a low moan to her lips.

She barely heard Blake's voice. "Do you feel how beautiful you are to me?"

"Yes."

Then her hands were gently pulled away, as she felt him press his mouth between her breasts, his lips trailing lower, lower until his tongue was warm and soft against the folds of her hidden place. She gasped as he licked and teased her into new thrills of heavenly pleasure. What was this new way of making love? She might have been embarrassed, but the sensations he was creating in her left her too weak to resist. Instead, she ran her fingers through his hair and pulled him closer, rocking against the movement of his mouth, driving the thrills that vibrated through her deeper and deeper, until she thought she'd faint from the pure excitement of it.

Then Blake's mouth was moving in a path of kisses from her thighs to her hips to her breasts and shoulders, as he rose and braced himself over her. He entered her slowly, and she felt the length of him sliding inside her in one delicious, silken movement. The intense sensuality she'd experienced earlier mounted as he held himself over her.

She opened her eyes to find him looking down at her. He watched her as he withdrew almost entirely, then his mouth came down over hers as he glided inside her again. She heard him moan when she grasped him tightly around the neck, matching the hunger of his kiss, the heat of his rhythm with every fiber of her body. As the knot of desire tightened, stretching so thin it would snap, she was finally released from its bonds, and she felt the love she had for Blake ebbing and flowing from her body into his.

Holding him tightly, she felt as if she could cry at

how happy she was. She remembered the lovers she'd seen in the parks in London, holding hands and gazing into one another's eyes, some secret passing between them. She'd never known what it was that made them look at each other so intensely. Now she did. It was this closeness, these words, these caresses, the private joy discovered in each other's bodies. That had been their secret. How much she'd been cheated of in her marriage to Baxter.

And how much Blake had given her in the past few hours.

She closed her eyes, exhausted, and wishing she could make this afternoon with him last.

Chapter Twenty-one

Just before sunset, they'd returned to the ship. Blake had left Lydia in the captain's quarters to take a nap and had gone up top. It was late now, and moonlight streamed through the porthole above the bed. Awake and waiting for Blake's return, Lydia sat on the bed, hugging her knees, in deep and dreamy thought about the past two days.

They'd confirmed her feelings for Blake; she was in love with him. No matter how many times she reminded herself that he was a pirate and a rogue, she'd remember his arms around her, the feel of him next to her, and she'd forget everything else.

The problem was, what was she going to do about it? Could she marry him? No doubt it would shock her family. And for a moment she pictured herself standing before her father and relatives, Blake on her arm, dressed to the hilt as a pirate. The look on Gwendolyn's face would be one of jealousy at Lydia's having found such a handsome man. Her father would be red with rage at his inevitable fall from society with a pirate for a son-in-law. And Aunt Phyllida would simply faint into Uncle Ambrose's arms.

She giggled at the thought. She could marry him just for the simple pleasure of shocking them.

But more importantly, she wanted to be with Blake. Being without him was unbearable. She remembered how lonely Bellefleur had been in his absence. And besides, Brigitte was right. What did it matter that he was a rogue? She loved him.

But would he want to marry her? The thought gave her pause. When she looked in his eyes, did she see love or only desire? She cursed her lack of experience with men, because she could easily recognize desire in their looks, but love was a different sort of thing. Maybe one couldn't see love exactly. One could feel it in oneself, she reasoned, but how did one know that another felt the same way? It was confusing, to say the least.

She lay on the bed, thinking about this, gazing out at the moon.

Her love for him was all mixed up in her feelings of desire for him. That much was certain. Hadn't she been the one responsible for them making love the first time? She'd felt this way about him even then, yet it was her body's curiosity that had pushed her into tumbling into bed with him.

But their first night together had been more than she could have dreamed possible. He'd been so gentle and loving with her. If he hadn't any feelings for her, would he have been so patient and giving? Or had it all been part of his desire to make love to her? Brigitte had said once, in her typically matter-of-fact way, that a man would do and say anything to get a woman into bed, even make her think he loved her. She'd said that desire and love were separate things when it came to men, but women confused the two all the time — always thinking the man was in love with her, simply because he'd bedded her.

Was that how it was between her and Blake?

Lydia frowned. She simply didn't know.

But Brigitte had said something else. And remembering her words gave Lydia some hope. Brigitte, so much younger, but wise in the ways of love, had said that it was the desire that attracted the man and woman to each other, and that sometimes love could grow out of that attraction. Maybe Blake could learn to love her as she loved him?

Lydia hoped so with all her heart. She hoped that he loved her even now, and that someday he'd tell her so. She didn't have the nerve to ask him. Somehow *not* knowing was less painful than knowing he felt nothing for her. She would bide her time and wait for him to feel the same about her. If he married me, she daydreamed, then the house would be *ours*.

Wondering what was keeping him away, she walked to the door and laid a hand on the knob.

It didn't move. She tried again, then realized it was locked. He'd locked her in the cabin! Her stomach turned. Did he still mean to keep her here as his mistress until she signed the deed—even after all that had happened between them? She jiggled the knob again, more furiously than before, pulling on the door and hoping it was just stuck.

But it was definitely locked. The door remained shut.

She stood stunned for a moment, then kicked the door. Damn him! He did mean to keep her here! Last night and this afternoon had had no bearing on his plans whatsoever. It was as Brigitte had said. He'd spoken all the right words, touched her in all the right places, simply to bed her. How dare he treat her in this abominable way after all they'd shared? And what a fool she'd been to think he might have loved her. It was clear, she meant nothing to him. Bellefleur was his only concern. He wanted the damn house, that was all—and if he could get her into bed in the process, how much the better!

Her heart wrenched in her chest, and she felt tears welling in her eyes. A sob threatened to escape, but she swallowed against it. She wouldn't shed a single tear over him, if she could help it. When she saw him next, she would demand to be released. If he refused, she would find a way to escape. And then she would get as far away from him as she could.

She raised her fists in hurt and anger and began pounding on the door. "Blake Spencer, you despicable bastard! Let me out of here this instant! Do you hear me? I want out of here *now!*"

She continued pounding on the door and yelling until she heard footsteps outside the door. She ceased, her hand in midair, listening. If it was Blake, she'd serve him one stinging slap the minute he walked through the door.

But instead a young voice came from the other side. "What is it, mum?"

"Who's there?"

"Simon's my name."

From the sound of Simon's voice, Lydia thought him to be the same scowling young boy she'd seen on deck when she first arrived. He had appeared to be about twelve years old, with white blond hair and big brown eyes, a face too sweet to be among the riffraff she had encountered on board. But perhaps he could help her escape. She really didn't think she could face Blake. It would only make her feel worse to hear from his own lips how he intended to keep her there until she signed over Bellefleur. Besides, she didn't trust her feelings for him when she was with him. For all she knew, he'd have her in his bed again, and she wouldn't be able to resist him!

Crossing her fingers, she asked Simon, "Do you have a key to this door?"

"No, mum, only Captain's got the key. In his pocket he keeps it."

"Do you think you could take it from him without his

knowing?"

"No, mum. That would be stealin', and I ain't no thief," came his affronted reply.

"You could borrow it from him, and when you've let me out, you could return the key."

There was a pause.

"Simon?"

"Mum?"

"Please. He's locked me in here, and he won't let me out until I sign a piece of paper. And, Simon, I do want to get out and go home. Do you think you could help me? I'd pay you half a crown." She waited for his reply, then continued, "You wouldn't want to be shut up inside a cabin all day, would you?"

Again there was a pause.

"No, mum, but if the captain don't want you to get out—"

"It's stuffy and cramped in here, and there's nothing to do. I'm bored. You don't like being bored, do you?"

"No, I don't at all," he cried with emphasis.

"Then could you borrow the key for me? I would be ever so grateful to you. And remember, there's half a crown for you, if you can get me off this ship."

"Well—"

"Simon, please."

"Half a crown, mum?"

"I'll make it a full crown. Please."

"Very good, mum! I 'spose borrowin' the key wouldn't be like stealin' it."

She heard his footsteps retreating down the hall at a run, and leaning against the door, her mind raced for what she would do once she was outside the cabin. They weren't far from shore, but where were they? Blake had said they were near another island. But how close was it to Jamaica? And would there be a town on this island with a ship that could take her back to Port Royal? She hoped Simon would help her. He seemed rather loyal to Blake. Maybe her bribe would change his mind. She

271

could pay him when she reached Bellefleur. And at this moment, she would pay any sum on earth to get back home and as far away from Blake Spencer as she could possibly get.

Blake was leaning against the rail of the ship, when he felt a tugging at his pocket. He turned and grasped the small hand that had nearly lifted the ring of keys.

Surprised, he peered down into the face of young Simon. "What are you doing?"

The boy looked at the ground and shuffled his feet. "Borrowin' your keys, Mr. Spencer."

"Usually, when people borrow things, they ask first."

Simon considered this. "May I borrow your keys, Mr. Spencer? I'll return 'em when I'm done."

"And why do you want to borrow them?"

The boy didn't answer right away, only looked out over the side of the ship.

"It's fine, Simon, you can tell me," Blake encouraged.

"There's a lady in your cabin what wants to get out. She's bored in there, and she says you won't let her out, until she's signed some paper. She wants to go home. Why did you lock the lady in your cabin?"

Blake laughed and ruffled Simon's hair. "It's a long story." He handed the keys to the boy. "You may borrow my keys to let the lady out. And here." He dug into his pocket and withdrew a piece of eight, depositing it in Simon's hand. "If you get the lady safely to Port Royal, there will be another one of those waiting for you."

Simon's eyes widened at the sparkling coin. What a lucky night for him! "Thank you, Mr. Spencer." He turned to go, but Blake caught his arm.

"Get the lady *safely* back to Port Royal. Take her to the Boar's Head Inn. I'll send someone with some clothes for her. Someone she knows. Do you remember the path I showed you once?"

Simon nodded.

"Good. One other thing. Don't tell the lady that I let you borrow the keys. And don't tell her you talked to me at all. It will be our secret. Now run along. I'll lower the boat for you. Do you think you can manage her?"

Simon raised a somewhat scrawny arm, flexing what might someday be a muscle. "I'm strong as an ox, Mr. Spencer. I can manage her."

"Good."

And then Simon was racing down the deck back to the cabin.

Blake turned to the rail and regarded the smaller craft hanging alongside. With a heavy sigh, he began lowering it to the water below, then dropped a rope ladder over the side of the ship for their descent. When he finished, he gathered together a lantern and matches, some blankets and a skin of water, setting them on the deck of the ship in plain sight. They might need them, he thought, then retreated into the shadows to watch their departure.

They came up from below, quickly sighting and grabbing the things he'd left for them. Soon they were scrambling over the side of the ship. Blake held his breath, hoping neither would fall from the rope ladder. And when he heard the thud of their feet onto the boat below, he exhaled slowly. Not long after, the sound of Simon's uneven strokes and their hushed whispers reached his ears, and he knew they were on their way.

Moving out of the shadows, Blake stood by the rail, watching them go, two silhouettes in the moonlight, one small, the other slender and sitting straight. He watched the slender one. "Good-bye, lovely Lydia," he whispered.

He pulled a cigar from his pocket, but didn't light it, only chewed on one end thoughtfully. He'd been doing some thinking of his own in the last few hours, and he was satisfied with his last-minute decision to let her escape. He needed some distance from her. He found he

273

couldn't think straight when she was near him. And she'd done nothing but distract him since she'd arrived. He was still no closer to retrieving Bellefleur from her. That was what he'd set out to do, wasn't it? Get back what was rightfully his?

When they'd returned to the ship that evening, he'd debated on whether he should lock the cabin door or not. How long had he stood there, keys in his hands, trying to come to a decision? He had weighed the consequences carefully. If he locked it, he would be back in control of the situation, letting her know in no uncertain terms that he intended to keep her there until she signed over the house. And if he didn't turn the lock —

The meaning behind that had been too confusing. But he'd come very close — too close — to walking away without locking the door.

He scowled. How did she manage to muddle up his brain like that? He'd brought her here to scare her into signing the deed, and the whole damn thing had blown up in his face. Instead of being frigid, as he'd imagined her, she'd turned out to be the most passionate woman he'd ever come across. The discovery had caught him completely off guard. When he should have been keeping his mind on getting the deed signed, all he could think of was how much he wanted to make love to her. Then she had slipped his shirt from his shoulders and told him she wasn't afraid. To a man who'd been without a woman as long as he had, the words were welcome, especially coming from her.

It was all those months of living with her in the same house, he reasoned. *A man would have to be made of stone not to want her as much as I did.*

But even after he'd satisfied his need with her, why hadn't he been able to keep his desire in check this morning? He'd awakened with every intention of getting back to the signing of the deed, but then in her sleep, she'd pressed her body up against his, and his reason had flown straight out the window. His impulsive decision to take her to the falls that afternoon had been another mistake — not one he regretted, however.

That was the trouble. He didn't regret a single moment he'd spent with her here. He'd thoroughly enjoyed being with her. She'd been the warmest, most exciting woman he'd ever met.

But she has your house, damn it!

He gritted his teeth. He had to stop thinking about her. Even now, as she was being rowed out of sight, she could still cloud his reason.

His fist came down on the rail. "No more," he said aloud to her retreating silhouette. "You may have won this battle, sweet Lydia, but you haven't seen the last of me yet."

Chapter Twenty-two

When she opened the door to the room at the Boar's Head Inn, Lydia threw her arms around Brigitte, never so happy in her life to see someone she knew. "Brigitte, thank God, it's you! I was so frightened when you knocked, but when I heard your voice—thank heavens, you're here!"

Surprised by such a welcome, Brigitte pulled away from Lydia, then gasped. "But *Madame* has been crying."

It was true. Since Simon had brought her to the inn, Lydia had done nothing but cry. She felt miserable and almost wished she hadn't been so successful in escaping. Yet everything had gone off without a hitch.

The *Tiger Lily* had been anchored off the shore of Jamaica, a few miles east of Port Royal. It had hurt somewhat to know that Blake hadn't been completely truthful about their location, but it was a relief to find out she was closer to home than she'd thought. She and Simon had walked half the night along an overgrown path, until they reached the Boar's Head Inn. It was a tiny, well-kept establishment, on the outskirts of Port Royal.

The moment they arrived at the inn, Simon had curled up in a corner, where he still lay sleeping. Lydia, unable to even close her eyes, had lain on her mattress, staining it with her tears, until the early morning light had crept through the window.

Brigitte pulled a handkerchief from her pocket and gave it to Lydia. *"Mon Dieu,* I have never seen such tears!"

Lydia wiped her eyes. "I've been crying all night." Her lip quivered and a new stream of tears rolled down her cheeks.

"This is not what I planned at all."

Perplexed, Lydia sniffed and looked at Brigitte. "What do you mean, 'what you planned?' And how did you know I was here?" She'd been so happy to see a familiar face, she hadn't even questioned the fact that Brigitte had turned up out of nowhere. And then she saw the gown—one of her own!—rolled up and tucked under Brigitte's arm. She was still wearing the men's breeches and shirt Blake had given her the morning before. How did Brigitte know she would need new clothes?

Lydia eyed her suspiciously. "You had better explain yourself."

Brigitte's eyes snapped, and Lydia realized she was furious. "I was indeed a fool, *Madame!* I actually helped to kidnap you because I thought you were in love with *Monsieur* Spencer. *And—"* She paused, heaving in indignation, "all because I am a romantic, me!"

"Brigitte! What do you mean? You *helped* kidnap me?"

"Yes, and all because I wanted to spend time

277

with my lover, and—"

She burst into a storm of sobs.

Lydia put her arm around Brigitte and led her to the bed. "For heaven's sake, don't you start crying, too. I'm not angry with you. Really, I'm not."

Brigitte looked up. "Do you mean it?"

"Of course, I do." Then Lydia had to choke back a sob. "Thanks to you, I had the most beautiful time I've ever had in my life. I'm glad you did it. It was Blake that ruined everything, not you."

"I am so relieved you are not angry with me, *Madame*."

"You said it best, you're a romantic."

"But what do I know? Things did not turn out so well for me with my lover either," she said, and burst into another round of tears, more furious than the first. "What a *stupid* romantic, I am."

"Thank heaven for stupid romantics."

Brigitte giggled through her tears, and soon Lydia laughed, too. They faced each other, a bit embarrassed by their sudden confidence in one another. All sniffles, runny noses, and puffy eyes, they laughed again to cover the awkward silence that ensued.

"But what happened to you and *Monsieur* Spencer? I thought for certain you would fall in love," Brigitte asked.

Lydia felt her cheeks heating up. Brigitte's confession had put their relationship on a different footing, one that Lydia felt better about, but she wasn't ready to tell her what had happened with Blake—it was far too intimate.

Lydia looked away.

Brigitte sensed the familiar wall rising up between her and her mistress. She dried her eyes with her handkerchief. Then straightened her shoulders. Perhaps, if she talked about her troubles with Jacques . . .

"Look at me," she started, "crying my eyes out like a baby. And for what? That rogue, Jacques Noir? I would like to strangle that one. He romances me for two nights. Then this morning as I am ready to leave to find you, he tells me he cannot live without me, and for the hundredth time he asks me if I will sail away with him. And stupid as I am, I think this is a proposal of marriage. I ask him if he is proposing, and do you know what that scoundrel says to me? He says, 'Why should I marry you, when you are already my *mistress?*' I slapped his face and walked out."

"Jacques Noir—the pirate—is your lover? And you were with him just now?"

"*Oui.* It was part of the plan. Jacques and I were on another ship anchored near the *Tiger Lily.* We were to wait until *Monsieur* Spencer called for us, then I was to accompany you back home." She shook her head. "I would have been better off waiting for the moon to turn green than to expect to marry Jacques."

"But how did you know where to find me? Blake couldn't have known I would come here."

Brigitte furrowed her brow. "I received a message early this morning to bring a gown for you to the Boar's Head, where I would find you and the boy, Simon." She nodded in the direction of the sleeping figure in the corner. "I assumed it was from *Monsieur* Spencer."

Biting her lip, Lydia let out a sigh. She got up from the bed and walked to the window, looking out at the street below. Her escape had been far too easy. She remembered how everything had been prepared for their departure, and how vague Simon had been about how the boat had been lowered. And then there had been the lantern and blankets. Blake had clearly commandeered the entire escape.

"I'm sure the message was from him."

Her voice sounded cold, but Brigitte saw the tear that slid along Lydia's cheek. She moved to her mistress's side, wanting to console her, but not knowing how. "I know it is hard for you to admit it, but you love this man. It makes you sad to know the message was from him."

"He let me escape. He arranged it."

"And now you know he will not come after you."

Lydia said nothing. Her feelings must be as transparent as glass. Wasn't that exactly what she'd hoped he would do? Come after her?

Brigitte pursed her lips. "Then he is a fool. For now, we will take you back to Bellefleur. I will wake Simon and send him to hire a coach for us. And if you are worried about *Madame* O'Hare, I have already told her you were with the *comtesse*. Now quickly, here is your gown. You must get dressed."

But Lydia couldn't move. None of it made any sense to her. Her time with Blake had been so wonderful, and then he'd locked her in the cabin like a prisoner. He still wanted the house. But then why did he let her escape?

She heard Brigitte's matter-of-fact voice from behind her. *"Madame,* if I may be so bold as to offer you some advice. A man never understands the value of a woman who loves him, until she is gone. Let *Monsieur* Spencer think about what he has lost. He will be back. Besides, *you* are mistress of Bellefleur. That thought alone will drive him mad. If he wants his precious house, he will *have* to come back, no? It would not surprise me if he is waiting there now."

Lydia's heart lightened. Could Brigitte be right? Blake waiting at Bellefleur? She'd been right about so many other things concerning men, she had to be right about this. Of course, he would return.

Maybe not today, but he'd come back sooner or later, if for nothing else but Bellefleur. And the thought of merely seeing him was enough to make her smile again.

"How did you come to know so much about men, Brigitte?"

"*Madame,* when you have four older brothers, who fall in love as many times as the sun rises, you begin to know things about men—things you would much rather not know, believe me!"

"What of your own experience with men? Hasn't that taught you a thing or two?"

"*Madame,* that goes without saying."

Lydia laughed, and hands trembling with excitement, she began to get undressed. She could hardly wait to get home. Blake was coming back, she would wager the house on it.

Blake was not waiting at Bellefleur that afternoon, nor did he come the next day or the day after that. Two months passed, and as each day came and went, Lydia felt less sure of his return. Brigitte did her best to keep her spirits up, encouraging her to plan parties, teas, and excursions into Port Royal, and Moira would take up these suggestions with zeal, arranging everything.

But in the end, Lydia's heart was simply not in it.

If the house had seemed empty after Blake's initial departure, it was even more so now. Any pleasure she had found in it while he was there, was nothing more than bittersweet memories. And she would have given anything to have him back with his silly rules and stubborn ways.

She felt positively numb.

But then rumors of the exploits of the *Tiger Lily* began circulating around Port Royal.

281

A Spanish galleon had fallen prey to the pirate ship whose captain was *rumored* to be French. But Lydia was sure she knew better. When she heard the gossip about the attack, Blake's allowing her to escape finally made a little sense. She reasoned he'd undoubtedly gotten word of the galleon and wanted to go after it. And, of course, couldn't be bothered with a woman! It wouldn't have surprised her if he looted the ship to be able to offer her more money for Bellefleur.

Then she could hardly wait for him to return with his offer, simply so she could refuse him and his pirate money. But then another galleon was attacked, and she felt herself growing a little impatient, until she heard how much the two ships had brought him. Then she was furious with him. The sum was enormous! *How much did he need to buy back Bellefleur, for heaven's sake?*

When the third ship was sacked, the possibility that he'd given up the house entirely began to gnaw at her hope that he would return.

She was miserable again. The house, her actions, the things people said to her lacked the spark they had had when Blake was around.

Even the party that she planned for this evening was lifeless, and she knew it was because he wasn't there. She invited the Grandmires, the governor, and Andrew Ames in the hopes that some of their previous evening might be recaptured. Secretly, she hoped they might have some information about Blake. But thus far, the conversation had steered a wide berth around the subject of Mr. Spencer.

They were sitting in the drawing room after dinner, and Lydia was trying to concentrate on their discussion.

"My dear, your mind is wandering again." Lady Grandmire's voice interrupted her thoughts.

She looked up to see Winnifred Grandmire peering at her curiously. "I'm sorry. It must be the heat. You were saying?"

"I was asking if you'd heard anything from your sister. When will she be coming to Jamaica?"

"No, I haven't heard anything yet." Lydia felt she should say more, but nothing would come out of her mouth.

"Well, I must say, you are the most exhilarating conversationalist this evening, Mistress Collins."

"Winnifred!" chided Lord Grandmire.

Lydia held up a hand. "Please, Lord Grandmire. I'm used to your wife's candor. She's right. I'm afraid I'm all out of sorts these days. I'm sure it's just the heat."

Lady Grandmire patted her hand, then gave her a sly look. "Has anyone heard *anything* about Mr. Spencer? I do say, I have missed him terribly to-night."

Lydia felt her heart skip a beat at mention of the one subject she had wanted to talk about all evening.

Andrew Ames spoke up. "He's disappeared, you know. Told O'Hare he was going away on business. I believe the last time I saw Spence was when Bellefleur's ownership was decided. Have you seen him since then, Mistress Collins?" asked Ames.

"No," she lied, her mouth dry all at once. She thought of her time with Blake on the *Tiger Lily*. If any of them knew of what had happened to her then, they would have understood the warm flush that rose suddenly to her cheeks. She wet her lips before finishing calmly. "I haven't seen him since he left Bellefleur."

The governor grunted. "But have you any word of when he might return? My asking is rather selfish. We were working on a plan to encourage planting on the island. Without his support, I'm afraid I'm a fish out of water."

"He didn't tell *me* when he was coming back. Did he say anything to you?" She turned to Ames, trying not to sound too obviously concerned, but she was anxious to know if Ames had heard anything. But his answer was disappointing.

"Not a word. I'd say Spence has done a good job of covering his tracks. He didn't tell *anyone* where he was going. Not even O'Hare."

"Devilish quandary I'm in," the governor began. "The buccaneers are at it again — and with a vengeance, I might add. I'm sure you've heard the rumors going about. Three Spanish galleons in the last two months! The *Tiger Lily*'s captain recruited some thirty soldiers from Fort Charles — soldiers that were sent here to be farmers, not bloody buccaneers. Pardon me for swearing, but it is so very frustrating."

What would you think, dear Governor, if I told you the captain of the Tiger Lily *was Blake Spencer?* Lydia wanted to say to him. But instead, she asked, "Do you know the captain's name? He's rumored to be French, is he not?"

"I didn't know you had such an interest in pirates, my dear," drawled Lady Grandmire. "Thinking of writing a history?"

"No, I'm just . . . curious." She turned to the governor again. "I hear the captain is French?"

"Yes, supposedly, though it's not unheard of for one of our own countrymen to perform acts of piracy under a French name. The Crown is at peace with Spain, after all. It wouldn't do for our ally to think we're looting her ships, now would it?"

Lydia smiled. "No, indeed."

"But I seriously think this fellow *is* a Frenchman."

I wouldn't stake my life on it, Governor, she thought. *Your captain is as French as I am.*

"Really?" Lydia raised a brow. "I thought perhaps this captain might be Mr. Spencer."

She looked around the room for her guests' reactions.

Lady Grandmire gave an incredulous laugh. "My dear, I do think the heat is getting to you. Mr. Spencer? A pirate?"

"It's possible. How long has Mr. Spencer been 'missing'?" She looked to Andrew Ames.

Ames grinned, obviously aware of where she was going with this line of questioning. "It's been almost two months."

"And three ships were sacked in the last—what did you say, Governor?"

The governor laughed. "I believe I said the last two months."

Lydia was enjoying this. Blake, that scoundrel! Everyone here thought him so very respectable. She knew she couldn't tarnish his reputation among her guests, but it was fun to give voice to her own suspicions, without their having the slightest inkling of its possible truth.

She gave everyone an impish grin. "Hmmm. Mr. Spencer mysteriously disappears two months ago. Three Spanish galleons, sailing the area have been looted . . . also in the past two months . . ."

"And don't forget, the man *does* wear an earring!" chimed in Lady Grandmire, and everyone burst out laughing.

"Blake Spencer, captain of the *Tiger Lily*. It's an interesting thought, Mistress Collins, but how do you explain his interest in farming?" questioned the Governor jokingly.

"It's a disguise," she returned quickly. "To cover up his privateering activities."

"Then he'd do well to remove the earring, don't you think?" asked Lord Grandmire.

"Perhaps he can't. Perhaps he's sworn an oath to

wear the ring that binds him to his brother pirates," she replied with mock seriousness.

"Simply charming! If you haven't considered
writing a history, you would do well to think about
it, my dear. What an interesting history it would
be. If Mr. Spencer were written as a pirate, I
shudder to think what you might make of me!"
crowed Lady Grandmire.

The others laughed and joked about the possible
roles Lydia might cast them in, and by the end of
the evening, Lydia's mood lightened considerably.

The next afternoon, Moira came rushing out
from the kitchen, waving a small envelope. "Mistress Collins, there's a letter here from your sister."

"From Amy?" Lydia rushed to meet Moira.

"Aye, Mistress."

Overjoyed, Lydia took the envelope. "At last!
I'm going upstairs to read it now. Thank you,
Moira." She took to the stairs, calling down to
Moira. "Amy's probably on her way!"

In her room, she could barely wait to read the
letter. She broke the wax and unfolded the parchment.

Dearest Liddy,
I cannot come to Jamaica! Liddy, I do so
detest writing to you about all this, but I
don't know what I shall do.

Her heart sank as she read on.

Father's offered my hand in marriage to a
man. Lord Calvert's his name, and he's almost
ancient! He scowls all the time when he's talk-
ing with father, and his voice booms like a
cannon. He frightens me nearly out of my

286

wits!

I wish I was as brave as you. Then I could talk to Father like you did when you went to Jamaica. But every time I open my mouth, my knees start knocking. I'm such a coward.

Father's being completely unreasonable, and I'm afraid I'll be forced to marry this Lord Calvert. Please, Liddy, you've got to come home on the very next ship and help me!

I don't know how I shall know if you've received this letter in time. I only hope and pray to find you on the next ship from Jamaica.

Your loving sister, Amy

Lydia' fist came down on the arm of the chair. She rose and began pacing.

Damn her father! How could he do this to sweet Amy?

Her heart went out to her sister entirely. She remembered all the fear she felt when her father announced to her that she would marry Baxter. She remembered how loathsome Baxter had seemed to her and shuddered at the memory.

There was no doubt in her mind about what she must do.

"Brigitte!" she called.

In a moment Brigitte appeared in the doorway. *"Oui, Madame."*

"Send someone immediately tonight to book me passage on the next ship back to England."

"England, *Madame?"* Brigitte looked startled.

"Yes! Then come back here and begin packing. My sister's in trouble, and I have to go home."

"You—you will be coming back?"

Lydia frowned, distracted. "I don't know—"

What Brigitte said next came as a complete surprise to her.

"Then, *Madame,* I am going with you!"

Within a week, Lydia and Brigitte were on board the *King's Bounty*, sailing for the open seas.

It had not been easy to prepare for the journey. The next ship bound for England hadn't been scheduled to leave for another two weeks, but Lydia had persuaded the ship's captain—with a handsome bonus—to put out to sea early. He'd been more than obliging when he saw the pouch of gold she offered.

Then Brigitte had dragged her heels about the packing, and Lydia had the feeling her maid was beginning to have second doubts about leaving. She imagined it was because of Jacques, and Lydia's heart went out to her. Her own feelings about leaving the Caribbees behind—where she might still have a chance to see Blake again sometimes—were unsettling and regretful.

But she had to get back to help Amy. She tried to make it the one thing that occupied her mind during the preparation. Purposely, she would push aside her thoughts of Blake, trying to convince herself that he'd left for good and wasn't coming back—that there was no use staying in Jamaica to wait for him. Especially when Amy needed her.

Now she and Brigitte stood at the railing of the *King's Bounty*. Jamaica had disappeared on the horizon, and the ship had just sailed past the western peninsula of Hispaniola. She finally breathed a sigh of relief—relief that the last week's hurried preparation was over.

But there was also the feeling of sadness to be leaving the island behind. So much had happened to her there. She'd discovered independence, love, new friendships. She knew she would return!

As she gazed out over the trail of waves the ship

left behind, she heard Brigitte gasp and heard a sudden excitement from the other passengers on deck.

"Pirates!" a man shouted and the others hurried to the rail of the ship.

"It's the *Tiger Lily*!" one woman exclaimed, pointing over the stern.

Lydia followed the woman's finger. Sailing some distance behind them and following the same course as the *King's Bounty*, was a ship, and Lydia immediately recognized it. It *was* the *Tiger Lily*! It's brilliant blue and gold colors, waving atop the main mast, gave it away.

Her heart skipped a beat.

"They're sailing straight for us!" another passenger cried as the ship tacked into the wind, steering a course due north.

"Do you think they'll board us?" the first woman asked.

"What will we do?"

Another woman gave a startled shriek, "My jewels!" and began removing her necklace and stuffing it hurriedly into the bodice of her gown.

"No need to fear, dear ladies," came the captains' voice as he moved among the passengers. "The *Tiger Lily* is partial to the Spanish. I doubt very much if her crew will board us."

But Lydia noticed he continued to watch the progress of the *Tiger Lily* with a look of concern. She waited, almost without taking a breath, secretly hoping it *would* sail for the *King's Bounty*. Blake was on the ship, she was sure of it. Had he heard she was leaving Jamaica and come after her?

What a dramatic reunion it would be! She could see Blake, climbing over the ship's rail, sweeping her into his arms, kissing her for all on deck to see. She would tell him about Amy, and he would come with her back to England to help her with her sister. Joshua Lyndham wouldn't stand a chance with the both of them together.

She watched as the *Tiger Lily* drew nearer. Her shoe slipped from her foot and twirled on the end of her toe beneath her skirts.

Lydia didn't realize it, but Brigitte was holding her breath, too.

Brigitte thought she was going to faint. *Jacques, I knew you could not let me leave!* she thought, and her mind raced with the fancy of him climbing on deck, searching for her frantically among the other passengers. He would take her in his arms and carry her off the ship with a kiss and promises of marriage.

She clutched Lydia's hand on the rail and waited.

The sails of the *Tiger Lily* luffed, then filled with air. The pirate ship tacked east then began to slowly disappear behind the peninsula of Hispaniola.

"You see, it is as I told you. The *Tiger Lily* only sets her sails for the Spanish." The captain laughed in nervous relief and moved off down the deck.

"Thank goodness!" said one woman, retrieving her necklace from her bodice.

"I was never so frightened in my life!" the first woman said, holding her hand to her throat. "I would have fainted dead away at the sight of a pirate!"

Lydia and Brigitte watched as the ship sailed from sight. Then both women exhaled with a disappointed sigh. Each heard it coming from the other, and looked guiltily at one another.

Lydia cleared her throat. "What a relief. I must say I was . . . frightened too."

"For a moment, I hoped it might be my Jacques—" Brigitte said in a strangled voice. "I must forget him! It is a good thing we are sailing for

England where there are no pirates. It will be much safer for our hearts there, no?"

Why she was still protecting Blake she would never know, but Lydia simply couldn't bring herself to tell Brigitte that she knew who really was the captain of the *Tiger Lily*!

"Yes," Lydia agreed, but the thought wasn't as comforting as it should be. She gave one last look to where the ship had disappeared. *Good-bye, Blake,* she thought sadly, and set her sights on England.

Chapter Twenty-three

The skies were soft and gray, the air held a faint chill. Now and again, a patter of rain sprinkled down on the crowds of people gathered to meet the passengers disembarking from the *King's Bounty*. The waiting people were huddled in dark cloaks and wide hats against the rain, a sea of hues that looked as depressing to Lydia's eyes as the drab sky and dark buildings.

The scene held none of the bright colors, the sunshine, the freedom of the people of Jamaica. These people looked overdressed to her, bundled against the weather as they were, folded in upon themselves, and she felt as mournful as the scene. She didn't want to be here. She knew now she belonged to a white house set like a diamond among tropical flowers, to a place where one moment the sun could be shining, the next the winds blowing with hurricane force, a place as wild and elemental as the man who had captured her heart.

But she had not captured his heart in turn. What they had shared together had meant nothing to him. The happiness she'd felt in his arms had been like the passing sun, soon enough blotted out by storm clouds.

Brigitte and she had not been very good company for each other on the voyage, but it had been comforting for each of them to not be alone. They were both mourning the loss of the men they loved—and mourning their own foolishness for giving their hearts to handsome rogues who had never intended to give their own love in return.

She shook her head as she followed her sister Amy through the crowds to the coach waiting for them. She'd had enough of such thoughts on the voyage, she reminded herself. Blake was far behind her, half a world away, and she was here to help Amy, and to try to put a new life together for herself.

Amy had come alone to meet her, wanting to have some time to talk to her privately before they were surrounded by the family. They were all staying in the London town house, and two coaches waited to take them there, one for her and Amy, and a second for Brigitte and her trunks.

Lydia and Amy hurried into the coach as the rain suddenly pattered down harder. They settled into the seats, throwing back their hoods, and as the coach started off, they clasped hands tightly and exchanged a long, emotion-filled look.

Amy was no longer a girl, but a lovely young woman, Lydia saw, feeling her throat tighten with love for her sister. Amy had filled out into curves, and was richly dressed in a becoming shade of forest green, with her light brown curls done up in a fashionable mass of ringlets around her heart-shaped face. But her big brown eyes were anxious, and she was biting her lip.

"Oh, Liddy! I am so frightfully glad you're back!" Amy threw her arms tightly around Lydia's neck and held on as if she would never let go.

"Darling, and I am happy to be here to help you. Now don't cry! You must tell me everything, for your letter was not very coherent. Do you think I'd let Father marry you off for gain the way he did to me?" she added fiercely, breaking the embrace and looking sternly at Amy, who was still sobbing. "Here, take my handkerchief. And tell me why you wrote so infrequently, and kept putting off coming to me in Jamaica. Was it Father's bullying that was frightening you?"

Amy gulped, and looked somewhat guilty. "Oh, Liddy—it *has* been awful lately. But it wasn't Father's bullying that kept me here. He hasn't been bullying me at all, until the last few months. It was that I met someone—someone I care for."

Amy looked at her sister pleadingly, as Lydia stared. "Why didn't you tell me in your letters? You mean you are in love?"

"Please don't be hurt, Liddy, that I never wrote you about him! It was just that for a long time, I didn't know whether he cared for me or not, and I was shy of writing it in case he didn't! It is only recently that I have come to believe he cares for me, for he actually asked Father for my hand! And I wouldn't have even known about it, except that Gwendolyn, that hateful cat, came and told me that I'd had a suitor—and that Father had sent him packing and told him not to ever call again!"

Amy sobbed freshly into her handkerchief, and Lydia felt nonplused that Amy—who was, after all, almost like her daughter—had grown up enough to be in love, to have her own heartbreaks! With a start, Lydia realized she had been dwelling so much on her own affairs of the heart that she had not given much thought to the fact that Amy would have changed a great deal in the year that had passed since she'd left her behind in England.

"Darling—who is this young man? How did you meet him?"

At first, Amy could barely speak for sobbing, but as she got her story out, she calmed somewhat.

"His n-name is Christopher Fletcher, and I m-met him at a dinner party after w-we'd taken up residence in London. Father wanted me to start meeting some young m-men, so we've been going to all kinds of parties. But Christopher is only a draper's son! And even though his family is rich, once this Lord Calvert came calling, Father put a stop to it at once, for his family is in trade, while Lord Calvert has a title!"

Lydia drew her brows together, feeling a rising indignation. "Tell me about this Lord Calvert who wants to marry you," she said coldly.

"Oh, but he doesn't want to marry me, Lydia," said Amy, opening her eyes wide and staring despairingly at Lydia. "He wants to marry *you!*"

Lydia had a feeling of uncanny familiarity as she walked into the drawing room, prepared to do battle with her family. Granted, it was a very different room than the one at Lyndford Hall. Amy had told her that Gwendolyn had redecorated the town house in the latest and most elegant fashion of ornamented white plaster walls with Grecian-style columns; the effect was bright and airy, rather than dark and overornamented as Lyndford was. But the scene was much the same as the one when she'd announced she was going to Jamaica.

They were all there. Her father, looking much less the country squire and more the London man of fashion, she noted. Startingly, he was wearing a flowing brown wig with rolled side curls that were tied back with a silver ribbon, perhaps in an attempt to look younger for his wife. But his reddened face and cold, pale blue eyes were not softened by his fashionable garb, and she thought it made him look every one of his years. Gwendolyn sat at his side, in a daffodil gown of such elegance that Lydia knew she must be spending a fortune at the dressmaker's; her blond hair was artfully arranged, and she wore more paint than ever on her face, which emphasized the fine lines that were beginning to appear there. But still, she was as poisonously pretty as ever.

And Aunt Phyllida and Uncle Ambrose occupied a sofa, with a nervous Amy sitting next to them. Phyllida also hadn't changed a bit, except that her overflowing frame was covered with puce sarsanet, which made her look larger than ever—and made Uncle Ambrose, beside her, look thinner by contrast.

Lydia had greeted them all earlier, then pleaded fatigue from her journey and retired to her room to change. And to plan. Her blood was still boiling at the outrageous story Amy had told her, as she walked into the drawing room and surveyed her family with an assumed calm.

Joshua Lyndham jumped up. "Ah! There you are, Lydia. Take a seat, child. I know you must still be weary from your voyage."

So he was trying to be cordial! Lydia narrowed her eyes at him as she sat. The hypocrite! "I am not weary, Father, but am ready to discuss this proposed marriage for Amy to this Lord Calvert—

whoever *he* is."

Her father sat, regarding her with a pleased smile that had a flicker of cruelty in it. "Yes. I imagine your sister told you that he had first offered for you . . . not for her?"

"She mentioned it. What I don't understand is why a man who has never met me would offer for me in marriage? Nor why there is any talk of affiancing Amy to him, if it is me he is interested in—though I cannot see how he *can* be interested in marrying me, as I am a total stranger to him! Or perhaps," she added with a steely challenge, "I *have* met him and do not remember him?"

She knew this was not true, because Amy had described him to her in the coach. "He's quite old, Liddy—only think, he has *gray* hair! Oh, I shall die if Father makes me marry him, and not Christopher!" she'd finished, crying anew. Lydia had never met any elderly peers, either when she was married to Baxter or in the days when her father had been searching for a husband for her. The aristocracy had been above their station in those days.

"Really, Lydia," said Gwendolyn in a voice of acid impatience. "I do not see how you can have reached the age you are and be quite so naive. Lord Calvert has no need to have met you to be interested in marrying you. You may choose to forget it, but you are one of the wealthiest widows in England. Lord Calvert, though titled, is in need of money . . . as so many old families are."

"Now, now, Gwendolyn," cut in Joshua, after a glance at Lydia's face told him she was furious. "You are making it sound as if the man doesn't care for anything but money. That is not how he came to offer for you at all, Lydia. I met him at a bear-baiting, and we hit it off at once. He was

297

gracious enough to attend a supper we had here in London — most condescending of him, I thought. We got to talking, and he confided he was in search of a rich wife. It was then I thought to show him your portrait — the one painted of you before you married Baxter."

Lydia winced inwardly, remembering how much she had hated to sit for that portrait, how miserable she had been at the prospect of marriage to a man she didn't love. The portrait was most unflattering, she thought, for the painter had captured the melancholy in her eyes all too accurately. It had hung in the London house, and after Baxter's death, she'd wanted nothing to do with it.

Evidently, she thought bitterly, her family had found a use for it.

"Calvert was most struck by the portrait," her father was going on, and there was a glitter in his eye that told her he was triumphant as he at long last backed her into a corner. "It was then that he offered for your hand — but I told him with some regret that you had removed to Jamaica and had no intention of coming back."

"He was simply crushed, Lydia," trumpeted Aunt Phyllida. "Naturally, we'd told him all about you, emphasizing your virtues and, of course, not bringing up your faults, such as how headstrong you are. He was most set on marrying you."

Joshua Lyndham's eyes gleamed. At last he had her where he wanted her! In a moment, she'd learn that she had no choice but to bend to his wishes. It had taken a long time to bring her to heel, he thought, but now he'd show his wayward daughter that his will was not to be set aside lightly.

"Well," he said briskly, pretending regret, "of course, I had to tell him that I doubted you'd come back from Jamaica. But, of course, Lord Calvert, I said, I *do* have another daughter. One as lovely as the eldest, if not quite so rich. I decided a large portion for Amy was worth giving up, to have a lord as a son-in-law. With such connections, I can easily make up for the money I settle on her. Well, let us just say Lord Calvert was willing to listen. Seems he is in most desperate need of money. Creditors, I believe. I imagine he'd agree to have the banns called for Amy this week, if I pressed him."

Lydia clenched her fists in her skirts and stared at him with hatred. Damn him! "And what is the point of this discussion, if you have already made up your mind to marry Amy to him?"

"Why, naturally, Lydia," purred Gwendolyn, looking at her with mocking green eyes, "we thought you might want to meet him yourself, now that you are actually here. He is quite presentable, and after all, *you* are his first choice. But if not—" She shrugged, and smiled at her husband.

"If not, then we can go ahead with Amy's wedding plans at once," he said, with a hard look at Lydia.

Lydia glanced across the room at Amy, who looked terrified, and far too timid to speak. She turned back to her father. "Then, in essence, you are proposing to blackmail me into marrying this lord? If I do not agree to his suit, you will force Amy into marrying him?" she said coldly.

Joshua's eyebrows rose. "I have said no such thing," he said craftily. "You, as you told me in no uncertain terms, cannot be *forced* into anything, now that you are of age and wealthy in your own right. But you must be mad if you think I am going to let an advantage like this one for our family pass us by. It is not every day that a peer of the realm wants to marry so far beneath him."

"If only you would be *sensible,* Lydia," Aunt Phyllida put in with distaste in her voice. "This notion of marrying for love is mad. Marriages are made in every family because of advantage—which is how it should be. And I do not see how you can object to your sister marrying a man you have never even met. You are prejudging this match most unfairly!"

"Besides, girl, it's a father's place to decide his daughter's marriage, and as Amy is still just sixteen, he has that right, and all your haughty words won't stop him from doing his natural duty, which is ordering this family's affairs!" said Uncle Ambrose warmly.

Under her gown, Lydia slid off her shoe and began to twirl it with a stockinged toe. She could never, never let them see how upset she was—how she wanted to jump up and scream at them that they could never get away with it—that she would protect Amy!

But the truth was, they could and would get away with it, unless she stayed calm and thought of a way to stop them.

"Perhaps, Father," she said frigidly, "you would consider a bargain. Allow Amy to refuse this suit, and choose her marriage partner herself, and I am willing to be most generous with you. The properties in Scotland—"

"I don't need your money." Her father spoke venomously. "Not any longer. The rebuilding of London since the Great Fire has been the making of me, for there is a demand for Cotswolds stone that cannot be kept up with. The quarries on Lyndford are kept busy from morning till night. Sir Christopher Wren himself used Cotswolds stone to rebuild St. Paul's, for since the fire, only a madman would rebuild with wood. Because of Wren's

300

example, I am becoming richer every day. But money can't buy me what an aristocratic connection can, as you well know. The real wealth is made at Court. No family in trade can ever become one of the powerful ones, no matter how much money a man may have."

Gwendolyn watched Lydia's face as she took this in, and smiled her cat smile. "But Lydia, dear, it seems to me you are making much of little. Of course, it's as much as I expected from your regrettably stubborn temperament, but bear in mind nothing has been settled yet. We are not asking you to marry Lord Calvert, nor has it yet been agreed that he will marry Amy. All we are asking . . ."

She paused, and her eyes glowed with triumph, though when she went on, it was in the sweetest and most reasonable of voices, ". . . is that you *meet* Lord Calvert, before you leap to judgment about him. I think when you do meet him, you might even find you are not adverse, after all, to his suit. We are having a ball this very week that he plans to attend, and all we are asking at this moment is that you be there."

The clock on the mantel ticked loudly into the silence as Lydia stared at Gwendolyn, then at her father. At last she looked at Amy, and saw the tears that were trembling on her lashes, the hands tightly folded in her lap.

She let them see defeat in her face. Slumping her shoulders slightly, she said, as meekly as the old Lydia long ago would have, "I see, then. I—perhaps I *have* been unfair. I—I will agree to come to this ball, and at least meet Lord Calvert. After all . . ." She heaved a sigh, and looked down at her hands, "I *do* have to marry again sometime. It has not been easy, being an unprotected woman on Jamaica, I have found."

She looked up, and as they all began to speak at once, she saw from their faces that they thought they had beaten her into submission, that she had succeeded in presenting a picture of one who was totally cowed.

But what they couldn't see was that, before she'd begun to speak, she'd slipped her shoe firmly back onto her foot.

Chapter Twenty-four

"This despicable weather!" Casting an irritated eye at the low gray clouds that were letting down a steady drizzle of rain, Brigitte pulled the hood of her cloak more closely around her hair and hurried down the front steps of Lyndham's town house.

Really, I do not see how these English can stand to live in London! she thought, hoping her mistress would decide to go back to Jamaica before much longer. It had been a mistake to leave Jacques behind, she saw that now, for her heart was breaking without him, while at this very moment he was probably finding consolation with some Port Royal lightskirt, forgetting all about her—

And, worse, in the sun!

Oh, why had she ever let her temper get the better of her? she wondered miserably, shivering in the cold as she ran down the front walk and unlatched the great wrought iron gates to the street. And why did her mistress make such a fuss over her sister marrying a lord? *Dieu,* what did it matter if he was as old as the devil? These rich women did not know when they were lucky, she thought scornfully, piqued that she had been sent out in this *incroyable* cold merely to fetch some perfume for the ball that was in two nights—

Yes, she is mad, she decided, *for what does she want perfume for, when she doesn't want to marry this lord in any case?*

With a small startled shriek, she ran headlong into someone. She had been so busy with her thoughts, head bent against the rain, she had not been looking where she was going.

"*Mon dieu!* Excuse me, *Monsieur,* I—"

And she gave another shriek, not so small this time, when she saw who she had run into.

"*Monsieur* Spencer!" she gasped.

He squinted at her through the rain, looking as startled as she was. "Brigitte? Then—she is here?"

"Yes—but *Monsieur* Spencer! What are *you* doing here? In London! Is Jacques with you?"

He frowned, and, giving a quick glance in both directions took her arm. "Come—we can't talk out here in the street—I don't want to be seen. Duck into this doorway with me."

Unable to take her eyes from him, Brigitte obediently ran a few steps with him until they had reached the shelter of a servant's entry, set deep in a high stone wall that surrounded one of the other houses on the street. The door was closed and barred behind them, and the rain cut them off effectively from whoever it was he did not wish to be seen by.

She regarded the roquelare he wore with deepening astonishment. But, you are looking very fine! Is Jacques—"

He laughed then, and she couldn't help admiring the way he looked, even if her heart did belong to

Jacques — *Dieu,* he was a sight, dressed as a gentleman!

"No, Jacques is not with me. There, you are not going to cry, are you?"

"No," she flashed, though tears *had* started. For a moment, she had so hoped . . . "But what are you doing here? And why are you dressed like that?"

He dismissed his clothes with a wave of the hand. "When in London . . . Listen, Brigitte, can you keep a secret for me, from your mistress? I don't want her to know that I am in London — at least, not *yet.*"

"You have come here to see her?" Brigitte's interest was piqued. Really, did her mistress not know how lucky she was, to have a man like Blake Spencer chasing her halfway across the globe? "But this is most romantic, *Monsieur.* Perhaps you find you miss her after all?"

He grinned at her. "Perhaps. Then you won't tell her you have seen me?"

She pouted, but let her eyes dance at him. "And why do you think I would be so disloyal to my mistress? But there! I have always had a soft corner for lovers, and also for you, *Monsieur* Spencer. Perhaps you will tell me news of Jacques, if I promise to keep your secret . . . and also, you will keep the fact that I miss the rascal a secret when you see him again, in exchange?"

"Done." They smiled at each other in perfect understanding. Then Brigitte sighed and widened her eyes at him.

"But first, I think I must tell you, that you may be too late. My mistress is being courted by an English aristocrat . . . a Lord Calvert, no less. If you have come here to win her back . . . or even to propose to her . . . you had best hurry, for I think she means to accept him at a ball in two days' time."

His jaw tightened most satisfactorily at this piece of news, she saw.

"A ball." He considered her, broodingly, for a few moments. "Where?"

"Why, at the town house where we are staying. The same place you were going just now, *Monsieur*," she teased him. "But perhaps this ball might be a better way of surprising her than trying to ring the bell. For I warn you, her whole family is there—and they are terrors, those ones! I do not think you would be able to make a romantic impression . . . *or* get her alone . . . if you called. Or perhaps you have just been walking up and down in the rain, hoping she will come out?"

He scowled at her. "You are a minx, Brigitte." Then suddenly he laughed. "A ball, eh? So she means to accept him, does she? Maybe I'll come after all, if you can get me an invitation."

"It depends, *Monsieur,* on what you can tell me about Jacques," she said demurely.

He looked at her with some humor. It was blackmail, no less! But well worth it.

Worth it for news of Lydia.

But Devil take it, what on earth was he supposed to tell her about Jacques? The last he'd seen him, he'd been drunk as two lords in a Port Royal tavern, with a pretty wench on his knee. Drowning his sorrows at Brigitte's departure. "The best way to forget her, *mon ami*," he'd confided in Blake. "It has never failed me before." And Jacques had barely listened to Blake's plans to sail to England, it seemed, too caught up in his own cure for a wounded heart to care what Blake did.

Mustering all his diplomacy, Blake sighed and began, "Well, I think I could say that he misses you . . .

Chapter Twenty-five

It was the morning of the ball, and Lydia and Amy sat in the drawing room, eagerly awaiting a certain visitor. At this hour, Gwendolyn and their father were inevitably still abed, so their caller could come in secret. They should be safe in receiving him as long as he didn't stay long.

"Here he comes—his carriage has just driven up!" Amy turned from the window, her pretty face flushed with excitement, her brown eyes sparkling. Lydia smiled at her.

"Thank you again for letting him call on me today! I should never have had the courage to ask him to come here without you, Liddy!" Amy exclaimed, positioning herself on the settee and turning rapturously to the door.

It was so wonderful that Amy was in love, Lydia thought. Now if only this young man was worthy of her.

She didn't have long to wait to find out. The footman appeared in the doorway. "Mr. Christopher Fletcher," he announced, and withdrew.

A young man was on the footman's heels, tall and quite handsome, with soft brown curls that she saw at once were a most fashionable wig, a splendid suit of deep maroon with a jacket long enough to brush the tops of his knee breeches, and immaculate white hose and silver-buckled shoes that showed not a spatter of street mud.

He actually blushed when he saw Amy, and managed a deep bow to both of them that was, though practiced, somehow awkward at the same time. "Miss Lyndham! May I present my compliments. I am honored that you would receive me today," he said earnestly, his large brown eyes fixed adoringly on Amy.

Who was blushing herself, her eyes cast down modestly. Lydia hid a smile as she saw her sister manage to raise them to meet his, and murmur softly, "I am delighted you could call on us. May I present my sister, Mistress Collins? Mr. Christopher Fletcher."

"I am very pleased to meet you, Mr. Fletcher," Lydia said, smiling warmly to put him at his ease, for he was clearly nervous. "Won't you please be seated, and allow us to serve you some refreshments?"

"I believe I told you, Mr. Fletcher, that my sister has just returned from Jamaica . . ." Amy offered as he seated himself, and Lydia was glad to answer his interested questions about the Caribbees, for it both put him at ease and gave her a chance to study him.

It was touchingly obvious that he adored Amy

. . . and that she adored him. When a servant brought in the tray, Amy made a fuss of serving everything perfectly, pouring a glass of canary wine for him and tea for herself and Lydia, while he looked at her with admiration. As Amy handed him his wine and offered the plate of biscuits, their eyes kept touching briefly.

After a few moments of conversation, during which he barely sipped his wine, he rose. "I—I must be going, Miss Lyndham . . . Mistress Collins. I—"

He was about to say something more, but Lydia rose, too, cutting in smoothly, "I shall see you to the door, Mr. Fletcher. Thank you for calling on us today."

He sent her a startled look, then colored again, merely nodding to Amy before following in Lydia's wake as she swept out of the room. Lydia had to bite off a giggle at his dejected expression, for obviously he believed he had not won her over and that he was being given a set-down to his pretensions.

She walked down the hall to the front door, where the footman stood at attention. "You may go, James. I shall show Mr. Fletcher out," she said.

She studied him as they waited for the footman to leave. Yes, he was perfect for Amy, as sweet as she was. He was a serious young man, once he'd gotten over the initial tongue-tied state Amy had produced in him. She hazarded that his fine and fashionable dress was donned solely with the hopes of impressing her family that he was a worthy suitor.

She smiled at him. "Mr. Fletcher, I must tell

you—"

He sighed, looking more dejected than ever. "I know . . . you need not say it. My father is merely a draper, though we have more than enough in the way of money. I shall not call on Miss Lyndham again, if that is her family's wish. But Mistress Collins—" Suddenly his brown eyes flashed with a desperate defiance she liked very much, "I must tell you that I have come to love your sister, and that I am devoted to her happiness—"

"I know." She smiled even wider at his dumbstruck expression. "And I enjoyed hearing you tell me that, even though you guessed wrong about what I was going to tell you. I was merely going to tell you that you *must* come to the ball tonight." He stared at her as if he could not believe what she had said. She took an invitation from her pocket and pressed it into his hand . . . and was rewarded by his smile.

She cut short his delirious thanks with a laugh. "It is merely an invitation to a ball, Mr. Fletcher. There is still my father to handle—and besides, *have* you asked her yet?"

"No, but I think she—that is—but you can't sacrifice yourself for Amy's happiness by marrying this lord!" he burst out. "It wouldn't be right! I—"

Again, she cut him off. "I have no intention of marrying him, so set your mind at rest, Mr. Fletcher. And now, I really must go and dress for that ball." She gave him a last dazzling smile and left him standing in the hall, looking after her as if she were a saint.

As she went up to her room, she reflected with

a light heart that he had looked at her *almost* as adoringly as he did at Amy.

Now her only problem was Lord Calvert, but she smiled at that thought, too. Because she had a solution at last.

"Liddy! I cannot believe you told Christopher to come to the ball tonight!"

Lydia looked up from the mirror and smiled. She was just putting the finishing touches on her dress.

"Of course I did, darling. Wait until he sees you in that dress! He will lose no time asking you to be his wife." Amy looked angelic in pale blue satin caught up over sapphire silk.

"But what about Father? He will be livid when he sees Christopher at the ball!"

"I think not." Lydia smiled, thinking she looked her best tonight . . . and she wanted to look her best, or at least good enough to be able to bemuse an elderly lord. Her gown was a dusky rose satin dress, pinned up over a petticoat of copper lace, cut daringly low. She fastened a topaz earring in her ear under a cascade of ringlets as she spoke. "Father will be too happy to see me at Lord Calvert's side all evening to care if Christopher is present or not."

Amy gasped. "You don't mean to *encourage* Lord *Calvert!?*"

"I mean just that. And don't look so alarmed. It is the perfect way to put Father off the scent . . . and to see that you and Christopher can get married. You see, I intend to become engaged to him."

311

"Engaged! Oh, Liddy, you can't, just to save me, when—"

"Just what your Christopher told me," she answered, smiling fondly at Amy. "Really, you two *are* made for one another—you even think alike! Don't worry, I shan't have to marry him. But if I encourage him, and tell Father I have found him to my liking, I am sure you will be allowed to marry Christopher."

Amy sat down abruptly on the bed, not seeming to care she was creasing her gown. "But he'll never believe you!"

"*That* is precisely why I must take care to dazzle this Lord Calvert, *and* to seem to be dazzled by him tonight. I plan to hint to him that I am amenable to his proposal . . . and tell him that I will accept him, on the condition of a *long* engagement. Which will not be announced except privately, to the family. I will give him my permission to speak to Father about it in a day or two. I shall speak to Father myself first. I shall tell him I will only consider the marriage if he allows you and Christopher to marry—and without delay."

"But, Liddy! Will it work? And I hate to think of you suffering some strange man's attentions for my sake."

"Of course it will work. As soon as you are married, I shall break the engagement. It's all this Lord Calvert deserves, after all, for trying to arrange to marry me just for my money!"

"What will father do when you break the engagement?" Amy was round-eyed, but beginning to look hopeful.

"What *can* he do? I'm not afraid of his temper. And besides, darling, I shall be returning to Jamaica once I have seen you safely married." Lydia crossed to her sister and kissed her cheek. "There will be no place for me in your new home as a busy draper's wife, though I promise to come back and visit once my first niece or nephew is born."

Amy's arms were tight around her neck, and Lydia heard Amy give a little cry of dismay. "But, Liddy, why won't you stay here? I know Christopher would want you to live with us as much as I do—or at least *near* us, and—"

Gently, Lydia freed herself from Amy's embrace and took her hands. Could she ever make Amy understand, she wondered. It was a poignant joy to know that Amy had found true love . . . and that she herself had come so close, only to lose it by loving the wrong man. She thought of the respectful way Christopher had looked at Amy and knew a twist of her heart, for Blake Spencer had surely never looked at her that way.

No, he'd looked at her in a very different way . . .

A way that had brought fireworks to her veins that she had mistaken for love.

The truth was, she didn't want to stay in London . . . or even England. She had never been happy in England, and wouldn't be happy on the fringes of Amy's life.

She wanted to make her own life. Running her businesses would help her forget Blake. She had come to love Jamaica, and maybe in time, she would find a love as true as Amy's there.

Or do you want to go back there because you know Blake is there? Fool, her heart whispered.

She managed a bright smile. "Darling, I know you may find it hard to believe, but I love Ja-

313

maica. In fact, I hope that you and Christopher will take a trip to visit me after you are married. Perhaps you two will love it, and decide to settle there! Port Royal needs drapers, too, after all! But enough . . . no tears yet. We are far ahead of ourselves. Christopher hasn't even proposed to you yet — and I haven't dazzled Lord Calvert! And neither will happen if we go down to the ball looking like a couple of wilted, crumpled roses with red-rimmed eyes!"

They laughed together then, and Amy jumped up and flew to the mirror. "Oh, Liddy — you are right! But I can hardly bear to think of you having to face this Lord Calvert! He frightens me so that I can scarcely speak a word in his presence! Besides, he is so old that I can't think of a thing to converse with him about . . . but I'm not half as brave as you!"

"Then he is quite an ogre?" Lydia frowned, hoping he wouldn't be *too* formal and impossible to talk to . . . or so elderly that she would feel strange flirting with him. Well, if she had to come baldly out and tell him she accepted his offer, so be it.

"Not precisely an *ogre*," admitted Amy. "Perhaps it is just that I am so shy with men, but he is very silent with me, and he has the most unnerving way of looking at people! Even father is not himself around Lord Calvert! He almost seems scared of him, if I didn't know better." Amy sounded awe-struck.

"Doubtless because he is impressed with his title," Lydia said tartly.

"Why Lord Calvert ever offered for me when he barely speaks to me or looks at me . . . ? Well, perhaps you will do better with him, Liddy," Amy finished doubtfully.

"Don't worry. On Jamaica, I played hostess to the governor himself, so I am not intimidated by a mere lord." *And learned to speak up to drunkards, and pirates . . . and Blake Spencer,* she finished silently, though she couldn't tell Amy such things.

Glancing at the clock on the mantelpiece, Lydia took a deep breath. "It is time to go down," she said. "Amy, since I want to make an impression on him, when we hear his name announced, I shall make an excuse and go out onto the terrace. Find a way to bring him out to me there, so I can meet him for the first time without Aunt Phyllida, Gwendolyn, and Uncle Ambrose surrounding us. Not to mention Father. And then . . ." Lydia favored the mirror with a confident smile, but took the precaution of crossing her fingers behind a fold of her skirt. "I shall take it from there."

"He's here!" Aunt Phyllida clutched Lydia's arm as the footman announced Lord Calvert's name in ringing tones.

"So it would seem." *Drat it, the man couldn't have shown worse timing!* Lydia snapped open her fan and fanned herself with a nonchalant air. She was standing on the sidelines with Aunt Phyllida and Gwendolyn, and now she had to make her escape. She knew it would take him a few moments to make his way to them, for her father was doubtless greeting him. She detached her sleeve from her aunt's grip.

Their eyes riveted on her, and she gave them an encompassing smile. "I am going to absent myself

315

for a few moments to freshen up. I *do* want to make a good first impression, and the dancing and the heat have wilted me a trifle."

Aunt Phyllida gave her a look of the deepest suspicion.

"I must say you look lovely tonight, Lydia, I do not see the need," Gwendolyn commented acidly.

But Lydia was already starting away from them. "I shall come back here, so wait for me so you can introduce us. Perhaps Amy will entertain him until I am back," she called over her shoulder. "I shall only be a few moments, I promise."

She had to stifle a laugh at their expressions as she turned back to lose herself in the crowd, and then she was slipping through the side door they would expect her to leave by if she were really going to visit the ladies' closet.

She hurried down the hall, pausing only long enough to glance at herself in the mirror and see that not a hair was out of place. She was making for the library at the end of the hall, for it had a door that opened out onto the terrace and there would be no one in it at this hour. Perhaps later, when couples went in search of some privacy, it would be occupied, but the ball had been underway only an hour and she hoped she would find it deserted.

She was in luck. There was no one in the library, though the fire was burning and several braces of candelabra were lit. She took a last glance behind her to make sure Gwendolyn or her aunt hadn't followed her into the hall, and shut the door behind herself. Then quickly, she crossed to the terrace door and was out.

Thank God it is a warm evening, she thought,

or he'd think me mad to be out here without a wrap. There were a few strollers and small groups on the terrace, laughing and looking out over the gardens, and she scanned them quickly, hoping to find no acquaintances among them. Again she was in luck.

Now it was up to Amy to maneuver him out here. Where should she stand? Quickly she considered, then chose a spot not far from the library door, where the light from a silk lantern fell in soft shades of gold and rose. Perfect. The other people were all near the ballroom, and the light would flatter her gown and hair.

She walked to the spot and turned her back to the town house, resisting the urge to glance over her shoulder. Unseeing, she stared down at the small formal garden below, at the pretty light the lanterns strung there were casting. No one was in the garden . . . yet . . . but perhaps later, she could take Lord Calvert there or to the library, so she could let him know she would accept his cold-hearted proposal.

She heard footsteps on the stones of the terrace and bit her lip, but didn't turn. It sounded like a small crowd of people. Maybe if she pretended to be absorbed in the view, whoever they were would pass by without speaking to her.

"Lydia? May I present Lord Calvert to you?"

It was Amy's voice, sounding extremely timid and shaky. So she had succeeded! With a mental cheer for her sister, Lydia fixed on her most brilliant smile and snapped open her fan. Let him see that she was not on fire to meet him.

Slowly she turned around, to find Amy before her, looking incredibly timid, her fingers lightly

317

resting on the fine pewter velvet sleeve of Lord Calvert's coat.

Except that he wasn't Lord Calvert.

He was Blake Spencer.

He smiled at her, a long slow smile laden with mockery, and took her hand, which was as frozen as her smile, in his.

"At last," he said, bending to kiss her hand, "We meet." He straightened, not releasing her trembling hand, and his ice gray eyes fixed hers. "This is a pleasure I have long been anticipating."

Chapter Twenty-six

"You!" she gasped. "What—"

He cut in smoothly, stopping her before she could finish her sentence. "You are much more lovely than your portrait," he said, arching a black brow toward Amy, who was staring at Lydia's face with an expression of utmost puzzlement. He gave Lydia a meaningful look. "Perhaps you will do me the honor of dancing with me so that we may become . . . better acquainted?"

But it wasn't Blake's warning words that recalled Lydia to her senses; it was her father's voice from behind them.

"So, at last you've met my eldest daughter, Calvert! Since my daughter Amy seems to have forgotten the formalities, allow me. May I present my eldest daughter, Lydia Lyndham Collins—Lydia, meet Anthony Blakely, Lord Calvert."

Lydia's head snapped up, and to her horror, she saw her father and Gwendolyn standing just behind Blake. This couldn't be happening! She glanced briefly from her father to Amy, who was looking at her with trepidation.

She stiffened her spine and forced herself to smile at Blake, and tried her best to speak evenly — though she longed to shout. "I am pleased to meet you, *Lord Calvert.*" But as hard as she tried to speak calmly, she simply couldn't keep the sarcastic emphasis off his name.

"Well, *at last* she speaks," she heard Gwendolyn murmur, in a meant-to-be-heard aside.

Blake offered his arm. "Shall we dance?"

She took it, feeling she was going into battle, and armed herself with her best ballroom smile. "We shall," she answered, as Blake took her hand with as courtly a gesture as if she were royalty, and escorted her off the terrace toward the lighted dance floor.

She registered her family's faces as she swept past them, her father beaming at her docility, Gwendolyn looking greenly envious, Amy staring at her with a worried frown.

And then, with a formal curtsy on her part, a bow any courtier might have envied on Blake's, they faced off like duelists and joined the dancing.

There were two lines of dancers and, temporarily, they were separated by the formal intricacies of the dance. As Lydia tried hard to look as if she were not both furious and also about to faint, she was glad the dance was keeping them apart, for it gave her a few moments to collect herself.

But she found that looking at Blake across from her was doing anything but helping her collect herself. Her heart was beating faster at the mere

320

sight of him, and it dismayed her. Would she never be able to shake this hold he had on her heart? And was it only because he was so impossibly handsome?

She hadn't been able to resist him on Jamaica— but the sight of Blake masquerading as a lord took her breath. He was wearing a pewter velvet coat and satin breeches, and the lace at his throat and wrists made his tanned skin look all the darker. For all his fashionable attire, he wore no wig, and was one of the only men in the room without one. The silver at his temples contrasting with the darkness of his hair made him look at once distinguished and formidable. Compared to the fashionable, bewigged fops in the room, he also looked uncivilized. There was an air of danger about him.

His earring caught the light.

But the most astonishing thing of all was that he was dancing as if he had been born a peer, instead of the convict and pirate she knew him to be!

The dance brought them together, and as he took her hand and pirouetted her perfectly, she murmured through her smile, "What the *hell* are you doing here, *pretending* to my family that you are a lord?"

He looked at her mockingly. "But I am not pretending anything, my darling Lydia. I came here to see you."

"What do you mean? You know you have come here simply to devil me, but why you should involve my family—and my *sister*—"

"Temper, darling," he smiled, and to Lydia's frustration, the dance separated them again.

Oh, he was impossible! The rogue! She glanced

321

hastily at the sidelines and saw her family watching them avidly as they danced. She scanned the crowd for Amy, and saw that she had too joined the dance ... and that her partner was Christopher! Damn it, Blake was absolutely right. Whatever he *was* doing here, she couldn't enact the scene she longed to in front of them.

"I demand to be told what you are doing here!" she said, under the cover of a smile, when the dance brought them together again.

"And I look forward to telling you," he smiled. "Perhaps when the dance has ended, we might find someplace to be alone? I do not think your father would object ... He is most anxious that you accept *Lord Calvert's* proposal."

He gave the words the same sarcastic emphasis she had earlier. And just what did he mean by *that?* But she really had no choice. "Very well," she said scathingly.

His eyes were sparkling with amusement as they took their places across from each other for the final figure of the dance. He made an elegant leg to her, and she pasted on a brilliant smile for the benefit of her family, as she dropped into a deep curtsy.

He extended his hand and raised her, then proffered his arm. "I think we had best make our escape immediately, if we do not want to be surrounded by your family. Have you someplace where you usually take your suitors to be alone?"

She shot him a glance through her lashes, but his face was bland, though there had been a slight edge to his question. She wouldn't give him the satisfaction of rising to his bait. It was obvious he was trying to make her lose her temper.

"Where on earth did you learn to do the min-

322

uet, Blake? In the hold of a ship? I imagine it must have been difficult to learn with chains around your ankles. We can go to the library, to answer your question. I imagine it is quite deserted at this hour ... though later in the evening, it is a favorite haunt for lovers in search of privacy. This way."

She felt the muscles of his arm tighten under her fingers, and wondered which of her barbs had hit home.

"Must I point out that it is Lord Calvert?" he said in a steely tone, as they threaded their way through the crowd, and he nodded at someone she did not know.

She smiled at the stranger, then said in an undertone, "If you think I am going to aid you in keeping this preposterous deception—"

But he cut her off. "Calling me by my first name will only add to *your* troubles, not mine, if someone should overhear you, Lydia darling. Wouldn't they think you rather forward, considering we have just this moment met?"

With relief, she saw the door ahead. "Then why are you calling me *Lydia darling?*" she hissed as they walked into the hallway.

"Because I don't give a damn about your reputation," he answered.

She controlled the urge to yank her hand off his arm, as there were a few knots of people in the hallway. She knew they would be shocked to see her going openly into the library alone with a man and shutting the doors—it was expected that lovers absent themselves more discreetly—but this was an emergency. In a moment, there would be a much more scandalous scene for them to talk about, if she didn't get this blackguard alone!

She opened the library door. It was deserted, and the moment they were both inside, she slammed the door behind them and whirled to face him.

He had the gall to laugh at her. "I must say that I enjoy it when you look at me so scathingly—"

"Enough! Blake Spencer, I demand that you tell me this minute what you are doing here in London! And pretending to my family that you are a lord—! Anthony *Blakely*, indeed! Couldn't you have made up something more original? I gave you credit for more imagination than that. After all, you have *imagined* that this whole deception will work, but I tell you, I won't keep quiet about who you really are. How *dare* you pay court to my sister!"

"I did *not* pay court to your sister. I am afraid that was all your father's idea. I merely called on him privately, telling him I was interested in marrying his eldest daughter, as she was reputed to be wealthy and besides . . . very beautiful. Imagine my disappointment when he told me that she lived on Jamaica and had no plans of returning to London."

"You—" Lydia was speechless for a moment at the outrageousness of it all. "But I *told* you that my father wanted one of his daughters to marry a peer—and you knew how he would react!"

"Let us just say I hoped."

Lydia felt a wave of sickness and betrayal. So he had used her confessions to him—made that day on the beach when she had believed they were so close—against her. "To terrify my sister Amy into thinking you were courting her . . . *just to get me to come back from Jamaica?*" She was perilously close to tears.

"I deny that I ever terrified her—though she *is* very timid. It is hard to believe that you two are sisters," he remarked, for all the world as if he didn't see her hurt or her anger. "Why don't you sit down and stop striding up and down the room? We don't have all night to be alone, and I am perfectly willing to tell you why I am here."

She stared at him angrily for a moment, then sat with a flounce. "Begin, then," she said coldly.

He took a few paces and stopped in front of an ornate mirror, looking at his reflection with a slight expression of distaste. "First of all, I must set you straight on one thing. Revolting as I find this costume to be . . ."

A brown hand flicked the lace at his throat, and then his eyes met hers in the mirror, ". . . I did not deceive your family into believing I am a lord. The shameful truth is that I am . . . indeed . . . Lord Calvert. And that the name that is made-up is not Anthony Blakely . . . but Blake Spencer."

"You're lying! I heard all about your exploits on the *Tiger Lily*!"

He laughed. "The *Tiger Lily* is Jacques Noir's ship, not mine. You were so damn sure I was a pirate, that I borrowed the *Tiger Lily* to play the role."

She wasn't convinced.

"My darling Lydia . . . why would I lie about this to you? But if you don't believe me, you can learn the truth easily enough. You see," he turned from the mirror and took a chair across from her, "I was born a Blakely, and I am afraid that Blakelys have never amounted to much. Drink and gambling took care of what money we once had . . . but through the dissipation of our fortunes,

325

we always managed to hang onto the title some-how . . . and onto the manor house that had been in the family since the time of William the Con-queror."

There was a bitter twist to his mouth as he spoke, and Lydia thought his eyes held a shadow . . . or was it merely a trick of the candlelight?

"I was the third son—and born many years after my older brothers. My mother died when I was a boy, and after that, I grew up at Blakely, watching it fall down around our ears . . . while my father and brothers were up in London, gambling the last of what little money we had away."

He smiled, a cold smile that made her heart twist. "I am afraid I was not very close to my father," he added, in an ironic tone of understate-ment.

Her heart contracted with pain. What kind of childhood must he have had! So like her own . . . but at least, she had Amy's love, she thought, wanting to ask him questions, but not daring to speak for fear of stopping him.

Then he shrugged, dismissively, as if it were of little consequence. "When I was eighteen I'd had enough, and I ran away to Paris. When my father learned that I was making my living gambling, he disinherited me." He looked at her, and there was a gleam in his eyes that could have been amuse-ment. "It was then that I decided I wanted no more to do with my family's name . . . that I would make my own name in the world. And took the name Blake Spencer. My full name is Anthony Spencer Blakely, you see."

"So when you were caught dueling . . ."

"I preferred not to go to my family for help. And by the time I started serving my indenture, I

had decided that I would stay in the new world
. . . and carve out a new place for myself there. I
learned in the fifth year of my indenture that my
father was dead, and my oldest brother had come
into the title . . . and that Blakely was gone, sold
to pay the debts. So you see, there was nothing
for me to go back for. It wasn't until a year
before I finished my indenture that I received word
that the title had come to me. Both of my brothers had died in an epidemic that swept London,
though I've no doubt that starvation and drink
had something to do with their deaths. And I had
no intention of claiming the title . . . until now."

With a start, Lydia realized she had completely
forgotten that she was angry at him.

"And what made you decide to claim it?" she
asked, though she was sure she knew the answer.

He stretched his long legs out before him and
gave her a lazy look. A look that said mockingly,
As if you really don't know?

"You, of course. I realized that you might prefer to sell me the house . . . rather than have to
marry me. Or see your sister pressured into accept-
ing my suit. Of course, I shall drop it at once.
For a price."

"You would use Amy against me?" she gasped,
leaping to her feet.

He stood then, too, and it was his smile that
did it. A moment ago, she'd been ready to sell
him the house and be done with it forever, but
he'd brought her back to her senses. If Blake
dropped his suit, Amy would never be allowed to
marry Christopher. Damn him, if he wasn't above
using her, she wasn't above using him.

"Then I accept your proposal, Lord Calvert,"
she said through clenched teeth. "If you want the

house so badly, you can get it by marrying me . . . as you have threatened. That should satisfy you!"

I could see how Amy could have thought he was frightening—but how could Amy ever thought he was old? were her dizzy thoughts, as he took a furious step toward her.

"You mean it?" he grated. "Or have you just lost your temper again?"

"I mean it!" she flashed. "What must I do to prove to you I am as serious as you are?"

"Kiss me," he said.

His hands grasped her wrists, and though she meant to resist, what she saw when she looked at him drove all thought of resisting from her mind. His mouth was grim, but what she saw in his eyes was desire, not anger, as he pulled her against him.

"If I must," she breathed, feeling the hard length of his body molded so closely to her that it seemed as if her dress were of the merest silk rather than layers of satin.

His mouth came down on hers in a possessive and punishing kiss that seemed to release all the pent passion between them. She gave herself up to it, opening her mouth under his, answering his kiss with a surrender that lit a blaze in her heart and a fire in her veins.

And then he was pulling back from her, breathing as hard as she was. "Damn you, Lydia. You think you can make me forget what I came here for! It worked once before—but I tell you, it won't again. You say you want to marry me?"

She felt as if she'd been slapped. Was that what he thought—that she'd made love to him before only so she could keep the house?

"Yes — I will marry you!" she shouted.

"Good!" he blazed back at her. "Then we shall announce our engagement right now, before you have a chance to change your mind!"

With that, he dropped his hold on one of her wrists, and keeping a tight hold on the other, dragged her after him to the door. He opened it and gave her a glittering look.

"Smile, my darling," he said. "You're going to marry a lord."

Chapter Twenty-seven

"Brigitte! Blake Spencer is here—in London!"

Lydia slammed the door to her bedroom behind her as if she were being pursued by demons, and stood panting, staring wildly at Brigitte.

"And I am engaged to him!"

Brigitte leaped up, clasping her hands together. "You are engaged to him?" she cried. "But this is wonderful news!"

"No, it is not! Help me out of my stays. I feel like I am going to faint."

"Oh, *Madame*—you do look white! And very wild! Here, let me help you!"

As Brigitte rushed to her and started undoing the lacings of her dress, Lydia felt she really would faint if she didn't get to lie down for a moment. Had she ever been through an evening as racking as this one?

"But . . . you are not happy!? To be engaged to *Monsieur* Spencer? How did it happen?"

Lydia winced. Not at the dress Brigitte was pulling off over her head, but at the memory. How did it happen! Would she ever be able to forget the unreal dazzle of candles in the ballroom, the glittering throngs of people all turning as Blake, his hand clamped over hers in what looked like a gesture of affection and possession, led her up to the orchestra?

The way he'd smiled down at her, looking for all the world like a man out of his mind with happiness . . . but she'd seen clearly enough the little muscle in his jaw that told her he really meant to go through with it . . . and, she knew he was giving her one last chance to back out.

And yet, she'd actually believed he wouldn't *really* go through with it . . . until he turned and called for silence and a hundred interested faces lit up, turning to stare at them as they stood together in the front of the ballroom.

"I have a most happy announcement to make. Mistress Lydia Collins has just agreed to make me the most fortunate of men — by becoming my wife."

And then! Amid the shouted congratulations, the buzzing of the crowd, the laughter, he'd not answered any of them but turned, caught her in his arms and kissed her — most indecently — for everyone to see!

Then they'd been surrounded by a crowd, and she'd had to endure all the congratulations. So *many* of them had told her that Lord Calvert was so delightfully *unexpected,* so refreshingly *informal,* and she'd had to smile and laugh until her face ached . . .

She groaned as Brigitte finished with her stays, and sat down abruptly on the bed. "How did it happen? Brigitte — it was awful. He dragged me up to the front of the ballroom and kissed me in front of everyone."

"But that is most romantic!" Again, Brigitte clasped her hands together and looked transported. "You are going to *marry* him! What does it matter if he kisses you in front of the world? If Jacques were to do this to me, I would be the happiest woman on earth! But what did Lord Calvert do? Was he mad with rage that you are marrying a handsome young man instead of an old, shriveled-up—"

"That is the *worst* part—what I haven't told you. Blake Spencer *is* Lord Calvert. He—"

Brigitte shrieked. *"He* is a lord? *Madame,* it is impossible! But *mon dieu,* if that is really so—?"

Lydia nodded dully.

"Then all your problems are solved! Marry him! He has money, he has position, and he will keep your father from deviling you and your sister! But this is much better than *I* thought when I learned he was in London—"

She abruptly clapped one hand over her mouth. Above it her black eyes were wide.

"You *knew* Blake was in London and you didn't tell me?" Lydia said awfully.

Startling Lydia, Brigitte knelt at the side of the bed. "Oh, *Madame,* forgive me—I *knew* it wasn't right not to say anything, but—I saw him just a few days ago on the street. I thought he followed you here because he loved you, so I did not tell you. He begged me not to. But you are upset, so perhaps I did the wrong thing? I thought you loved him, too!"

Tears welled in Lydia's eyes, and for once she didn't fight them. "But he didn't follow me here because he loved me. He came to get the house. It's all he wants or cares about," she said sadly.

"Oh *Madame,* then you really do have a problem," Brigitte said sympathetically, and tears started to run down Brigitte's cheeks too. "Like the one I have with Jacques. He will not say he loves me either. I am sorry I have been so bad to you. I should have told you at once he was here—"

Lydia took Brigitte's hand, and for a moment, both their grips tightened. "Oh, Brigitte—I forgive you. You did what you thought best—and how could you know any better, when I never tell you anything? Maybe it's time for you to stop calling me *Madame* and call me Lydia instead—and time for us to be friends, if we are going to sit here together and sob over men!"

Brigitte gave a little hitching laugh through her tears. "But what men they are, *Madame*—I mean, Lee-dy-a! No?"

Lydia found herself laughing, too, and felt the torrent of tears slow. "Try Liddy. It's what my sister calls me, and it might be easier for you to say. And do get up off the floor and sit on the bed."

At once, Brigitte got up and sat down next to Lydia on the bed. She reached in her apron pocket. *"Voilà.* A handkerchief for each of us."

They both wiped away their tears, though not without a few final sobs. If Brigitte was the least bit self-conscious about being suddenly elevated from maid to friend, she didn't show it. Ruefully, Lydia thought, *That is because I am the one who has much to learn about how little social position really means—not Brigitte.*

"Li-di. And you must call me Gitte, then. So that rapscallion came here to get the house? Is that what he told you?"

Brigitte still pronounced her name with an accent, but Lydia liked the sound. It made her plain name sound exotic. "That is what he told me," she said heavily, then giggled.

"And what is funny?"

"You ought to have seen my family's faces when the engagement was announced! Even though Aunt Phyllida wanted me to marry a lord—! She was torn between being pleased and utterly shocked by the way Blake kissed me in front of everyone. And what will I tell Amy? When I saw her face—and Christopher's—"

"What is there to tell them?" Brigitte asked scornfully.

"Oh, you don't understand! They think I am doing it so they can get married, sacrificing myself, and—"

"Then they are getting married?" Brigitte's eyebrows shot up in amazement.

"Yes." Lydia laughed, a trifle wildly. "Father himself announced their engagement after he was finished congratulating us. Father turned to them as they were standing there, staring at me in dismay, and said, 'Well, Fletcher, you've been asking for the hand of my other daughter. This seems a propitious evening to give you my consent and announce it to the world, eh?' How awful for Amy! Thank God she loves Christopher, for Father didn't even ask her what her opinion was, or—"

She broke off, thinking indignantly: *Very much the way he married me off to Baxter!*

"So? Why are you so worried about your sister! She is happy to be marrying this man, is she not? You can tell her the truth about you and Blake later."

"But I do worry about her—I suppose it's because I've always been a mother to her—"

"No longer, *non?* If she is old enough to marry a man she loves, she no longer needs a mother."

It was as if a great weight lifted somewhere in the area of Lydia's chest. These words were so simple, made so much sense! Why hadn't she seen it for herself? She laughed shakily.

"Thank you, Gitte. You are absolutely right. As for my father . . ." For a moment, Lydia's voice tightened, then she heard herself and shrugged it off with another laugh. "If he knew Blake had spent seven years as Baxter's indentured servant! Shall I tell him?"

Brigitte giggled. "That would be revenge indeed, *Madame*—I mean, Li-di. And what of his *coquette* wife?"

"She was nearly green with envy. It is just the kind of catch she wishes she could have made for herself—

a rich *young* man, a *lord*—and one as handsome as Blake! You ought to have seen the she cat dancing with him! If she had stroked his lapel one more time, I would have— But listen to me!" Lydia broke off, startled at herself for being so venomous. It was just that Gwendolyn brought out the worst in her, she told herself quickly.

"Yes, listen to you! 'As handsome as Blake.' You speak like a woman in love—and you will not admit it."

Lydia bent her head and looked at her hands, tightly folded in her lap.

"I will admit it. I love him, but what good will that do me when he does not want me, and only wants the house?"

Brigitte jumped up. "Pah! This is silliness I will not hear! *Monsieur* Spencer does not *only* want the house! He wants you, too—or he would not go to all this trouble! And do not tell me I do not know Blake Spencer, as Jacques always does! I know men, me. Why not stay engaged to him for a time, and see if you two can put this silly house behind you, and learn if you are really in love or not?"

"Why not?" Lydia whispered. Then she turned to Brigitte with a new energy of purpose. "What should I do?"

Brigitte's eyes sparkled. "First, tell me *everything*. How else can I advise you? I have not done very well so far by guessing!"

Lydia laughed again, a laugh of blessed relief. Thank God, at last she had someone she could tell the whole unvarnished truth to—and not have to hide *anything* for fear of disapproval! Or embarrassment, she admonished herself.

"Very well. I will tell you *everything*—but on one condition. When I am finished, you must tell *me* everything about Jacques."

Brigitte threw her a wide smile of delight and sat

335

down again, this time in a chair. "Agreed!" She kicked off her shoes with a sigh, rubbed her stockinged toes for a moment, then pulled up a footstool, and put up her feet, adding, "Then maybe, we can decide what to do."

She shrugged, a twinkle of mischief in her eyes. "Or maybe not. Jacques has not been moved by any of my decisions — yet! Men have a most annoying way of doing what they please, no matter what we women do."

"I begin to suspect," Lydia smiled, with an answering twinkle, "that they say the same about us."

Chapter Twenty-eight

"*Monsieur* Blake is downstairs! Are you ready?"
Lydia jumped at Brigitte's sudden entrance to the room, feeling her heart speed up. So Blake had arrived! Just the announcement had the power to make her as excited as the actual sight of him.

"It would be strange if I were not ready, seeing that you have been doing nothing but dressing me for the last six hours!"

It was a week later, and tonight was Lady Montfort's ball. The Lyndham town house had been in an uproar ever since Blake had asked to escort her to the event. After all, her father had stated again and again, *royalty* had been known to make an appearance at Lady Montfort's soirees. Gwendolyn had hardly been able to hide the fact that she was envious both of the invitation and the dress Lydia was to wear.

The gown was really more Gwendolyn's style — a

dashing affair of black velvet and white tulle that Lydia was wearing with her diamond necklace and earrings. Their frosty shimmer set off the black and white, and the dressmaker had been ecstatic when Lydia had asked her to tighten the bodice of the gown and lower the neckline. Now the dress was only saved from indecency by the barest filmy whisper of tulle that veiled her bosom and just skimmed her shoulders.

"I am still nervous about this dress, Gitte. I think all these diamonds will only remind Blake of the fact that I am a wealthy woman. You know how he is always throwing it in my face that he thinks I do nothing but visit the dressmaker and —"

"Tut. In *that* dress, Lidi, he will not even see the diamonds. Besides, what else would you wear to Lady Montfort's? A simple calico shift and some beads made of shells, perhaps, to show Blake you really wish to go back to Jamaica?"

The good-humored mockery in Brigitte's voice rallied Lydia. Yes, it was too late to change the dress now, and besides, wasn't this how she'd planned to get Blake's attention tonight? She didn't give a straw for royalty or the glories of Montfort House. This was her first chance to be alone with Blake since he'd announced their engagement. Tonight Blake Spencer was going to realize that there was no use looking at another woman, because once she had his full attention, she absolutely meant to keep it.

I hope there is someplace I can get him alone, she thought.

"What are you doing, standing there so cool as if you are of ice? You English! Go down and

338

show him that dress before—"

Lydia picked up her fan, a fanciful affair of black velvet and white swansdown plumes. "I am going to make him wait for a bit," she smiled, practicing an enigmatic smile in the mirror. *Besides, it will give me a moment to settle these butterflies!* she thought, before adding with a lilt, "I believe it's called making a grand entrance."

Her grand entrance didn't go at all the way she had planned . . . and imagined. For the last few days, she had pictured Blake striding impatiently up and down the intricately patterned marble tiles at the foot of the winding staircase; she would pause at the top of the stairs and he would look up at her, his face lighting up at the sight of her.

And she would read love in his eyes.

But when she made her pause, the sight she saw below made her actually stop, not merely pause. Blake was there at the bottom of the stairs, and looking every bit as magnificent as she'd imagined, in a black velvet coat with silver braid—but his back was to her, and Gwendolyn was with him.

A stunningly dressed Gwendolyn, in a crimson satin ball gown fine enough for Lady Montfort's. She saw the flash of rubies around Gwendolyn's neck. Well, it wouldn't do her a bit of good, for without an invitation she wasn't going to be going. But it galled her to see Gwendolyn put a very white hand on his sleeve and say something that made him laugh.

And then Gwendolyn lifted her lazy green eyes over Blake's shoulder and saw Lydia at the top of the stairs.

"There she is at last," she trilled. "Lydia, Lord Calvert has been here for some time . . . but I have managed to keep him entertained during your absence."

The witch managed to make it sound both as if Lydia had committed an unpardonable rudeness by being late . . . *and* that she hadn't been missed one bit.

At last, Blake was turning around, and when his eyes met hers, they did light up exactly as she had imagined. But the fact that Gwendolyn's hand was still on his sleeve robbed the moment of any thrill.

"Lord Calvert. Gwendolyn. Good evening. I am sorry to have kept you waiting." And with that she started down the stairs.

"What the devil is the matter with you tonight?" Blake demanded in an irritable tone.

The ride to Montfort House was almost at an end, and Lydia abstracted her attention from the strings of flambeaux lighting the crowded drive, and the press of coaches ahead of them, slowly dropping off scores of guests.

"I should think it is *you* who are in a mood," she said composedly. "Look! We are nearly there. There are only four coaches ahead of us."

"Why the hell we can't just get out and walk—" Blake muttered, then turned his attention back to her, drawing his brows together. He didn't look much like a lord despite his black velvet coat, for he had one heel hooked on the edge of her seat, careless of her skirts, and one arm along the back of his seat. "You know what I mean. You haven't said a word to me tonight except to tell me I'll

340

wrinkle my coat if I sit like this. What's gotten into you?"

She flashed him a brilliant smile. "Excitement, I expect. I can scarcely wait to get to Lady Montfort's. I know so many people who are going to be there."

His scowl deepened as he studied her.

"Do you have a wrap?" he demanded abruptly.

"No, it's such a warm night, why on earth should I need a wrap?"

"Don't you think that dress is a damned sight too revealing? I don't see why you think you have to go out in public dressed like—"

She laughed. This was promising! Oh, Gitte had been right. Blake was acting like a jealous husband. "It is the style, Lord Calvert. Or didn't you notice Gwendolyn's dress? Mine is not nearly so—"

"Yes, I noticed it," he said tightly. "So that's what has gotten into you. You are jealous of Gwendolyn, is that it? But I wouldn't recommend modeling yourself after her at places like Montfort House, for she has no more idea of how to act in society—"

She knew her eyes were sparkling, and she laughed again, lightly. "Jealous—of Gwendolyn? You mistake my excitement. I am merely in the mood for dancing. After all, now that we are to be married—even if it is a marriage of convenience—" She shrugged and felt the way the tulle slid dangerously over her shoulders. Blake's eyes widened at the sight, then narrowed.

"Go on."

"Well, you know my experience of marriage. I find that it is very restrictive for a woman. So

341

tonight I intend to dance every dance I can . . . though naturally I hope many of them will be with you," she added sweetly.

The coach halted, and there was a jouncing as the footman jumped off the back. Lydia twisted in her seat, pretending she didn't see the expression on Blake's face. "We are here! Doesn't it look exquisite with all the lanterns in the gardens!"

The door swung open, and she felt Blake brush past her to climb out and help her alight. She gathered up her skirts and fan in one hand, and extended the other for Blake to take.

Pausing on the top step, Lydia took in the lighted front of Montfort House, the press of arrivals, as if the sight delighted her. She sighed, "I know I shall enjoy myself tonight."

"Do not," came the growl, pitched too low for the footman to hear, "enjoy yourself too much."

She looked down at him, and his eyes were stormy, his jaw set. She felt a sensual jolt all the way through her, and gave him a languid smile. Then, greatly daring, she reached up one finger to slowly run down the line of his cheek. She saw his mouth tighten into an even grimmer line under her touch.

"I won't, my darling Lord," she said softly, "if you intend to stay in this foul mood."

With that, she laughed, and throwing a brilliant smile at her startled footman, started down the steps.

Chapter Twenty-nine

"Such a lovely evening, is it not, Lord Calvert?"

Blake barely heard the question of the hopeful woman at his side, then realized she had spoken and gave her a distracted glance. She was watching him expectantly, he saw, and struggled to remember her name. Lady Something-or-other, with a mass of raven ringlets, large dark eyes, and an enticing figure. Once he'd never have had any trouble remembering the name of a woman as attractive as this, but now . . .

His eyes returned to the dance floor. "Yes. It is a lovely evening."

His companion followed his gaze, then sighed. "She *is* very lovely, Lord Calvert. And it is evident that you are very much in love with her, for you cannot even take your eyes off her to make the most boring conversation about the weather. When is the wedding to take place?"

343

Blake started, tearing his eyes away from the sight of Lydia dancing and laughing with a very rakish-looking blond man. "The wedding? I am afraid we have not set a date yet. And I am afraid I have been remiss in letting a lady as lovely as yourself suffer for the lack of my attention. Shall we dance?"

The lady sighed again as he led her out onto the dance floor, thinking about the sudden spark in his eyes when she'd mentioned the wedding date, the way his mouth quirked in a cynical twist. Obviously it bothered him that his intended was dancing with a rake like the Viscount. After all, they weren't married yet, she thought happily, and if his fiancée didn't have the sense to see that there wasn't another man in the room like Lord Calvert, well!

But Blake, though being gallant by habit, hardly knew whom he was dancing with. His eyes were on the gown of black and white that went in and out of his vision in a maddening way. The sight of her in another man's arms was making the blood seethe in his veins. But he told himself it was only because of that damned dress—only because she was making a spectacle of herself, behaving like the most outrageous of ligthskirts, the way she was letting the Viscount hold her too tightly—

"The gardens are ravishing this evening, Lord Calvert. Perhaps you would like to take a turn in them for some fresh air when we have done dancing?"

Blake hardly heard the leading question, nor saw the pout when he didn't answer. Lydia was dancing past within earshot now, and with growing rage, Blake saw that the Viscount's hand had moved from Lydia's rib cage to her waist, and that he was staring unashamedly down at her near-exposed breasts, and saying, "But those diamonds are gorgeous . . . I have never seen any sight that I think is more fetching than the dazzle of those stones. Why, I cannot imagine, for I see diamonds constantly, but yours are . . . different," the Viscount finished with a wicked grin.

And instead of blushing, Lydia tilted back her head to laugh, exposing the lovely line of her throat to the Viscount's hungry gaze.

"Lord Calvert, you haven't answered my question about going out for some air," the woman he was dancing with reminded him.

To her surprise, he dropped her hands in the middle of the dance floor, and gave her the shortest of bows. The look in his eyes!

"An excellent suggestion," he said shortly. "Some air is exactly what I need. Excuse me."

The disappointed lady watched him stride off through the dancers, not for the balcony doors, but straight for the Viscount and his fiancée.

Ah well . . . she is a fool, but a lucky one at that, she sighed to herself, and then she laughed. Well, after all . . . that was what she liked best about Lord Calvert. He was never dull.

From the corner of her eye, Lydia saw Blake's sudden departure from the gorgeous raven-haired woman and breathed a sigh of relief. It was high time he came and rescued her from this disgusting libertine she was dancing with, but she had begun to worry that he was enjoying himself with that woman.

And now, maybe I can get him alone in the gardens for a few moments, she thought, saying aloud, "I have enjoyed your company, Viscount, but —"

"*But!* I am slain. With words like that you wound me. I had hoped you enjoyed my company

345

without reservations, so much so that you would consent to *enjoying* it still more this evening."

His inference was unmistakable, and Lydia laughed nervously, wishing to find a graceful way to disentangle herself from his grasp before Blake arrived. Strange, this was very much how Blake had behaved when she first arrived on Jamaica, but Blake had never made her feel as if she were a plate of sweets to be devoured.

"May I have this dance?"

Blake's voice stopped them.

The Viscount drew himself up, but didn't drop his grasp on Lydia's waist. A mocking smile twisted his mouth. "Ah. Lord Calvert. I believe you can see that I am presently in the midst of dancing with Mistress Collins. The next one, perhaps."

Lydia turned to look at Blake. His eyes were the color of slate and as hard. "Excuse me, Viscount, but perhaps we can finish our dance later—" she began.

Blake's hand went to the hilt of his sword. "She is finished dancing with you for the evening, Viscount," he said pleasantly. "She is coming with me into the gardens. Now."

"I think she can make her own decisions, Calvert."

By now an interested group of spectators had gathered.

"It seems, Viscount, I am going for a walk in the gardens . . . and I assure you, of my own free will," Lydia said hastily, wriggling out of the Viscount's grasp.

Blake's eyes locked with hers for a moment, and then briefly, with the Viscount's. Whatever the Viscount saw there, he released Lydia's hand and stepped back. Blake offered her his arm as he had on the night of their engagement, and as she took it, he pressed her hand to his arm with his free hand, as if to hold her there. There was a buzz of conversation around them as they left the Viscount standing with an insulted look on his face in the middle of the dance floor.

"You do not," said Lydia conversationally, with a glance up at his profile, "have to drag me."

"I do—to stop you from making a spectacle of yourself."

"I am coming with you quite willingly. But where are you taking me?"

There was no answer. They reached the edge of the ballroom, and heads turned to follow their progress as they exited into the main hall. She was enjoying the feel of Blake's muscles under the velvet coat sleeve. "We are creating a scandal, Blake," she said with a ripple of laughter.

"Why are you laughing? Have you been drinking punch with that cursed scum you were dancing with?"

"I haven't. I am only thinking of the expression on Gwendolyn's face when she hears of it."

He stopped abruptly, giving a startled laugh. "Damn it, Lydia, you are actually enjoying this, aren't you? Did you plan this just so I would drag you off and create a scandal to devil Gwendolyn?"

"No," she said demurely, letting a small smile play at the corners of her mouth. "But I admit it is an unexpected benefit of your impetuous temper, Blake. I believe you were dragging me off somewhere so you could lecture me? Please don't stop. I had hoped," she finished shyly, looking at him through her lashes, "to be alone with you sometime tonight."

There was a silence in which she could clearly hear his indrawn breath.

"You . . . *want* to be alone with me?"

She nodded, thinking, *Now* he will take me out

347

to the garden!

"Very well, then," he said, starting off down the hall at such a pace she was hard put to keep up. Ahead was a great double staircase that curved to an upper landing, and small groups of laughing guests were going up and down, stopping to admire the huge gilt-framed paintings that lined the upper gallery. Heads turned as Blake and Lydia went up in an indecorous hurry, and Lydia laughed recklessly. "Where are you taking me? Blake!"

Not, it seemed, to the garden!

Down the long upper gallery, past open doors and closed doors, he was looking into every room. At last he seemed to find what he was looking for, because he strode inside a double set of open white and gilded doors and stopped.

Before her stretched a bedroom of elysian proportions. The carpets were all gold and white, the walls a deep shade of blue.

"Blake," she protested, still laughing, "but this must be Lady Montfort's bedroom. We cannot—"

He walked over to the great balcony doors, closing them and pulling the drapes shut. "We can. I doubt Lady Montfort will be requiring her room at the moment."

"Blake, are you mad?" she cried, running after him as he crossed the room to the hall doors and started to pull them shut. "There are other places we can go to be alone besides Lady Montfort's bedroom."

The lock clicked shut and he turned, catching her in his arms. All at once Lydia didn't care anymore that this was another outrageous scandal that would be the talk of London by morning.

"It is time you started behaving as if you were engaged to me," he said grimly. "First of all, that dress."

"Don't you like it?" she questioned softly, and felt his arms tighten. "I wore it for you."

"And for half of London. The woman I marry will not—"

She laughed up at him.

"Damn it, Lydia, aren't you listening? I brought you up here so we could talk."

"Must we?" she said softly, letting her eyes caress him. "We have already talked so much . . . and it has solved nothing."

"Lydia—" She saw the anger leave his face, and felt his breath coming faster. She raised her hand to the necklace at her throat and let her fingers trail slowly over it, watching his eyes follow her motion.

"The Viscount admired my diamonds . . . but perhaps you think they are too much with this dress?"

With a convulsive movement, Blake let go of Lydia and his hand stilled her hand at her throat. His other hand was moving up her back. His fingers met at the clasp on her bared neck. She felt the clasp coming undone, felt the cold diamonds on her skin as the open necklace slowly slid down her neck and over her chest, then came to rest just above her bodice.

She shivered as his lips moved over the path the necklace had taken.

"Are you trying to seduce me?" she heard him whisper, his lips against her breast.

For an answer, she tilted her head back and arched her breast against his lips, and felt the necklace slither down into her bodice. "We have lost the necklace," she breathed. "It seems you will have to undress me to find it again."

Blake propped himself on his elbow to look

down at Lydia, sleeping beside him on the soft rug before the fire. There was no sound in the room except for the crackle of the flames, and the distant strains of laughter and music from the rooms below. Their clothes were tossed haphazardly around the room, and he watched her with a kind of awe, remembering their passionate lovemaking.

The firelight gave her skin a warm glow and picked up red glints in the diamond necklace around her throat. He felt his breath quicken at the memory of how, once they were both naked, she had knelt in the fireglow and let him take down her hair until it fell in a molten river around her shoulders, and then she had put the necklace back around her neck.

She had looked like a goddess in the firelight, with nothing but that diamond collar around her neck, her skin like golden silk in contrast. For a moment, he'd only been able to marvel at her as she knelt there, and then she had reached out and run her hands over his muscles, as if she were as struck by the sight of him as he was by her.

And then they had come together in a blaze of passionate urgency. She'd been as uninhibited as Aphrodite, letting him explore every inch of her body with his hands and then, with his mouth—and she had done the same to him. In fact, she had seduced him—utterly.

And this was the woman he'd once believed to be afraid of lovemaking.

In sleep, her face was sweet, trusting; she awakened a protective feeling that was as strong as the passion they'd shared but a moment before. But her sleeping face made him think of her face when, to his wonder, she'd moved on top of him and guided him deep inside her; her face as he held her slender waist and watched the necklace sparkling above her breasts as she moved above him until they were both crying out with passion.

Even though she was sleeping with such a glow of contentment on her face, he couldn't stop himself. He put his hand on the warm curve of her skin and ran it gently upward to the swell of her breast.

Her eyes fluttered open, filled with the softest look he'd ever seen, and she smiled.

"Yes," she whispered. "Again?"

As Lydia pulled on her garter, she threw Blake a playful look. He was standing across the room, donning his shirt, but he'd paused in the act, and was staring at her legs as she worked the garter up her silk stocking. "Really, Blake, we must finish dressing before someone comes," she reminded him.

"Must we? If you persist in doing that . . . damn it, now where the devil is my shoe?"

She laughed at the sight of him stooping to search under the armoire. "You'd best find it, or whatever will Lady Montfort think? Besides, how will we go downstairs without it? We *have* been in here for almost two hours."

He grinned at her. "Found it. I think I'll just toss the thing in the fire in any case. Why these fops in London wear high-heeled shoes . . . in fact, maybe I'll throw this cravat in with it. It's worth burning. *Was* it two hours? It seemed much shorter to me."

Smiling at him, Lydia saw what she had long dreamed of in his answering gaze. Surely that was love in his eyes. *The moment Amy is married,* she thought, *I shall give him the deed. Less than a week. And then . . .*

And then she would ask him to marry her in

earnest — and find out at last if he truly loved her!

"To me it seemed longer. Blake, honestly, you must come and lace up the back of my dress. Otherwise we shall never get downstairs."

He walked to the balcony windows and pulled aside the curtains, then unlatched the doors and looked out. "Fortunately, it's dark down there. Yes, and I see an easy climb down. Forget your shoes. Let's escape this ball, shall we? I'll climb down first and you can toss me the rest of our clothes, and then we'll find a way to get out of the garden without anyone seeing us."

"But what about the coach?" She was giggling again, but the mad idea appealed to her. It was far better than trying to go down to the ball with her hair in disarray, and she knew Blake would be hopeless at helping her put it up again.

"We'll walk, and I'll pay some servant to come back here and tell the coachman we've gone. It isn't far to my lodgings."

"Your lodgings, Lord Calvert? Then you are proposing I do not go home tonight? I fear you are trying to compromise me, sir."

"I fear, Madam, that it was you who compromised me tonight, if I may refresh your memory," he said solemnly. "My reputation is forever ruined. And," he added, "do you really want to go back to face your Aunt?"

They both burst out laughing, and she jumped up and ran to his side, presenting her back to him. "Then lace up my dress, for I can't climb down this way."

He was just starting to tug at her laces, with a few distractions of kissing her neck, when there was a noise on the balcony. They looked up, startled, as there was the sound of footsteps and the unlatched balcony door swung open.

"I don't think you can climb down this way in

that dress, for I have had a hard time climbing up," said a deep male voice.

Lydia screamed and jumped.

"It is about time I found you. I have been searching for you for two hours," the voice went on, and the intruder stepped into the room—and into the light.

"Jacques!" cried Blake behind her. "What the devil are you doing here!"

Chapter Thirty

Jacques strolled into the room as if he owned it . . . and indeed, he looked as if he might have. He was splendidly dressed in a coat of amber velvet, with spills of point lace at his throat and wrists. His knee breeches were adorned with gilt ribbons, and a large topaz winked in the lace of his cravat. He would have looked like a duke, were it not for the gold hoop just visible in his ear, beneath the blond curls of the periwig he wore.

He put a fist on his hip and struck a pose for them, grinning. "Do I not look *magnifique?* Clothes fit for London, no? But, what am I doing here? I have sailed all the way from Jamaica and that is all you can say?"

Blake laughed and crossed to his friend as Lydia grabbed at the bodice of her dress to keep it from slipping off her shoulders. The two men pounded each other on the back as they exchanged good-natured insults.

Jacques—here? she thought, staring at him in amazement. Brigitte would be overjoyed!

"What the hell is that on your head?" Blake grinned. "And what are you doing here? Has Jamaica gotten too hot for you? Or did the governor finally banish you?"

"Nothing of the kind. And as for my dress, you are hardly one to talk." Jacques eyed Blake's undone shirt pointedly. "As for this . . ." he indicated the wig with a deprecating gesture. "When I called at your lodgings, your manservant said you were at this ball, so I thought perhaps the wig might be in order. Only a barbarian like yourself would think of appearing in such fashionable company without one. But then, if we are leaving by the balcony, I will not be needing it any more."

Jacques pulled the wig off his head, revealing his own sandy hair, tied back in a plain black ribbon. He tossed the wig carelessly onto a brocaded loveseat, and then turned to Lydia and made a bow.

"Forgive me, Mistress Collins, for not greeting you sooner. You are looking most radiant tonight." His brown eyes were dancing as they took in her *dishabille*.

Lydia was crimson, all too aware of the state of the room, her half-undone dress. But Blake didn't seem the least embarrassed at being caught by his friend after an obvious bout of lovemaking.

"And just how did you get in here without an invitation? I was told this was a most exclusive affair," he chuckled.

"They let you in, did they not? But such things are nothing for the son of a *vicomte,* eh, Lord Calvert? This Lady Montfort welcomed me effusively when I sent up my card."

The son of a *vicomte?* Was he jesting, or was

every criminal in the Caribbean an aristocrat? As Lydia tried unobtrusively to back away from the mirror over the mantel, where her unlaced back was reflected, she thought that if it were true, Brigitte would be more than ever determined to marry her Jacques.

Her maneuvering was in vain, for Jacques turned to her, his grin fading. "But enough of these stories for now. I'll tell you all about my voyage later. *Naturellement,* I sailed the *Tiger Lily* here. But I have a question that is most urgent for Mistress Collins."

Jacques turned to Lydia and anxiously searched her face. "Where is Brigitte? She is still with you?"

Lydia broke into a smile, forgetting all about the state of her dress for the moment. So he *had* come for her! How romantic! "Brigitte? Yes, she is still with me. She is at my town house this very moment."

"Diable!" Jacques suddenly sat down on a chair and wiped his brow, with an expression of profound relief. "I was afraid I'd find her gone—that I'd come too late. She is really in London?"

"She is really here," Blake said, sounding amused.

"And has she any . . . admirers?" Jacques asked fiercely.

"Well . . . she is not *married,*" Lydia allowed. "So you came here . . . all the way to London . . . to find her?" Brigitte wouldn't thank her if she made it too easy for him. Let him worry that she had admirers, even though she'd done nothing but pine for Jacques since she'd arrived here.

Jacques stood up with an air of decision. "I came here to marry her," he announced. "So come, Blake. Finish lacing up Mistress Collins's dress. I shall wait on the balcony while you do. I am most impatient to see Brigitte, for I counted

356

the minutes on the voyage, and I am in no mind to wait any longer than I have to. You were leaving in any case, I believe? A most dull sort of ball, I thought. Not a single sword fight," he finished, winking at Lydia, and then was gone through the open balcony door.

It had been quite an adventure, getting out of the Montfort's ball unseen. It was easy enough for Blake and Jacques to climb down the stonework of Montfort House, and would have been for Lydia, were she not in a ball dress. They'd ended by sending Blake down first to scout the gardens, and then she'd had to toss down her lace petticoats one by one and hitch up her dress. She had stared at Jacques meaningly, but he'd just grinned at her and refused to turn his back, so she'd swallowed her embarrassment and, turning her own back, hitched up her skirts to unfasten her petticoats.

Once they'd reached the gardens, it had been easy enough to skirt the lights and people, staying to the dark bushes until they found a tradesman's entrance in the wall. A piece of silver, and the footman there had been happy enough to let them out, and he'd vowed several times, clutching the coin, that he'd never seen them! . . . probably believing they were thieves!

The three of them, laughing, had linked arms and taken to their heels, careless of who looked at them as if they were mad as they passed. They had stopped at Blake's lodgings, and he'd grabbed a black cloak for her, one with a hood that would cover her tumbling hair and her dress . . . and the fact that she'd left her petticoats in Lady Montfort's garden.

She was exhilarated. It was an evening to remember.

She paused for a moment in the lighted doorway of the town house and glanced back at the two broad-shouldered shapes waiting across the street, and thought, *Give me reckless men!*

To think she'd once looked down on Blake for his wild ways. Her reputation was ruined, she had doubtless caused a scandal . . . and she had never been happier. Tonight, she had learned how much fun it was to be a rogue.

She turned and went inside, and luck was with her. The hallway was deserted. Clutching Blake's black cloak close about her, Lydia took the stairs two at a time, hardly able to wait to break the news to Brigitte.

"There. She is inside." The front doors of the Lyndham town house closed behind Lydia, and Jacques turned to Blake with a satisfied air. "I hope it will not be long before she sends Brigitte out. Shall I call on you tomorrow?"

Blake smiled at this obvious hint that his presence was no longer wanted. "Don't worry, I'll disappear the moment she comes out. But I imagine we have a few minutes—knowing women, she'll probably want to change her dress. Or keep you cooling your heels. If she comes out at all."

"Not my Brigitte! She would never . . . Do you really think she will not see me?" he added fearfully.

Blake looked at his friend, his curiosity piqued. Was this the same Jacques who had sworn a thousand times never to marry? "So you really mean to marry her?"

"If she'll have me." Jacques spoke fervently, staring at the house as if he were willing Brigitte to come outside that moment. Then Blake's earlier remarks at last penetrated Jacques's lovelorn anxiety. "But what do you mean, 'knowing women'? Once it was me who thought he knew everything about women, and *you* who claimed to know nothing," he pointed out, needling Blake. "But it is astonishing! Being in love has reduced me to ignorance. Though I surprised you in a most passionate moment, you must not be in love with her . . . since you claim that you know her, eh?"

"Know her?" Blake laughed shortly, but he was thinking seriously, disturbed. By Jacques's definition, he *was* in love with Lydia, because he never knew from one moment to the next what she would do.

She was always a surprise to him. A picture of her at Bellefleur came into his mind . . . the poised and correct woman, looking gorgeous and untouchable, cool to any man's advances, a shadow of fear in her eyes whenever he touched her . . . or kissed her. The same woman who'd tonight taken him into Lady Montfort's bedroom and made the most uninhibited love to him he could imagine.

One moment she'd fight him with the courage of any man—the next she'd be laughing with him like a child. He hadn't, he thought, his eyes narrowing as he looked up at the house, laughed that way with anyone else . . . ever.

"She has some surprises about her that even I would not have guessed, I admit," he said gruffly.

This got Jacques's attention away from the front door long enough to give his friend a derisive look. *"Oui.* I'd never have thought she would *really* climb down the balcony with us, eh? And I was surprised that she took off her petticoats in the end . . . though she seemed most embarrassed about it. Though why, I shall never know, as that one has legs no woman should desire to hide."

Blake strangled a sudden urge to leap on his

friend. "Damn it! Do you mean to tell me you *watched* her? Couldn't you have turned your back?"

"Mon ami!" Jacques's attention was now completely on Blake, for he knew that particularly furious voice meant business. "But why should this bother you, unless you are in love with her? I apologize with abjectness, but when you left Jamaica, you told me most clearly this woman was only an *affaire* to you, and that you despised her, that she was your adversary and had stolen your house! I did not imagine you would mind if I looked at her legs," he finished ingenuously, with a guileless look.

But Blake's jaw was still set. "You must congratulate me . . . for I am engaged to her." The words came out tightly, and he stared at Jacques with unequivocal threat.

"Diable! Why did you not tell me this! I should never have looked at her smallest finger, if I had known you had fallen in love with her!"

Blake felt the tight coil inside his abdomen relax. In love with her? He didn't know if there was a word for what he felt about Lydia.

Fascination, perhaps . . . or infatuation? He'd come all the way from Jamaica telling himself that he was doing this to get the house, his anger fueled by plans as to how he would best her this time.

It had been an upsetting revelation when at last, after so many weeks, he'd seen her standing on the terrace, her back to him, and been thunderstruck by the way the sight of her made him feel.

As if he couldn't breathe. As if there was no one else in the room.

What should have been his moment of triumph after so many months of planning was meaningless the moment she turned around and he saw those long, tilted eyes looking into his.

He'd forgotten how beautiful she was.

Or had he? When not a moment had passed since he'd sailed that her face had not haunted him? The memory of her silken skin under his hands—of how it had felt to worship her glorious body, hold her close—had given him nothing but restless nights.

And the night he'd finally seen her again after so long of plotting and planning, it had all gone wrong somehow.

In the library, he'd found himself telling her things he'd never told anyone before . . . not even Jacques. For a few moments, he'd almost forgotten what he'd come there to do. He'd felt a closeness to her he'd never before felt with any other person.

Now, he winced inside as he remembered how hurt she'd been, how angry, when he'd steeled himself to remember his purpose. Steeled himself against the sight of her facing him, with eyes sparkling with defiance, her mouth set in resolute lines, looking unutterably desirable to him—as she set him back on his heels and accepted his proposal!

As happened so often with her, he'd lost his cursed temper . . . and found himself an engaged man.

And to his surprise, he was enjoying every moment of it. Even Bellefleur seemed not so important now. But love? The man who had become Blake Spencer and left Lord Calvert behind was of a resolute mind. Too many years of making decisions on his own and holding his heart free from any entanglements made his mind shy away from the very word. If in truth he'd fallen in love, he'd admit it first to himself . . . certainly not to Jacques.

"Suffice it to say that I am engaged," he said. "An engagement of convenience, you could call it. But while she is my betrothed, I will not have other men looking at her."

"But I am astonished! You must tell me what happened. Your plan did not work?" Jacques well understood that Blake's pride would not allow him to have another man looking at a woman he was engaged to, even if he had not the least intention of marrying her. "Then she accepted your proposal?"

"It seems I did not count on the fact that her sister wishes to marry someone else," Blake replied dryly. "She accepted my proposal—to my surprise—in order to get her father to allow her sister to marry this other man." Briefly, Blake outlined events since he had arrived in London.

"Then she intends to break the engagement to you when her sister is married—and *still* not sell you the house?" Jacques was outraged. "But Blake, she is using you! And you are allowing her to do this?"

Jacques sounded as if he could not believe his ears, and Blake gave a wry inward smile. *Ah, but what I have not told you is how much I am enjoying this 'being used,'* he thought. Aloud he said only, "For the time being. We shall see what happens after her sister's wedding. It is in a week."

Jacques looked at his friend shrewdly. "Then what? Will you hold her to this engagement and marry her to get the house? From what I saw tonight, it looks as if she would not be adverse." Jacques's opinion of Lydia had sunk ten notches. So the scheming wench was using Blake to save her sister, and it seemed, her sexual charms to twine him round her fingers! He'd seen a hundred men with their heads muddled by beautiful and heartless women, but in a thousand years, he

362

would never have bet on it happening to Blake Spencer.

Diable, just look at the way his friend was smiling. A smile he'd never seen on Blake's face before—the completely foolish smile of a man who was infatuated and didn't know it!

"Marry her?" Blake suddenly seemed to come to himself with an almost visible mental shake, and gave Jacques one of his old sardonic looks, a look that brought relief to Jacques's troubled heart. "I suppose it might have to come to that in the end, if I am to get that house back."

Then Blake gave an ironic nod toward the house. "But I'd stop worrying about my betrothal and start worrying about your own, if I were you. Here she comes. I wish you luck, my friend."

And with a brief clasp of his hand on Jacques's shoulder, Blake turned on his heel and walked off into the night, hardly missed by the two lovers who were running into each other's arms.

Chapter Thirty-one

"Oh, Amy darling, I am so happy for you!"

It was just dawn on Amy's wedding morning, and the two sisters clung tightly together, both of their eyes wet with tears. They were sitting on the bed in Amy's room, both still in their wrappers, their hair in braids down their backs.

"Liddy, I will miss you so. Tell me you've changed your mind about leaving," Amy sobbed.

Lydia gently set Amy back and looked at her. "I haven't. But it's your wedding morning, and that brings me to something I want to tell you before we start to dress you. I am afraid that before I went to Jamaica, I told you something I have since discovered is untrue. That — " she hesitated, a little unsure of how to go on, of what to say.

"That making love to a man is a terrible thing," she finished in a rush.

"Liddy!" gasped Amy, blushing as the implications of what Lydia had said sank in. "You've—"

"Yes, I have. And enjoyed every moment of it," Lydia said firmly. "I would not have told you, except that I did not want you afraid to go to your marriage bed with Christopher."

And then Amy startled her sister. "Well, I *did* think you must be wrong," she said shyly, "for I must confess, Christopher took me in the garden one night and kissed me, and we . . . well, he did more than just kiss me. He opened the bodice of my dress, and . . ."

Amy was by now blushing furiously.

"Go on," said Lydia, fascinated.

"Well, it was very nice!" she finished in a rush. "He was terribly apologetic afterwards, but it made me think of how you once told me that it would be different if you loved someone. So you love Lord Calvert?"

"Lord Calvert! How did you know that he was the one—"

Amy laughed. "It's the way you look at him, Liddy. Besides, I must tell you there have been some rumors about the night you went to the Montfort's ball . . ."

"And *you* heard them?!" Lydia turned on her sister, amazed.

Amy's eyes were twinkling. "I am not so naive as I was when you left me. After all, this morning, I am going to become a married woman, am I not?"

They laughed together then, and Lydia sat down on the bed with a bounce. "Then I see that my guardianship of you is really at an end, Amy dear. And in that case, I owe you the truth. The truth about Lord Calvert . . . and our relationship. I imagine you remember that I often mentioned Blake Spencer in my letters?"

"The man you hated!" Amy nodded vigorously. "The man who was after your house."

"That man, Amy, is the man I hope to marry—and he is one and the same with Lord Calvert."

Fifteen minutes later, an astonished Amy was staring at Lydia, having heard the whole story. "And so . . . you say you've had the solicitors draw up the deed to the house in his name?"

Lydia took a deep breath. "Yes. I had it done yesterday. And I plan to give it to him today, after you're married and gone. Then—"

"Then! Oh, Liddy—you really love him?" Amy searched her sister's face anxiously, afraid for her.

"I am afraid I do. With all my heart and soul," Lydia said, a trifle sadly.

"And if he does not marry you? What will you do then?"

Lydia smiled tightly. "I will sail to Jamaica in any case. I booked passage on a ship that sails tomorrow. Brigitte helped me pack my trunks before she left me. She is on the *Tiger Lily* now with her Jacques, and they are planning to marry once they reach the islands. Perhaps Blake and I will be going with them together . . . or perhaps I'll be leaving by myself." She shrugged. "In any case, I shall not stay here. But why shouldn't we have hope? This is your wedding day! We have to dress. With so many weddings, how can I help being lucky? After all, you and Brigitte are both marrying the men of your dreams. Maybe by tonight, I'll be doing the same thing."

"Oh, Liddy! I so hope you will! For you deserve a happy ending to your story!" Amy cried fervently. "As happy an ending as you have made for me and Christopher!"

Chapter Thirty-two

The Lyndham town house had never looked better than on the morning of Amy's wedding breakfast. Shafts of sunlight came down through the round, open cupola over the stairs and lit the Grecian columns that rose to the second floor, the festoons of flowers, and the fruit plasterwork that edged the top of the columns and the border of the ceilings, in a blaze of white so bright it hurt the eyes. The sunlight coming through the open cupola and from the tall sash windows on the second floor fell on Amy and Christopher, not near as bright as the happiness the two so obviously shared.

The house was full of guests dressed in their best, satins and full wigs, white hose and silver-buckled shoes. They were admiring the wedding gifts set out in the drawing room, the heavy silver plate, the Delftware, six Louise Quatorze chairs, a fine spring clock for the mantel that amazingly could be set for an entire year, and (naturally, considering Amy had married a draper's son) an array of cloth and linens of English and exotic manufacture. Amy would never want for velvet to make her bed-curtains, English wool to warm her in winter, nor India muslins to adorn her windows.

Lydia lingered for a moment at the railing that encircled the second-floor cupola, looking down at Amy and Christopher. They seemed to fairly glow as they looked at each other, as they laughed and greeted their well-wishers. Amy was wearing a simple gown of pale blue satin, and Christopher beside her was splendid in a coat of midnight blue with silver buttons.

Lydia sighed, thinking of the lovely ceremony in the church, how she'd stood at her sister's side and watched the Reverend marry them; the tears had come then, tears of joy for Amy—and tears of emotion for herself. Christopher had looked down at Amy with such overwhelming pride and joy when they'd been joined in wedlock. Would Blake ever look at her that way, standing at the front of the church?

Lydia's doubts came back for a moment. She could never picture Blake being so humbled by love, so adoring. Did that mean what he felt for her was not love? Then she shook her head, dismissing such thoughts. It was time to bid Amy and Christopher good-bye, to wish her sister happy as she drove away from her life as a Lyndham to the new house she and Christopher would be occupying in the city.

And—perhaps—later today Lydia would have her answer. Because in a desk drawer in her room was the deed to Bellefleur, made over to Blake. Just two days ago she'd gone to her solicitors and had them draw up the papers for her.

Bellefleur would stand between them no longer. But would she gain Blake? Or lose him, too?

She squared her shoulders and started down the stairs, her eyes on the happy couple. If Blake married her, it would be because he wanted to. Not because of the house, nor because he felt forced to . . . but because he loved her.

"Really, I think that this tulip vase is most vulgar," Aunt Phyllida said in an undertone, surveying a tureen-sized piece of porcelain brightly decorated with scantily clad nymphs and crusted with gilt scrolls. "It is a shame that you allowed dear Amy to marry into such a common tradesman's family, Joshua, but I suppose the money will help."

Lydia stiffened, indignant at this comment, stopping in the door of the drawing room. It seemed her father and Aunt Phyllida thought they were, for the moment, alone as they counted over the display of gifts in what to her was the most "vulgar" manner imaginable!

Her father, his face redder than ever with the quantities of sack he'd drunk already at the breakfast, replied with a derisive laugh, "Yes, Phyllida, the money *will* help. Do you think I give a damn for the lad's origins, when I made my fortune in Cotswolds stone, eh? But rest your mind, woman. We've done well enough with the elder one, have we not?"

"I suppose so, Joshua. If her behavior at Lady Montfort's has not ruined everything. Gwendolyn told me the most dreadful rumors! It is fortunate for us that the aristocracy has a much more *worldly* view of these things. I gather the episode was looked on as amusing." Phyllida heaved a sigh, and Lydia clenched her fists at her sides, feeling her cheeks redden with anger and embarrassment. She'd known people were discussing the night of the Montfort's ball, but to hear her own Aunt speak so of her!

"Has Calvert told you where he plans to make his home?" Phyllida went on. "I hope he will consider building something in London that will rival Montfort House. Possession of such a residence will make everyone forget the scandalous way the two of them have behaved during their engagement quickly enough."

"Aye—and there are fortunes to be made with the goodwill of those at Court," her father said in a voice in which greed was apparent. Then he puffed out his chest, visibly full of the plans he had for the future. "Did I tell you I am considering having Gwendolyn's portrait painted by Lely, once Lydia has become Lord Calvert's wife? All the best people, it seems, have this chap paint them. He's painted the Queen, no less."

"Did I hear my name?" came Gwendolyn's voice. Lydia stepped back behind the lintel, out of sight, as Gwendolyn entered the drawing room by another door, and her father and her aunt turned to greet her.

"Darling Joshua! You really mean to have the great Lely paint *me?*" she purred, and Lydia clenched her teeth. The scheming wench! Out for anything and everything she could get! "How flattering. For he has painted the loveliest ladies in England, they say. I fear I hardly belong in their ranks."

"Of course you do, my darling." How besotted her father sounded! "The moment my daughter is married to Lord Calvert, we can—"

"And has Anthony told you when the wedding will be?" said Gwendolyn sharply. "For I don't think it's wise to count on anything until they are actually wed, and if you ask me, the chances of that are slim now, When she was keeping him panting after her—" Gwendolyn's voice was full of malice, and Lydia stifled a gasp at her next words. "But now she's let

370

him into her bed, slut that she is, and all of London knows it. Why should Anthony marry her now that he's bedded her? I advise you to hurry the nuptials along, if he has not already lost interest, for there are a score of ladies in London pursuing him this moment. With *his* looks, he can have his pick, I tell you."

"Really, Gwendolyn! Someone might overhear you!" hissed Aunt Phyllida. "We have done our best to scotch this scandal that that idiot girl has caused, but after all, Calvert is here, is he not, and was most attentive to Lydia at the wedding breakfast, so I am sure your fears are nonsense!"

"Anthony—as you term him—" began her father angrily, "promised to speak to me this morning, and—"

"And has come, as promised," said Blake's voice from behind Lydia's shoulder.

She whirled to find Blake standing at her elbow. How long had he been listening? From the set of his jaw and the ice gray of his eyes, long enough. He looked down at her, just a moment's glance, but the glance told her that the famous Spencer temper had been lost.

"Come, darling," he said with an edge, taking her elbow and steering her out from behind the lintel and into the doorway. "It is time we had a chat with your father about our marriage plans."

Three pairs of eyes looked up, as startled as Lydia was. The wheels turning were almost visible for a moment. Aunt Phyllida gave a small shriek and put her hand to her ample bosom, Gwendolyn narrowed her green eyes and flicked them from Blake to Lydia, and Joshua's eyes were suddenly cold and shrewd as he obviously wondered how much had been overheard.

And then Joshua's expression changed to a bluff and hearty one so quickly that the assessing look might never have been there.

"Lord Calvert! Then witnessing one wedding has made you anxious for your own, eh?" Joshua boomed, in a heavy-handed attempt at humor.

Never had Lydia felt so proud as during the short walk into the drawing room on Blake's arm. She didn't know what was about to happen, but she knew that Blake was as angry as she was—and she had a feeling that, for once, someone was about to take her part against her father.

Blake dropped her arm and gave a short, ironic bow.

"Impatient indeed. So impatient, that I would like your permission to marry your daughter today. And I might add that I intend to marry her whether you give me your permission or not."

Today! Oh, God, Lydia thought wildly, this wasn't how she'd wanted it to happen. Not before she'd had a chance to give him the deed!

"Blake—" she protested, but he didn't even look at her.

Her father said in a placating tone, as if he were reasoning with a madman, "But I must remind you, Lord Calvert, that the banns have not been called. In three days, we can have the wedding take place in the same church, and—"

"It will take place today." The words brooked no argument, and Lydia couldn't take her eyes off him as he paced up and down the length of the room— defending her. Angry enough to marry her because of what he'd overheard! Oh, it wasn't the way she'd wanted it to happen, but it was wonderful all the same.

She thought her heart might burst from love as she watched him, his raven black hair with the silver brushstrokes at his temples, his eyes so hard with anger, his muscled shoulders making a mockery of the elegant coat he wore, his long legs made for striding the deck of a ship, not for the parquet floor of a drawing room. The Blake she loved, laying down the law in his inimitable fashion.

"Banns are not required for shipboard weddings — and it just so happens that a friend of mine, captain of a ship, is anchored in London. I'm sure it won't take him long to hunt down a Reverend willing to marry us. But first, Joshua, I think I should set your mind straight on a few minor points."

Blake smiled, a rapier smile.

Joshua Lyndham was beginning to look nervous.

"I believe you were concerned as to where we are going to live. There was some mention of a residence in London?" He deepened that discomfiting smile for Aunt Phyllida's benefit, and she goggled, turning crimson. "I am sorry to disappoint you, but Lydia and I will not be making our home in London."

Gwendolyn looked sick.

"Not in London?" burst out Lydia's father. "No need to make a hasty decision, Lord Calvert."

And Lydia, as if in a dizzy dream, heard Blake say words that transported her back to another drawing room, another confrontation with her father.

"We are going back to Jamaica," he said.

"Jamaica!" shrilled Aunt Phyllida.

"Really, Anthony —" protested Gwendolyn, throwing Lydia a glance of jealous and defeated anger. Then she thought quickly. Perhaps this hellish situation could still be salvaged! She forced a smile and went on in a sugary voice, "Lord Calvert, you have simply lost your temper because of some words you overheard, but there is no need to react so angrily. I apologize. I fear my jealousy for Lydia's good fortune led me to spite. I am sure if we all talk, we can settle this without such drastic measures!"

"Now, look here, Calvert —" her father began in a

threatening tone.

"I have not finished." Blake's eyes were storm clouds as they measured Joshua Lyndham, and for an endless moment, the air crackled with challenge between the two men. "I'm afraid I've neglected to tell you my history. Shameful of me, but then, the time has come to be honest. I don't have any intention of using this title of mine that you seem to prize so highly. You see, I have another name on Jamaica, one that I think may be familiar to you, Lyndham. Blake Spencer."

"Blake Spencer?" Joshua Lyndham stared. "Do you mean you were—"

Blake laughed. "Baxter Collins's overseer . . . and former indentured servant." He gave a mocking bow. "One and the same with Lord Calvert, I confess. I came into the title only recently, and I find that it bores me. So I think I shall drop it when my wife and I arrive on Jamaica. Titles are of little use there."

His wife! He'd said the words as if he meant them, Lydia thought, staring at him in disbelief.

"What the hell do you mean by this preposterous story, Calvert!" Her father had found his voice. "Do you mean to tell me that you were actually indentured for a crime—and that you think you can just spirit my daughter off to some ship and marry her without my consent? I warn you—"

"And how do you intend to stop us, Lyndham?" inquired Blake silkily. He turned to Lydia and held out his hand. She took it and stood at his side, looking up into his eyes. "Can you be packed in an hour?"

"In less than an hour," she breathed.

"If you try this nonsense, I'll have that ship boarded! I'll—" her father was blustering.

"Have we heard enough of this, darling?" he asked her. When she nodded at him, dazzled, he

374

tucked her hand through the crook of his elbow and surveyed her father with a glint of steel in his smile.

"Make the attempt, if you like, but I feel it's my duty to warn you that my friend is a French pirate, and his ship is well-loaded with cannons. And his men are spoiling for a fight."

"A pirate!" Aunt Phyllida gasped, unable to keep still a moment longer. "You are talking about marrying my niece aboard a pirate ship? Lydia—have you lost your senses? This man is telling us he's a criminal—and you stand there on his arm? Are you actually thinking of marrying a *pirate?*" she finished with a wild shriek.

It was too much for Lydia. She laughed, then leveled sparkling eyes on her shocked Aunt.

"It seems that—apparently—I am."

Blake took her arm and they walked together to the door.

At the door, she paused, turning back. "I almost forgot to say farewell, Father . . . Aunt Phyllida . . . Gwendolyn. Since marrying off your daughters didn't make your fortune, Father, I wouldn't scorn piracy, if I were you. It seems to me it's a profession that the three of you are well suited for."

And with a reckless toss of her head and a smile that took in the three outraged faces staring at her, she walked from the room on Blake's arm.

Chapter Thirty-three

The pennants on the three masts of the *Tiger Lily* snapped gaily in the breeze, as Lydia's coach arrived at the wharf. The sun had come out from behind the scurrying clouds, illuminating the wooden sides of the ship, the high square stern, the brightly painted figure of a woman adorning the bow. It had a festive air—and it was the most beautiful sight in the world to her today, never mind that it was not a church!

It was the place she was going to marry Blake Spencer, and somehow, a pirate ship seemed fitting! She laughed, thinking of the magnificent way Blake had stood up to her father, had said they were going to live on Jamaica. Her heart thrilled to think that Bellefleur at last would be *their* home!

Of course, he still hadn't told her he loved her, but . . .

With hope, she touched the deed to the house,

tucked into the decolletage between her breasts.

The deck of the *Tiger Lily* was fraught with activity, as men came and went, loading water casks, barrels of meal and salt bacon, supplies for the voyage back to the New World. With a smile, she thought of how frightened she'd been of those same men the night Blake had kidnapped her, and looked among the moving figures hoping to catch a glimpse of Blake. And then she caught sight of a small, black-haired figure waving excitedly to her from the rail.

"Brigitte!" she called, leaning out of the coach window and waving as it stopped. She opened the door and jumped out, not waiting for the driver to put the steps down, and then she was running up to the gangplank with a heart that sang.

Brigitte met her halfway down, and they embraced, laughing and exclaiming.

"Is it not wonderful, Lidi? Only think, our rogues are going to marry us at last!"

"Oh, Brigitte—I cannot believe it! I think I am dreaming! But where are they, Jacques and Blake? They are not on the ship?"

"*Non.* Jacques went off to fetch a priest, and Blake to his lodgings to get his baggage . . . though he swore he was burning all his London clothes!"

The two women walked arm in arm up the gangplank, oblivious to the crew, giggling.

"I have told Jacques he must give up pirating," Brigitte confided with a twinkle.

"No! And don't tell me he agreed?!"

"But, of course, for my Jacques would do anything to please me, now that he has at last come to his senses!" Brigitte laughed. "We are going to be respectable tradespeople, like you and Blake. Besides, I think he is afraid that otherwise, I will decide to marry a planter instead!"

"But how wonderful!" They had reached the deck, and Lydia was momentarily carried away by a vision of how it would be, if Blake also 'came to his senses!' "You can build near us — a house as lovely as Bellefleur — and we can be neighbors!"

"And raise our sons and daughters to be business rivals?" Brigitte teased.

Lydia threw her an affectionate smile, but then she sobered. "That is . . . if I *do* marry Blake."

"What do you mean? You are not still being an idiot about it, when —"

Lydia drew the paper out of her bodice and opened it. "The deed to Bellefleur. In Blake's name. You see . . . he still has not told me he loves me. And when he knows he need not marry me to have the house —"

"Tut! This I will not hear! He will marry you anyway, or my name will not be Brigitte Noir!" Brigitte actually looked as if she believed this indignant threat, and Lydia folded up the deed and replaced it in her bodice.

"And my name will not be Lydia Spencer," she said solemnly. "In fact, those will be neither of our names, as they are assumed. So what makes us think our marriages will be lawful in any case, I ask you?"

Brigitte stared at her for a moment, then giggled. "Oh! You! But you are right. We must ask the priest if we must be Brigitte DuNoir and Lydia Blakely to be truly wed! Now come," she said excitedly, "We must dress for our weddings tonight. Wait until you see the dress Jacques bought me! It is gorgeous! And what are *you* going to wear?"

And deep in their feminine chatter about dress, they walked down the deck to Brigitte's cabin, all of Lydia's misgivings forgotten in the excitement of planning what to wear for her hoped-for wedding to the man she loved.

The sun was westering as Lydia and Brigitte finished helping each other dress, both stooping and turning this way and that to see themselves in the small glass that hung on the cabin wall. Brigitte wore a rich gown of deep pink velvet with bursts of white lace at the elbow, looped up over a scarlet petticoat embroidered heavily with pearls. Proudly, she'd told Lydia that the petticoat was spoils of a Spanish galleon, no doubt meant for some viceroy's wife. But no haughty Castilian beauty's black hair and eyes could have been set off any better by the scarlet; and Brigitte's cheeks were as pink as the velvet with excitement. She wore a rich necklace of seed pearls and gold, also spoils of the galleon.

As for Lydia, she wore an amber silk dress she'd had made in the last weeks, hoping to wear it should Blake actually decide to marry her. It was an exact replica of the dress he'd cut off her that night in the cabin—the first time they'd ever made love. True, it was not as magnificent as many of the gowns he'd seen her in, but by wearing it, she wanted to tell him that she'd loved him from the first, and never regretted that night—or any other.

There was a knock on the door. *"Dieu!* Are we ready?" Brigitte squealed, flustered.

"Just a moment!" Lydia called. Distractedly, she looked at Brigitte. "I wonder if Blake is back? Where is that damned deed?"

"Or Jacques—with the priest! Oh, Lidi, I am so nervous!"

The folded deed was lying on top of the desk, among the litter of jewels, rouge, and perfumes they had used while dressing. *"You* are nervous? I am terrified!" she said. With shaking fingers, she tucked it in her bodice, then went to the cabin door and unlatched it.

"Simon!" she cried.

The white-haired lad grinned at her, unchanged except that he'd shot up and now was all elbows. "Yes, mum. I've come to let you out of the cabin again, only this time I don't need no key. I've a message for both you ladies—the Captain and Mr. Spencer are waitin' for you up top. I hear there's to be a weddin'," he added with a shy grin. "Congratulations, mum."

Lydia laughed, but before she could reply, he ducked his head and scampered away down the deck, and she saw him toss his hat in the air.

Jacques and Blake walked a little distance from the raucous crew, who were celebrating in advance the unusual event of the weddings on the *Tiger Lily* by passing the grog. Even the priest was joining in.

"Mon ami, I wanted to speak to you alone," said Jacques with some urgency.

"What about?" Blake leaned a casual arm on the rail and faced his friend.

"I am concerned about you. Me, I am marrying for love. But you—to gain a house. There is no need for you to take the drastic step of marrying Lydia. Now that I am in love, I have learned that one should marry *only* for love, though I often enough told you to marry her to get the house. There is still time to think of another way—"

"No more of your plans, Jacques! None of them have worked, and—"

"But this one will! Look at the boatswain—he is

380

drunk already, and I know he would agree to impersonate a priest for you—"

Lydia and Brigitte stopped in their tracks as the men's conversation clearly came to their ears. Brigitte's hand reached out and clutched Lydia's in a convulsive grip as they stared at the two men leaning on the rail, backs to them and unaware of their arrival.

Lydia's heart plummeted at what she'd just heard—he didn't want to marry her at all! And he still didn't love her! Frozen, she clutched Brigitte's hand back, as Blake spoke.

"You are incorrigible! No more! What you do not understand—because I have never told you—is that the house doesn't matter a damn to me anymore."

Bellefleur didn't matter to him? Her heart, so heavy a moment before, soared as she and Brigitte exchanged an ecstatic look.

Lydia laughed, and the two men turned, startled. "If the house doesn't matter a damn to you anymore," she said, withdrawing the deed from her bodice, "I don't know what to do with this."

She stepped forward, as Blake's eyes locked with hers, proffering the deed. His gaze swept the dress she was wearing, and then a smile that made her knees weaken curved his lips.

"And what," he said, "is this you are offering me?"

Though Brigitte and Jacques were watching, to Blake and Lydia, it was as if they were alone.

"Bellefleur," she said. "It is yours. I never had any intention of forcing you into marrying me. I was forced into marriage myself, and I would never do that to you."

Blake grasped the hilt of his sword and drew it. It flashed in the sunset, as it came up and neatly

381

speared the deed. Lydia let go, laughing, as he tossed it into the air off the point of his sword. The blade flickered, and the deed drifted to the deck, cut cleanly in two pieces.

He stood on the deck of the pirate ship, her reckless lover, and his gray eyes were alight. With love.

"It is you that matters to me. Not Bellefleur," were his heart-stopping words. "Would you marry for love?"

"Yes!" she cried, as he dropped the sword and swept her into his arms. "And only for love!"

Their lips met, and Lydia was filled with a joy she could barely contain. She was hardly aware of Brigitte's squeal of delight and Jacques's applause.

She pulled back and looked at Blake tenderly. "But you haven't told me you love me," she teased.

"I think I loved you from the moment you fell into my arms, but I was too headstrong—and too much of a fool—to admit it. I'll not make such a mistake again. I love you, my darling and stubborn Lydia!"

"And I found I lost my heart to my adversary," she sighed. "I love you, Blake. I thought you would never come to love me as I did you."

They kissed again, rivals no more, but blissfully united by the magic created by love.

At last they turned to see Jacques and Brigitte also sharing an embrace. "What are we waiting for, Jacques?" Blake called. "I believe the priest is impatient!"

"And so am I, *mon ami!*" A grinning Jacques kept his arms possessively around his bride as he started off down the deck, to where the crew was waiting.

Lydia's eyes misted as she saw the crew form two lines on the deck and lift their swords, forming a glittering arch for them to walk under. The priest waited at the end, and Blake took her hand and brought it to his lips.

"Shall we? I am most impatient to get this wedding done with, so I can be alone with you, my love," he smiled.

"Oh, Blake, I am so happy! I never thought I could feel like this!" It was true. At last she had found the true love she had dreamed of for so long, and Blake had been the right man from the first. Her heart had written the story. Blake was her hero, and she would never doubt it again.

Then his eyes danced down at her, with a devilish glint in them, and she saw that love hadn't changed him in every way!

"And if you think I didn't notice the dress . . . I hope you haven't grown too fond of it, for I think I shall have to take my sword to it the moment we are alone!"

Laughing, she threw her arms around his neck and kissed him. "We shall have the whole voyage . . . and I have plenty of dresses with me this time."

"And then," he said. "We will go home. To build a new life together . . . at Bellefleur."

Home! As Lydia and Blake walked down the deck together, both of them knew there had never been a sweeter word.